IN THE DARKNESS

OTHER TITLES BY MIKE OMER

ZOE BENTLEY MYSTERIES

A Killer's Mind

GLENMORE PARK MYSTERIES

Spider's Web
Deadly Web
Web of Fear

IN THE DARKNESS

MIKE OMER

This is a work of fiction. Names, characters, organizations, places, events, and incidents are either products of the author's imagination or are used fictitiously. Any resemblance to actual persons, living or dead, or actual events is purely coincidental.

Published by Thomas & Mercer, Seattle
www.apub.com

Amazon, the Amazon logo, and Thomas & Mercer are trademarks of Amazon.com, Inc., or its affiliates.

ISBN-13: 9781503990425 (hardcover)
ISBN-10: 1503990427 (hardcover)

ISBN-13: 9781542040594 (paperback)
ISBN-10: 1542040590 (paperback)

Cover design by Christopher Lin

Printed in the United States of America

First edition

IN THE DARKNESS

CHAPTER 1

San Angelo, Texas, Friday, September 2, 2016

A measure of sand trickled into the grave as he hoisted himself out. The tiny grains hissed, sprinkling onto the lid of the box, dirtying it. For a moment, he was irritated. He wanted it to be clean as he observed it from above. He smiled to himself as he realized the absurdity. He was about to bury the box under a few tons of soil. What did it matter if a bit of sand littered it?

He took a moment to think of the other participant in this experiment. She might have heard the sand scattering above her. It was possible she even understood the implication. His heart pounded excitedly as he imagined it: the sound amplified in the small space, accompanied by the absolute darkness within.

He picked up the shovel, jamming it into the mound of dirt, and then paused. *Stupid. So stupid.* He'd been so excited by the actual act that he'd forgotten the important part. He laid the shovel aside and turned to his laptop. He hooked it to the external battery charger, making sure the charger worked. Didn't want the battery to run out halfway through the experiment.

The loud sound of a truck's engine behind him made him tense up, and he gritted his teeth. He had chosen this spot with a lot of care, making sure that it was hidden from view by a wall of cacti, trees, and shrubs. The road was hardly used, but the occasional vehicle still drove by. The distractions grated on him. This was a great occasion. It deserved his entire focus.

He activated the video feed and scrutinized the screen. The angle seemed a bit too high. He went over to the camera, adjusted the tripod's height, and then checked it again. Perfect. He hesitated for a second, the pivotal moment nearly robbing him of his breath. Then he clicked, starting the broadcast.

He picked the shovel up again and dumped the first batch of sand and gravel onto the box. The camera lens watched him, and he forced himself to ignore it. *Smile for the camera*, he could hear his mother's voice say. She never gave up on trying to pose him for the family photo album when he was a young boy.

When he hefted the fourth batch, the muffled thumping began. The truck's growling had probably woken the young woman, and now she was banging on the lid. Trying to push it open. Screaming. The craving took hold of him, and he nearly dropped the shovel as a sudden wave of heat flashed through his body.

Focus. There would be plenty of time for that later.

After five minutes, the lid was gone from view, though he could still hear the thumping and screaming if he tried hard. Was anyone watching the feed already? Probably. That was the whole point, after all. What were they thinking? Did they stare, waiting for the punch line? Assume this was a practical joke? Or were they even now calling the police, trying to explain what they had seen?

His mind and body were consumed by raw excitement, the moment cathartic. He couldn't concentrate, couldn't remember the details of the plan. He had to stop, just for a moment. Had to let off some steam.

He thrust the shovel into the ground and hurried to his van, taking the laptop with him. Once he was done, he cleaned up, put the gloves back on, and got out of the van to resume digging. He hoped his viewers hadn't missed him too much.

He'd heard somewhere that the average attention span of an online video clip viewer was thirty-seven seconds. He competed with videos of drunk cats, movie trailers, and porn. He had to be fast. That was why he'd prepared the bins.

He went over to the rightmost large bin and tipped it into the grave, watching with fascination as the soil poured inside in clumps. He emptied the bin completely, using the shovel to scrape the caked earth in the bottom. Then he went to each bin in turn and repeated the action, captivated by the view of the hole filling up, disappearing. Once he was done, he shoveled a bit more dirt over the grave to cover it completely. The shouts and thumps were gone now, silenced by the blanket of earth. Nevertheless, the audience at home could still hear it easily. He had made sure of that.

He took a moment to appreciate his handiwork. The ground was almost uniform. They wouldn't find this location in a hurry.

He stretched, giving his aching back a rest, and glanced at the lens.

Smile for the camera.

And though he knew it couldn't catch his face, he did.

CHAPTER 2

Quantico, Virginia, Monday, September 5, 2016

Zoe Bentley sat in her office, holding a photo between her thumb and forefinger—a man and a young woman smiling at the camera, their heads leaning close to each other, nearly touching. A casual observer wouldn't pay the photo any attention—just another selfie—but Zoe could see the tiny details that indicated otherwise. The man's empty eyes, the thin hostile smile. And the girl's face—innocent, naive. Ignorant.

The girl was Zoe's sister, Andrea. The man was Rod Glover, who had raped and strangled several women to death.

It'd been one month since Rod Glover had made his appearance in Dale City. Showing up for a single creepy photo op and fading away like a malicious phantom.

Zoe put the photo inside her desk drawer and slammed it shut. She knew she would retrieve it again later. She couldn't help herself. She'd done it several times every day since she'd gotten the photograph back from the tech lab.

When she was a young girl, Glover had been her neighbor. Zoe had found out about his crimes and alerted the cops. Unfortunately, by the time they'd paid any attention to her, Glover had fled. Since then he'd maintained a connection with Zoe, sending her envelopes containing gray ties, the item he'd used to strangle his victims.

His obsession with Zoe had escalated last summer. While she'd been investigating a serial killer in Chicago, Glover had begun following her and later attacked and nearly killed her. Not long after, he'd sent Zoe the picture. He'd approached Andrea in the street, and she had agreed to pose for it, not knowing who he was. Since then he'd disappeared completely.

Zoe got up and paced her small office in the FBI's Behavioral Analysis Unit, back and forth, brain buzzing. She had a hard time concentrating, partly because she was sleeping badly, nightmares and anxieties swirling in her skull.

She sat down at her desk and logged into ViCAP, the Violent Criminal Apprehension Program. It was the bureau's database responsible for documenting violent crimes to aid the search for serial offenders. She searched for any crime that involved rape and strangulation in the past twenty-four hours. She got one hit, and her pulse quickened as she read the report. A forty-five-year-old woman had been raped and strangled to death in her own home in New York City. Nothing fit the profile, not even remotely. The victim was too old, the strangulation was done with bare hands, and the location was off. It wasn't him.

Where are you, Glover?

If she could, she'd place Andrea in protective custody, preferably in a secure locked compound, until Glover was caught. But she couldn't. It had taken Zoe several weeks, and numerous loud arguments, to get her sister to move in with her temporarily.

The FBI agent in charge of the case didn't see eye to eye with Zoe on the matter. Neither did the police. They believed Glover was long gone. That he'd never risk staying in close proximity to either of the Bentley sisters. Zoe *knew* they were wrong. She'd seen the way he'd looked at her the last time they'd met. Heard his voice. This obsession wasn't going away.

She gazed at nothing, lost in trepidation. Her desk lacked any pictures or accessories. She had tried to bring in a potted plant two times, but the first had died within two days. The second, a cactus, had managed to survive nearly a month before succumbing. She was pretty sure the problem was the lack of water and sunlight, though Tatum, her coworker and friend, theorized that she'd scared the plants to death with her stare. Now, instead of plants, she personalized her desk with mess, and there was plenty of it.

The sound of familiar brisk footsteps tapped outside her door, and Zoe lunged from her seat and hurried to the corridor, catching up to the unit chief, Christine Mancuso.

"Chief, can I have a word?"

Mancuso barely glanced at her, her strides fast and purposeful. "Make it quick, Zoe. This week barely started, and I already have six different places I need to be." Her dark hair was pulled back, her suit crisp and clean. Everything, down to the beauty spot by her lips, spoke of authority and efficiency.

"I want to start working with Agent Caldwell on the Glover case." Like Zoe, Dan Caldwell worked in the BAU profiling serial criminals. Zoe had been furious when he was assigned to the case instead of her, but Mancuso had refused to reconsider.

"We've discussed this. No."

"I think my firsthand knowledge can be a valuable asset in building this offender's profile. We should work with everything we have, especially since there are indications that it's only a matter of time before he strikes again."

Mancuso paused by a large printer that spewed pages and glanced at the topmost page, then grunted in frustration. She turned to look at Zoe. "Which is why Agent Caldwell has spent two days interviewing you, working over everything you know and remember from your acquaintance with Glover."

"I don't think . . . I believe I can be objective in my—"

"You can't." Mancuso's tone was final.

"Then I need a vacation."

"So you can go after the man like some sort of bounty hunter? I don't think so. I need you here."

"Why?" Zoe's voice came out almost shouting. "I'm working on cases that are ten or fifteen years old. Why is that so urgent?"

Mancuso pursed her lips. "You're forgetting yourself, Bentley." She turned back to the printer and thumbed through the printout, grabbed a few pages, and began marching back, not bothering to check whether Zoe was following.

Zoe hurried after her, almost running to keep pace. "Christine . . . I can't concentrate with that man threatening my sister. I can't do my job. Please give me a few days. That's all I need. A few days and an analyst."

Mancuso slowed down. Zoe had used the one weapon she'd held ever since she'd started working at Quantico. She'd never called Mancuso by her first name. Never alluded to their past familiarity, working together in the field office in Boston. This was not something she'd be able to use again anytime soon.

"Tell you what," Mancuso said. "There's another case I need you to look into. Once you're done with it, I'll give you five days, as long as you work directly with Agent Caldwell."

"Okay." Zoe nodded quickly, not believing her luck. "What's the case?"

Mancuso paused by one of the office doors. "I'll forward it to you. There's no case file yet. It only arrived this morning."

"No police file?" Zoe asked, surprised. "Then what do we have?"

"A link to a video. Of someone burying a woman alive."

"I don't understand. If this is a serial killer, we should have other cases of—"

"It's the first one."

Zoe blinked. "But we deal in *serial* killers."

"I believe there are going to be more."

"Why?"

Mancuso gripped the doorknob. "Because the title of the video is 'Experiment Number One.'"

CHAPTER 3

Christine Mancuso opened the door of Tatum Gray's office and slid inside, shutting it forcefully behind her before Zoe had time to follow her. Though Christine cherished Zoe, the woman was slowly driving her insane. For the past month, Christine had borne an endless assault of emails, phone calls, and visits from Zoe, all concerning the same damn serial killer. She needed a few Bentley-free days.

Tatum raised his head, surprised to see her in his office. "Good morning, Chief. How was the weekend?"

"Short." Christine sat down in front of him.

He had an open case file on his desk and had been reading it when she'd interrupted him. Gray had joined the BAU recently and still lacked most of the knowledge and experience that Christine expected from her profilers. But she had to grudgingly admit to herself that he compensated, at least partly, with sharp instincts. Even better, he possessed an almost-unheard-of ability to actually *listen* to what other people had to say.

Tatum had already proven himself a month before, working on the Chicago murders case with Zoe. Though Christine had some reservations about the way the investigation had been conducted, there was no ignoring the fact that they'd prevented the massacre of an entire family.

She was glad to see that his usual grin was missing. Though she was sure that some people found his grin charming, she personally thought it made him look smug and adolescent. Right now, his expression was focused on her with interest.

"What can you tell me about Glenn Wells?" she asked.

Tatum blinked in confusion and leaned back, his wide shoulders tense. After a moment, he said, "Wells was a pedophile I investigated in LA. He targeted young girls on their way to school. He'd grab them, rape them, and threaten them to keep silent about it. He also took pictures. We found photos of over thirty young girls in his laptop. One of the girls tried to kill herself."

She watched her agent as he spoke. He radiated a calm demeanor, but his lip curved, and his right fist clenched.

"It was hard to get solid proof. It was all circumstantial. We had him followed for a long time and finally had him when he grabbed a thirteen-year-old girl in the street. He was dragging her away, and we closed in to arrest him."

"What happened?"

"He bolted. I chased Wells into the alley. He stopped halfway inside, turned around. I aimed the gun at him, told him to put his hands over his head. Instead, he shoved his hand quickly into his shoulder bag. I shot him. Three shots."

"And what did he have in his shoulder bag?"

"Just a camera. We think he wanted to delete the photos on it before we grabbed him."

"And he died."

"There was an investigation. They cleared me."

"It might be reopened," Christine said softly.

Tatum's eyes widened. "Why?"

"Apparently there's a new witness. Someone saw the shooting and came forward."

"Why did he wait until now?"

Christine shrugged. "Why does anyone do anything? I got a phone call this morning from a special agent in the IIS. A guy named Larson.

Do you know him?" The IIS was the FBI's Internal Investigations Section. Christine could have done without that damn phone call.

"Yeah, I know him." Tatum clenched his jaw.

"I think he dislikes you. I really don't know how you manage to piss so many people off."

"Perseverance," Tatum suggested.

"Well, he was positively gleeful when he told me about it. He wanted to alert me that you were about to be summoned for an interview."

"Did he tell you when?"

"We didn't get that far. I told him that you were investigating a time-sensitive case and that you needed a few days."

"I'm not working on any investigation right now."

She sighed. "Of course you are. Why would I tell Larson about it otherwise?"

Tatum seemed at a loss. "What do you want me to do, exactly?"

"I want to know more about this internal affairs case," she said. "And I'm working on it. But I need time. You have to lay low for a few days, at least, until I can sort this out."

Tatum nodded, but Christine noticed that now both his fists were clenched. If she had to guess, in less than twenty-four hours, Tatum would start making calls, trying to handle this mess himself. And that would make this much worse.

CHAPTER 4

The news about the reopening of the internal investigation left Tatum with a bitter taste. He'd thought he was done with this. Now the whole thing was crawling back from the murky past.

He spent an hour or so trying to bury himself in work, finally giving up and trying to find comfort in the office kitchenette. But hoping for anything uplifting in the kitchenette was an exercise in futility. Munching a dry, hostile cookie, he walked back, past Zoe's office, then paused, thinking that he could use a friendly face.

He knocked on the door. Behind it he could hear a disturbing muffled sound, as if someone was crying.

"Come in," Zoe answered, and he opened the door. She sat behind her desk, transfixed by her laptop.

She was much smaller than Tatum—or most women, for that matter. Her eyes were the most prominent fixture of her face, green and mesmerizing. Tatum had once overheard one of the agents call Zoe "the Vulture" behind her back, and he could see why. Her gaze had a predatory look to it, and it almost seemed like she was able to look through people, reading their innermost thoughts. And her nose was long and slightly curved, like a beak.

The crying sound he'd heard emanated from Zoe's computer. She glanced at him, then hit a key, pausing it. Tatum relaxed his shoulders as the crying stopped.

"Sorry. I can come back at another time," he said.

"Okay." She turned back to the screen.

Tatum raised an eyebrow. She hadn't seen him since Friday; it would have been nice if she at least showed a passing interest in his well-being. He turned to leave, deciding that if he was looking for a friendly face, perhaps Zoe's office wasn't the best place to find one.

"Tatum, hang on."

"Yeah?"

"I could use another pair of eyes here. Would you mind taking a look?"

"Sure." He blinked in surprise. Zoe usually worked alone. He circled her desk and peered at her screen. It showed a video clip paused at 43:32. The entire length of the video was just under an hour. The paused frame was of a young woman lying inside a tight, dark space, her face twisted in fear. The video was in black and white, and Tatum guessed it had been taken using a thermal camera. Zoe restarted the video.

The video started with the screen split. The bottom half showed the same woman in black and white, lying in the dark space, but now she was screaming. The top half showed sandy terrain, perhaps a desert. There was a rectangular pit in the ground that looked like a grave. The lower part of a man's body moved around the hole as the man appeared to be shoveling sand into it.

The woman's screaming was unbearable. Tatum glanced at the office door. He'd left it open. He hurried over to the door and shut it.

"Can you lower the volume, please?" he said.

Zoe nodded, clicking her mouse, and the screaming's volume decreased slightly. Tatum looked back at the screen. The man filling the grave went over to a large bin. He tipped it over with his foot, and soil dropped in clumps from the bin into the large hole. The man scraped the bin with the shovel. The woman thumped with both her hands on whatever was on top of her.

The dissonance between the cool, calm movements of the man on top of the screen and the hysteria of the woman on the bottom made Tatum shudder. He leaned over Zoe and paused the video. The screaming stopped, and he sagged in relief. "What is this?"

"It's a video of a woman being buried alive. Or at least, that's what it looks like."

"Where did you find it?"

"Mancuso forwarded it to me. It was sent to the FBI by the San Angelo police, in Texas. She asked me to take a look and tell her what I think." Zoe's hand moved to resume the video.

"Wait," Tatum said hurriedly.

Her hand hovered for a second over the mouse, then retreated.

"What do we know?" Tatum asked, staring at the screen. The caption below the video read "Experiment Number One." The uploader's user name was displayed in gray beside the caption—Schrodinger. A time stamp for the upload read "09/02/16 08:32." Those were the only details on the screen beyond the video itself. The rest of the web page was blank. Tatum glanced at the URL on the top—it appeared to be a random sequence of letters and digits.

Zoe switched to her email account and quickly scanned the email displayed. "The buried person in the video was identified by the San Angelo police as Nicole Medina. She's nineteen years old, lives with her mother in San Angelo. She was reported missing three days ago by her mother. Then, a few hours after she was reported missing, this link was sent to eight bloggers and two journalists from a temporary mailbox."

Tatum read the email from behind her shoulder. "They haven't found her yet."

"No, they haven't." Zoe pointed at the email, a few lines below where Tatum was reading. "Her mother said that she would never have disappeared like that."

"Could be a publicity stunt. Faking this video. The mother could even be involved."

"It could be."

"But you don't think so."

"I don't know yet."

"Let's see the rest."

Zoe resumed the video clip. Nicole's screams filled the room again, and Tatum listened to them, gritting his teeth. He forced himself to look away from the tortured face and focus on the man filling the grave instead. The top half of the video was the important one. Any clue there could help them identify the location where the video had been recorded. The camera was positioned so that the only things visible were the ground, the man's feet and hands, the bins, and the slowly filling grave. He was dressed in jeans and a long-sleeved shirt, his hands covered in thick gloves. No part of his skin was exposed. The sound of the feed originated solely from the video of the woman, who had stopped screaming and begun sobbing in fear.

Something in the grave drew his attention. "Look." He pointed at one of the grave's corners, where something snaked upward. "A cable."

"You're right. Maybe it's for air?"

Tatum scrutinized it carefully. "I don't think so," he finally said. "It looks like an electrical cable. It could explain how the feed from the buried woman is streamed. If she's really in there."

"Why use a cable? Why not just send it via Bluetooth or something?"

"If she's buried under a lot of earth, it would interfere with reception."

"Right." Zoe nodded, intent on the screen.

The man worked at emptying the bins for seven minutes. At one point he stepped out of the frame, and the top half remained still for a few minutes, while on the bottom, Nicole screamed again. He finished tipping the bins of soil into the grave, then tidied the ground with a shovel. They could hardly see any indication that there was anything there. He then paused and turned to the camera.

"What's he doing?" Tatum asked.

"I think he's just resting, but hang on—look."

The man approached the camera, taking something from his pocket. A phone. He flipped it to display the mobile's screen. Tatum frowned. It was footage of the president talking behind a podium. The only sound was the soft exhausted sobs of Nicole Medina.

"Is this . . . some sort of political statement?"

Zoe shook her head. "The video was posted on Friday morning." She pointed at the time stamp of the "Experiment Number One" video. "The news footage was live and streamed at the same time. He's proving to us that his own video is a *live* video."

Tatum glanced at the date again, his pulse racing. If the police could have located him as he was streaming the video, the entire thing would have been over almost before it had begun.

On-screen, the man lowered the phone and pocketed it. He then leaned toward the camera, and the top half of the footage went black. Nicole's crying got louder and more hysterical as she thumped on the wood on top of her again.

"In a minute or two the video will adjust itself to show her on full screen," Zoe said.

"You watched the whole thing?"

"Yeah."

Tatum cleared his throat. "What happens in the end?" The question sounded crass and dumb in the context, and he was disgusted with himself for asking.

Zoe moved the cursor to the video progress bar and dragged it to the right. Flashes of the video flickered as she dragged it up to 57:07. When she released the button, Nicole was mostly silent, occasionally sniffing. After ten seconds, the video went dark.

"The feed just stops," Zoe said.

Tatum frowned. "I'd expect him to leave it on, show us how she suffocates."

"Maybe she doesn't suffocate."

"Right."

"And maybe Nicole isn't really in that grave. Even if Nicole isn't pretending, this could still be a very sick practical joke. She could be locked somewhere else."

"Maybe the video of Nicole trapped wasn't live footage," Tatum suggested. "The man only showed the live news footage in the top half of the video. There's nothing that necessarily connects it to the bottom half that showed Nicole."

"It's possible that there's a reference to Schrodinger's cat." Zoe pointed at the uploader's name, Schrodinger. "I don't know the exact details, but Schrodinger's cat is an experiment where you trap a cat in a box."

"And you don't know if it's alive or dead. So it's both."

"And here we have a woman trapped in a box, and we're left to wonder if she's alive or dead." Zoe leaned back in her chair. "So what do you think?"

"What do you mean?"

"Is this really a woman being buried alive? The video is called 'Experiment Number One.' There could be more."

"Let's assume it's real . . ." Tatum's heart suddenly lurched. "She could still be alive."

Zoe shook her head. "Not if she was left there. That's the first thing I checked. I called Lionel and asked him to take a look."

Tatum nodded. Lionel was one of the analysts working with the BAU.

"He managed to approximate the grave's size by comparing it to the man's legs and the box's height by comparing it to Nicole's head. At most, if the box is big enough to fill the entire grave, it would be about ninety inches long, thirty inches wide, and twenty-five inches tall—probably just slightly larger than a coffin. According to Lionel, even if we factor in a large mistake in his calculations, Nicole would have suffocated within thirty-six hours at the most. And considering the fact that she was quite hysterical at first, she probably consumed much more air than she needed. Lionel thinks she was probably dead after twelve hours."

Tatum sat on the edge of Zoe's desk, atop a few papers. "So . . . Mancuso wants you to discern if this is some sort of deranged prank or a killer, right?"

"Could be something else. Maybe someone really took Nicole but didn't kill her. The caption 'Experiment Number One' could just mean it's the first of many videos that will feature Nicole."

That thought was somehow the worst so far, and Tatum flinched. "So how can you figure that out?"

Zoe was about to answer when the door opened, and Mancuso stepped in.

"Oh, good," she said, glancing at Tatum. "You're here. I was about to ask you to join us. Did you see the video?"

"Parts of it," Tatum answered.

Mancuso nodded, satisfied, and turned to Zoe. "Any initial thoughts?"

"I need to talk to the detective in charge to understand the details of the case better. It would help to know more about Nicole Medina. And surely there's technical data in the video with which we can—"

"So you think we should investigate this a bit more thoroughly?"

"Even if this is a prank, Nicole is not likely a willing participant," Zoe said. "At the very least, this is a case of kidnapping."

"Okay. I want you both to go there," Mancuso said. "As early as possible in case Nicole Medina is still alive. I want to do what we can to help the San Angelo police."

Tatum frowned. "Chief, I doubt this requires us to fly to Texas. I'm sure a few phone interviews would be more than enough—"

"I'd really prefer to have people there," Mancuso said smoothly. "This feels like a case that has the potential to escalate, and I want to be prepared in case that happens."

"But Chief." Zoe's face registered both surprise and worry. "My sister—"

"Your sister is fine, Bentley. Buy flight tickets, for tonight if possible." Mancuso's voice was hard, not to be argued with. "I want this unit to be involved in the Nicole Medina case."

For a few seconds, Zoe and Mancuso stared at each other. Tatum fought an urge to lean away from their glares.

In a moment of clarity, he realized that the chief's decision had additional reasons other than Nicole Medina's safety. Mancuso didn't want Zoe interfering with the Glover investigation anymore. It was common knowledge in the unit that Zoe and the agent who was assigned to the case were constantly arguing about Glover's profile—to the point that the agent complained that Zoe was making his job impossible.

And, of course, the chief also wanted Tatum temporarily out of the way and far from the clutches of Larson and the internal investigation.

Finally, Zoe glanced away, pursing her lips. "Anything else, *Chief*?"

"Contact the San Angelo police to inform them about your arrival. I want constant updates on this case."

CHAPTER 5

Tatum could hear Marvin, his grandfather, shouting even before he opened the door to the apartment. The old man sounded furious, and Tatum wondered who had peed in his cereal. It was usually Freckle, Tatum's cat. In fact, Tatum wouldn't have been surprised to find out that the cat had literally peed in Marvin's cereal. He peeked inside carefully. Lately Freckle had decided that his new bed was in front of the door. Opening it too fast resulted in a very angry cat, and in Freckle's case, an angry cat meant bleeding calves for all humans involved. Today, though, the miniature tiger prowled somewhere else, and the entrance was cat-free.

The shouts emerged from the kitchen. By their one-sidedness, Tatum concluded that Marvin was talking on the phone. Or ranting on the phone, in this case.

"Look, miss, just let me talk to your supervisor or anyone else there that has more than two brain cells. I want to . . . well, of course I want health insurance—that's why I called, right? No, I'm not talking about senior citizen health insurance, damn it! I specifically asked for . . . hello? Hello!"

Tatum rolled his eyes and walked into the kitchen. Marvin sat by the table, a half-empty cup of tea in front of him. His sharp glare immediately met Tatum's.

"Goddamn insurance agents! Bloodsucking leeches! They want your money, but god forbid they actually have to *work* for it. Think out of the box for once!"

"I'm glad you're finally handling this." Tatum fixed himself a cup of tea. He had been nagging Marvin to get his health insurance in order for weeks.

"Yeah, well, it doesn't look like it's going anywhere!"

Tatum nodded. His grandfather was old school. He wanted to do everything face to face and refused to fill out online forms. Any phone conversation that took more than five minutes made him cranky. Tatum could sympathize. Things changed too quickly for Marvin these days. He poured the hot water, refilled his grandfather's cup as well, and sat in front of him.

"Want me to handle it for you?" he asked. "I know how these people think."

Marvin hesitated. "Yeah?" he finally said, grudgingly. "You'd do that?"

"Sure. What do you need?"

"I'm trying to get insurance for my skydiving course."

Tatum coughed and spluttered as Marvin stared at him, folding his arms. Tea is most unpleasant when it runs up the nose, especially when it's still hot.

"Skydiving course?" Tatum finally said, amid sneezing.

"I have a skydiving course in three days, already paid for and everything. But now it turns out they're not happy with my age. Their insurance doesn't cover it, so they said I had to get external insurance if I want to participate. Can you believe their nerve?"

"I can, actually." Tatum wiped his mouth with a kitchen towel. "You can't do a skydiving course."

"Why the hell not?"

"Because you're eighty-seven years old."

"So what? All I have to do is fall from a plane. Gravity works the same for old people, Tatum."

"Who cares about gravity? You'll have a heart attack five seconds after you jump from the plane."

"My heart is as strong as an ox's. Don't be absurd."

"You already *had* one heart attack!"

"More than ten years ago, Tatum. What doesn't kill you makes you stronger. I don't have a lot of time left. Thirty or forty years max. I want to jump off a plane before I die. Is that too much to ask?"

"Can't you just play bridge or go fishing like a normal grandfather?"

"Look, you said you'd help me. Are you going to make the call or not?"

"Absolutely not."

Marvin got up angrily and stomped away. Tatum sighed and gazed upward. He wondered if his grandmother was up there in the sky watching them and laughing her ass off.

He stood up, taking his tea with him, and followed his grandfather to the living room. Freckle, the orange cat of death, sat there, his tail swishing as he glared at the fishbowl. The one fish inside the glass bowl swam back and forth calmly, circling the beer bottle that served as his sole fish tank decor. The fish's name was Timothy, and the cat and he were engaged in a constant mind battle.

Tatum wasn't sure how it had happened, but a few weeks ago, in the middle of the night, he had been woken up by a large crash. Bolting to the living room, gun in hand, he'd found Freckle dazed, completely drenched, and a potted plant upturned. Timothy had been swimming placidly in his fishbowl, which was half-empty. Since then Freckle often prowled around the fishbowl, eyeing it with hate, while the fish . . . did what fish usually do.

Marvin sat on the couch, frowning in anger. Tatum knew if he didn't fix it now, his grandfather would find an even more dangerous way to pass the time than skydiving. He was about to fly to Texas, and he didn't want to return to a funeral. He needed to find a way to keep the man busy.

"Listen." He plopped on the couch next to his granddad. His tea swished dangerously in the cup but miraculously stayed mostly inside. "I'm flying to Texas tonight. I need a favor."

"Oh, you need a favor now? Well, I'm not in a generous mood, Tatum."

"You know Zoe Bentley? The woman I work with?"

Marvin glanced at him, his interest clearly piqued. "Yeah."

"They still didn't catch the guy who attacked her. You know, the serial killer—"

"Rod Glover. I know, Tatum. I'm not senile."

"He's threatening her sister. Maybe stalking her. And Zoe is worried about leaving her sister alone. Do you think you could . . . drop by, check up on her?"

"Hmm. Why don't the police do anything?"

"Well, Glover has been gone for over a month, but Zoe thinks he might still be around. Just drop by occasionally. It would make her and her sister feel a lot safer."

"Sure. I have a gun."

Tatum blanched. "Uh . . . right. No need for that. You can leave your gun at home."

"And do what, Tatum? Hit the serial killer on his head with my walking stick if he shows up?"

"You don't have a walking stick."

"Damn right I don't! You know what I *do* have, Tatum? A gun. You can tell Zoe I'll take care of her sister. Unlike *you*, I'm glad to help when I'm needed."

CHAPTER 6

Zoe lay on her bed, watching the burial video again on her laptop. She ignored the bottom half of the feed, where Nicole Medina thumped the lid, screaming for help. After Andrea had entered the room earlier, asking about the disturbing noise, Zoe had muted the sound.

She stared at the man with rapt attention, fascinated with the casual movements—unhurried, calm. Or so he appeared. Watching closely, she could see that as he filled the grave, his movements accelerated, acquiring a fast, excited pace. That clumsy walk of a man struggling with an uncomfortable erection. He was sexually stimulated.

Which further convinced her this wasn't a prank. This man was enacting a fantasy. What excited him more? The fact that he filmed it for everyone to see? The screams and thumps from below? The act of covering the grave?

Too early to tell.

Andrea knocked on the door. "Zoe? Aren't you hungry?"

She was starving. Pausing the video, she frowned at the screen for another moment. The man on top was paused while smoothing the sand above the grave. Below, Nicole's face was captured in the midst of a terrified scream, her mouth wide.

She shut the laptop, got off the bed, and opened the door. The smell of deep-fried food made her stomach rumble ravenously. Andrea was just about to knock again. She was pale, her eyes lacking their usual spark, and a wave of sadness washed over Zoe. She hadn't seen her sister like that for a long while. Andrea was a wildflower, a blaze of color, cheerful and full of life. But when faced with perpetual fear, she wilted, her energy drained.

"What are we eating?" Zoe asked, fake cheer in her voice.

"I made schnitzel and mashed potatoes."

"Schnitzel? Sounds European."

Her sister turned and shuffled to the kitchen. "I think it's Austrian."

Zoe followed Andrea to the kitchen, where two steaming plates sat on the red-and-white-plaid tablecloth. A large piece of what Zoe assumed was chicken lay on each plate, covered in brown, crispy bread crumbs. Next to it was a dollop of buttery mashed potatoes topped with a decorative green leaf. A slice of lemon sat on the edge of each plate. It looked and smelled delicious.

Andrea pulled two beers from the fridge as Zoe sat down, her mouth salivating.

"Put some lemon on it," Andrea said.

She did, squeezing it above the schnitzel. She cut a piece and put it in her mouth. The bread crumb layer spoke of pepper, and flour, and comfort. The meat, definitely chicken, was thin and well done, and Zoe's teeth sank in it easily. The lemon mingled well with it all, and Zoe breathed through her nose as she chewed slowly.

"Good, right?" Andrea smiled, and for a moment Zoe could glimpse the enthusiastic, happy sister she usually was.

"It's amazing," Zoe said and swallowed.

"I wouldn't go that far. It's chicken breast in bread crumbs. Hardly worthy of a Michelin star."

"Well, it gets a Zoe star."

"You're just hungry." Andrea blushed slightly as she cut her own schnitzel.

Zoe sipped from her beer. "What are you doing home? Weren't you supposed to work tonight?"

Andrea shrugged, eyes on her plate. "I got fired."

"What?"

"Frank called me earlier. He said he found someone to replace me." Andrea spoke casually, but her voice had the grainy quality that came when words were laced with tears.

Frank was the owner of the restaurant Andrea worked in. Zoe digested the news and realized her immediate gut reaction was relief. The night shifts in the restaurant were a constant source of tension between Andrea and her. They placed Andrea at unnecessary risk. Glover could be waiting for Andrea to step out and throw away the trash behind the restaurant. He could follow her when she returned home, grabbing her as she got out of the cab.

"Why did he fire you?" she finally asked.

"Why do you think?" Andrea asked bitterly. "He said he couldn't pay a waitress who wouldn't do three night shifts a week."

"I'm sorry, honey, I—"

Andrea dropped her fork, and it clattered on the table. "I can't take this any longer, Zoe. It's been over a month, and no one saw him, not even once! And Agent Caldwell says—"

"Agent Caldwell is wrong. He got him all wrong," Zoe spat angrily. "He doesn't understand how Glover—"

"He said that Glover is too careful. That he'd never risk direct contact."

"He's wrong. Glover's fantasy is—"

"I don't care what his fantasy is, Zoe! What if he's really gone? What if he intends to hide for another year? Or two? Or five? I won't keep living like this." The tears she'd managed to hide so far materialized, and one dropped on her schnitzel, absorbed by the bread crumbs.

"Andrea." Zoe reached for her sister's hand, but Andrea pulled it away.

"Forget it," she said. "It was a shitty job anyway."

Unsure how to make Andrea feel better, Zoe ate in silence. Andrea wiped her tears with her hand and began eating.

After a few minutes, Zoe said, "Tatum called earlier. Would you mind it if his grandfather dropped by occasionally while we're in Texas? He's an old man, and Tatum says he gets very lonely."

Andrea fixed her with a sharp look. Though unlike Zoe, she hadn't inherited their mother's crooked nose, her sister had gotten their father's intense green eyes. Zoe met her stare, and they sat in silence for a second. She couldn't tell if her sister believed her innocent explanation.

"Sure," Andrea said. "He's a nice man, right?"

"Yeah, and he doesn't know a lot of people here." That was a blatant lie. In the six weeks since Tatum and Marvin had moved to Dale City, Marvin had already made the acquaintance of several people, some considerably younger. He had thrown two parties in Tatum's apartment, each one resulting in property damage and police complaints from nearby residents.

"It's not like I have anything to do now that I don't have a job or an apartment of my own."

"You'll find another job."

"I'm tired, Zoe. I don't want to be scared anymore."

Zoe nodded, the delicious mashed potatoes in her mouth suddenly tasteless. Andrea didn't deserve this. Unlike Zoe, she did her best to stay away from violence. Andrea couldn't stand to see anyone hurt, even on TV. And now this twisted person had invaded her life because of her connection to Zoe.

"When I come back, I'll fix this." Zoe hoped she could keep her word. "Mancuso promised me access to the case. I'll find that bastard Glover and put him behind bars."

"And if you don't?"

"We'll find a solution."

CHAPTER 7

San Angelo, Texas, Tuesday, September 6, 2016

The blast of hot, dry air that struck Zoe as they left the airport momentarily took her breath away. The air-conditioned atmosphere inside the terminal had been very misleading. Every molecule of water in her skin dissipated, leaving behind a dry, crinkling parchment. She shadowed her eyes with her free hand as she peered around her, the bright sun blinding her. She quickly took off her black jacket, folding it and placing it in the crook of her arm. She'd left her sunglasses back home. She'd packed late at night, when the concept of sunlight had been far away. She'd have to buy a new pair, or she'd spend the entire time in San Angelo squinting at everything.

"Our car should be over there." Tatum gestured. He looked like the perfect FBI agent cliché—dark suit, large black sunglasses, shiny shoes. If the heat bothered him in any way, it didn't show. "A silver Hyundai Accent. They said it's parked on the northern side of the parking lot."

Zoe glanced at the parking lot. It was dozens of yards away. She wasn't sure she'd make it that far.

"Do you have water?" she asked, her voice croaking. She hazily remembered seeing him buy a bottle inside the terminal.

Tatum nodded, rummaged in his bag, and located the water bottle. He held it to her, a bead of condensation slowly trickling down the plastic container. Zoe took it, unscrewed the cap, and tipped the bottle to her mouth, throwing her head back.

"Feel free to"—Tatum stared as Zoe gulped the entire thing—"finish it."

"Thanks." She licked her lips, relieved.

As they paced between the cars, the sun boiled Zoe's brain, turning it into soup. All thoughts of serial killers were gone, replaced by a confused shopping list of things she'd need to survive the heat. A hat; a large bottle of water; short, thin clothes; a portable icebox to live inside.

"There." Tatum unlocked the car. Zoe hurriedly stepped inside. The heat in the car was stifling, far from the relief she'd hoped for.

Tatum switched on the engine, and the car's air-conditioning blasted them with hot air that quickly cooled into icy goodness. Zoe aimed the vents directly at her face, feeling her brain slowly kicking into gear again. She'd have to stay in air-conditioned rooms constantly if she was expected to think.

As Tatum checked how to get to the San Angelo police station on his phone, Zoe turned on the radio and flipped the stations until she heard Taylor Swift singing "Begin Again." Pleased, she leaned back, waiting for Tatum to drive.

"Yeah . . . we're not going to listen to that, right?" Tatum raised his eyes from the phone.

"Yes, we are."

"I can't really do that, Zoe."

"Sure you can. Come on—drive."

"Tell you what." Tatum brightened up. "We'll take turns, okay? I'll choose the songs for this ride, then you'll do the next one."

"Fine."

Tatum plugged his phone into the auxiliary input and fiddled with it a bit. "Okay, we're listening to Genesis."

"I like Genesis," Zoe said, feeling satisfaction that Tatum's attempt at patronizing her musical taste was foiled. "I had the cassette of *Invisible Touch* when I was younger."

"I'm sure you did. But I'm talking about Genesis before Peter Gabriel left and everything went to hell. This is *Selling England by the Pound*, and it's a masterpiece."

He hit play and began to drive, the hum of the car engine intermingling with a lone singer's mournful tone.

Zoe gazed out the window, the music washing over her. The land on her side was a flat endless field, dotted with an occasional tree. The other side of the road was hidden from sight by a wild growth of similar trees and cacti.

Her mind turned to Andrea. What was her sister doing right now? Still sleeping, probably. She had said she'd start looking for a new job today. Zoe did her best to ignore the pang of worry that instantly awoke when she thought of Andrea driving around Dale City by herself. Zoe had left her the car keys, so Andrea wouldn't need to take cabs or public transportation. That, Zoe hoped, would keep her sister safer and difficult to follow.

"You don't seem to mind the heat," she said, glancing at Tatum, trying to distract herself.

"I grew up in Arizona."

Zoe nodded. "Did you like growing up in . . ." She hesitated, suddenly unsure where exactly he'd grown up in.

"Wickenburg? Yeah, I guess I did. It was a really small town, so everyone knew everyone. I had the same three friends from kindergarten all the way up to high school. And the pace was different than it is in the city. We'd hang around outside for hours playing ball or just chatting until my parents or Marvin would shout at us to go do something useful."

"You lived close to Marvin?" Zoe asked.

Tatum smiled. "He moved next door to us after my grandma died. My dad and Marvin used to shout at each other through the window. The houses were still a bit apart, so they had to shout really loud. Drove the neighbors insane." Tatum deepened his voice in imitation. "Hey, Marvin, coming to watch the game? Sure, Tolly, what's for dinner? Marvin, we already ate dinner an hour ago. What? And you didn't call?" Tatum snorted. "They'd keep shouting until my mom would bang the window shut."

"Tolly?" Zoe asked.

"Tolliver. But everyone called my dad Tolly. Check this out. This part of the song's brilliant."

Zoe didn't share his excitement with "this part of the song." The style kept changing, making it annoying to follow.

"My parents hardly ever shouted. They always worried about what the neighbors think," she said. "When they'd have an argument, my mom would walk around the house, making sure all the windows were closed, while screaming at my dad."

"Ha! My parents sometimes shouted at each other because there was nothing good on TV. It was like a family pastime."

Tatum drummed on the steering wheel, the smile still on his face as he listened to the album. "What did you do as a child?" Tatum asked after a few minutes. "Before you started chasing serial killers, I mean."

"Read, mostly. Anything I could get my hands on. We had a nice library in Maynard, and I'd go there on my bike a few times every week to borrow books."

"I had you pegged for a bookworm."

"I wasn't like a recluse, hiding in the attic with my books," Zoe said, annoyed. "I'd hang out with my friends . . . well, one friend."

"Your BFF?"

"I don't know what that is."

Tatum glanced at her, surprised. "Best friends forever. Everyone knows that."

Zoe shrugged. "Well, obviously not forever—I haven't talked to her in more than five years. But we were very good friends. We would go to each other's house all the time on our bikes. Now that I think about it, I went *everywhere* with my bike. I don't think I've ridden a bike since I left Maynard."

"I used to ride my bike everywhere too," Tatum said. "Whenever I think about my childhood, I remember pedaling hard, trying to get the bike as fast as I could. I'd ride to school and back every day, timing myself, always trying to break my own records. I'd ride with my friends a lot too, racing down the street, ramming into each other. Sometimes we'd go to Turtleback Mountain . . . I don't even think it's a proper mountain, but it seemed huge. We'd ride to the top, then drive as fast as we could to the bottom."

"Sounds like it's a miracle you survived childhood."

Tatum laughed. "Once I moved in with Marvin, supervision became a bit lax."

The image of teenage Tatum took shape in Zoe's mind. She found herself fascinated with it. She wanted to find out how little Tatum had grown up into the man she was slowly getting to know.

"What happened to your parents?" she asked. They'd never talked about it before. She just knew that Marvin had raised him.

"They died in a car accident when I was twelve. Drunk driver rammed into them."

"I'm sorry."

"Thanks. The driver who killed them died as well, which I think was lucky. Because otherwise, Marvin would have hunted him down and killed him. Instead, he took me in and did a pretty decent job of raising me."

"I'd say he did more than a decent job."

"Well, you weren't around for the famous eleventh-grade curfew time war." Tatum flashed her a grin. He slowed the car down as they entered the parking lot of the San Angelo Police Department, a large flat brown structure.

"So?" He switched off the engine. "What do you think of the album?"

"There's no chorus, no rhythm, and the singer's voice is a bit annoying when he yells. But I liked the instrumental section in the first song. If the entire album was like that, it would have been great to listen to."

Tatum's mouth twitched. "You have to listen to it several times to really—"

"Tatum, I'm never listening to that album again. And it's my turn to choose next time." She got out of the car and closed the door behind her.

CHAPTER 8

The Criminal Investigation Division of the San Angelo Police Department was on the first floor, on the far end of the long hallway that emerged from the lobby. The open space was split into an assortment of cubicles, their walls beige, just low enough that Tatum could peek over the top into each of the small enclosed spaces. Lieutenant Peter Jensen, who escorted them inside, paused for a moment and looked around him, as if noticing the cubicles for the first time.

"This is where our detectives work." He gestured grandly around his kingdom. He was a short man, not much taller than Zoe. "Over here we have the investigation whiteboard," he continued, showing them a large whiteboard. "We fill it with our most pressing cases."

The whiteboard was empty except for one corner, where someone had played tic-tac-toe, and the top, where it seemed someone accidentally had begun writing with a permanent marker and then realized his mistake and stopped. The letters *Gib* were the result, etched for eternity. Jensen glared at the whiteboard in frustration, clearly upset there was no pressing case to demonstrate.

"That's very interesting." Tatum hoped to interrupt the tour. "Where do you want to talk about the Medina case?"

"Let's go to my office. It's just over there."

He led them through a small door at the edge of the cubicles to a cramped corner office with a large desk, its surface entirely clean. On the wall opposite the door were several framed letters that thanked the police for their hard work and one photograph of Jensen with an official-looking man Tatum assumed was the police chief.

Jensen sat behind his desk and entwined his fingers. "Please. Sit down."

Over his years as an FBI agent, Tatum had learned to sense when he was not welcome. Jensen clearly wasn't happy they were there. He had a certain air of a man preparing a long speech that could be summarized as "Go away."

"I am really happy the FBI is taking this case so seriously," Jensen said. "Quite frankly, we informed you about the video because we wanted to update you that we had a situation that could, under certain circumstances, escalate."

Tatum translated Jensen's sentence in his mind. *Someone called the FBI without asking me first.*

"That's why we're here," he said brightly. "To prevent escalation."

"Of course! And we're very pleased. Interagency collaboration is something we value very highly in the San Angelo Police Department."

We handle our shit ourselves. All other law agencies should mind their own damn business.

"However, it might have been premature to send an FBI team over."

You want to take our case away. That will happen over my cold, dead body.

"Premature?" Zoe interrupted. "A young woman seems to have been buried alive. Do you really have the expertise to handle such a case on your own?"

"Well . . . obviously we're looking into all aspects. The video is quite disturbing. But we suspect it doesn't necessarily represent the whole facts."

The video is a fake, just like you two.

"What kind of facts? What are you talking about?" Zoe asked in a tense voice. Tatum struggled with the dilemma, unsure if he should intervene. On one hand, if Zoe exploded, they might be kicked off the case and out of the station. On the other hand, it would be amusing. Decisions, decisions.

"Nicole Medina's father, Oscar Medina, is incarcerated on possession with intent to sell. He has clear connections to the Mexican Mafia. We have an informant claiming a local gang is trying to exert leverage on a large supply chain, and it's very possible the video is a threat aimed at Oscar Medina."

"You think a local gang buried Nicole alive while filming it to . . . threaten her father?" Zoe's eyes narrowed. "And then what? They dug her back up?"

"We need to examine all possibilities. And we really want to hear the FBI's take on it, of course."

Tatum's bullshit-interpretation skill overloaded and crashed. Zoe took a deep breath, preparing for assault. Tatum decided that as funny as it would be to see her verbally disintegrate the lieutenant, they could at least justify the trip to Texas. "Who is the detective handling the case?" he asked hurriedly.

"He's our most experienced investigator, so I assure you we're taking this case very seriously."

Tatum resisted the impulse to point out that it hadn't gone on the very-serious whiteboard. "Of course. Can you point us to his cubicle? We'll just talk to him, see we're on the same page, and be on our way."

Jensen's face relaxed, and a small smile twisted his thick lips. Clearly the words "be on our way" were what he'd wanted to hear all along.

CHAPTER 9

Detective Samuel Foster had rich black skin, his face sporting a full dark beard with spotty touches of gray. Zoe estimated he was about forty, perhaps slightly older, the lines of age starting to materialize on his forehead. Someone had once told her cops aged faster, and though it was a ridiculous generalization, she often saw instances in which it really was true. He chewed a pencil, half gazing at his monitor when they showed up in his cubicle, led by Lieutenant Jensen. The screen displayed the video page of the live burial of Nicole Medina, the frame frozen halfway through the video.

"Detective, these are Agents Gray and Bentley from the FBI." Jensen's voice was businesslike, but Zoe could sense a vague snappishness in it, as if this whole situation had offended him in some obscure manner. She didn't bother correcting him about her actual title.

Foster swiveled his chair to look at them. His face was impassive and calculating. He took the pencil from his mouth. Teeth marks marred the pencil's entire surface.

"FBI agents?" Foster said. "Why are they here?"

"They came after we informed them about the Nicole Medina case."

"We did?" Foster's eyes widened. "I'm glad you changed your mind, Lieutenant."

"They're just here to offer some advice." Jensen's jaw was clenched so tightly that it was a wonder he managed to form syllables. "I would appreciate it if you give them a rundown of what we have so far."

"Absolutely, Lieutenant."

Jensen nodded curtly and left without saying another word.

The detective's face broke into a wide, warm smile. A second before he had been a jaded, angry cop. Now he metamorphosed into a pleasant, friendly, welcoming man. "Thanks for coming. I'm frankly relieved the FBI is showing such an interest in our case."

"Are you the one who notified the FBI about it?" Tatum asked.

"Me?" Foster put his hand on his chest theatrically. "That's not my decision to make. I suggested we call the feds, but ultimately, *only* the lieutenant decides if the case warrants outside intervention."

"Well, it's good that someone notified us," Zoe said, impatient to start. "I hope we'll be able to help narrow the suspect list."

Foster motioned at an extra chair beside him. "Sit down. You can grab a third chair from the cubicle over there. O'Sullivan is on vacation—he won't mind."

Zoe sat down while Tatum went to the adjacent cubicle to get the extra chair. It was crowded in the cubicle, which hardly had enough room for two people, not to mention three.

"I assume you saw the video?" Foster placed the pencil he'd chewed in a small cup already containing half a dozen mangled pencils.

"Yes." Zoe said. "Lieutenant Jensen told us that you think Nicole Medina was being used to threaten her father in some capacity—"

"I'm sure the lieutenant has some wild theories, but I assure you he didn't get them from me," Foster said.

Zoe exchanged looks with Tatum. "The lieutenant said he has an informant who told him that."

"Rufus 'Blacky' Anderson. Blacky *always* has a tip for us, especially since we started paying forty dollars per tip. Some of his tips pan out, and some make great bedtime stories." Foster shook his head. "I don't believe for a second this is drug or gang related. There's a sick bastard behind all this."

"What can you tell us about Nicole Medina's disappearance?" Tatum asked.

"Her mother reported her missing on the morning of September second," Foster answered. "Nicole had gone to a party the night before, told her mother she'd be home by midnight. In the morning, when her mother saw she never came back home, she called us. We talked to her friends, and they claimed she rode with them and that they dropped her at her home. Their accounts match, and we have red light camera footage of the four of them in the car. Nicole's face is visible in the back seat."

"How does she seem in the footage?" Zoe asked. "Drunk? Sleepy?"

"You tell me." Foster leaned forward and grabbed the mouse. He double-clicked an image file on an open folder. The image opened on-screen, displaying an image of a Toyota driving down the road. The image's resolution was poor, but Zoe could spot the hazy face of a girl staring out the passenger window. It was impossible to see her features clearly.

"She's conscious—that much we can tell," Foster said. "Nothing much beyond that. I can show you the actual footage from the red light cam later."

"What then?" Tatum asked.

"According to her friends, they dropped her off at her home and drove away. I went to her home with the driver, and he showed me exactly where he stopped the car. We went door to door in the vicinity. No one saw them dropping her off, but like I said, their accounts match, and they look like nice kids. The street is dark, and there's a gravel path to the door."

Zoe frowned. "You think someone grabbed her there?"

"There are some scuff marks on the path that could indicate a struggle." Foster shrugged. "Not conclusive. No blood found on scene. In fact, the mother couldn't tell us for sure that Nicole *didn't* return home. It's possible Nicole came home, went to sleep, and left in the morning before her mother woke up. But it isn't likely. We couldn't find anything that would indicate Nicole came home after the party."

Zoe tried to imagine it. Nicole being dragged off a few steps from the entrance to her home. It sounded remarkably risky, but she could see the advantages. The girl would be less alert, already feeling safe. Zoe resolved to see the house for herself.

Foster sighed. "The lieutenant has some wild theories, but to his credit, he took it seriously, as did the chief. We talked to everyone, did an extensive search in the vicinity. And then, in the evening, a local kid named Ronnie Cronin sent us the link to this video." He gestured at the monitor, his face weary. "I watched this thing several times. It keeps me awake at night."

Zoe could sympathize. Even with the image frozen, the frame blurry, caught in the midst of motion, it was unpleasant. The wide, panicky gaze; the gaping mouth, paused midscream; the claustrophobic space the young woman was in. "This local kid," she said. "How did he find the link to the video?"

"Got it by email. He has a YouTube channel where he talks about . . ." Foster rolled his eyes. "I have no idea about what, frankly. I watched several of his videos, and I couldn't understand half of what he was talking about. Anyway, he said someone sent this to him and a bunch of other people. He forwarded the email to me. The email is from a temporary mail address and just has the video link. It was sent to ten different email addresses. Eight of them, including Cronin, are popular YouTubers from San Angelo and nearby towns. The other two are local reporters. I talked to a few of them, and they all said more or less the same—they watched a few seconds, decided the video was a distasteful prank, and stopped watching."

"Did you check Cronin?" Zoe asked.

"He was doing an all-night live broadcast of himself playing a video game with a bunch of friends. We checked it out, and it's rock solid."

"Any other leads?" Tatum asked.

"The mother gave us a handful of contacts, mostly friends of Medina. Then I went to the prison and talked to the father. He seemed very worried and told me there was no way this was gang related. We had a lot of ground to cover, and time was ticking."

Foster adopted the glazed look of a man looking back into the past, regretting his decisions. "I should have insisted right then that we involve you people. But I thought we'd uncover something fast. Then someone talked to Blacky. And since then . . . well, we're still looking. But the case is going in the wrong directions. And now, if the girl was left buried, there's a good chance she's dead."

"You want us to find her," Zoe said, the realization sinking. "That's why you involved the bureau in the first place."

"Of course. You guys have ways to trace the video, right? Find out who posted it. Our cyber unit got nowhere with it, but the feds should be able to do it easily."

Zoe gritted her teeth in frustration. She didn't have Foster's faith in their cyber capabilities. But even worse, Foster's call for help had gotten to the wrong place. All the detective needed was someone from the FBI field office in San Antonio to take a look. Instead, his request had somehow been routed to the BAU, wasting valuable time, ending up with the wrong people showing up. Had anyone in the bureau even made a serious attempt to locate the video's source?

Foster's eyes shifted between them. "So can you talk to your analysts? Do some FBI magic?"

Zoe shook her head. "That's not what we—"

"We'll do whatever we can," Tatum said.

CHAPTER 10

As far as Tatum was concerned, the entire bureau had only one tech analyst—Sarah Lee from the LA field office. He was vaguely aware of other people sporting the title "analyst" walking around, and it made certain sense. After all, Sarah couldn't do everything, and other people had to be hired to pick up her slack. But if he needed *anything* at all, he called Sarah. If he had a question about explosives, he called Sarah. Tricky tool marks in a crime scene—Sarah was the first one he dialed. Couldn't figure out how to fix his internet router at home after Marvin broke it? A quick phone call to Sarah.

Sitting in the empty cubicle across from Foster's, he dialed her private number, not bothering to go through her office number.

"Tatum?" She sounded half-delighted, half-aghast to answer his phone call.

"Sarah!" He grinned at the sound of her voice. "How are you?"

"I'm fine. It's nice to talk to you. How are the things in the BAU?"

"Still learning the ropes," Tatum said, dutifully taking part in the small talk ceremony. "How's Grace?" Grace was Sarah's dog, and Tatum had been regaled with stories about her more times than he could count.

"She's good. She ate cat poop yesterday."

"Awesome. Listen, Sarah, I need a favor."

"Tatum. You can't keep calling me for favors."

"It's a real emergency."

"Don't they have people in Quantico to help you?"

"They're all idiots. And whenever I ask one to help me, they want me to fill out paperwork."

"Be still my beating heart," she remarked dryly. "Paperwork? What is the bureau coming to?"

"Form 212B this, Form 42A that—"

"Those are not real form numbers. Did you ever fill out *any* lab form?"

"I don't need to, because you are above all that."

"I'm not above it—you just can't seem to do it."

"It's like I'm James Bond and you are Q, full of technological wonders."

"I bet even James Bond filled out some request forms every now and then."

"You are like an oracle who has all the answers."

"Okay, okay, stop that. What do you need?"

He filled her in on the details, simultaneously emailing her the video link from his laptop. He heard her tapping on her keyboard, and after a minute he heard the faint screaming of Nicole Medina coming from her side of the phone. Sarah's breath hitched.

"What do you need from me?" she asked. The screaming stopped as she either muted or paused the video.

"I need to trace that video."

"I can do some digging, but it'll take time, and I'm not very optimistic." There was some furious typing going on. "I'll also try and figure out who the domain name belongs to—maybe I can find it through there."

Tatum drummed on the desk. "Is there any other way you can get the location of the video? Maybe use aerial photos to search for it?"

Sarah snorted. "And look for what? Cacti, pebbles, and sand somewhere in Texas? I doubt that would narrow it down."

"Then maybe you could—"

"Maybe *you* could let me do my job in peace. You're just as irritating as you were when you were working here. Hovering over my shoulder with your endless suggestions."

There was some tapping in the background as he waited on the line.

"I just skipped ahead a bit," Sarah said. "What's his deal with the president?"

"This isn't about the president. He's just using the live feed of CNN to—"

"The CNN feed is live?"

"Yeah."

"I'll call you once I have something, okay?" She sounded suddenly excited.

"Thanks, Sarah. I really appreciate it. You're my—"

"I'm your oracle, your Q, your technical wizard—I know. I'll call you." She hung up.

Amused, he turned to Foster and Zoe, who were sitting in Foster's cubicle going over the case's timeline again.

"I want to talk to Nicole Medina's mother," Zoe told him. "And I want to see the place where she supposedly disappeared."

CHAPTER 11

Tatum followed Foster's car—a battered silver Chevy—to Nicole Medina's home. Foster had offered to give them a ride, but Tatum preferred to drive and get a bit of a feel for San Angelo on the way.

The ride would have been relaxing as well if it hadn't been Zoe's turn to choose the music. She inflicted Taylor Swift's *Red* upon him and pointed out that she was skipping some of the songs because she wanted him to hear the best ones. As far as he was concerned, this didn't improve the experience.

Finally, Foster's car parked on the side of the street. Tatum slowed down, pulling to the side behind him. The road's edges met with grass and dirt, no sidewalk anywhere. There was a large cluster of wild bushes and foliage to their right, and beyond it, a gravel road.

He switched off the engine and stepped out of the car.

Foster waited for them with his hands on his hips, his eyes hidden by a pair of dark shades. He indicated down the gravel path. "That's the house."

Tatum looked down the road. The house was small but seemed well maintained. The grass in the front yard was mowed, and clusters of flowers grew around it. The sprinklers were running, painting the air in a misty hue. He thought of Sophia Medina, Nicole's mother, worried sick about her daughter.

"No streetlights," Zoe said by his side.

"And the house is about fifteen yards from the road," Tatum pointed out. "No immediate neighbors."

"He could hide here easily." Zoe pointed at the foliage and then gestured back the way they had come. "With his vehicle over there, just a few yards down the road. There's a spot no one would notice."

Her cheeks and forehead were turning pink, but she didn't seem to notice the sun at all. Was she even aware the sun was up? Or did she see the street as it was, late in the evening, four days ago, when Nicole Medina had been taken? She took a few steps to the thick foliage, crouched between the low trees and bushes. Tatum eyed her position. She was right: if the kidnapper had hidden there, he would have been practically invisible in the dark.

The door to Nicole Medina's home opened abruptly, and a woman half marched, half ran to them, her entire body rigid with tension.

"Detective," she said. "Any news about Nicole?"

"No, Mrs. Medina, I'm sorry," Foster answered gently.

The woman's body slumped, and she turned to look at Tatum.

"This is Agent Gray." Foster gestured. "From the FBI. He's here to help us investigate your daughter's case."

Tatum was used to seeing a spectrum of emotions on people's faces when realizing that a fed had entered their life. But the only reaction he saw from Sophia Medina was a slight measure of relief.

"Thank you," she said. "She's been missing for four days."

"I understand," Tatum said. "The detective—"

"She went with her friends to a party. They dropped her off here." Her words rushed out of her mouth, frantic, urgent. "They're nice kids; I know them all. Gina practically grew up in our house. She's Nicole's best friend. And they dropped Nicole here. She was right here. But I don't think she entered the house. She didn't use her toothbrush, and her clothes weren't in the laundry. She always changes her clothes, always brushes her teeth before going to bed. I can give you the phone numbers of all her friends. And her teachers. Her teachers all love her—they can tell you—"

Tatum raised his palms in a reassuring gesture, and the torrent of words died. The woman stared at him pleadingly.

A rustle came from the bushes, and Sophia's eyes shifted as Zoe stepped out from them.

"This is my partner, Zoe Bentley." He intentionally neglected to add Zoe's title. He really didn't want to explain to Sophia why a forensic psychologist was investigating Nicole's case.

"Mind if we come in?" Foster asked.

Sophia nodded and led them inside, past the cool haze of mist from the sprinklers. The house was dark, most of the blinds shut, the lights turned off. Only one of the windows was open, facing the street, a single chair by it. An ashtray and several empty mugs of coffee were scattered on the floor next to the chair. This was Sophia's sentry post. She probably sat there, waiting for the police to show up. And maybe hoping that Nicole would stroll down the gravel path and come back home.

"Could you take us to your daughter's room, please?" Zoe's voice was subdued. The silent dark house felt like a place of mourning. Loud voices did not belong.

"Her room's over here." The woman led them to a small room. The walls were painted a soft yellow, and the bed's sheets had a cheerful floral pattern. A smooth wooden desk stood by a small window, and on it were a few notebooks, a small desk lamp, a scented candle.

"Did you tidy the room after your daughter disappeared?" Zoe asked.

"No," Sophia said. "Nicole likes it organized."

Tatum walked over to the far wall, where a small shelf hung, covered with figurines of turtles. They were different sizes and shapes, made of wood, glass, plastic, cloth. He picked one up, a handmade clay turtle.

"It's Nicole's collection," Sophia explained. "She started collecting them when she was twelve."

"Does Nicole have a boyfriend?" Zoe asked.

"No. She broke up with her boyfriend six months ago," Sophia answered.

"Who was he?"

"A boy from school."

"We talked to him," Foster said. "He hadn't seen Nicole in a while."

Zoe glanced at Foster, raising her eyebrow doubtfully. "And no other boys? No one she dated? Not even once?"

"No. She would have told me," the mother answered.

"Any new people in her life?"

"She always had a lot of friends, but I don't think there is anyone new. She spends all day messaging them on the phone. It keeps pinging, driving me insane. I . . ." Her voice broke. Tatum was willing to bet the absence of the phone's pinging had just occurred to her.

"Is she popular?" Zoe asked.

"She is. She's very friendly and sweet. She has a knack for making friends."

Zoe grilled her about Nicole's habits—what she did during the day, whom she interacted with, whether she often returned home late at night. Tatum wandered around, examining the room, half listening to the woman's answers. The missing girl's presence was everywhere—pictures of Nicole on top of a dresser, a hairbrush with a bunch of hair bands wrapped around its handle discarded on a shelf, a pair of pink flip-flops in one of the corners. After a while Zoe stopped asking questions and just listened as Sophia told her stories about Nicole. How Nicole loved swimming. How she'd been afraid of monsters under the bed until she was six. The time Nicole had bought her a birthday present with all of her allowance.

Finally, she seemed to run out of steam. Tears were running down her cheeks, her words submerged in fear and worry.

Foster thanked her, and they stepped outside, closing the door behind them.

"Where did you spot the scuff marks?" Zoe asked.

Foster stepped to the edge of the path. "Over here." He crouched. "It's hard to see now, but we have a few photographs."

Tatum's phone rang. He checked the display. It was Sarah Lee. He stepped aside, letting Foster talk to Zoe, and answered the call.

"You found something?"

"That CNN video was live, right? So we know when the video was taken."

"That's right." Tatum watched Foster and Zoe as they straightened. Foster pointed at the street, saying something.

"I contacted the mobile providers covering the area," Sarah told him. "And asked for CDRs of users who browsed to the CNN live feed page around that time."

Tatum digested this. It took him a few seconds to remember what CDR stood for—call detail records. When the man had browsed to CNN, the mobile company maintained a record of the activity, which had to include the domain name as well as the cell base stations that serviced the request. And that could be translated to an approximate location. Fortunately for them, this information was not protected by the Fourth Amendment and could be accessed by Sarah without a warrant.

"That list must be huge."

"It was." Sarah had an undertone of smugness to her voice. "So I narrowed it down. Just the perimeter around San Angelo. Got the exact time of that specific video on CNN and limited myself to CDRs of users who started watching the live stream within five minutes of that time. The list became quite short."

"How short?" he asked, his voice tense.

"Eighteen phone numbers in San Angelo or the vicinity. And out of those eighteen, seventeen were deep in San Angelo, so they obviously aren't our guy, right? Our guy was in the middle of nowhere."

"Sarah . . ." Tatum felt his heart pound. "You have a location for me?"

"I'm sending you the GPS coordinates. And I already checked satellite images, Tatum. The location's accuracy isn't great, but the surroundings are a perfect match for the video."

CHAPTER 12

Zoe looked at the gravel path and its surroundings, trying to picture that night. It would have been almost pitch black without streetlights. The car with Nicole's friends had dropped her off. She'd waved goodbye, and they'd driven away, leaving her in darkness. She'd probably moved fast to the door. The man who had taken her had hidden in the bushes by the yard—she was almost 100 percent sure. That was the most likely place. No chance he'd lurked there by accident. This had been planned.

"I have the location!" Tatum's excited voice jolted her out of her reverie. He pointed at his phone emphatically. Foster was by his side in a second. Zoe hurried over to join them.

"Where?" Foster asked, breathless.

"Spillway Road," Tatum said, indicating the map on the mobile's screen. "It's an approximate location, within five hundred feet." He switched to a satellite image. They waited for a few seconds as the phone's slow connection downloaded the image. Most of the area was covered with cacti, bushes, and trees.

Foster looked at the phone's screen. "In that case, it could be Chalimar Road as well."

"Not likely," Zoe interjected. "Too close to the farm over here." She indicated the farm.

"Five hundred feet along Spillway Road here?" Foster traced the satellite image with his finger. "Can't be the northern part of the road—the foliage is too thick. He buried her in a clear patch of dirt. Has to be around here." He pointed at a small area on the map, about fifty feet in diameter.

"I think you're right," Tatum agreed.

"I'll send a patrol over there right now. If she's there, we'll find her."

"No, wait!" Zoe blurted. "You have to get crime scene technicians with you to process the area."

"You're kidding." Foster glanced at her, incredulous. "The girl might be suffocating in that box right now. There's not a moment to—"

"If she's in there, she's been dead for three days," Zoe said decisively. "Rushing to get a corpse out will only hurt our efforts to catch whoever did this later on."

Foster glanced at the house as if worried Nicole's mother was listening in on their discussion. "You don't know that," he hissed in a low voice.

"I do. Our analyst gave Medina a maximum of thirty-six hours."

"That's just conjecture."

"It's actually called math."

Foster exhaled and shook his head. "I'm digging the girl up as soon as possible." He marched away.

"Let's call the lieutenant," Zoe said urgently to Tatum. "We need them to preserve the crime scene."

Tatum glanced at her, scrunching his eyebrows. "This is not our case," he reminded her. "We're just here to advise. And we definitely don't want to get on the detective's bad side."

"But they might storm to that grave site with patrol cars or heavy machinery and trample any shred of evidence we'll be able to use later."

"It's not our decision to make."

CHAPTER 13

It was a thirty-minute ride to Spillway Road, since Tatum made a wrong turn somewhere. By the time they arrived, it was easy to see that the police had found the exact location already—there were already two patrol cars there. Zoe groaned by his side when they saw them, four officers hard at work, digging. Three of them had spades; the other was digging with his hands, shoveling handfuls of earth out of the pit.

Tatum swerved off the road, the car's tires scraping on the gravel. He opened the door and half jogged toward the four officers. As he got closer, one of the officers turned to face him, probably about to tell him to stay away.

"Agent Gray, FBI," Tatum said, flashing his badge. "I'm just here to help."

The officer seemed confused for a second, then shrugged and returned to the growing hole. The men were digging fast, almost frantically, and Tatum felt their excitement. He reminded himself Zoe was probably right. If the girl was underneath all that sand, she was long gone. His only hope was she wasn't there at all. That the video had been fake, or that after burying her and pausing the video, the man had dug her up again. Why else pause the video? The only reason he could think of was that the man wanted to hide something.

Before he could think it through, Tatum was in the pit alongside one of the officers, scooping earth with his hands. It was easy to dig; the earth wasn't compact, hadn't had time to harden in the few days since the man on the video had spilled it into the grave.

As he tossed handful after handful of soil out of the pit, he tried to recall how deep the grave was. How much did they need to dig? It was about three or four feet, no more. The pace they were going, they could get there in ten minutes.

One of the men cried in pain, and they all paused. A shovel had hit his hand as he scooped dirt.

"Watch it, Ramirez!" the man snapped at the officer by his side.

"Sorry!" Ramirez apologized, taking a step sideways.

"Nearly took my finger off," the hurt officer complained, but he was already shoveling sand again, ignoring the red streak of blood on his palm.

After a few minutes another car showed up. Tatum raised his eyes to see Detective Foster getting out of the car, holding a bunch of shovels. He hurried to the grave, gave a small pause as he saw Tatum in it, and then, with a curt nod, handed him a shovel.

Just seconds later, one of the shovels hit wood, emitting a loud thunk.

"I hit it!" Ramirez shouted. "It's here."

Tatum dug faster, feeling the buzz of frantic activity as the people beside him did the same. Soon he could see the wood—unpolished planks, pale and dirty. He found the shovel to be a burden since the thing kept bumping into the planks. He tossed the shovel out of the pit and began removing dirt with his hands again. All the other officers followed suit.

Scoop, straighten, toss, crouch, scoop, straighten, toss . . . Tatum suspected his back would hurt like hell later.

"Okay!" Foster called. "That's good enough. Everyone out of the pit."

The box's lid was now mostly visible, covered by small mounds of sand in just a few spots. The only thing that prevented them from opening the thing were the four men currently standing on top of it. Tatum scrambled out, and the rest of them followed. One of the officers, a tall bald man with wide shoulders, bent into the pit, grabbing the edge of the box's lid. For a moment it didn't budge, the weight of the sand on it keeping it shut. But the man grunted, and with a sudden creak, the lid came off.

The smell that hit them told Tatum all he needed to know. As the people around him groaned, one of them running into the bushes to throw up, Tatum glanced into the coffin, looking at the discolored, bloated body.

Nicole Medina had been in there after all. And she was long dead.

CHAPTER 14

Zoe had been told repeatedly throughout her life that she was insensitive and tactless. Nevertheless, when Tatum turned to face her for the first time since they'd arrived at the grave site, she knew it was a good time to bite her tongue. His suit, which was usually straight and immaculate, was now dusty and smudged, the fabric creased, one of the buttons of his white shirt open. His hair was ruffled, and his face was tired and sad. For a moment, she felt an urge to hug him.

He walked over to her. "She's been dead for two days at the very least."

Zoe gave him a short nod. A few yards away, Detective Foster took charge, telling the men to step away, to establish a perimeter around the crime scene. Because that was what it was now, of course: a murder crime scene.

She approached the grave. Peering inside, she scrutinized the body. Medina was fully clothed in the outfit she'd presumably worn to the party. Zoe made a mental note to verify with her friends that it was indeed what she'd worn. Her shirt was disheveled but intact. Her eyes were shut. Perhaps she'd mercifully lost consciousness long before she'd completely run out of air. Her veins and arteries were discolored and dark, crisscrossing the pallid skin. A fly landed on her face, but it was the first one. No insects crawled around the body. Perhaps it had been buried too deep, or maybe the soil was too dry for insect life.

A small device was embedded into the box just by the body's head. The camera. Zoe crouched to look at it more carefully. A bit of the wire snaked out of it, through a hole in the box. She examined the uneven side of the dug hole, seeing two sections where the wire had been partially uncovered. She wondered where the tip of the wire broke through the ground.

She frowned, looking back at the box and the body. The box was a bit taller and significantly wider than the body was. Maybe these were standard measurements—she would have to check. But she had a hunch that the box was larger than it needed to be.

Had the killer had Nicole in mind when he'd built the box, or had he built a box that would fit any random victim?

"Agent, do you mind signing this?" Foster was by her side, handing her a clipboard and a pen.

She glanced at it. It was a crime scene log. "Of course." She plucked the pen from his hand and scribbled her name under Tatum's. "I'm not an agent, Detective Foster. I'm a civilian consultant."

Foster nodded distractedly, the distinction far from his mind. He peered down at the grave. "What sort of monster would do something like that?"

"It's not a monster," Zoe said automatically. As Foster narrowed his eyes, she added, "It's a man you're dealing with. Not a monster. He can be studied and understood. He can be caught."

"Do you think there'll be more? Is this a serial killer?"

She considered it. "I think it's best to talk once we have a thorough report on the crime scene."

Foster looked up at the sky, the setting sun. "That'll happen tomorrow. We'll do what we can in the darkness, with spotlights, but I think we'll want to do another sweep in the morning." His phone rang, and he stepped away to answer the call.

An officer, his uniform dusty from the digging, twisted crime scene tape around the low bushes that surrounded the grave. Zoe moved away, scanning the area around her. A wall of trees hid the grave site from the road, their branches contorted and thorny, covered in nettles. Cacti growing between the trees supplied additional camouflage, their thick green arms creating an almost-impenetrable wall. The road itself was a long narrow stretch with almost no traffic, everything beige or gray or dusty green. It felt like a road to nowhere.

The perfect place to bury a body. Or, in this case, to bury a living victim.

She turned around, looking back. There was an opening in the wall of cacti and trees about six feet wide. Two patrol cars were parked in it, one after the other. Zoe sighed. Obviously, this was the path the killer had used to get his own vehicle through. They'd probably eliminated any tire marks. She stepped to the narrow path and crouched, frowning.

"What is it?" Tatum asked behind her.

"There were plants here as well." She pointed at a branch protruding from the ground. "Someone clipped them."

"You think it was the killer?"

She stood up. "Probably. See how the path leads directly to the grave site? He'd prepared a driveway."

"He had the grave site planned in advance," Tatum said. After a second he added, "He probably dug the grave before he even kidnapped his victim."

"But why here?" Zoe asked. "We're in the middle of the desert. There are probably a million places to bury someone. Why choose a place where he had to work so hard just to get it ready?"

Tatum didn't answer, inspecting the clipped branch closely. Finally, he stood up and turned to her. "I just updated Mancuso. She wants to know if we think there'll be more victims."

"It's too soon to say."

"But you have a hunch, right? I know *I* do."

"We can't act on a hunch."

Tatum sighed. "What does your gut tell you, Zoe?"

She bit her lip. "There'll be more. This wasn't about killing Nicole Medina. This was about burying someone alive. This was a fantasy."

"That's what I think as well," Tatum said. "And if the killer called this experiment number one—"

"There's a good chance he's already planning experiment number two."

CHAPTER 15

He was disappointed by the internet. Though he hadn't thought his video would be an instant viral success, he'd assumed watching a woman being buried alive would elicit a bit more than the paltry 1,903 views his video currently had.

None of the ten blogs and reporters he'd originally sent this to had published anything about it. The majority of his views came from a website that collected videos of people getting hurt and dying, and even there, his popularity was quite low. One of the users said it was lame that they didn't get to see the woman suffocate to death. Another commented this was clearly staged and that both participants were lousy actors.

It didn't matter. The next one would get their attention.

He switched to Instagram and began scrolling through his targets' feeds. He almost never followed them in person anymore. Why risk getting caught when women went out of their way to do his dirty work for him? He took in the new selfies, the poses, the teasing captions. He made notes of the ones who had new boyfriends and the ones who went out to party because they were "free at last."

Those were his preferable targets. Boyfriends made things more complicated.

He paused for a moment over a profile of one Gloria King. Gloria had just tagged herself in a picture with friends on a night out. In the selfie, the three of them were holding bottles of beer, smiling at the camera. Gloria wore a sleeveless pink shirt, leaving her golden skin exposed. The picture was recent, uploaded only twenty minutes ago.

A night out, getting drunk. She would return home wasted, well beyond midnight, her parents long asleep. He knew where she lived, of course. They had a dog, but it was tied up near the front door. And the path up to her house was long and dark, the neighboring houses too far to matter.

An opportunity there. He considered it. Gloria King's fate hung by a thread.

It was too soon. He wasn't in a hurry. He had plenty of time.

He minimized the browser and double-clicked the video thumbnail on the desktop. The face of the young woman appeared on-screen, just as she slowly woke up. He could already sense the excitement building up inside him as she screamed her very first scream. He tried not to watch this video too many times. Anything could get dull with repetition, even this. But for now, it was still almost as exciting as being there for the very first time.

He'd watched the entire video from start to finish only once. It was fourteen hours long. It wasn't even the director's cut—it was just the raw material, and some of it wasn't great. The whole part between 7:08:00 and 11:32:00 was just her lying motionless with her eyes closed. And after 12:35:23, the woman stopped moving altogether.

But all in all, it was definitely good material to work with. He estimated his personal edited version would be about three hours long.

Right now, for a bit of release after a long day, he knew of several good segments he could watch. He could start with 3:42:00.

As Nicole Medina thumped the lid, starting to scream again, he grabbed the box of tissues on the desk, breathing hard.

CHAPTER 16

Harry Barry sat by his desk, staring into space. The incessant noise of the *Chicago Daily Gazette* office served as a background music for his thoughts, something he almost didn't notice anymore. The sound of a printer spewing pages, the endless tapping of his coworkers' keyboards, the daily loud phone conversation between Rhonda and her husband. It hadn't changed for the past six years. Six years of sameness. Six years of writing what his editor liked to call human interest stories and Harry called addictive trash. Celebrity news and sex scandals. Sometimes he mixed it up with some celebrity scandals and sex news.

He'd used to like it. He was good at it.

But he'd gotten a taste of something different, and now his everyday life adopted a bland flavor. Like someone who ate meatloaf every day, and liked it, but then had a onetime encounter with a juicy steak.

He pondered this as he recalled the short conversation he'd had on the phone just an hour earlier. He'd received a tip. The tantalizing hint of a good story, one that he'd been working on for over a month now. And the next chapter of this story was not in Chicago, where he worked.

It was in San Angelo.

The problem was how to get there.

The idea of taking a vacation and paying for the trip himself sat uncomfortably with him. No, much better for his boss to pay for the trip and for Harry's expenses. And infinitely better if he didn't spend his precious vacation days but instead got paid for his time. How to convince his editor: that was the issue he mulled over in his head. He couldn't see any way to solve that conundrum. It made him quite upset.

He browsed to his latest online article, where he'd outed a famous local college football halfback's affair with a cheerleader. The title of the article—"Give Me an F-L-I-N-G"—made him quite proud. It was a short article, written in a somewhat bemused manner, like all his "human interest stories" were. He'd signed it, as always, as H. Barry. Because Harry Barry wasn't an acceptable name for a reporter. In fact, it wasn't an acceptable name for anything. It was an indication of parental laziness. As if his mother had said, "Let's not think of a whole name—let's just figure out one letter to switch."

Now, as he often did when he needed a fun distraction, he scrolled down to the comments. He enjoyed the miasma of trolls, angry readers, and loneliness that accompanied the comments in general, but what he loved most were the outraged readers. Nothing was as satisfying as a reader who read the article from beginning to end in fascination and then hurried to comment about everyone's obsession with sex or violence and moan about the decline of American values.

One comment in particular, posted by ConcernedCitizen13, caught his eye. *Trash. The "writer" of this article should be ashamed of himself.*

It drew his attention first and foremost because it was the only comment with no spelling mistakes and with actual punctuation. But more to the point, because of the sentiment.

That he should be ashamed of himself.

He stared at it long and hard, a grin forming on his face. Shame, now there was a thing.

He checked the time. He should have sent the draft of his next article to his editor ten minutes ago. Which meant he would appear just about—

"Harry. Where's the draft?" Daniel McGrath stepped into his cubicle.

Harry didn't answer, staring at the screen, his gaze far away.

"Harry. Hey!"

Harry blinked, glancing back at his longtime editor. "Oh. Daniel. I didn't hear you."

"Where's the damn article? You told me you had something good planned for today. The nude paparazzi pictures of that Russell woman."

"Paparazzi. Right." Harry let out a long sigh.

"Well? Where is it?"

"Daniel, did you ever stop to consider what we're doing?"

The editor blinked in surprise. "Is this about not hiring our own paparazzi photographers again? I told you, it's way cheaper to—"

"No, I mean . . ." Harry gestured sadly at the screen. "Everything."

"The paper?"

"Those articles I write. Those people. I was sitting here writing that article, and I suddenly thought, Cassy Russell has parents."

"She . . . well, what difference does that—"

"She has a mother and a father."

"That's how parents usually work, yes."

"Can you imagine opening the newspaper on Sunday morning, and your daughter's bare chest is on the front page?"

"Don't flatter yourself. It's on page eight, Harry."

"How it must feel. The same girl you bounced on your knees . . ."

"And we pixelate those breasts, you know that."

"The girl you told bedtime stories to . . ."

"What are you talking about?"

"How it wrenches his heart, his daughter exploited that way."

"Exploited? I . . . didn't you tell me *she* was the one who called the paparazzi photographers in the first place?"

"Didn't you ever make mistakes when you were young? We were like hyenas, waiting for her to fall. So what if she called them? She's still young."

"She's twenty-six."

"She's twenty-six." Harry shook his head, shutting his eyes. "Twenty-six."

Daniel nudged closer, lowering his voice. "Harry, what's going on?"

"We don't make the world a better place."

"A better place? What are you saying? We provide entertainment. We make people happy."

"We need to hold ourselves to a higher standard." Harry began to enjoy himself. "It's my fault. I got addicted to the attention. But now that we have a strong platform, we can *use* it. I write human interest stories, right? Let's make them count."

"Make them count?"

"You remember that email? The nurse who took care of that homeless person with the cancer? Let's write a piece on her."

"Are you trying to avoid writing this article? I can give it to someone else. I have a dozen junior writers dying to write the Russell woman's boobs article."

"*Cassy* Russell. She has a name. She's a human being, Daniel. A human being with feelings." That was an actual quote from a comment on one of his articles.

"She's a human being whose husband embezzled millions and now bared her boobs to get some attention."

"I want to write about that teacher who tutors illegal immigrants in English."

"People don't want to read that!"

"They *should*! I don't want to be ashamed of what I do." He considered thumping his chest and decided it would be going too far. "I'm going to write good human interest stories. No more exploitation."

Daniel's eyes shifted. Anxiety flickered in them. Harry was the paper's most popular journalist by far. Not just because of his topic material but because he knew how to use it. The worst thing that could happen was for him to be *ashamed*.

"Listen, I see you're going through a phase here, Harry. Tell you what—you need a vacation."

"No. I want to write stories." He shifted the papers on his tables. "I had something here. A vet who adopted a three-legged dog. You'll really like it."

"Tell you what," Daniel blurted. "How about a follow-up with that profiler? Bentley? You've been nagging me with it for a while."

"Bentley?" Harry quirked his eyebrows. "The FBI profiler from last month?"

"You were interested in writing about her at the time."

"Write about crime? And serial killers? I don't know, Daniel."

"Try it. You can make it a positive article. A young profiler trying to make a difference. It's a nice story, right?"

"I don't think she's available for an interview. She just went to San Angelo following a case."

"Well . . . fantastic!" Daniel brightened. "Fly there. See what she does. Write about that. That's not exploitation, right? And maybe the change of scenery will do you some good. Get you to see things in a better light."

Harry sighed heavily again, his shoulders slumping, while in his mind, he was doing a victory lap, the crowd cheering wildly.

CHAPTER 17

Zoe lay on the motel bed, her hair still wet from the shower, wearing a pair of underwear and a long baggy shirt that had the logo of an indie rock band Zoe didn't know. The shirt belonged to Andrea, and Zoe was pretty sure that *she'd* actually taken it from one of her boyfriends back in Boston.

But it was comfortable, and comfort was what Zoe needed right now.

They'd left soon after the crime scene technicians had shown up on the scene. Zoe had offered to drive, Tatum seeming tired and unfocused. He'd insisted he should drive, and she hadn't argued. He'd taken them to a motel that was reasonably close to the police station. They'd both been silent during the car ride. Once she'd closed the motel room's door behind her, the images and sensations had begun to break through. They were leaning against the wall of detachment that she protected herself with. As soon as she was alone, that wall always became paper thin.

She could walk out of the room, search for distractions, but she knew from experience it would only result in horrific nightmares. Her mind needed to vent, and it would do it one way or another. Best do it now, when she was mentally prepared.

The body had triggered this. Before she'd seen it, there could be numerous theories about what had happened. But once they'd found the body, got a visceral glimpse of its state, those realities had merged into one. Nicole Medina had been kidnapped, placed in a box, and buried alive.

Zoe had a knack. She could crawl into the mind of a killer, think like he did, sometimes even guess what he'd do next. But it was a gift with a price. She'd often find herself trapped in the mind of the victim as well. See their last moments, feel them almost as if they were her own.

And in Nicole's case, her imagination didn't even need to try hard. For the first time, she'd actually *seen* the victim suffering. Sliding into Nicole Medina's mind at that nightmarish juncture was as natural as breathing.

It would have been dark in that box, pitch black. She'd been lying on her back, and whenever she moved, she'd feel the walls around her. The air would feel stale, dusty, and as time went by, she'd have trouble breathing, which would trigger panic.

The walls closed around her, the horrifying knowledge that she was trapped with nowhere to go.

As a child, Zoe had once gone on a tour with her family to Laurel Caverns. It was a large group of people, and Zoe had been excited, waving her flashlight around. Then, midtour, as she crawled through a tight tunnel, the woman in front of her got stuck. Behind her, the rest of the group kept closing in, not realizing the way forward was blocked, and Zoe could feel the weight of their bodies approaching. Walls all around her, people blocking her way forward and back—she suddenly had trouble breathing. Andrea, who was right behind, pushed her to get her to move, and it had taken all of Zoe's self-control not to kick back.

She always avoided caves and tunnels after that day, and small elevators made her uncomfortable.

She lay on the bed, imagining the sensation of being trapped in that tiny space, a mountain of dirt all around her, her heart pounding in her ears, her breath coming out in short, panicky bursts.

CHAPTER 18

Tatum stood in the shower, his back aching, palms burning from a dozen bruises and scratches. One of his fingernails was broken, a thin line of blood underneath. He let the hot water wash over him, thinking of Nicole Medina lying in the box. Remembering the girl's screams on the video.

He observed the water pooling around his feet, gray with dirt. Sighing, he opened the motel's customary soap bar's package and began scrubbing.

Once he was clean, he got out of the bathroom, toweling himself, leaving wet footprints behind him on the parquet floor. He shut the blinds, then let the towel drop, considering his very limited wardrobe.

It was almost evening, but murder scenes weren't generally conducive to a healthy appetite, and he wasn't prepared to consider dinner. He thought of watching a bit of TV, but the idea of being cooped in the small room wasn't attractive either.

The motel had a small swimming pool, and Tatum decided a short swim would be perfect, both for his back and his appetite. He hadn't packed his bathing suit, so he went through his shorts. The white boxer shorts were a big no-no for obvious reasons. The black ones were a bit too tight, and while it wouldn't be a problem as long as he stayed in the pool, once he left it, they'd cling to his privates like plastic sandwich wrap. The blue ones were probably fine. He put them on, threw a towel over his shoulder, and left the room, locking it behind him. He ignored the panicky voice in his mind telling him he was outside in nothing but his underpants. He wasn't. He was wearing a bathing suit.

The swimming pool wasn't large by any standard, and the water sparkled in the setting sun's light. The surface was still, begging for someone to dive in. Tatum dove headfirst, which almost resulted in a concussion since the bottom was much closer than he'd initially estimated. He swam underwater to the other side of the pool and resurfaced, taking a long breath.

He did some laps. They were ridiculously short, a bit like doing laps in the bathtub, but for a while he concentrated on nothing but his body's movement in the water, on his breath, on pushing himself away whenever he reached the pool's edge.

After a few dozen minilaps, he felt someone watching him. He paused and lifted his head. It was Zoe. She stared at him with her piercing eyes, like a bird of prey considering a fish for dinner.

He gave her a cheery wave. "Come for a swim?"

She wrinkled her nose. "I don't like swimming."

"The water is really nice and cool." Despite the fact that the sky was already a dark blue, the air was still stifling hot. "You can dip your feet."

To his surprise, she actually sat down by the pool's edge and took off her shoes. She put one foot in the water and then the other. Then she let out a long sigh.

He swam to her side. Her face seemed far away and troubled. For a second he almost splashed her with water, recalling from his college days that it was a sure way to get a shrieking laugh from a girl, a playful "Stop it!"

But then, looking at her face, he thought better of it. Zoe didn't seem like the type to let out a shrieking laugh. She'd probably just give him a withering, chilly stare. Or possibly kill him.

"You okay?"

"Yeah." She let out a small shiver. "I just needed to get out a bit. I've been thinking about Nicole Medina."

Tatum nodded. After a few seconds he asked, "Why don't you like swimming?"

She eyed him speculatively. "Didn't you see *The Wizard of Oz*? Water makes me melt."

Tatum grinned at her, and she smiled back.

"I just don't like swimming," she said. "I don't like cold water, and my hair gets all tangly after I swim. The chlorine in swimming pools makes my skin itch."

"Gotcha. Swimming's the worst."

"Andrea was on her high school's swimming team," Zoe added. "She'd spend every day in the pool if you'd let her." She fumbled in her pocket, retrieving her phone. Her lips pursed as she tapped at its screen; then she put it aside and gazed at the water.

"How's Andrea doing?" Tatum asked, guessing that was what Zoe had checked.

"I wouldn't know." Her tone was testy. "She isn't responding to my text."

"Did she see it yet?"

"Well . . . no. But I've seen her ignore texts all the time. She doesn't open the ones that she ignores. She's sneaky like that."

"I'm sure she's fine." Tatum knew fully well it was an empty gesture. He'd been present during the discussions about Rod Glover's last letter to Zoe, his picture with Andrea. But since that day, no one had seen or heard anything from Glover. If Zoe heard his words, she didn't give any indication of it. She checked the screen again.

"Andrea is a smart girl," Tatum said. "She wouldn't—"

"Andrea doesn't know what people like Glover are capable of. If she did, she would never leave the apartment. But *I* know. And you do too. They construct elaborate fantasies and obsess about them, making them more intricate, more *alive*. Until the urge is impossible to resist. And then they act."

"Yeah, but Rod Glover never trailed a specific girl. *You* told me that. He always acted on opportunity. Targeting girls who were alone. He didn't stalk *anyone*."

"He stalked me," Zoe pointed out.

A month before, during the Strangling Undertaker case in Chicago, Glover had followed Zoe until she was alone. And then he'd pounced. Luckily, she'd managed to fight him off. Tatum knew that in Zoe's position, he wouldn't be able to calm down. To be aware that it was possible one of the people they routinely profiled could be targeting your family . . . it was a sickening feeling. Like an oncologist finding symptoms of a brain tumor in his child—knowing what those symptoms could potentially mean. Ignorance sometimes really was bliss.

He looked up at Zoe, noticing her rapid blinking, the tremor in her lip. Sitting at the pool's edge, her feet in the water, she suddenly seemed like a lost girl looking for her parents.

"There's an internal investigation on one of my cases," he blurted, searching for a distraction. Any distraction.

It worked. Zoe focused her stare on him, her eyes widening. "What case?"

"Wrongful shooting of a suspected pedophile."

"Oh." She nodded. "I remember—you told me about it. The guy reached for his camera, and you shot him, right?"

"He reached for his *bag*, and I shot him. Later, we figured out he reached for the camera. He had no weapon in the bag."

Zoe seemed to mull that over. Feeling a bit chilly, Tatum swam to the other side of the pool, then back.

"Why did they reopen the case?" she asked.

"There's supposedly a new witness."

"Could the witness have seen anything that would reflect badly on you?"

"No," Tatum said flatly. "They'd have seen what happened. I had no way of knowing that he wasn't going for a gun."

"Did you say anything before you shot him?"

"Just told the man to put his hands up."

"Did you call him by his name?"

"What?"

"Did you call the man by his name or simply tell him to put his hands up?"

"What difference does it make?"

"It's perceived differently. Which was it?"

Tatum pulled himself out of the pool, the water trickling on the white stone. He grabbed his towel from the nearby plastic chair and dried himself while verifying his shorts stunt still worked. He tugged at them a bit, then sat by Zoe, towel over his shoulders. "I think I called him by his last name. It was Wells. So I said something like, 'Wells, put your hands up.'"

"Just his last name? Did you say anything else? Were you speaking clearly?"

"It's no big deal, Zoe. Someone's just kicking up some dirt. Don't worry about it."

"If they reopened the case, they have a reason. It *is* a big deal."

"No pressure or anything," Tatum said irritably. He wished he hadn't brought the subject up.

"You were chasing him, right?"

"Yeah. He grabbed a young girl on the street while we were watching."

"How long did you chase him?"

"I don't know. A couple of blocks. The guy wasn't exactly an athlete."

Zoe's phone blipped. She snatched it from the ground, the screen lighting her face. Her shoulders sagged, and her lips twisted in a small smile.

"Andrea?"

"Yes. She's fine. Your grandfather came by to see her today."

"Yeah?" Tatum raised an eyebrow. "And she survived it?"

"She said he was a nice old man."

"Then I don't think it's the same guy. It's probably someone else's grandfather."

Zoe laughed. It was a surprising burst of happiness, and Tatum was aware it wasn't due to his razor-sharp wit. It was a laughter born of pure relief. He smiled at her warmly.

"Do you want to grab something to eat?" he asked. "I'm starving." And he was. His stomach gave a sudden rumble, cheering at the mention of food.

"Sure." Zoe stood up, water drops trickling down her legs. She picked up her sandals from the ground. "Aren't you worried at all? About the internal affairs investigation?"

"Nah. It'll blow over. It's just a bit of static." He stood up as well, turning toward the staircase.

"Did you really think it was a gun?"

The question made him pause in utter surprise. He glanced back at Zoe. Her face was calm, but her eyes bored into his, unblinking.

"Of course," he answered. "I shot him."

"And he was a pedophile. You were working on the case for a long time. A difficult case. A sexual predator who targets children."

"Yes." The word dragged in his mouth. Tatum tensed, feeling the anger bubbling below the surface. He tried to contain it. She was just asking a simple question. "And I really wanted to catch the guy. I wanted him arrested."

"Pedophiles are frequently repeat offenders. If he went to prison, he'd be out in a few years, free to molest kids again. You knew that. And then you cornered him. And he wanted to destroy the evidence he had with him."

"I didn't see—"

"Even in that moment, after chasing him, adrenaline pumping in your veins, you called him by his name. He wasn't just a threat. He was a very *specific* threat."

"Zoe, drop it."

"You have conviction," Zoe said. "You want to make a difference. It's possible that when you had to make a snap judgment call, you made a rash action. Maybe you even convinced yourself that—"

"Are you . . . profiling me?" Tatum asked in disbelief. Up until that moment he'd thought she was talking about the way the case was perceived. But no, she was actually analyzing *him*.

"It's totally understandable. If you *believed* he had to be stopped—"

"He was going for a gun."

"It was a camera."

"I thought it was a gun!" Only as he heard his words echoing back to him from the motel buildings around him did Tatum realize he had shouted.

Zoe gaped at him in surprise. "Why are you angry? I didn't say—"

Tatum raised his hand to quiet her, trembling with fury. "Never profile me. You got that? I'm not one of your subjects."

"I just want you to be ready. If they ask you difficult questions—"

"There are no difficult questions, Bentley. Because I defended myself. Against a man who I thought was armed. I would *never* shoot an unarmed man. And you should know that."

"I'm not saying you did anything wrong. I'm just saying they could point out that you reacted more aggressively than you should have."

"This isn't about them at all. This is what *you* think."

"I wasn't there."

"Exactly. You weren't. And you could try and take my word for what happened there." He brushed past her, gritting his teeth. His appetite had left him, and despite his recent swim, his body pulsed with heat.

CHAPTER 19

San Angelo, Texas, Friday, May 9, 1986

The boy hid in his room. Not the best hiding spot, but when you were scared, you went to your safe place. This was his tortoise shell, his bunker, his haven. Where he could curl, clutching his E. T. doll, guarded by Superman, who stood sentry from a poster above the boy's bed.

Did they know?

His dad's binoculars had always mesmerized him. A simple object, though surprisingly heavy. And when he held them to his eyes, wonders happened. The boy could read the license plate of a car driving down the road. Could see the faces of the people entering the hairdresser's salon at the end of the street. With his dad's binoculars, he developed a superpower—superhuman eyesight.

There was a rule, of course. Always with Daddy, never alone. But what sort of superhero went with his daddy everywhere?

And besides, Daddy never let him look at the neighbor. And that was his favorite pastime with his superhuman eyesight. Mrs. Palmer lived just across the street, and he could glimpse fragments of her bedroom with the binoculars, a fact that excited him whether she was there or not.

He broke the rule. And the more he did, the more he needed to do it again. Always careful, never when his parents were around. Weekends were the best, because they slept late, and so did Mrs. Palmer. He could watch her uninterrupted.

But that morning, when she'd woken up, about to get dressed, she'd suddenly turned to the window, frowning. For a second she'd just stood there, looking straight at him. He couldn't have moved even if he'd wanted to.

And then she'd lunged for the drape on the window, pulled it shut, and he knew he'd been caught.

He had bolted to his room, a panicky, uncontrollable response. He was muttering silent prayers, promising God that if Mrs. Palmer didn't call his parents, he would never watch her again. He'd never touch the binoculars again.

The binoculars. They were still in his hands. He needed to put them back in place, before—

The phone rang, a shrill loud noise from the living room. He could bolt there, answer before his parents. Tell them it was a wrong number. Maybe he could convince Mrs. Palmer that he was looking at birds.

Instead he curled tighter into the corner. His bed stood adjacent to his green desk, and if he sat just right, his feet held close to his chest, he was hidden from the door. If his parents came into the room, they wouldn't be able to see him.

Another superpower he had. Invisibility.

His mother answered the phone. He could hear her sleepy voice as she answered, her tone becoming sharp and alert as the conversation went on.

He had to come up with a plan, but his mother's steps and angry voice clarified it was too late.

She called his name, her voice shrill, furious. The sound of a storm approaching. Tears of fear clogged his throat.

The door flung open. For a second his mother just stood in the doorway, muttering to herself, "Where *is* he." Invisibility. Best superpower ever.

But then she stepped inside the room, and the spell was broken. Her face was ruddy and furious. She screamed his name again, shrieking about the neighbor. About the binoculars.

He went for the only course of action left: denial. What neighbor? He was watching the birds.

"And now you're *lying* to me?" his mom yelled in disbelief.

She grabbed his arm, began dragging him across the room, out of the door. For a moment he tried to struggle, dragged his feet.

But superhuman strength was *not* one of his superpowers. He wailed and begged and said he was sorry. That should be the magic word, right? Sorry? He was sorry. He was so, so sorry.

She took him downstairs to the basement. He needed to be punished. He needed time to *think* about what he had done wrong. As if he hadn't just spent the past twenty minutes thinking nonstop about it.

Other parents, he knew, hit their children when they misbehaved. Robby from his class once told him his dad spanked him on his bottom *a hundred* times.

But his parents didn't hit their children. Hitting children was wrong. His parents believed a punishment had to be educational.

His mom always said he needed time to *think* about his actions.

A broom closet lurked in the basement. A dark place within a dark place.

Please, Mommy—he was sorry. He was so sorry. He would never do it again. He'd learned his lesson. He would apologize to Mrs. Palmer. He was sorry.

She pushed him into the broom closet and slammed the door, latching it. He heard her footsteps as she strode away, climbing the stairs, closing the basement door behind her. The tight space above him smelled of cleaning supplies, dust, mold, and nightmares.

He sobbed and thumped the door and screeched that he was sorry.

It was dark in the broom closet. So dark it was almost like going blind.

This wasn't the first time he'd been there. He often needed time to think. It always smelled the same. He could always feel the terror clogging his throat as the darkness closed in on him.

Why did Mrs. Palmer have to call his mom? He wasn't hurting anyone. She could've just closed the blinds. Or if she wanted him to stop, she could've talked to him. He would have listened. It was *her* fault he was here. *She* did this to him.

In the darkness, all he could do was listen, hearing his mother's footsteps somewhere above him. Hearing the phone ring. Somewhere faraway, a radio, a snatch of static and music.

A third superpower. Superhearing. And he needed all the superpowers he could get.

Because in the darkness, the monsters came.

CHAPTER 20

San Angelo, Texas, Wednesday, September 7, 2016

Zoe was exhausted. After Tatum's sudden outburst the night before, she'd eaten alone and then tried to go to bed, but sleep had refused to come. She'd mulled over the conversation, trying to figure out what had triggered Tatum. She'd finally decided he was dumb, that all male federal agents were dumb, and in fact, men in general were dumb. When she'd managed to fall asleep, she'd had a nightmare about Andrea and had woken up before sunrise. Luckily, they had a Starbucks just across the road from their motel, and by the time Tatum came to tell her tersely he was leaving for the police station if she wanted a ride, she had drunk a Grande Americano.

The ride to the police station was short and tense. Tatum remained stony and impassive for the entire drive. Zoe tried several times to talk about their strategy when working with the San Angelo police. But his responses were so snappish and unpleasant that she finally stopped trying and resolved to get Uber rides for the remainder of the visit. If Chief Mancuso complained about the additional expense, Zoe would tell her she was welcome to ride with Tatum herself.

Lieutenant Jensen intercepted them both as they entered the division. He seemed to be dressed in a brand-new suit, his hair carefully combed, his shoes shiny. "Agents, good to see you're here. We were just about to start the task force meeting."

"What task force?" Tatum growled.

"The chief of police instructed us to form a task force to investigate the Medina murder case," Jensen explained. "We were hoping you'd be able to join and provide your opinion on how to proceed."

"Right," Tatum said dryly. "Provide our opinion."

"Through here, Agents." Jensen walked down the hall.

"I'm not an agent." Zoe followed him. "I'm an FBI consultant."

"Oh?" Jensen said in disinterest. He strode at a brisk pace, but his short legs made it easy for her to walk beside him. Tatum stomped behind them, a dark maelstrom of discontent.

"I'm a civilian consul—"

"In here." Jensen marched through a door into a large room. Most of the space was taken by a large off-white rectangular table and two rows of chairs. There was a large whiteboard on which someone had written *Nicole Medina, September 2nd*. Three people sat by the table. Detective Foster sat on the right side next to a redheaded woman, her hair swept back into a ponytail. On the other side sat a bald man, his bushy eyebrows intersecting into one perfect unibrow. The brow seemed like a bird in flight, and the man raised it a fraction when Zoe looked at him, making the bird flap its hairy wings. It was very distracting.

Jensen closed the door and clapped his hands together. "Right," he announced. "Now that we're all here, we can start. First let's introduce everyone. You've already met Detective Foster. That's Detective Carol Lyons . . ."

The woman nodded at Zoe and Tatum.

"And you probably know Agent Shelton." Jensen gestured at the man with the birdlike eyebrows, apparently assuming all federal agents knew each other.

"No, we never met," the man said. "Brian Shelton from the San Antonio field office."

"Oh?" Jensen said. Zoe suspected it was his response whenever things went off script. "Well then. These are Agents Gray and Bentley. I mean, Agent Gray and . . . uh." He seemed suddenly at a loss of words.

"Dr. Bentley," Zoe said frostily.

"Now we all know each other." Jensen clapped his hands again.

Zoe sat down by Agent Shelton. Tatum sat down next to Detective Lyons. Zoe met Tatum's gaze, and he glanced away, clenching his jaw.

"Let's go over the details of the case," Jensen said. "Detective Foster?"

Foster cleared his throat and launched into a summary of the case, ending with the discovery of Nicole Medina's body the day before. Consulting the pages in front of him, he began to detail the initial findings.

"The cause of death is assumed by the medical examiner to be environmental asphyxiation," Foster said. "He estimates the time of death to be between two and eight a.m. on September third, though we'll know more once he concludes his autopsy. The victim was buried inside a wooden handmade box. A small infrared camera and a microphone were mounted inside the box to capture the video. They were connected to a cable that ran out of the grave. The cable's other edge was clipped and covered with earth, presumably to hide it once the murderer finished recording the video. We found a lot of fingerprints inside the box, and we're comparing them to the victim's fingerprints. No fingerprints on the camera, the exterior of the box, or the cable. We also collected some DNA samples from the interior of the coffin, mostly hair, a broken fingernail, some blood . . ." He glanced at Agent Shelton.

"Our lab will be processing those samples shortly, comparing them to the victim's DNA and checking them against CODIS," Shelton said.

"We have some tire marks from the scene, but . . ." His eyes darted toward Zoe for a short second. "They were mostly covered and erased during our attempt to rescue the victim."

Zoe's face remained blank, and she didn't bother to point out she had told them as much the day before. She never understood people's urge to say, "I told you so." It was like taking pride in the fact that you weren't convincing enough.

"The crime scene technicians are doing a second sweep this morning, collecting shoe impressions from the ground. However, the topmost soil is thin dust, and it was very windy two days ago. Add to that the people who were digging up the grave, and I'm not optimistic."

Jensen cleared his throat. "Our top priority had been to save Medina's life, if it was possible, of course." It was an obvious attempt to avoid accusations of professional inadequacy.

Zoe tried to catch Tatum's eyes, knowing that on any other day he'd roll them comically. But he focused on Foster, ignoring Zoe.

"The autopsy is scheduled to start in the afternoon," Foster said. "Our crime scene technicians are currently working on the box, trying to get as much information about it as possible."

He glanced at his papers. "The mobile phone the killer used is offline, so we can't track it. It seems it was turned on for the first time near the grave site, so we can't use it at the moment to analyze his movements *before* the burial either." He tapped his pages on the table, aligning them into an orderly stack. "That's what we have so far."

"Good, please send your summary by email to all the participants of this meeting," Jensen said.

"Yup, will do."

"I guess the most important question on the agenda is obvious. Is this a serial killer?" Jensen glanced at Tatum and then at Zoe expectantly.

"A serial killer is defined as a murderer who kills at least two people on separate occasions," Tatum answered. "So far, we have no evidence that's the case."

"Doesn't it take at least *three* victims to define a serial killer?" Jensen asked.

"No." Zoe answered a fraction of a second before Tatum and Agent Shelton said the same. Zoe leaned forward. "We changed it back in 2005. The definition is an offender who kills *two* or more victims in separate events."

"The video that he published is titled 'Experiment Number One,'" Jensen pointed out. "Should we expect another victim in the future?"

"We have absolutely no way of knowing that yet," Zoe said. "We need to investigate further. There's a clear possibility it really is a serial killer."

"There's a press conference in"—he checked his wristwatch—"thirty-two minutes. What do we tell them?"

"Nothing. You cancel the conference."

"That's impossible. They already know a body has been found. Someone will connect it to the video. We need to stay in control of the situation."

"I agree completely." Zoe clenched a fist under the table. She now understood why Jensen was dressed so nicely. "Which is why you *must* avoid involving the press for as long as you can. At least until we know more."

"As I said, that's impossible." Jensen turned to Tatum, like a patient looking for a second opinion. "Our aim is to reduce rumors and panic."

"If this *is* a serial killer," Tatum said gravely, "he might react to the press interest in him. It might prod him to kill again. I agree with Dr. Bentley."

"Oh?"

Zoe suspected the press conference would happen no matter what. "Give them the barest details. With no room for interpretation. If you want to reduce panic, you should refrain from using the term *serial killer.*"

"Right." Jensen clapped his hands again. "That's settled. Now, for our next steps, I think we have some promising leads. The Mexican Mafia for one. We should talk to Medina's father—"

"If I may, Lieutenant," Detective Lyons interjected. "I have an additional inquiry line in mind."

"Oh?" Jensen blinked at her in surprise.

"We are currently working under the assumption that Medina was kidnapped right after being dropped off by her friends, before she entered the house. We should make sure this assumption holds. Interview all her friends again, get our timeline as detailed as possible. Also, if she really *was* taken then, the killer either waited for her by her home, or he followed them from the party. We should check the red light camera footage for any vehicles that went by in close proximity to the friend's car."

Foster kept his gaze on Lyons, his mouth twitching in a slight smile. They were playing the lieutenant—Zoe was sure of it. Lyons did the talking because they knew, for whatever reason, that Jensen would be more susceptible to it.

"Also, once we have the tech results," Lyons continued, "it's likely we'll have a lead on the box's maker. If the killer didn't make it himself, we could follow that lead. And of course, we'll try to monitor the killer's phone number."

Jensen blinked and cleared his throat. "Of course. That sounds like a reasonable course of action."

"We're trying to determine the digital traces that the killer left," Agent Shelton said. "We'll let you know if anything pops up. And there's the issue of the upload origin."

"Yes." Jensen's face was blank. "Upload origin."

"The video was uploaded on-site." Shelton scrunched his forehead, and the eyebrow bird folded its wings as if about to dive. "The murderer must have used a cellular modem."

"He could have used his phone as a hotspot," Foster pointed out.

"We already checked all the phone's activity," Shelton said. "The CNN footage is the only thing it was used for. We'll pull all the data we have on the nearby cell towers. Since the crime scene is in a remote area, that won't be a very long list. If he uploaded from the site, we'll find the record for it, and then we might be able to use it to track the killer."

Jensen kept nodding throughout that explanation. Satisfied, he glanced at Tatum. "Agent, anything you want to add?"

"Dr. Bentley and I will start working on an initial profile," Tatum said. "We would appreciate full access to all the evidence collected from the crime scene, including the photographs."

"Of course." Jensen made an elaborate gesture. It would have looked reasonable on a king granting his subjects' wishes but was utterly absurd in this context. "Let's get to work."

CHAPTER 21

Tatum was almost by the door when Zoe grabbed his arm.

"Can you hang on for just a second?" she asked.

He went rigid at her touch. "Sure."

They stood by the doorway as the rest of the meeting's participants walked out the door. Agent Shelton was the last to leave, and he gave them a querying look. Tatum nodded at him and gave him a small polite smile. The agent shrugged and left as well.

"We need to decide how to approach this case," Zoe said. "There's a lot of work to do."

Tatum had guessed she wasn't about to talk about what she'd said the night before, let alone apologize. Still, he felt a pang of anger and disappointment. He *needed* to vent. If she'd told him to stop acting like a child, at least he'd have a good opportunity to snap back. He'd spent half the night before thinking of all the things he should have said when Zoe had casually called him a murderer. But saying them now would be pointless. Comebacks had a very limited expiration date.

"Of course," he said. "We need to look at past crime reports in the area. Assuming the killer's fantasy has a claustrophobic angle, we can check anything that involves shutting people in small cramped spaces."

"Maybe see if any prostitutes reported anything like that. A customer who made them lie in a closed box for a long time or a car's trunk."

"Okay. I'll look at past cases in the area."

"I'll try ViCAP." Zoe sighed.

Tatum understood her tone. ViCAP should have been perfect for this kind of investigation. The FBI's Violent Criminal Apprehension Program was supposed to be a database of all violent crimes across the country. If the killer had committed violent crimes in other states before, it should have been reported and logged. Theoretically, all Zoe would need to do was to search for other incidents of people being buried alive, and voilà, she'd get a list of similar cases.

Except there were a few snags. The major one was that less than 1 percent of all violent crimes were logged in the ViCAP database. The second problem was, of course, that there was no checkbox in the ViCAP entry form for "buried alive." However, Tatum's sympathy ran low at the moment, and he didn't offer to help out with the workload.

"The nickname of the uploader is Schrodinger, and it's probably not a coincidence. We should both study Schrodinger, as well," Zoe said. "If he's really referencing Schrodinger's cat, we should understand the experiment better."

"It's pretty straightforward. You put a cat in a box, you close the box . . . and for some reason the cat might die at some point. So the cat is alive . . . but also dead."

"Why is he alive and also dead? He's either alive or dead."

"I mean . . . because we don't really know. It's a physics thing, I guess."

A second of silence.

"We should both study Schrodinger," Zoe said again.

CHAPTER 22

Zoe sat alone in the meeting room, her laptop in front of her, papers and printed photographs scattered all over the table. She'd asked Jensen earlier if she could use the room to work, and after a lot of hemming and hawing, he'd agreed. Tatum was in the detective division, sitting in the cubicle belonging to the man who was on vacation. This worked out nicely as far as Zoe was concerned. With Tatum's present state of mind, she found him quite unbearable.

The laptop was open on the ViCAP search screen. She'd run eight different searches that morning and ended up with over two hundred cases that could be connected to the Medina case. Sifting through them was both difficult and unproductive.

She had questions she needed answered. How had the victim been taken? What did the toxicology report say? Where was the box from? Questions that would be answered in due time, but Zoe was used to being consulted when a case stalled and all the immediate questions had been answered already. One of the things she'd heard a lot in the BAU was "If only they'd called us sooner." As if the profilers could show up after one act of violence, point out the guilty party like some sort of real-life Poirot, and prevent all the other crimes that followed. And now here she was, pretty much as soon as she could possibly be, and it turned out she was as clueless as the rest of them.

She massaged her forehead, knowing she wasn't in her element. She was distracted by Tatum's anger and by her distance from Andrea. At the thought of her sister, she instantly imagined Andrea carelessly going to the parking lot, not noticing the dark figure waiting by her car, holding a gray tie in his clenched fists.

She clenched her jaw and grabbed her phone. She tapped a quick message to Andrea. Hey, how are you this morning?

To her surprise, the chat window indicated that Andrea opened it almost instantly—a significant change for the better.

Fine. How's the case?

Zoe sighed and answered, A bit messy. And Tatum's angry at me.

What did you do?

Nothing. He's just being a baby.

Andrea sent an emoji with its eyebrow raised, and Zoe found its suspicious expression quite annoying. I need to go back to work, she tapped. Talk later?

Sure.

Feeling relieved, Zoe stood up and paced the room. It was time to change tack, to start again. She couldn't figure out anything conclusive yet, but she could theorize. Nicole, in all likelihood, had been killed by a stranger. If she'd been killed by someone who knew her for one of the common motives—say, greed or jealousy—the killer wouldn't go to all that length of burying her alive, filming it, posting it online. No. The drive that had propelled the killer here was different.

A couple of markers lay by the whiteboard. Taking one, she began to make a list.

Buried alive. Remote location. Online video.

After circling the words *Buried alive*, she drew a line from it, ending with the word *Claustrophobia.* Then, hesitating, she checked online for the term for the fear of being buried alive and wrote it down—*Taphephobia.* She'd already seen indications that the killer had been sexually stimulated. Now she sat down in front of the laptop, clicked the video file, and followed the killer's actions.

Twice during the video, the killer stopped filling the grave and disappeared from the frame. In the second instance, it took him three minutes to return. By the third time she watched the video, she was positive. When he left, his posture was rigid and hurried. When he returned, he was relaxed and calm.

He'd stepped out of the frame to masturbate.

Her confidence bolstered, she connected two more words to the diagram. *Dominance* and *Control.* These two drives were common with sexual serial killers and certainly applied here.

She moved on to *Remote Location.* She drew new lines from it and wrote down *Planning* and *Van.* Time for the third bullet—*Online video.*

This was what concerned her the most, and it was the main reason she wanted the police to keep a lid on the press as long as possible. She could think of only one reason for him to post the video, and she wrote it down, underlining it three times. *Fame.*

Some serial killers weren't just driven by fantasies. They were driven by the desire for fame. The Son of Sam and BTK were classic examples, sending letters to the press, boasting of their actions. And now, with the internet's wide grasp, the killer didn't even need to reach out to the press.

But in this age of endless distractions and TL;DRs, he couldn't just post long rambling letters like the Son of Sam had. No one would read them. He had to move on with the times. He'd posted a video.

This could have serious consequences for his killing rate. When a serial killer acted on his fantasies, there would often be long stretches of time between the killings. The memory of the murder and its reenactment in their mind was good enough to curb the compulsion to kill, at least for a while.

But if a killer murdered for attention, he might kill again whenever he felt he was losing the focus of the crowd. And these days, when news went stale fast, it meant he'd start getting that frustrating sensation very soon.

The meeting room door opened, startling her out of her focus. Foster and Lyons stepped into the room.

"Bentley, there you are," Foster said. "The autopsy is . . ." The words faded as he inspected the whiteboard. "Is this the profile?"

Zoe shook her head. "No. Just ideas. I won't have anything concrete until tomorrow."

"What's taphephobia?" he asked.

"The fear of being buried alive," Zoe answered.

"Specific." Lyons quirked her eyebrow.

"You think the killer is taphephobic?" Foster asked.

"I don't know. But he's sexually aroused by the act of burying a woman alive. It's common for fear and sexual stimulation to be connected. I'm almost certain he masturbated at a certain point in the video . . . off camera, of course."

"Really?" Lyons twisted her mouth in disgust.

"You should canvass the crime scene with a UV camera, search for spots of semen. We might get lucky."

"Lucky," Foster remarked dryly. He exchanged looks with Lyons.

Zoe ignored their reaction. She had no patience for coddling them. "This is a sexual killing, through and through." She frowned at the whiteboard, focusing on the word *planning*. "Except . . . something here doesn't fit."

"What?" Lyons asked.

"Serial killers usually harbor their sexual fantasies in a sort of gestation phase until something stressful happens. We call it the stressor.

It could be a relationship ending or getting fired . . . something that weighs heavily on them. The stress gets too much, and they snap and kill, fulfilling their original fantasy. Once they cross that barrier, make that first killing, the next one comes easier. They plan it more thoroughly, think of all the things they could do to improve their technique. But that first murder is almost always an impulsive act."

"No planning." Foster glanced at the whiteboard.

"Exactly. *This* murder was elaborately planned. He had to build or order the box, find a location, get the website ready. He was very careful with his burner phone and cleaned up after himself as well. These are not impulsive actions. I believe it took him a month or two to do some research and plan them out."

"Maybe this killer is different," Lyons suggested.

"He could be." Zoe shrugged. "But there's a simpler explanation. Something stressed him. He snapped and killed, probably on the same week. And then, after a while, he planned his next murders."

"Then . . . are you saying—"

"There's at least one more victim we haven't found yet," Zoe said.

"But . . . he called this experiment number one," Lyons pointed out weakly.

"I wouldn't subscribe too much to that. There could be endless reasons why he did that. I think there's a good chance he buried another girl sometime in the past. Not too long ago. A few months."

Lyons seemed pale. "Excuse me," she said faintly and left.

Zoe considered asking Foster what was wrong with Lyons, then decided it was none of her business. If the woman got a fainting fit whenever murder was involved, perhaps she was in the wrong line of work.

"I actually came here to tell you the autopsy is done," Foster said. "We were about to talk to the medical examiner. Do you want to tag along?"

"I'll come in a moment." Zoe regarded the whiteboard. She wanted to think this through while the ideas were fresh in her mind.

CHAPTER 23

Tatum followed Detective Foster into the autopsy room. It was the first time since they'd landed in Texas he'd felt chilly. He wore a thin white buttoned shirt and immediately regretted the absence of his jacket.

But then, as the smell hit, his discomfort with the temperature took a back seat. The scents of formalin, disinfectant, raw flesh, and blood all mixed together into an unbearable stench that had him breathing shallowly through his mouth. He never got used to this smell. A box of face masks stood on a shiny steel cabinet by the door, and Foster snagged two, handing one to Tatum.

Nicole Medina's body lay naked on a steel bed in the middle of the room, a Y-shaped scar of an autopsy operation covering her torso. The body's skin was gray in the room's cold light, but even in its current state, Tatum could easily see the girl from the video.

The medical examiner was hunched over a microscope. He was dressed in white coveralls, stained brown in several places, and his mouth and nose were covered by a mask as well. His head was bald, and the white fluorescent light made his scalp seem even paler than it was. As they stepped closer, he straightened, peering at them through a pair of thick glasses.

"It's freezing here, Curly." Foster rubbed his hands together. "How can you work like this?"

"I wear warm socks," the man said. His eyes crinkled, and Tatum guessed he was smiling under the mask.

The door to the autopsy room opened, and Zoe strode briskly inside. She paused two steps in, presumably as the smell hit her, her face gaining a slightly sickly look. Tatum wondered if Zoe's nose, which was a bit longer than most, made her more vulnerable to the surrounding aroma.

Before he could remember that he was furious at her, he gestured at the box by the door. "There are face masks over there."

She turned back and quickly retrieved a face mask.

Foster motioned at Tatum. "Curly, this is Agent Gray and Dr. Bentley. They're consulting on the Medina case. And this"—he pointed at the medical examiner—"is our medical examiner, Curly."

The medical examiner rolled his eyes and turned to Tatum. "Curly is my school nickname. I'm Dr. Clyde Prescott. Nice to meet you."

Foster turned to Zoe. "Curly was just about to walk us through the autopsy report."

Curly picked up a clipboard from the counter and scanned it. "Nicole Medina, aged nineteen. The cause of death is almost certainly asphyxia due to environmental suffocation—"

"Almost certainly?" Foster asked.

"There is no evidence of any serious trauma to the body, and considering the location where the body was found, environmental suffocation is the reasonable conclusion. However, to be sure, you'll need to wait for the toxicology report."

He pointed at the body's hip, which had a greenish-black hue. Tatum looked away after a quick glance at it. "The early putrefaction started on the iliac fossa. This, combined with the potassium concentration in the vitreous humor, led me to deduce that the victim died approximately eighty hours before discovery."

"How approximate?" Foster asked.

"The victim was young and healthy, and the body was kept in a relatively clean environment, protected from insects and heat. So it's accurate within four hours."

This was actually a much better approximation than Tatum had assumed they would get. He made a quick calculation. "Between six a.m. and two p.m. on September third."

"That's right. Lividity marks over the back of the body indicate the deceased died lying on her back and that the body wasn't moved after death."

He walked around the autopsy table, looking down at Medina's body. "Multiple scratches and bruises on her knees, palms, elbows, and feet all seem to be consistent with repeatedly hitting and kicking a hard wooden lid. There were three old fractures, probably from early childhood. Two on the left leg, one across her right wrist. All three fractures healed well. The stomach was empty, which is not surprising, since it's likely she didn't have access to food in the last twelve hours of her life."

"Any signs of a sexual encounter, either forced or consensual?" Zoe asked.

"I swabbed the mouth, vaginal and anal cavities, and checked for foreign elements, but there were none. There is a large stain on the victim's trousers, but it's urine, not sperm."

He pointed at the body's neck, and Tatum craned forward. A thin long scratch marred the skin.

"This scratch is fairly new," Curly said. "Examined closely, it looks like a sharp and smooth object cut the skin. It didn't cut deep."

"Someone cut her with a blade?" Tatum asked.

"Yes, but I don't think the intention was to kill her. My guess is someone held a blade to her throat, and it cut her. See the angle? This probably indicates whoever did it stood behind her. If you look at her left arm, you'll see a bruise there. That's where he grabbed her."

Tatum pictured it in his mind. Nicole getting out of the car in her home's driveway. The street is dark. She starts walking toward the entrance when someone grabs her left arm fiercely, and holds a knife to her throat.

"The man who did this is right handed." Foster echoed Tatum's own conclusion. This wasn't a big surprise. The man on the video was right handed as well. "Any signs of struggle?"

"Nothing visible. I clipped her fingernails and sent them for testing."

"No sign she was tied either?"

"No."

Tatum considered this. "Make sure the toxicology test includes date-rape drugs. It could explain why the victim didn't struggle, even when he put her in a box." Date-rape drugs weren't always in the standard toxicology test to save costs. It was best to make sure.

Curly made a note. "I'll make sure they test for it. Ketamine and Flunitrazepam would definitely show traces in the hair samples."

Tatum couldn't wait to leave the autopsy room, but he forced himself to take one last look at the victim. Nicole Medina had probably lost consciousness before she died, and her eyes were shut, face serene.

But there was no question regarding the terror she'd felt shut in the dark, cramped space. It must have seemed to her that no one could hear her as she screamed. Ironically, her screams had been heard by many people, but no one could help her in time.

CHAPTER 24

"I wasn't sure how you drink your coffee."

Zoe raised her eyes from her laptop, looking at the speaker. It was Detective Lyons. She held two cups of coffee in one hand, balancing a pink pastry box in the other, looking as if it required no effort. Zoe knew if she tried this acrobatic feat, she'd end up with a large coffee stain on her crotch and a bunch of pastries on the floor.

Lyons stepped into the room, putting the cups and the box on the table. She then took one cup and drank from it. "I didn't add sugar."

"That's fine, thanks." Zoe took the other cup. She sipped from it and kept her face carefully blank. The coffee was so weak that it was nearly like drinking tepid water.

Lyons opened the box. It had four doughnuts in it, two chocolate frosted and two vanilla frosted with sprinkles. She took one of the chocolate ones and motioned for Zoe to dig in.

"Thanks," Zoe said again, taking a vanilla doughnut.

"A young woman disappeared in San Angelo six weeks ago," Lyons said. "Her name is—"

"Maribel Howe, aged twenty-two."

"How did you—"

Zoe turned her laptop around so Lyons could see the screen. It displayed the NamUs missing persons database. "I looked through some databases, searching for missing persons in Texas," Zoe explained. "Of all the people who were reported missing in San Angelo in the past six months, Maribel Howe is the only one still missing."

"I'm investigating the Howe case," Lyons said. "Though I hit a dead end early on. She went out to see a film with some friends on Saturday evening . . . you don't want the other chocolate doughnut?"

"I'm good."

"I'm addicted to chocolate doughnuts. I really should stop, but when the craving hits me, my stomach takes the steering wheel. Cops and their doughnuts, right?"

"Right." Zoe didn't recall ever working with a cop who regularly ate doughnuts. But someone probably had to perpetuate the myth.

"Anyway," Lyons continued, taking the second doughnut, "she disappeared in a similar fashion. She'd gone to see a movie with a friend. They shared an Uber ride on the way home—they live on the same street, just a few houses apart. The driver dropped them by the friend's house, about thirty yards from Howe's home. Howe said goodbye to her friend and walked to her own house. In the morning she didn't show up for work. Her boss called her several times, got worried, sent one of her coworkers to check up on her. There was nobody in her home, and after a few hours of repeatedly phoning her, they called the police."

"You think she was taken like Nicole Medina, near her home?"

Lyons shrugged. "Maribel Howe wasn't Nicole Medina. She was twenty-two, lived alone. Her friend told us she hated this city, hated her job, always talked about leaving. She didn't get along with her parents; she left home when she was eighteen. And she disappeared soon after two of the detectives from the division had retired, so we were seriously understaffed. I'm not saying I stopped searching, but I had half a dozen cases to juggle, and when push came to shove, it was easy to assume she just decided to skip town."

Lyons put her half-eaten chocolate doughnut back in the box. "I checked her Instagram page occasionally," she said after a few seconds, her voice thick. "She used to update it *all the time*. Like, a few photos every day. But after she went missing, there was nothing." She took out her phone, tapped it a few times, and handed it to Zoe.

It was Maribel's Instagram account, and the last image was from July 29. Maribel and another girl, smiling at the camera, their heads tilted slightly toward each other. The caption read, "Alexander Skarsgard, here we come."

Zoe glanced at Lyons. "Who's Alexander—"

"Hot movie actor."

Maribel was beautiful. She was one of those girls who knew how to put on makeup so it looked effortless and perfect, her lips glistening red, long thick eyelashes that seemed almost natural, her black hair cut short and pixie-like. She wore a strapless green top and had a mischievous smile, as if hinting that when Alexander finally met her, he'd forget about Hollywood and move to San Angelo.

"Her mother still calls me every week," Lyons said. "She wants an update, and I have nothing. But you know what I think now?"

Zoe didn't answer.

Lyons's eyes were misty. "I think she's buried somewhere around here."

CHAPTER 25

Delia Howe was doing the dishes, scrubbing furiously. Every day the same thing, Frank with his damn bacon and eggs. She kept telling him to rinse the dish once he was done. It's not rocket science. You put the dish half a second under the faucet, and that's it. But she was lucky if he even bothered to put the plate in the sink once he was done. And by the time she got to it, the egg leftovers hardened, becoming a discolored yellow stain, and she had to scrub it endlessly to get it off the plate. Tomorrow, she'd let Frank eat off a dirty dish; maybe he'd finally get the damn message.

He probably wouldn't even notice. She shook her head, her lips pressed to a fine line.

Frank was hardly even talking to her since Maribel had disappeared. He acted as if it was all her fault. Her fault Maribel had left home. Her fault Maribel didn't watch out for herself. Her fault that—

The plate she was washing hit the edge of the sink hard, with all the force of Delia's angry scrubbing. It cracked and split into three pieces. Delia clutched a third of the plate, a triangular pie-shaped fragment, and for a moment, just gaped at it stupidly.

Then she noticed the blood running from her palm. Mixing with the soapsuds and the water, a pink trickle of blood dripping on the sink.

She let go of the plate and wrapped her hand with a nearby towel, which quickly turned red. Her palm tingled with pain, but she didn't mind. Pain had become a friend these recent weeks. Pain drove the hollowness away.

A knock on the door. She trudged over and opened it. Detective Lyons stood on the welcome mat, her expression severe. An unfamiliar woman stood by her. Another detective? Delia had been discouraged when she'd found out that a woman had investigated her daughter's disappearance. Sure, women were great, and they deserved equality and all that. But it was basic evolution, wasn't it? Men were hunters; women were gatherers. She wanted a hunter to find her daughter.

And now here was another woman involved. Perfect.

"Detective Lyons," she said dryly. "What a surprise."

She could inject meaning to her words like the best of them. *What a surprise*, in this case, meant she knew that the police didn't take the disappearance of her daughter seriously. Half the questions they'd asked her had been if Maribel had a reason to leave town without telling her. As if Maribel would just disappear.

"Any news about Maribel?" she asked after a second. Because she couldn't not ask it. Because even after all these weeks, after all the false hopes and deep disappointments, she still dared to have faith.

Two weeks ago, her cousin had called her to tell her he'd seen Maribel in New York. She worked as a clerk in the nearby supermarket. Delia hadn't even asked her cousin to make sure, to send her a photo. She'd bought plane tickets and was about to fly over when her cousin had called again apologizing. He'd been sure it was Maribel. But it had been a trick of the light.

She hadn't been able to get a refund on the flight tickets. Frank was probably furious about the tickets' price, but he hadn't said anything.

"No," Lyons said. "Not yet. I'm sorry. Mrs. Howe, this is Zoe Bentley, from the FBI."

Delia blinked and regarded Bentley. The FBI? The woman didn't look like she was from the FBI. She was short and thin, her cheeks pink. Her neck was so scrawny it could probably break with one twist.

Her eyes, though—for a second Delia found herself staring into the woman's eyes. Then she looked away, her heart pounding. What was the FBI doing here? Was this about Maribel?

"Mrs. Howe, can we come in and—are you okay? You're bleeding!"

For a second Delia glanced down at her shirt, as if the dull hollow throb in her chest had finally developed into a bleeding wound. But no, the detective was talking about her hand. "I'm fine," she said, taking a step back, gesturing for them to come inside. "I cut myself on a broken plate."

"Let me see that," the fed said, and before Delia could react, she grabbed her hand, removing the towel. It was a long gash, and Delia stared at it vacantly, then realized it was near the burn marks, and she snatched her hand away.

"It's nothing." Had the woman seen the marks?

"You should put some disinfectant on that," Bentley said.

"Are you here about Maribel?" Delia resisted the urge to hide the hand behind her back.

"Yes," Bentley answered. "I wanted to ask you a few questions about her."

Lyons shut the door behind her and walked past Delia to the living room. Delia followed her, feeling out of place in her own house. She vindictively decided not to offer them anything to drink. Lyons took the armchair, and Bentley sat on one side of the couch, leaving the other side for Delia. It was the only place left to sit, and Delia took it, made uncomfortable by the close proximity of the fed.

"What do you want to know?" she asked.

"Did your daughter go out a lot?"

"She went out sometimes," Delia answered guardedly. "She isn't some sort of slut, if that's what you're implying."

"I'm not implying anything, Mrs. Howe. She went out with friends? In the evening?"

"I guess so. She doesn't live here anymore. She has her own home."

"Why is that?"

"Because she's stubborn. I told her endless times to come back. I didn't want her out of the house."

"Why did she leave in the first place?"

"We argued a lot. She said we were . . . that *I* was driving her insane. I was just looking out for her." The arguments popped in Delia's mind, like they often did lately. She and Maribel couldn't seem to agree on *anything*. The way Maribel dressed, the people she met, the way she kept staying out late. They often argued about food. She'd tell Maribel to slow down, not to eat too much, to watch her figure, and Maribel would suddenly lose her temper. Or she'd talk nicely about Jackie's daughter and how thin she was, and Maribel would flip out, as if she'd said it to make a point. If Maribel had only listened, if she'd have been less sensitive about everything . . .

"On the street or any men she recently met?" Bentley was saying.

"I'm sorry?"

"I asked if Maribel had been mentioning any strangers she saw on the street or men she recently met."

"No. Why?"

"Is there somewhere your daughter frequented?"

"She went to her job. She worked at the supermarket near her home."

The woman kept asking questions. Endless questions, no answers. And throughout the conversation, Bentley seemed as if she were judging her, blaming her. Finally, Delia lost her temper.

"What do you want from me? I don't know anything about Maribel. Once she was eighteen, she just left, no thank-you, nothing! When we talked, we always argued. Is that what you want to hear? Yes, we argued. She would never listen to anything I said. I'm her mother, and she wouldn't listen. I just tried to help her grow up—that's all! If you find her, can you tell her that? Can you please tell her I just wanted to help?"

Her voice was strange, and her vision was blurry with tears. She didn't understand why they were there and what they wanted from her. She thought of the gas stove. Her eyes flicked to the kitchen's doorway and back to Bentley. The way this woman looked at her . . . she knew. Delia didn't know how, but she knew. She clutched her towel-wrapped hand.

"Thank you, Mrs. Howe," Bentley said, her voice softening. She drew a card and handed it to her. "If you think of anything else about your daughter, please call me."

They finally left. Delia locked the door behind them. Then she went straight to the kitchen and turned on the gas, the blue flames flickering. She touched her wrist to the fire. Just two seconds, maybe less. The sharp agony shot through her body, and she groaned, stumbling back, the emptiness and guilt hidden safely away behind a blanket of pain.

CHAPTER 26

Zoe sat on the motel bed, her back propped against the bulky pillow, laptop on her knees.

She'd spent the last couple of hours trying to understand Schrodinger's theories, reading some papers, even watching an online lecture. Though she understood the basics, the details quickly became incomprehensible. She became consumed by an irrational rage and hate against all physics and physicists everywhere.

Then her stomach grumbled. In all likelihood, her fury was mostly fueled by hunger. She was, like Andrea liked to say, hangry.

She could go grab a bite, but the thought of eating oily Chinese takeout as she did the evening before was depressing. She wanted to go out and eat somewhere. And she wanted company.

The obvious company was next door. But he was still sulking.

If she was honest with herself, it bothered her quite a bit. Tatum was usually easy mannered and pleasant. Sure, they had their disagreements here and there, and he could be a frustrating man to deal with, but she couldn't recall a single instance in which he was really angry at her.

It was time to talk to him. Though she wasn't sure what had made him fly into a tantrum, she'd make a blanket apology for the night before. She'd make amends, buy him dinner. The fact that she rarely ever apologized would only make it easier for him to understand she truly was sorry. She got up and rummaged in her bag and retrieved a short-sleeved white T-shirt and a pair of cutoff jeans. She put them on and glanced at herself in the mirror. She undid her hair, letting it drop on her shoulders. If anything positive could be said for the dry hot weather, it was that it made her hair look much better. Usually she struggled with spontaneous curls, knots, strange-looking clumps, and an overall fuzziness. But here, her hair was as straight and smooth as a shampoo commercial model's. She smiled at the reflection. Not bad at all.

After grabbing her purse and keys, she left the room and walked over to Tatum's door. She knocked on it. Her stomach rumbled. She knocked again.

He opened the door, looking tired and cranky. He wore a blue T-shirt and a pair of shorts. His eyes widened as he took in Zoe's appearance and attire. But then his jaw clenched tight, and he frowned.

"Hey." Zoe tried for a natural tone.

"I was just about to call you," Tatum said.

"You were?" she asked, feeling encouraged.

"I found one open murder case from eight months ago that could be relevant to our investigation. The body of a twenty-two-year-old prostitute named Laverne Whitfield was found buried a few miles north of San Angelo. Her arms were tied with an electrical cord, and she'd been stabbed several times."

"How did they find the body?"

"Wild animals dug it up."

"Any suspects?"

"One. A guy who used to be her pimp, named Alfonse . . . something." Tatum frowned. "I'll send you the case file. You can check out the exact details. It looked like a solid case, but when it got to court, the defense managed to point at some issues in the investigations. They'd missed a crucial witness, the time of death turned out to be wrong, and the main suspect wasn't Mirandized properly. A lot of the evidence was deemed inadmissible. The suspect walked."

"And you think it's relevant?" Zoe asked.

Tatum shrugged. "She'd been buried. But it was obviously done to hide the body, which isn't the case with the current killer. The stabbing doesn't match the current MO either."

"And she was found by wild animals, which means she wasn't buried deep."

"Right. I don't think it's the same guy, but I wouldn't rule it out either."

Zoe nodded, agreeing with his assessment. "I wanted to talk to you about something else. Regarding last night."

Tatum's face remained impassive.

"I'm really sorry you feel like what I said was hurtful. I was trying to help, but I can see how you would see what I said as criticism. I can sometimes be a bit too blunt." She expected his face to soften a bit, but it remained tense, full of hard edges and angry angles. "That thing in LA was years ago, and it's totally legitimate to want to avoid talking about it. I promise not to mention it again until you're ready."

It almost seemed as if his jaw clenched tighter. Had he missed the initial part, where she'd apologized?

"So anyway, I'm sorry. I was about to go get something to eat. Do you want to join me? My treat."

"You're sorry *I* feel that way," he said dryly.

Oh, he got that part after all. "Yes."

"You now realize you may have been too blunt."

This whole apologizing thing was not going as planned, and Zoe began to feel short tempered. "I really am sorry." *Third* time she said it. "So do you want to join me? I think there's a place—"

"I'm not hungry. Good night." The door slammed.

She stared at the closed door in disbelief. Then, just barely containing the urge to kick the door, she turned around and stormed off to get some dinner on her own.

CHAPTER 27

Harry sat in the motel's lounge, just about to give up on his stakeout, when he noticed Zoe outside, walking briskly toward the street. For a moment, he almost didn't recognize her, the T-shirt and the jeans so different from the pantsuits he saw her wear in Chicago. But then she turned her head, and there was no mistaking that face.

He lunged from the couch and dashed outside. "Dr. Bentley!"

She paused and turned around, looking at him distractedly.

"So nice to meet you here." Harry mixed innocence and surprise in his tone, walking casually toward her.

Her gaze focused, and he halted in his place, a bit unsettled. As a child he would often worry that some people could read his thoughts, know about all the dark corners of his soul. Zoe's eyes almost made him feel like that all over again.

"You," she hissed. "What are you doing here?"

"Oh, just traveling for work," he said. "I'm staying in this motel. What about you?"

She blinked, and dismay showed on her face as she realized they were staying in the same place. Now that the initial shock of facing her intense glare had abated, he found something unquestionably alluring about her. Her delicate neck and her rich dark hair gave her an almost Snow White quality. But that delicacy was shattered by her strange eyes and crooked nose, morphing her from "cute" to "mesmerizing." He made a mental note to mention that in his interview. He thought of other possible adjectives. *Captivating, gripping, spellbinding . . . no, spellbinding sounds ridiculous.*

"I'm here on . . ." She hesitated. Finally, she blurted, "Personal business."

"Personal business in San Angelo, huh? And Agent Tatum Gray is also on personal business, I assume?"

She glared at him for a long second. "I have nothing to say to you." She turned away and began marching.

Harry hurried after her. "No problem." He breathed hard. Damn, the woman could move fast. "Maybe just comment on the article I have for tomorrow's paper? I'm considering the headline, 'Serial killer expert consulting local police in San Angelo in wake of young woman's suspicious death.'" He wheezed as his heart and lungs screamed at the sudden unexpected effort. He hadn't moved so fast in years.

"I'll start by building the atmosphere." He raised his voice to overcome the traffic noise. She got farther away, and he hastened his steps, gulping air between words. "Dr. Bentley, famous for catching Chicago's Strangling Undertaker and the infamous Jovan Stokes, recently flew to San Angelo with her partner, Special Agent Tatum Gray. Though there was no comment regarding their presence, it is possible that it has something to do with the death of nineteen-year-old Nicole Medina . . ."

Zoe slowed her steps and then stopped. Breathing hard, Harry stopped as well. He felt like he was going to have a heart attack.

"Who was . . . found dead outside the . . . city." Damn those cigarettes. They'd be the end of him. "After . . . being reported missing . . ."

"Stop." She whirled around and strode toward him, looking like she might strangle him. "You can't print any of that. That's just provocation and misinformation."

"Misinformation?" He looked at her, hurt. "Aren't you in San Angelo with Agent Tatum Gray? Wasn't Nicole Medina found dead? They said she was found dead in today's news. Oh! I get it. You don't like the title *serial killer expert*. Fair enough. How about *renowned profiler*?"

"Mr. Barry, if you publish your article, the consequences might be . . . you can't . . ." She waved her hands helplessly, her gestures frantic and vague.

"Use your words, Dr. Bentley. I don't understand sign language." His heart rate was slowing down, but he was drenched in sweat. Maybe he should quit smoking. "What consequences?"

"Please wait one more day before publishing anything." She was not good at beseeching. Her tone made it sound more like an imperious order.

"So that all the local papers get the story before me? I don't think so, Doctor. Do you have a quote for me or not?"

She stared at him. He met her gaze calmly, but it was like having a staring contest with Medusa. He ended up glancing away first.

"There's a story for you here," she finally said. "But if you go public now, with my name and a list of all my so-called accomplishments, I swear you'll never hear *anything* from me."

He shrugged. "Doesn't seem like I'm hearing anything from you either way."

"I'll give you the whole story before anyone else. I promise."

"What if the rest of the press gets hold of it first?"

"You don't want to write about a dead girl in San Angelo. Your readers in Chicago couldn't care less about her. You want *my* angle on it."

"You can read me like an open book." He grinned at her.

"Wait with the article. I'll call you in a day or two."

He nodded. "I'll wait for your call. Just don't take too long."

She let out a long breath. "Good night."

"Did you eat dinner? We could grab something together."

"I'd rather dine with a rattlesnake, Harry Barry."

He watched her walking away, a bemused smile on his face. Then he rummaged in his pocket and took out a crumpled box of cigarettes. He tapped one out, put it between his lips, and lit it. He inhaled the smoke, shutting his eyes with joy. The hell with giving up smoking. He knew nothing better than the first cigarette after you snagged a good story.

CHAPTER 28

The girl's screams were background music as he browsed the local news websites. She was pleading for someone, anyone, to get her out. He listened to her for a few seconds, comparing this girl to Nicole Medina. He wasn't certain which one of them he found more engaging.

Shaking his head, he sifted through the websites again.

He'd been hoping that by now someone would make the connection, realize the girl who had died was the same one from the video he'd posted online. But all the articles just mentioned the bare facts. The dead victim's name and age. A selfie in a club the victim had posted two weeks ago on her Instagram account. The police statement that they were investigating it. No mention of a serial killer. No mention of the online video. No mention of Schrodinger. Article after article of bland, dry tidbits of information.

He smacked the table in a sudden bout of rage. How could they be so blind? He'd left them a blazing trail. Did he need to force-feed them every tiny detail?

He clicked the "Contact Us" link on the San Angelo Live website. Typing furiously, he pointed out the connection between the death of the victim and the video. He copied the URL. He pointed out the *name* of the video and stated there would be more. The police were helpless against him, and so were the FBI. There would be more victims, and no one was safe. They were all on his radar. There would be more. Dozens.

The cursor hovered above the "Send" button, and he paused.

He read the entire thing again. He literally had to *scroll* to do it, it was so damn long. Almost half the words were in all caps. He sounded deranged. He spotted no less than thirteen spelling mistakes. The number of exclamation marks was staggering. At one point he'd written *DOZENS!!!!!!*

Six exclamation marks. Capital letters. Like some frothing madman.

This was not the impression he wanted people to get, no matter how angry he was.

He got up from his chair and paced the basement, taking deep breaths. The space was a lot more cramped than it used to be. Boxes were stacked to the ceiling on the far side, their sizes uniform, each with a single hole drilled in it. Each box was intended for one subject. One experiment. Just looking at them calmed him down, made him smile.

Next to them stood bins full of soil. He had enough for five experiments, matching the different locations' soil. *This* was who he was. Someone who prepared. Who tied every loose thread. Who left nothing to chance.

He'd stick to the original plan. So what if the press was a bit slow. Soon, everyone would know about him. And everyone would be wondering who was next.

Because this girl wouldn't only make him visible. It would also clarify he wasn't about to stop with one or two.

Her screams echoed in the basement again. She was screaming for her mother.

And that gave him an idea.

He should have thought about it long before. These days, no one cared about what was happening right now.

All they talked about was what was *about to come*. There was always endless chatter about the trailers of future movies, the teasers, the hints and winks by the cast and the film crew. And after the movies screened, did anyone talk about them *at all* besides agreeing that they were kind of meh?

Teasers and trailers. Creating a buzz. The buzz was more important than the actual product. *That* would put him in the center of the public eye.

Who would have guessed that what a serial killer would need these days was a good marketing department?

He grinned as he left the basement. The idea was taking shape in his mind.

CHAPTER 29

Zoe sat by the bar, her fists clenched on her lap. She couldn't figure out how the evening had managed to go so badly. First Tatum's obnoxious behavior, then that shameless reporter from Chicago somehow finding her here, twisting her arm for a lousy interview. Ugh.

How had he even found her? He'd flown to San Angelo, and that meant he had a reliable source. Someone in BAU. She'd have to talk to Mancuso later, tell her someone was leaking info to the press.

"Here you go, miss." The bartender set three plates in front of Zoe. The first had a large thick steak, fried on a pan, looking promisingly juicy, a small piece of broccoli sitting next to it almost as an afterthought. The other dishes were the side dishes—a salad, the vegetables crisp and fresh in an assortment of green and red, and a baked potato with a mound of sour cream and slices of green onion on top.

At least one thing didn't disappoint tonight. If this food was half as good as it seemed, this would be a very satisfying meal.

She sliced a piece of the steak—the inside was as pink as she'd hoped it would be. She put it in her mouth, shutting her eyes.

Maybe life was worth living after all.

She chewed carefully, enjoying the juicy, tender meat, and then forked a piece of the potato, making sure that it came with some sour cream and a green onion slice. She ate the entire bite, a slight miscalculation there—the potato burned her tongue. But it tasted perfect.

"Everything okay?" the bartender asked politely as she put a glass of water by the plates, its surface foggy with condensation.

"Yesh, eesh great," Zoe said, breathing through her nose.

The bartender gave her an amused smile and walked away. Zoe took another bite from the steak. The night's events morphed in her mind. Harry Barry was possibly shameless, but he was also driven. She could appreciate someone who was dedicated to his job. And Tatum . . . well, Tatum was still obnoxious, but she knew his heart was in the right place. She was sorry he hadn't joined her. Food this good could work well with some company.

A sudden stab of guilt and fear shot through her as she realized that she'd been so busy working the case that she'd forgotten to check up on Andrea since that morning. Almost a full day.

She took out her phone. You okay? she tapped.

The answer came after a few seconds. Yes, stop bugging me. I'm eating dinner.

She sighed in relief and photographed the dish, sending it to Andrea with the caption, me too. After a moment, her sister sent her back a text—you think YOU are having a good dinner? Check out what you're missing—and an image of sad-looking ramen noodles. Zoe snorted and sent back the laughing emoji with the tears. Sometimes it was just tearful-laughing-emoji time.

After half the steak was gone, the bartender put a bottle of wine and a glass on the bar.

"Courtesy of the dude over there," she told Zoe, nodding to the edge of the bar. She placed a glass of wine in front of Zoe.

"Um . . . ," Zoe said. "I don't—"

"It's really good wine." The bartender raised her eyebrow.

It had been a while since someone had tried to pick her up in a bar, and she had to smile. "Okay, thanks."

She sniffed the wine, then tasted it. It really wasn't bad. She glanced at the man who'd sent her the glass. He had curly hair and a thick brown beard. He wore a checkered blue shirt that would have looked bad on most men, but not on him. He had a whole woodcutter vibe going for him. A small tattoo marked his neck. It seemed like initials, but Zoe couldn't make them out from this distance. He raised a glass of beer as a toast. She raised her own glass.

He seemed to decide that it was an invitation, and she wasn't sure it wasn't. He stood up, easily towering above most of the bar patrons, and ambled over, sitting down on the empty stool next to her.

"I like to see a girl who can enjoy her dinner." He smiled.

"Not really a girl—I'm thirty-three." She put down the glass. "Thanks for the wine."

"I'm Joseph."

Zoe offered her hand. "Zoe."

For a moment, when he took her hand, she tensed, thinking he might kiss it. But he just shook it firmly.

"You aren't from around here," he said. "Are you from Boston?"

She blinked in surprise. "Is my accent that obvious?"

He laughed. "I lived in Boston for a few years, so my ears are well tuned. It isn't very obvious, but it's there. Being *thirty-three* and all." His voice adopted a preposterous Bostonian accent, his smile mischievous.

Zoe returned a smile. "Well, I don't live there anymore either." She suddenly felt a strange jolt of homesickness. She took another sip from the wine.

"So what are you doing in San Angelo? Did you move here?"

"No, I'm here for work."

"What kind of work?"

Now there was a question. The words *forensic psychologist* had a certain curse to them. They made people either uncomfortable or intensely curious. Sometimes both. So naming her profession would either kill the conversation or shift it to revolve around homicide and rape.

She took a bite from her steak, thinking about it. Both possibilities didn't sound too good. She was content to enjoy her nice dinner and the so-far-pleasant company, and she didn't want serial killers intruding on it. "I'm a consultant."

"A consultant on what?" He took a long gulp from his beer.

"Oh . . . human behavior, mostly." She shrugged. "I just flew here yesterday. I'll be here for a few more days. What about you?"

"I live here." He smiled. "Born and raised in Sand and Jell-O."

It took her a minute to understand that it was a silly pun on the city name. She smiled back and ate a bite of potato with cream.

"I'm an electrician and an air-conditioning technician. It's a popular occupation." He leaned closer. "I don't know if you realize it, but the weather can occasionally get a bit warm around here."

She burst out laughing and then began coughing uncontrollably, the potato inhaled into her trachea. Joseph gaped at her in alarm and then quickly handed her the water glass. She took it from him, still coughing, her eyes watering, and drank a bit, finally getting her breathing in order. Smooth, Zoe. Very smooth.

"Are you all right?"

"Yeah." She wheezed and drank half her glass. "You just caught me off guard."

"Sorry, I'll try to be more serious when you're eating."

"So what were you doing in Boston if air-conditioning technicians are so much in demand here?"

"Followed a girl there—what else? Tried to start a business for lighting fixtures when I was there. It actually looked like it was booming for a couple of years. And then it wasn't." He picked up a beer coaster and began peeling it, scattering shreds of paper on the bar. "Broke up with the girl, so I came back home. And looking back, I don't know why I ever left."

Zoe sawed a piece of steak and chewed. She was over being hungry and ate mainly for the joy of it. She pointed at the initials tattooed on his neck. "Who's H. R.?"

He touched the spot of the tattoo. "Henrietta Ross. That was the girl from Boston. Kinda stupid, huh? You do the dumbest things when you're in love. Now I'm stuck with her name, and everyone asks me who that is." He frowned at the beer coaster he peeled.

Zoe had the feeling that if Andrea had been there, she would have managed to say something funny and turn the conversation around. She tried to think of something. She considered, *You could tell them it stands for Human Resources*, but was pretty sure it was as lame a joke as could be. She could start with, *Hey, at least her initials weren't* . . . but she couldn't think of a punch line.

She'd figure out something funny to say eventually. Three days from now, when she'd be trying to sleep.

"I don't think it's stupid," she ended up saying, feeling lame. "I think you loved someone and made a nice gesture."

He blinked. "Thanks, Zoe. That's a sweet thing to say."

Maybe humor was overrated after all.

Silence settled between them. It wasn't the comfortable silence of people who knew each other well. It was that tense silence, electric and sharp, almost tangible. As if there were an imaginary conversation ball they tossed to each other, and one of them had just fumbled, letting the ball drop.

He cleared his throat. "So who are the most important people in your life?"

It was a jarring question, unrelated to their conversation earlier, but Zoe could see it for what it was—the means to resuscitate the conversation, get it back on track. She was fine with that. "I have a sister. She lives with me."

"Really? Isn't that difficult? Living with your sister?"

"Maybe for her," she said lightly. "I love having her around."

"What about your parents?"

"My dad died a few years ago. And my mother can be a bit difficult." Her mother, always a controlling, passive-aggressive woman, had become almost impossible to bear in the last few years. "What about you?"

"I don't have any siblings, and my dad left Texas a few years ago, so it's only me and my mom. But we're very close."

"I bet she was happy when you came back."

"She was thrilled," he said. "Never wanted me to leave in the first place."

They talked a bit about Boston. Then the conversation veered left and right, with Joseph steering it and Zoe content to take the passenger's seat. He told her about his hobby of restoring old furniture for a bit, and Zoe did her best to act sufficiently impressed when he described the restoration of an ancient dresser. Her own experience of furniture building, constructing three chairs bought from IKEA, was not included in the conversation. Then they compared some favorite movies. Joseph asked for a wineglass for himself. After a while Zoe found that she was lowering her guard with him, words flowing more easily. When had she last just sat down with someone, talking with him about inconsequential matters, enjoying the company?

Long after the bartender took away her mostly empty plates and the wine's last drops had been sipped, Joseph asked, "What are your plans for the rest of the evening?"

Zoe tensed. It was nearly midnight. While she enjoyed Joseph's company, she didn't want the evening to continue. She still didn't know enough about him, except for the fact that he was very large and pretty charming. Then again, she knew of other charming men. Ted Bundy, Charles Manson, Richard Ramirez, Rod Glover. The list went on and on. For someone who dealt with psychopaths all day, charm became nothing more than dangerous camouflage.

"I think I need to sleep," she said. "I have an important day tomorrow."

"A day of consulting, huh?"

"That's right." She tried to smile but wasn't sure it came out right.

"Can you drive?" He glanced at her wineglass.

He didn't need to know that she had a room nearby. "I'll get a taxi."

He fished a business card out of his wallet. "If you feel like having another nice dinner tomorrow, give me a call."

She thanked him. He gave her another final smile that seemed to be a bit confused and left.

"Can I get the bill?" she asked.

"He already paid for everything earlier, when you were in the bathroom," the bartender said. "A real gentleman."

"Yeah," Zoe echoed. "A real gentleman."

CHAPTER 30

San Angelo, Texas, Thursday, September 8, 2016

Delia was folding the clean laundry, matching socks, when the home phone rang. All of Frank's socks were either gray or black, which meant she had to compare their length and fabric to make an actual pair. Sometimes she wouldn't bother, making pairs of short socks with long socks, woolly socks with paper-thin socks. That usually resulted in a litany of complaints, so right now she tried to do it right. For the life of her, she couldn't find the pair of the sock she held.

The phone's ring made her jump, her head turning left and right like a hunted animal. It wasn't only that she'd been deep in thought—it was that this phone almost never rang. Both she and Frank used their mobile phones, and everyone knew that was the way to reach them. In fact, the main reason they hadn't disconnected the phone line long ago was that Frank's mother, Gerta, would always call that number. Gerta had been an old woman, her memory dissipating, and Frank despaired of trying to make her call him by his new number. The president had a red phone to talk to Russia, and the Howe family had a beige phone to talk to Gerta.

Except Gerta had been dead for over seven months. Delia nestled her aching hand, her mind fuzzy with physical pain. It was a wrong number or a survey or a salesman with a deal she couldn't refuse.

Regardless, it was an annoyance. She decided to ignore it, waited for the ringing to end.

It didn't. It kept ringing and ringing maddeningly loudly. Those old-fashioned phones had been designed to ring as loud as possible so you'd hear them no matter where you were in the house.

Finally, impatient with the noise, Delia got up and picked up the phone.

"Hello?" Her tone was sharp, angry. Meant to clarify that she was not someone who wanted her time wasted.

Silence on the other end, and something soft, a hint of breath.

No, not breathing. Sobbing.

"Hello?" she asked, her voice softer, scared. And then, ever so faintly, "Maribel?"

For a second the person on the other line just kept sobbing. But then she called out, her voice broken and terrified. "Mommy . . ."

"Maribel? Where are you? Are you all right? Hello?" She waited for a second after each question, but Maribel only cried harder, apparently unable to answer. "Maribel!"

"Mommy!"

"Where are you? I'll come and get you—just tell me where you are."

"Get me out of here!" Maribel screamed. "Please!"

"Out of where? Where are you?"

The line went dead.

Delia stared at it in disbelief. And then, letting the phone drop, she rushed for her mobile phone, where she kept the phone number of Detective Lyons.

CHAPTER 31

Tatum was a few minutes late to the morning meeting and got an admonishing stare from Jensen, which he ignored with practiced ease.

"Right." Jensen clapped his hands. "Where's Lyons? I want to start."

"She'll probably be here in a moment," Foster said.

"Well, we can't wait for her. Where are we with the case? Detective Foster?"

Foster flipped through his notebook. "We talked to all the friends who were with Medina the night she disappeared. Between their testimonies and the red light camera footage, we feel safe saying she was dropped off in front of her house at one fifteen. All the neighbors were sleeping. The mother woke up at six thirty, saw Nicole never got home, reported Nicole missing at seven thirty-five after calling everyone she could think of. We're talking to eyewitnesses at the party and some of Nicole's other friends, but so far nothing stands out."

"Okay." Jensen clapped his hands again. "So maybe—"

"Lyons has been going through the red light cam footage," Foster continued. "Three vehicles followed the car Nicole rode in. Two of them belonged to teenagers returning from the same party. The third was a truck driven by a forty-seven-year-old man named Wyatt Tiller. We're looking into it, though I doubt he's our man."

Foster flipped a page in his notebook. "Some of Nicole Medina's friends had erected a small memorial shrine on her street. It looks harmless—there's nothing there that the press might have a field day with."

"Can you monitor visitors to the shrine?" Tatum asked. "The killer might visit it."

Foster considered it. "We can't have a man stationed there, but I see no problem with installing a small surveillance camera."

"What about the crime scene?" Zoe asked Foster. "Did you scan it with UV light?"

Tatum was mildly irritated, realizing she'd followed up on something that *he* wasn't privy to.

"The crime scene techs found no indication of any foreign fluids that show up under UV light." Foster paused for a second, letting it sink in, then continued. "Regarding the box, we consulted with an expert carpenter, and he said that he estimates the box was made by a professional. If our killer isn't a carpenter, he must have ordered it from somewhere. We want to follow that trail, but we frankly need more manpower."

"Well," Jensen said.

Tatum sighed. *And here begins the manpower mating dance.*

They argued for a bit. Eventually, a compromise was reached. Tatum wasn't sure what the bottom line was, but both Foster and Jensen seemed disgruntled and unhappy.

Then it was Agent Shelton's turn to speak, and he briskly outlined their efforts at tracking the killer via the online video he'd posted. It didn't sound promising. The hosting service had been paid for in Bitcoin; the domain was free and registered under a temporary email account.

"The unsub used a second burner phone as a hotspot to post the video, and that phone was switched on and off at the site," Shelton added, using the short term for *unknown subject*. "We're monitoring both phone numbers in case one of them is switched on again."

He glanced at his laptop, which was open in front of him. "Lab results indicate all DNA samples retrieved from the box belonged to the victim."

Jensen turned wearily to Tatum. "What about you? Any progress with the killer's profile?"

"We're searching for similar crime patterns," Tatum said. "So far, we found nothing. Dr. Bentley also pointed out we should probably look into Schrodinger and understand his theory—it might shed some light on the murderer."

"That's a good idea." Jensen beamed in a manner that made Tatum feel instantly suspicious.

"Well . . . yeah. I'll look into that today."

"I am friends with San Angelo's number one physics doctor at Angelo State University," Jensen said. "We know each other from college. I can set up a meeting."

"I have a bit to add," Zoe interrupted.

"Oh?" Jensen turned to her. "What did you find, Agent, uh, Dr. Bentley?"

"I composed a basic profile from what we know about the killer," she answered. "Nothing definite, of course, but I think I managed to pinpoint a few likely characteristics."

Jensen pursed his lips skeptically, but the two detectives focused on Zoe with interest.

"The killer is uncommonly careful, leaving no trace behind him, which leads me to believe he's at least thirty, probably even a bit older. Younger killers are usually more impulsive in their actions. However, he's in good shape: those bins on the video were heavy; that grave was hard to dig. He didn't seem in any discomfort during the video, despite the hard work. That makes me think he's no older than forty-five."

"I have an uncle who runs marathons, and he's sixty," Jensen said.

Tatum cleared his throat. "That's why Dr. Bentley said these are *likely* characteristics. We're not telling you to ignore anyone who's twenty. But we recommend that you prioritize your investigation according to our recommendations." For a second his eyes locked with Zoe's.

She gave a short curt nod. "The unsub was careful to avoid showing his skin in the video, wearing long gloves, high boots, a long-sleeved shirt. All this was probably done to avoid giving us any hint regarding his race. But the video was streamed live, and he must have assumed he might accidentally show a bit of skin during his hard work. This leads me to believe he wasn't too worried about it, didn't think that it would narrow down the search by much. Since San Angelo's demographic is mostly white, I assume it means he's white."

Foster scribbled in his notebook furiously.

"From the cleanliness of the crime scene and the quite elaborate murder, we can tell he has an obsessive personality, paying meticulous, often excessive, attention to details. If he has a job, it would be one where speed is not very important, but thoroughness is. That would probably mean he's not in customer service jobs or menial jobs. He's highly intelligent and is prone to show it off. This is almost certainly due to an inherent low self-esteem, which makes me think he was either belittled by his parents or bullied as a child. He probably endured some sort of abuse as a child."

The door opened, and Lyons entered the room wearing a haunted expression. Without saying a word, she sat down at the end of the table.

Zoe continued. "He has a van, and it would be the most common van around these parts." She shrugged. "I don't know about cars."

Jensen blinked. "That's very . . . detailed, Agent, uh, Doctor."

She didn't seem to hear him or care for his feedback. "He had a stressful event in his life a few months ago, which made him feel unappreciated and angry. It is likely job related; maybe he was fired, or something made him feel undervalued, demoted. We call this trigger a stressor."

"The stressor could also be a relationship ending," Tatum pointed out. "It's not necessarily job related."

"That's true," Zoe admitted. "But I feel like the video was a performance compensating for what he felt. He posted it online for everyone to see—he wants affirmation from the public. The name he gave himself—Schrodinger—as well as presenting the video as an experiment feels like an attempt to appear skilled and clever. Someone who deserved the appreciation of his superiors and peers."

Tatum wasn't sure he agreed with her assessment but decided to leave it.

"Also, I think it's likely Nicole Medina wasn't his first victim. The crime scene doesn't match the impulsive act of someone who killed for the first time. It looks like it was coldly planned by someone who killed before. Six weeks ago, a twenty-two-year-old woman named Maribel Howe was reported missing. The case file is still open. Detective Lyons and I talked to the mother yesterday, and I think it's possible Maribel is another victim."

Jensen glanced at Lyons. "Oh?"

Lyons cleared her throat. "I have news about that," she said, her voice haggard. "I just talked to the mother. She told me she got a phone call from Maribel. I couldn't get the exact details from her, but she sounded hysterical. I asked dispatch to send a patrol unit there to talk to her, and I'll go there myself to take her statement."

"Right." Jensen clapped his hands. "Meanwhile, Bentley and Gray will join me to hear what my physicist friend thinks."

Tatum was suddenly sorry for suggesting they learn more about Schrodinger. For one, he wanted to know more about Maribel Howe. And being with Jensen felt like having an unpleasant rash.

CHAPTER 32

Tatum frowned as he followed Jensen's car. It was a testament to how bad things were between Zoe and him that she'd said she'd ride with the lieutenant. Tatum was terrible at holding a grudge. He knew some people did it with ease, practically turning it into a hobby. His aunt could recall what her frenemy had told her in eighth grade as easily as if she was recalling an event from the night before. But Tatum had to make a constant effort to do it, and it exhausted him.

Jensen parked the car in the university's parking lot, and Tatum found a parking spot not far off. He joined Zoe and Jensen, and they all walked to the physics department. On their way, Jensen checked his messages and let out a curse. "The press found out about Maribel Howe's phone call."

"So fast?" Zoe asked.

"The girl's mother probably called them straightaway."

"She didn't strike me as the type," Zoe said.

Jensen didn't seem to be listening. "Some of them are hinting at links between Howe and Medina. This is blowing up in our faces. I knew we should have given them more at the press conference." His tone shifted, becoming accusatory.

Zoe pursed her lips. Tatum didn't try to intervene. Arguing with the lieutenant was useless, he knew. The man was already trying to find someone to pin this on in case he was blamed.

Dr. Cobb's office was on the third floor, and the door was open, but Jensen knocked on it anyway and said, "Knock, knock," in a way that was perhaps meant to be endearing.

Tatum glanced into the room. Dr. Cobb was far from what Tatum had expected a physicist to look like. Cobb was a thin, black-haired woman wearing a buttoned white shirt and a pair of jeans. Her glasses were neither thick nor round but delicate and square. She had a bright-red lipstick on, which instantly made Tatum think of one of his early crushes in high school.

"Ah," she said, her voice cool. "When you called, I thought I'd have some time to work before you showed up." Her voice and demeanor hinted that Jensen might have exaggerated when he called her a friend.

"How are you, Helen?" Jensen asked, beaming. He entered the room and seemed about to hug her.

The doctor, clearly anticipating the move, stuck out her hand, and Jensen, after a moment of hesitation, shook it. Zoe and Tatum entered the room, and Tatum shut the door. He took one of the empty chairs in the room.

"Helen, these are Dr. Bentley and Agent Gray from the FBI," Jensen said and then gestured at her, glancing at Tatum. "And *this* is Dr. Helen Cobb."

Dr. Cobb nodded at them. "Nice to meet you. I understand you need my help with a . . . case?"

"There's a killer who seems drawn to Schrodinger," Tatum said. "We need a crash course about the cat experiment."

Cobb sighed. "Well, it's more of a thought experiment. Schrodinger never actually tormented any cats, as far as I know. The experiment is aimed to demonstrate a problem in the two-state quantum system. In quantum physics, we say a quantum can be in two different separate states at once. We call that superposition."

Tatum could already feel his attention snagged by random thoughts. It was like being in school all over again, the drone of the teacher turning into a background noise as he fantasized about the girl who sat in front of him, about his afternoon plans, about frogs, about anything else, really.

"Schrodinger wanted to demonstrate that there is an inherent problem with superposition," Cobb continued. "So he formed this thought experiment. You put a cat in a box. In that box there is a flask of acid connected to a device that has a Geiger counter and radioactive matter. Enough radioactive matter that in one hour, there is a fifty percent chance one of the atoms decays. If it decays, the acid kills the cat. If it doesn't, the acid remains in the flask. With me so far?"

Tatum wasn't sure. He really tried, but he was momentarily distracted by Cobb's lips. How did her students ever manage to concentrate during class? He tried to pull his focus back together. A cat and some acid. Right.

"The matter in the device is in superposition. It decayed, but it also didn't decay. It's in two states at once. The cat was either exposed to the acid, or he wasn't. Which means he's both dead and alive at the same time. He's in superposition."

"But he is either dead or alive. He can't be both." Zoe sounded irritated. Tatum wondered why she found this so offensive. Perhaps she was averse to cruelty against imaginary cats.

"Well, the thought experiment states he's in superposition, because he's in a closed, unobserved device that is in superposition. So the cat and the device are in the same state."

"When you say unobserved, what does that mean?" Zoe asked.

"Superposition can only exist if the matter isn't measured. Once it's measured, it can't be in several states at once."

"What if we looked at the cat via a video?"

"Then it wouldn't be unobserved. So the cat wouldn't be in superposition."

"What if we observed the cat through a video, but then the feed was terminated?" Tatum asked, suddenly tense. "And then the experiment carried on without anyone observing it?"

Cobb hesitated. "After a while, the cat would be in superposition. He would be both alive and dead."

Was that why the killer had cut the feed, leaving them in uncertainty? Was it part of the experiment? Tatum clenched his jaw. Would he do other experiments?

"What if there was no acid in the box?" Zoe asked, rummaging in her handbag.

"Then the cat would presumably stay alive." Cobb scrunched her eyebrows.

"But he could die from lack of air." Zoe pulled out a copy of the case file and flipped through it, a pen in hand. She made a small notation on one of the pages.

"Yeah, but that's not a consequence of a quantum device, so he wouldn't be in superposition. He would be either alive or dead, not both."

"But we don't know which—doesn't it mean he's in superposition?"

"No." Cobb shrugged. "My husband is currently at home. He's either eating or showering or reading or whatever, and I have no idea which. That doesn't mean he's in superposition. Because his state isn't connected to a particle. And obviously, *he* isn't a particle. He's my husband. That's also part of the problem with the experiment. It has been proved a cat *can't* be in superposition."

"Why not?"

"Because he's too big. Big things can't be in superposition. It doesn't matter if the cat explodes or not—he would never be in superposition, because he's too big."

"Explodes?" Zoe asked. "You said he's killed by acid."

"Well, in Einstein's version, he'd explode. Einstein's experiment had a barrel of explosives. It really doesn't matter. The point is, it's something that kills the cat."

Apparently physicists liked to theoretically abuse cats in any number of ways. Perhaps Marvin would find that notion appealing, considering his long feud with Freckle. "So humans can't be in superposition either, right?" he asked.

"Of course not. Humans are bigger than cats."

"Dr. Cobb," Zoe said. "Was the experiment ever performed?"

"God, I hope not." Cobb shuddered. "What would be the point? The entire thing is intended to demonstrate a paradox. You don't actually need to trap a cat in a death machine to do it."

Unless the purpose of the experiment was different and wasn't about science at all.

CHAPTER 33

Andrea missed Boston.

That was the main thing she realized as she ran on the gym's treadmill. She missed jogging through Boston Common. Right now, the trees would be turning yellow, red, and pink, and running through that explosion of color would be—

"Ungh!" A loud grunt erupted behind her.

Much better than *this.* The man had been grunting intermittently for the past half hour as he tackled the various weight-lifting machines. Men weren't grunting around her when she jogged through Boston Common.

When she'd moved to Dale City, she couldn't wait to get away from Boston. But it wasn't Boston she wanted to escape from. It was her soul-crushing job as an insurance claims agent. It was Derek and their shambles of a relationship. It was her mother, less than an hour drive away, constantly nagging her to get married, ten times worse since Andrea's father had died.

So when Zoe had told her she was leaving Boston, moving to Virginia, all Andrea could think of was that she wanted to leave as well. She had a romantic idea of the two Bentley sisters conquering Dale City together.

"Ungh!" Another grunt pierced the air. Andrea rolled her eyes and increased her jogging speed, regretting leaving her earphones at home.

Reality had hit her fast. Zoe had a very busy job at Quantico. All of Andrea's work experience was at a job she'd sworn to never do again, so she'd ended up as a waitress in a mediocre restaurant.

The dating scene in Dale City wasn't much to talk about either. It got to the point that one sad evening, she'd called Derek to ask how he was doing. Worst. Phone call. Ever. Derek wasn't brokenhearted, pining for her. No. Derek was just *fine*. In fact, he had a girlfriend. He'd lost weight.

And now she didn't even have her job anymore. Her savings account was emptying at an alarming rate. Sure, Zoe would be happy to lend her some money. Hell, Zoe would be happy to just *give* her money—she'd actually offered to. But Andrea hadn't hit that rock bottom yet.

"Aggggh!" This time it was a woman grunting. What was with these people?

A month before, when she'd found out about Rod Glover, she'd been horrified. She hadn't remembered what he looked like, and he'd seemed like a nice, somewhat quirky man when he'd approached her on the street. Hugging her arm as he took the picture, thanking her politely later. Sure, she *knew* about that event when they were kids, the horrible night Rod Glover had tried to break in to the room while they huddled inside. Zoe had talked about it more than once. But she had no recollection of it.

Except, maybe, a fragment: her sitting on the bed, terrified of something outside, and Zoe hugging her, whispering, "Don't worry, Ray-Ray. He can't hurt us."

Now she knew. The man from the street had been the same monster who'd killed three girls in Maynard and at least two more in Chicago. He'd attacked her sister in Chicago as well, tried to rape and kill her. This was the man who'd told her "Smile" before taking the picture.

Sometimes her upper arm where his fingers had touched her tingled, as if hundreds of tiny insects were crawling on it. She'd have to take a shower for the sensation to pass.

"Ungh!"

"Agggggh!"

They were synchronized now, sounding like a couple engaged in the world's most uncomfortable and unpleasant sex act. The girl on the treadmill next to Andrea stopped running and left, a disgusted look on her face.

At first Andrea hadn't been able to sleep. She'd have nightmares and would wake up, listening to the building's noises, every creak, every neighbor's footstep, every unfamiliar sound—they all became *him.* Coming for her. To rape her and strangle her to death, like he had to those other girls. She'd found Zoe's notes about him, read some of them, seen pictures from crime scenes. These things were seared in her mind, impossible to scrub away. She'd been terrified.

But no one had seen him since that day. Slowly she'd become convinced he'd left. He'd wanted to freak her and Zoe out, and now he was far away. Agent Caldwell, Zoe's coworker, had explained that Rod Glover was an opportunistic sexual predator. He struck when an opportunity presented itself. He didn't target specific women. And he didn't want to get caught. They had no reason to think he was still around.

The fear had abated, though Zoe was still anxious, hovering over Andrea, suffocating her, to the point that Andrea had begun to resent her. And now she missed Boston desperately.

She had nothing going for her here. Running on this treadmill was a perfect metaphor for her life in Dale City.

Another grunt behind her, so ridiculously loud that Andrea shot a furious glance backward. A glimpse of something snagged her attention. She faced forward again, her mind sluggishly processing what she'd just seen.

A man was staring at her from the corner of the gym, partially hidden by one of the machines. Middle aged, lanky hair, a weird smile.

She'd looked at the photo enough times to know who he was.

Rod Glover.

He was here right now, watching her.

Her heart was racing, but she kept running, eyes locked forward. She was suddenly thankful for the grunting man and woman and the rest of the people around her. They all kept her safe.

Tears of fear filled her eyes as all the images from the crime scene photos popped into her mind. The dead, naked women, their bodies discarded on the ground. He was here, the monster who'd done this. Just behind her. Did he realize she'd seen him? Was he walking toward her right now, that sick smile on his face, hand wielding a knife? She couldn't look.

Her feet kept moving, running. She was living through that common nightmare—trying to run away from a monster but staying in the same spot.

Zoe had given her clear instructions for what she should do if she saw Glover. She should scream and run, fight if there was no other option. But if she screamed now, he'd just know she'd seen him. And then what? She tried to scream anyway, but her throat was clogged, empty of breath.

She had to get away from him. Her hand reached forward, stopping the treadmill. The machine slowed down, and she got off, walking away, doing her best to seem casual. She desperately tried to catch a glance of him from the corner of her eye. Was he following her? No way of knowing.

She hurried to the locker room. Her phone was in the locker room. She could call the police or the FBI or Zoe. She glanced at a mirror on the wall, didn't see him. She was trembling, lips quivering, trying to reassure herself by the people around her. Glover struck women who were on their own. He didn't want to get caught. She'd call the police, get cops to surround the place. They'd arrest him—she'd be okay.

She dove into the locker room, going for the lockers, momentarily confused. Which locker was hers? Then she found it, grabbed the combination lock, wrestled with it, fingers shaking.

The locker room was empty, she suddenly realized. She'd entered an empty room with only one door. She was essentially trapped.

She nearly bolted out right there and then, leaving her bag and phone behind her, but suddenly she wasn't sure he wasn't waiting for her outside the door. Wasn't it what he did? Hide, waiting for his victims to walk by?

The lock clicked, and she wrenched the door open. Fumbling in the bag, she found her phone and dialed 911.

"Nine-one-one, what's your emergency?"

"I . . . Rod Glover. There's a serial killer. He's following me. I'm in the gym."

"Ma'am, calm down. You're in the gym? Are there people around you?"

"Not right now." Her voice was high pitched, panicky. "I'm in the locker room. There's no one here. And there's a murderer who is stalking me."

"Can you get to somewhere public? Ma'am?"

She held the phone to her ear, unable to talk. The locker room door had a window of frosted glass, and a shadowy figure appeared in it, looming as it came closer. She quickly ran to the other end of the room, entering the farthest shower stall.

"Ma'am?"

"Please send cops over," she said in a low voice.

"Can you give me an address?"

She had no idea what the address was. "I'm at the gym. Uh . . . nearby Cheshire Station."

"Okay, ma'am, I'm sending a patrol over. Can you try and get to somewhere public until they arrive?"

Was the shadow still by the door? She didn't even dare look. "I'm scared." Her voice was hardly more than a whisper.

"I understand." The operator sounded calm, in control. Like Zoe always was. God, Andrea wanted Zoe there right now. "But if you're in the gym, where there are a lot of people, you're safe. Just go wait at the lobby for the police, okay? Keep me on the line, and walk to the lobby."

"Okay."

She crept toward the locker room door, her breath shallow, her heart feeling as if it were submerged in ice. She stepped softly on the wet floor, wiping the tears of fear from her eyes.

Footsteps. Movement at the frosted window. Someone was approaching.

"He's coming for me. Help. Help!" she screeched. The phone tumbled from her frozen fingers.

Scream and run. If you can't run, fight, Zoe had said. Andrea screamed, stumbling back, yelling as hard as she could. She couldn't run, and she didn't think she could fight. Only screaming was left. She screamed again, trying to summon anyone who could get there in time to save her.

A sweaty, fat woman stepped into the locker room, staring at Andrea in confusion and worry. Andrea fell to the floor, sobbing, the operator's voice calling her from the discarded phone on the floor.

CHAPTER 34

Zoe sighed and leaned back in her chair, the late-afternoon sun slanting through the meeting room window, blinding her. She moved around the table to a position where the sun wouldn't bother her or reflect on her laptop's screen.

The details about Maribel Howe's phone call to her mother were sparse and frustrating.

There was a record of an incoming phone call to the Howe residence. That much was true. However, they had no way of knowing who it was. Delia Howe repeatedly claimed it was Maribel but added the girl hadn't said much. And whoever it had been called her Mommy, which, Delia admitted, Maribel hadn't done since she'd been a small child. It all felt like there was a chance it was a prank call.

The phone she'd used was still on, but the accuracy of its exact position was poor. It was somewhere in south San Angelo in an area that contained over seven hundred houses. Cops were doing a door-to-door search, but they couldn't get a search warrant for seven hundred homes, and a lot of homes were vacant, their owners at work. And while they were doing *that*, other aspects of the investigation stalled.

Foster also told Zoe that the toxicology report had come back—the victim had traces of flunitrazepam in her system: Rohypnol. That clarified how the killer had been able to handle her and put her in a box without any struggle.

She mulled over it, distractedly doodling on the page in front of her. She was about to call Delia Howe to get the facts straight when Tatum entered the room.

"Hey," he said. "I wanted to talk to you."

"What is it?" she asked. She surprised herself with the eagerness in her voice.

"I had an idea about the case. I wanted to hear what you think."

"Shoot."

"You think this serial killer is obsessed with his own fame, right?"

"It's definitely part of his motivation."

"Could be a mind game he's playing with the police?" Tatum asked. "A way of establishing his superiority?"

Zoe considered this. "Maybe he wants to prove his superiority *publicly*. If it was just about being superior to the police, he'd have sent the video just to them, which would have been much safer."

"That fits the profile for the kind of killer who'd want to involve himself with the case, right?"

Many serial killers gravitated to the police investigation, making themselves part of it. A lot of times they were actually the ones who "found" the body, informing the police about it. Or they'd pretend to have valuable information about the case. It was a way to siphon information, and they also often erroneously believed it put them beyond suspicion. There was definitely a measure of superiority in that kind of behavior.

"I think you're right," she said.

"Let's not wait for him to do it. We need to start a volunteer hotline. Say we're looking for any info that might prove useful about the Nicole Medina case. And then the police can check the people that call as well as the leads. He might call."

Zoe considered this. "I think that's a good idea. We should suggest it."

A silence settled between them. For a few minutes, they had a taste of their previous bond. But now that the discussion was over, the tension was there again.

"I need to call Maribel Howe's mother," Zoe muttered, rummaging in her bag for her phone. "I want to know exactly . . ." The words faded as she gaped at the display.

She'd set it to silent when they'd visited Dr. Cobb and had forgotten about it. She had two missed calls from Harry Barry, three from Andrea, and one from Mancuso, as well as a message from Andrea asking Zoe to call her back urgently. She was dizzy as she dialed Andrea, listening to it ring, praying for her to answer already.

Finally, Andrea said, "Hey."

Zoe's heart plunged, hearing her sister's voice. She'd clearly been crying, and her breathing was heavy, frightened.

"Ray-Ray, what happened?"

"I saw Glover."

"Are you all right? Did he—"

"He didn't touch me. I saw him stalking me while I was at the gym. It was *him*, Zoe—I'm sure of it."

"Of course you're sure. I didn't think otherwise. Where are you now?"

"I'm at the apartment. I locked the door." Andrea hiccuped. "A patrol officer took me home and made sure the place was empty before he left."

"Did you talk to Agent Caldwell?"

"Yeah, I called him."

"What did he say?"

"He said the police will check the security cameras at the gym."

"Is there someone keeping watch for you right now?"

"I . . . I don't know. I don't think so."

Zoe leaned against the wall, feeling helpless and furious with herself. What was she doing all the way across the country from Andrea?

Her sister needed her right now. "Listen, I'll get home as fast as possible. I'll catch the first plane, okay? For now, I'll talk to Mancuso, make sure there's someone watching the place at all times. Did you latch the door as well?"

"Yes."

"And latch the windows too, okay? There's nothing to worry about, Ray-Ray. He won't get near you. Can you explain what happened, exactly?"

Zoe paced back and forth as she listened, ignoring Tatum's worried stare, her mind in an uproar. Glover was watching her sister. Clearly stalking her. Had he been doing it the entire time? Did he intend to hurt her sister, or was he just getting a thrill from watching her? Stupid question—Glover was way past voyeurism. If he stalked a woman, it meant he fantasized about attacking her. And Glover acted on his fantasies. She needed to keep Andrea safe. Maybe they could get her to a safehouse. Or fly her out of the country for a few months until Zoe could catch Glover, tear his eyes out, castrate him, and force-feed him his own—

"Hello? Zoe? Are you there?"

"I'm here. Okay, Ray-Ray, stay inside. Keep everything locked. I'll talk to Mancuso and get a flight out."

"Okay. I took your chef's knife."

It took Zoe a moment to figure out the context of what her sister had just said. "Oh. Okay."

"I'll sleep with it, just in case."

"Just be careful with it."

"I'll put it under the pillow."

"The way you toss around in your sleep? You'll end up impaling yourself with it."

Andrea let out a shuddering laugh.

"Hang in there. I'll call you back in a bit, okay?" She hung up.

Tatum looked at her. "Zoe, what—"

"Hang on." She dialed Mancuso.

The chief answered after two rings. "Zoe."

"Glover was watching Andrea. He was in the same *room* with her."

"We're checking it out—calm down. Caldwell is there right now looking at the security feed."

"You need to send someone to keep an eye on Andrea. She's all alone in my apartment. All alone! He could go there at any moment, Mancuso, and she won't—"

"Bentley, get a grip!"

Zoe shut up, surprised.

"There's a patrol car watching the entrance to your building right now. An officer already searched your apartment carefully. No one is letting anything happen to Andrea, okay?"

"She didn't know you were watching," Zoe muttered lamely.

"Your sister is scared out of her wits. I doubt she heard half of what Caldwell told her on the phone. She isn't a professional, and no one expects her to function under pressure. Unlike you."

Zoe ignored the remark, tapping on her keyboard, searching for flight tickets. "I'm flying back," she told Mancuso. "I can get on a plane tomorrow morning."

She expected the chief to argue with her, but Mancuso just sighed. "Fine. I doubt you have a lot more to do in San Angelo in any case. Gray can stay an extra day to help out the local police."

"Thanks."

"Andrea will be fine, Zoe."

Zoe didn't answer. Mancuso said goodbye and hung up. Zoe put down the phone.

"What's going on?" Tatum asked.

"Andrea saw Glover. He was stalking her." Zoe began to insert her details for the flight ticket.

"Is she all right?"

"Yeah. She's scared."

"I'll send Marvin over so she won't be alone."

"Thanks. I'm going back there first thing in the morning. Mancuso said you should probably stay another day to wrap things up here."

"Okay." A second of silence. "Do you want me to drop you off at the motel?"

"I'm fine. I'll take an Uber. You should go tell Foster about your hotline. It's a good idea."

Tatum cleared his throat. "I'm sure Andrea will be fine."

Zoe shut the laptop screen and stood up. "That's what Mancuso told me. I wish I knew where you two get your information."

CHAPTER 35

By the time Tatum had filled Foster in about the latest development and told him about the hotline, Zoe was already gone. Tatum almost called her to ask how Andrea was doing but decided to avoid bothering her. Instead, he walked out of the station and called Marvin.

"Guess what I did today, Tatum," his grandfather said without preamble.

Tatum could think of a bunch of options, none of them particularly good. "What?"

"I skydived."

Tatum groaned. "What about the insurance?"

"I found a company that agreed to insure me. It cost me an arm and a leg, but you can do without my inheritance, right?"

"I don't care about the damn inheritance. I just want you to be around for a while and—"

"I paid with your credit card, Tatum. Mine didn't work for some reason."

Tatum shut his eyes and lost himself to some calming murderous thoughts.

"I'll pay you back—don't worry," Marvin said. "And I got a discount for next time."

"Next . . . Marvin, there's no next—"

"I'm hooked, Tatum. You won't believe how great it feels. It's better than cocaine. It's almost better than sex. The only problem is it's short, Tatum. The free fall is less than a minute. Free fall. That's what we jumpers call the time between jumping and the moment the parachute opens. Georgette says I'm a natural."

"Who's Georgette?"

"The instructor. We jumped together. You should see her, Tatum. She's fantastic. If I was forty years younger—"

"Marvin, listen. Andrea just saw Rod Glover. He was stalking her."

"Aw, shit. Did he touch her?"

"No, but he was very close. Could you drop by, see how she's doing?"

"Sure thing, Tatum. I'll get there right now. Poor kid—she must be terrified. How's Zoe doing?"

"Shocked and worried. She went to the motel. She's flying back tomorrow."

"And where are you?"

"I'm at the police station. I need to finish up with some stuff."

"What's wrong with you, Tatum? Go help your partner—she needs someone to be there for her. She's probably worried sick."

"Thanks for your concern. Just see to Andrea."

"Tatum. Listen to me. Go be with Zoe. I don't care if you think she's fine. Trust me: she's not."

"You don't know her. She's the strongest person I know, and—"

"I swear your dad was an awesome kid, but he had no idea how to raise you. Go be with your damn partner!"

Tatum rolled his eyes. His grandfather was driving him insane. "Look, she's better without me anyway. We had an argument a few days ago, and it's a bit complicated right now. So I appreciate the advice, but—"

"What kind of argument?"

"It doesn't matter."

"What kind of argument, Tatum?"

"Just some dumb stuff she said. I told her about the case in LA. The one where I shot the pedophile."

"Oh yeah, I remember."

"The internal investigation has been reopened. Apparently there's a new witness."

"They're acting like shooting pedos is against the law."

"It *is* against the law. Anyway, Zoe said maybe I didn't shoot in self-defense. That I shot him because I thought it was the right thing to do."

"Yeah. So what did you argue about?"

Tatum frowned. "That's what we argued about."

"Oh, I get it," Marvin finally said. "You were hurt."

"Well, yeah."

"You thought she should know you better than that. I understand how you feel. You care about what she thinks of you."

"Of course I do." Tatum kicked a small rock, and it hit the station's wall. "Anyway. I should probably let her be alone. She doesn't need this right now."

"Uh-huh. But listen, Tatum."

"Yeah?"

"Are you a man or a wimp?"

"What?"

"Are you spineless? Are you a damn wuss? She hurt your delicate snowflake feelings? Is that what's the matter? You're lucky I'm not there, Tatum, or I'd do what your father should have done and wallop your ass!"

"Listen, Marvin—"

"Did you lose your balls, Tatum?" Marvin roared. "Did the vet accidentally take them off when you had Freckle castrated? Should I call the vet and ask for your balls back? Would that help you get over yourself and act like a man? What's wrong with you? Grow a damn spine and a pair of new balls and go be with your partner. She needs your support, damn it!"

"Grandpa, shut up!" Tatum shouted back. "I'm doing what I think is right. You don't know her like I do, and—"

"You're doing nothing right, Tatum! You get in your car, and you drive over there, and you comfort your friend, you got that? And I'm going over to see her sister, because one of us still remembers what it is to be a man!" The line clicked as Marvin hung up the phone.

Tatum nearly tossed his mobile on the ground. He shook with rage. That stubborn, daft old man and his old-fashioned clueless advice. What the hell did he know about anything? He had no idea. It was easy to yell and rant, but the bastard didn't even know Zoe, had no idea what made her tick. Zoe was the kind of person who needed time for herself. Tatum knew that. Marvin should respect his ability to know his partner.

Maybe she'd want some food, though. He should get her some take-out. Just hand it to her. Ask her if she needed anything else. Wouldn't hurt to ask.

He drove in furious silence, passing the time by thinking of things he could shout at Marvin next time they spoke. It took him some time until he found a restaurant that did takeout with reasonable-looking dishes. He got Zoe a nice hamburger and some fries. He then went to the nearby grocery and bought a six-pack. She would probably need the drink, and if she did want company, they could drink together. She wouldn't, but it was better to buy it, just in case.

The sun was low over the horizon when he reached the motel. He climbed the stairs and went over to her door. He knocked, then knocked again. He glanced through the window. The room was dark.

"She just left."

Tatum turned around to see a man walking toward him, smoking a cigarette.

"What?" he asked.

"You're looking for Zoe, right? I just saw her leave to grab some dinner. She had a guy with her. A giant, really. I think he was seven feet tall."

"Who the hell are you?"

"Harry Barry. Nice to meet you, Agent Gray."

CHAPTER 36

Zoe's apartment in Dale City had two bedrooms, and both bedrooms had windows overlooking the opposite building in the complex as well as the footpath that led to the building's entrance.

Andrea had latched the windows and shut the doors, positioning the couch in the living room so she could see both the entrance door and the living room window from the corners of her eyes. She now sat and stared at the TV, trying to concentrate on whatever transpired on-screen, while gripping the large knife she'd taken from Zoe's kitchen. She occasionally glanced down at it, taking comfort in the shining sharp blade.

The sudden knock on the door drove her heart up to her throat. She glanced at the time. It was a quarter past ten.

She made sure the door was latched, though she'd already checked half a dozen times. She got up, knife in hand, and crept to it, praying that whoever it was would just go away.

Another knock, harder this time. She winced and tried to call out, but all she could get out of her throat was a slight croak.

"Excuse me, sir?" she heard a firm voice say beyond the door. "Can I help you?"

It was probably the policeman watching the building's entrance. Agent Caldwell had called to tell her they'd checked the security footage and that there had definitely been someone looking at her, though it had been hard to identify his face. The agent had stressed several times that a policeman would be watching her home all night.

"Sir?" the voice said again. "Can you step away from the door?"

"I'm here to visit Andrea Bentley," a cranky voice answered. "Calm yourself. I'm not a goddamn serial killer."

"Sir. Please step away from the door."

"Listen, young man. I get that you're enthusiastic about your job, but . . . what are you doing? Put that down—don't be ridiculous."

Andrea unlatched and unlocked the door and yanked it open. Tatum's grandfather stood by the door, his back to her, a bag over one shoulder and a fishbowl in the other. He faced a uniformed cop, who held a gun in his hand, looking uncertain.

"It's all right," Andrea said hurriedly. "I know him."

"What did you think I was going to do?" Marvin asked in a loud voice. "Assault her with the goldfish?"

"Sorry, miss," the officer apologized. "I saw a man entering the building, carrying suspicious packages, and—"

"Suspicious? It's a fishbowl." Marvin shook his head. "Are you going to arrest the fish?"

"Thanks, Officer." Andrea smiled at him and opened the door wider. "Come in, Marvin."

The old man shuffled into the apartment, and Andrea closed the door behind him.

"Sorry." Marvin put the bowl with a dazed-looking fish on the table. "I called, but you didn't answer."

Andrea nodded dumbly. When he'd called, she'd been sobbing hysterically and wasn't in a state to answer the phone.

"I told my grandson I'd watch out for you," Marvin said. "And I'd heard you had some troubles, so here I am."

"Thanks. You didn't need to . . . why did you bring the fish?"

"If I'm going to spend the night here, I can't leave the fish with the cat. It won't end well for one of them. So it was either bringing the fish or the cat. And the fish didn't give as much resistance." Marvin lifted his arm, showing her three red claw marks that ran along his wrist. He then surveyed the room suspiciously. "Do you have cats here?"

"No," Andrea said weakly.

"Right." The old man unzipped his jacket and, to Andrea's horror, took out a large gun.

"Good thing that young cop didn't see this," he muttered, putting the gun on the table by the fishbowl. "Now, where's the kitchen? I need a nice cup of tea, and I gotta tell you, I think you do too. You're as pale as a bedsheet."

"Um, you really don't need to spend the night here." Andrea followed Marvin to the kitchen. "The police are watching my apartment, and—"

"Nonsense." Marvin waved his hand. "You can't stay alone right now. Don't worry—I'll sleep on the couch . . . where does your sister keep her tea?"

"I'm not sure she *has* tea. Zoe drinks coffee."

"There are times for coffee, and there are times for tea." He rummaged in one of the lower cupboards. "Ah, there we go. How do you drink yours?"

"I . . . well . . ."

"It's not a hard question. Either you drink it with zero spoons of sugar or one spoon or two spoons or, if you know what's good for you, three spoons."

"Half a spoon."

"Hmmmph. A bit of a wiseass, are you?" He shook his head as he made the tea.

Andrea glanced backward. The fish seemed to be eyeing the gun, as if it contemplated grabbing it. A beer bottle stood in the middle of his fishbowl, and it swam twice around it, then stopped in front of the gun again.

"It's not a goldfish," Andrea said.

"Eh?" Marvin shuffled over to her with two steaming mugs of tea.

"You called it a goldfish earlier. It's not. It's a gourami."

"It's gold, isn't it?" He sat by the kitchen table with both mugs, pushing one to the other side. "Sit down. Drink your tea. You've been through a nasty shock."

She sat down and sipped from the tea. He was right. She needed it. And the company. She felt her eyes moistening.

"How's your tea?"

"It's good," she croaked.

"I put two spoons of sugar in it." He waggled his bushy eyebrows.

Andrea snorted in laughter, then let out a sob.

The old man patted her awkwardly on her hand. "You're all right, aren't you? And I promise you that bastard isn't setting a foot near you while I'm around. Okay?"

"Okay." She wiped the tears with the back of her hand.

"You know what I did today? I skydived. What an experience! You can come with me next time. That minute of free fall until the canopy opens . . . *canopy* is what we jumpers call the parachute. Anyway, it's not as scary as you'd think. It's just exhilarating. Georgette says I'm a natural . . ."

She tried to smile and nod as he spoke. For the first time that day, she could relax. It was absurd, but the grumpy old man was just what she needed to feel a bit safer. And knowing he was about to sleep in the living room, no matter what she said, made her believe she could maybe fall asleep at some point during the night as well.

CHAPTER 37

"You don't like your ice cream?"

The question penetrated Zoe's fugue. She blinked, gazed down at the plastic cup in front of her. There was ice cream in it, or at least something that used to be ice cream. She'd let the thing sit untouched in the cup, and the heat had melted it to a milky goo. One lone pink iceberg, bobbing in a sea of orange. She wasn't even sure what flavors she'd asked for. Strawberry and . . . lemon? She toyed with the spoon a bit, then raised her eyes to meet Joseph's.

"I'm not hungry."

"What's hungry got to do with ice cream?" He grinned. His own plastic cup, which was decidedly larger, was completely empty.

She'd asked to meet him to distract herself. She'd been pacing her motel room back and forth, her thoughts an endless spiral of worry and guilt. Finally, she'd texted Joseph asking him to pick her up. He'd shown up in less than fifteen minutes. First, they'd eaten pad thai at Lemongrass before they'd wandered over for ice cream across the street.

All food tasted like ash in her mouth, and Zoe wasn't entirely sure whether she'd uttered a complete sentence for the entirety of their date. The whole time her mind projected thoughts about Andrea alone in the apartment while Glover prowled in the vicinity.

Zoe was no stranger to fear. But fear for herself was somehow different than fear for her sister. When her own life had been at risk, it propelled her forward, the survival instincts of fight or flight pushing her to save herself. But fearing for her sister was different. It was like her body was submerged in icy molasses, somehow slowing her down, her thoughts a jumble, chills constantly running through her. It made her useless.

Now, Joseph was eyeing her carefully. "I don't know you very well, but you seem like something is weighing you down tonight. Is anything wrong?"

Zoe dropped her gaze, stirring the ice cream with the spoon, creating swirls of pink and yellow. Usually, she wanted control over her life. She hated when someone else called the shots for her. But right now, she didn't trust her own judgment. For once, she wanted someone else to take charge.

"There is a homicidal sexual predator stalking my sister," she said, the words feeling lumpy in her mouth, as if they had an unpleasant texture. "He's obsessed with me, and now he's targeting her."

Joseph blinked. Clearly, he'd expected something else. A complaint about a bad day at work, an ailing relative, or an unpleasant encounter in the supermarket. Zoe didn't know the statistics, but she was quite sure the number of romantic dates in which a personal acquaintance with a serial killer popped up was low.

He didn't ask her if she was serious or bolt and run or laugh nervously. She had to give him that. He seemed to think it through, as if wondering how one reacted in those situations. It wasn't in the usual small talk protocol.

His eyebrows drew together. "How does he know you?"

"We were neighbors when I was a kid." She felt a sort of icy calm take over her. Facts she could deal with. Those were the stories of the past, not the horrors that might lurk in the future. "He raped and killed three girls in my town. I was the one who pointed him out to the cops."

"How old were you?"

"Fourteen."

He ran a hand over his beard, holding her gaze.

"And now I do this for a living," she carried on. She found something cathartic about laying everything plainly on the table. "I work for the FBI. In the Behavioral Analysis Unit. I'm a forensic psychologist. A profiler."

"Like in *Criminal Minds*?"

She sighed. "Yes. But real. The TV series isn't very accurate." There'd been a time she'd loved watching *Criminal Minds*, pointing out all the absurdities.

"You said you're here on business," Joseph said after a second.

"Consulting with the local police."

"About what?"

"About a murder."

"That girl they found buried? Near the Jackson farm?"

"I don't know where the Jackson farm is."

He shook his head in disbelief. "This guy you mentioned. He's stalking your sister?"

"Yes."

"But can't the police stop him?"

"They can watch her," Zoe said. "There's a patrol car in front of her building right now. But they can't stay there forever. They'll pull the surveillance sooner or later. In a month, in a year. And he'll be waiting for it. He's patient. He's been evading the police for over twenty years."

"What are they going to do?"

"Whatever they'll do won't be enough. I'll have to do it. I have to catch him." She sighed. "Can you take me to the motel, please?"

They drove back in silence. The motel wasn't far—she could've walked, but that would demand a measure of focus and orientation she wasn't sure she had tonight. He parked in the parking lot and opened the door on his side.

"You don't have to—"

"I'll walk you to your door," Joseph said resolutely.

She shrugged and got out of the car. She led the way, focusing on her feet, trying to keep the frightening thoughts at bay. She gripped her key in her hand as she crossed the parking lot and climbed the stairs to her room.

"Thanks. I'm sorry I've been such a . . ." She motioned vaguely. *Sorry for being me.*

Joseph shoved his hands in his pockets, looking almost sheepish. "No need to apologize."

She unlocked the door, stepping into the room. She turned, about to say goodbye, her hand already on the doorknob.

But once she closed that door, the thoughts would come swarming, buzzing and rattling in her skull. Like the ice cream swirls she'd had in the cup back at the store, it'd be a goopy soup. Helplessness, anxiety, and horrible what-ifs all mixed together, spinning endlessly in her mind, keeping sleep away.

"Do you want to come in?" she asked. A pleading note had entered her voice; she couldn't help it. She didn't want to be alone.

He furrowed his brow, surprised yet again. Somehow, this disastrous date had ended up in an invitation. He stepped in, and she shut the door behind him.

For a terrible moment, she thought he would start talking. But then his hand wrapped behind her back, pulling her closer to him. She stood on her tiptoes, her chest brushing against his, and she wrapped her arms around his neck.

He didn't kiss her yet, just stared into her eyes. They stood in silence, and Zoe's brain did what it always did when life paused: it filled up with thoughts. She tried to guess how far Glover was from Andrea. No more than three miles, probably. Waiting for the right moment. For them all to lay down their guard again. He was like a malignant, fatal tumor, waiting to erupt and destroy her sister. No way to find it and remove it.

She shivered, and Joseph held her fast, his brow furrowed.

As long as she focused on him, she could dim the volume of her own fears. Up close, she let her gaze roam over his features—the neatly trimmed beard, thick eyebrows, hazel eyes. His eyelashes turned blond at the tips, and only up close did she realize how long they were.

She pulled his face down, and he pressed his mouth against hers. The kiss started off tentative, like they were both unsure how the other person felt. He held back, making sure she really wanted him, and that made her more forceful. She drew his lower lip between hers, sucking on it for just a moment. His fingers tightened on her waist.

He smelled nice up close—wood shavings and polish. She opened her mouth to deepen the kiss, and her tongue brushed against his. He picked her up, and she let her thighs wrap around him as he carried her to the bed, as if she weighed nothing at all. It was just three steps away. Motel rooms were efficient for hookups that way, the bed never too far from the door.

They fell onto the bed, and it creaked under their weight. He pulled her into his lap, and she straddled him. His body was a sanctuary from her stormy thoughts. She could lose herself in this moment.

And right now, losing herself sounded like the best idea in the world.

CHAPTER 38

San Angelo, Texas, Saturday, November 10, 1990

Maine sat on his bed and exhaled heavily, gazing at the floor. The boy looked at her, wishing she'd go away. But that wouldn't happen anytime soon.

"Do you wanna play with my LEGOs?" he asked. He didn't want to play with her at all. But he knew from experience that his mother would later ask him what they'd done. He would have to demonstrate that he'd suggested a plethora of games, and Maine hadn't been interested in any of them. A good host always tried to entertain his guests, his mother told him *every single time*.

He never pointed out that a host was someone who invited his guests over. Not someone who was *forced* to have guests.

Maine rolled her eyes, as if the mere suggestion that they play LEGOs bored her.

Her real name was Charmaine, but he'd only heard it once, when her mother had been furious at her. The rest of the time, she was Maine. His mother and Maine's mother, Ruth, had been friends since high school. They met at least once a month, and Ruth always brought Maine with her. The two mothers would quickly tell them to go play, and they'd have to go to his room or outside together. He hated it. He knew Maine hated it, since she'd told him several times. He had no idea why Ruth kept bringing her over.

He wasn't even sure his mother enjoyed it. Before they would visit, his mother inevitably complained to his father that Ruth would find some way to look down at her. And after they'd leave, he often heard his mother say she was never inviting Ruth over again.

He used to feel a spark of hope when she said that. Not anymore. Ruth and Maine were a permanent fixture in his life. Like going to the dentist or waking up for church on Sunday or the basement closet punishments.

"We can play Monopoly," he suggested half-heartedly.

Maine snorted. "That's a game for little kids."

She was a year older than him. But she was almost a foot taller and would often point that out when they met, demonstrating how the top of his head didn't even reach her chin. When she took the time to establish that fact, he would stand perfectly still, his eyes locked on her chest. It bulged just a bit through her shirt.

He decided he'd covered his bases. He imagined the conversation with his mom in his head.

"What did you and Maine play?" she would ask, her voice slightly tense, as it always was after meeting her dear friend.

"Nothing," he'd say, cleverly omitting Maine's refusal. If he started out by explaining that she didn't want to play anything, it sounded defensive.

"You have to *suggest* things to play," his mother would say. "A good host always tries to entertain his guests."

"I did suggest things," he would say.

"What did you suggest?"

"Monopoly and LEGOs."

Check and mate. His mother would have nothing to say about that.

Maine exhaled again. She wore a nice perfume. The same one she'd worn last time. Its scent had stayed after she'd left and had almost made the visit worth it. He'd lain in bed thinking about her standing close to him, saying, "Look! My chin doesn't even touch your head. You're the shortest boy I know!"

Him standing motionless, staring at those bulges in her shirt.

He turned away and began to sort the matchboxes on his desk. Fifteen matchboxes, his prized collection. He loved playing with them, always feeling the fascination growing in him when he thought about their contents. His own little pets.

Beetles, spiders, cockroaches, but mostly flies. He'd catch them alive and put them in the matchboxes. Listen to the sounds as they scuttled in their tiny prisons. He'd put several in the same matchbox. The trick was, you opened the box just a bit, sliding the new captive inside, shutting it once he was there. Sometimes he'd mix and match. A spider with three flies. A cockroach and a beetle together.

Every once in a while he would shake each box and listen. If it made no sound, he'd empty it on a little strip of toilet paper. Eventually he'd make a small pile of little dead insects and just look at them, wondering how they'd felt, trapped in the box constantly looking for a way out.

"What are those?" The voice made him start. Maine stood behind him, leaning over his shoulder. He could smell her perfume.

"Just my collection. Of matchboxes." He'd stacked all fifteen boxes one on top of the other. A tower of prisoners.

"It's not very big." She sniffed. "And they're all the same type. Isn't a collection supposed to be of different types of boxes?"

"I don't know."

"You know what I like to do?" she said. "I like to light matches and let them burn. And then, when the flame almost reaches my finger, I grab them from the other side and flip them so they burn completely."

He licked his lips. "Okay."

She still leaned over his shoulder, her billowy shirt touching his neck.

"Here, let me show you." She grabbed the topmost box.

He didn't say anything, completely paralyzed by the moment. She straightened and opened the box. Her eyes widened as two flies shot out, flying around the ceiling. The dark feet of a cockroach wiggled out of the box.

She screamed, and the cockroach leaped out, climbing up Maine's hand. She shook her hand and stumbled, falling, knocking the tower of matchboxes to the floor. Still screeching, she stumbled to the door, yanked it open, and ran outside.

He didn't move, didn't breathe. Around him, dozens of prisoners scuttled and buzzed, their limbs and wings scratching against the cardboard walls of their cells.

CHAPTER 39

San Angelo, Texas, Friday, September 9, 2016

The alarm woke Tatum up seconds after he had drifted into sleep. At least, that was what it felt like. Dazed, he fumbled for the phone, knocking it off the night table and under the bed in one clumsy swipe.

The alarm got louder. Tatum had recently downloaded an alarm app that was designed for heavy sleepers. It couldn't be snoozed, and to stop it, he had to punch in a six-digit code. Its volume increased every few seconds. He had no idea what had prompted him to invite such a malicious entity into his life.

He got out of bed and crouched to get to the phone. He had somehow managed to knock the phone all the way to the center of the space beneath the bed—just far enough that it would be a nightmare to reach from all sides. He had to stretch hard to get it, nearly dislocating his shoulder in the process. The alarm was now blaring so loud it had probably managed to wake up several of the adjacent rooms as well.

His fingers snagged the phone, and he pulled it out, groaning. He tapped the required six digits, and the vile thing finally went quiet. He sat on the floor, holding it, recuperating from the traumatic wakeup call.

He sent Zoe a short message: Need a ride to the airport?

Putting the phone aside, he began dressing. Halfway through putting on his socks, he paused, one foot still bare, the remaining sock bunched in his hand.

Zoe hadn't responded yet. The night before, after lying awake in bed, thinking about Marvin's reprimand, he'd manage to cook up a vague sense of guilt for not rising to the occasion. He checked the phone and saw Zoe hadn't even opened his message.

That was a bit strange. She was awake for sure, and Zoe was obsessive about checking her messages. Doubly so now that Andrea was in danger.

That annoying reporter had told him last night that Zoe had gone to grab dinner with a tall man. At the time, Tatum had thought she might have gone with Detective Foster for some reason. But now he wondered.

Hearing the sound of the adjacent room's door opening, he hurried outside, intending to intercept Zoe before she left. He squinted in the sunlight, turning to Zoe's door.

A man was just leaving her room, the door shutting behind him.

Tall really was an apt description. The man towered even over Tatum. He scratched his beard and turned to leave, pausing when he saw Tatum. His eyes flickered for a moment to Tatum's feet, still clad in only one sock. He then brushed past, nodding at Tatum politely.

Tatum checked the phone in his hand. Zoe still hadn't seen the text. He suddenly felt a stab of concern. Who *was* this man who'd just stepped out of her room?

As he approached her door, he saw it hadn't quite shut, the latch jamming slightly. He knocked on the door. "Zoe? Are you there?"

No answer, not even after he knocked again. He hesitated, then pushed the door open.

The room was empty, but Zoe's suitcase was on the floor. The bedsheets were tangled in a way that made him think of a violent struggle. He could hear water running from the bathroom.

"Zoe?" he called out, and a second later, much louder, "Zoe? Are you all right?"

The running water stopped. "Tatum?" he heard her muffled voice through the door.

He relaxed instantly; then his mind interpreted everything again. The tangled sheets, the musky smell in the room, the man who'd left . . . he stood frozen, the simple jigsaw that he should have put together a few minutes before suddenly clicking in his mind.

"Tatum, is that you?" Zoe called from the bathroom again.

"Uh, yeah. Sorry. I just wanted to know if you need a ride to the airport." He shuffled uncomfortably, feeling awkward. "Sorry, you didn't answer the phone, and I thought . . ." He didn't finish the sentence. What *had* he thought? Why hadn't he conceived of the simple explanation that Zoe was momentarily indisposed?

"I'd appreciate a ride," she said. "I'll just be a minute."

Tatum was about to leave her room when Zoe's handbag grabbed his attention. It was open, and a gray folder peeked from inside. He took it out of her handbag and opened it. It was a copy of Nicole Medina's case file with some notations marked in Zoe's handwriting inside. He flipped the pages, getting glimpses of the familiar crime scene photos.

The bathroom door opened behind him. "Okay, I'm ready," Zoe said.

He turned around. Her hair was wet, her face paler than usual. A single drop of water ran down the side of her neck, and Tatum found his attention transfixed by it.

"Oh, yeah," she said. "Can you take the case file back to the police station? I forgot to return it before leaving."

"Sure. Did you talk to Andrea this morning?"

"She's much better." Zoe crouched and picked up her suitcase. "Your grandfather stayed the night, apparently."

"What? At your apartment?"

"She said he made her feel safe." She gave him a small smile. "He's a sweet man."

"That's Marvin," Tatum muttered. "The sweetest."

She began walking, dragging the suitcase after her.

"Let me," Tatum offered.

"I'm fine." She shouldered her handbag, then glanced at his feet. "Maybe you should finish putting your shoes on."

Tatum stared dumbly at his partially clad feet. "Sure. It'll just take a moment."

Zoe brushed past him as she left the room. She smelled of the hotel's shampoo. He hurriedly went to his room, putting on the other sock and the shoes. Then he left the room to follow Zoe. He hadn't gone to the bathroom or brushed his teeth since waking up. But he didn't want to ask her to wait. He'd have to avoid breathing on people until he could drop back by his hotel room.

"I hate to leave in a hurry, but there isn't much we can do here," Zoe said as they climbed down the motel's stairs. "You can help them with the press and kick off your hotline. Remember to make sure they have the Medina funeral closely watched. It should take place in a few days."

"Right." Serial killers sometimes showed up at their victims' funerals. It was good practice to take some photos of the funeral guests.

"I'll talk to you tonight, see how it's going."

"Just take care of your sister." He took the suitcase from her and hefted it into the trunk. They both slid into the car and shut the doors.

He started the engine. "I met that reporter friend of yours yesterday."

"Harry Barry?" She looked alarmed. "You didn't tell him about Andrea?"

"I didn't tell him *anything*," Tatum answered. They drove through the streets of San Angelo, which was slowly waking up. Tatum thought of pointing out that it was his turn to choose the music but couldn't find the words. It was as if the connection between Zoe and him had snapped, leaving them a couple of strangers. And maybe they *were* strangers after all. How long had he known her? A month? Was that really enough to know anyone?

His phone rang. Keeping one hand on the wheel, he answered the call. "Gray here."

"Agent Gray." It was Detective Foster. "The killer is streaming a new video. Experiment number two. It's Maribel Howe."

"Damn."

"I'm sending you the link. Get over here."

He hung up and glanced at Zoe. "We'll have to get you an Uber."

"What happened?"

"Experiment number two." His phone blipped. He pulled over by the sidewalk and glanced at the message. It was from Foster and contained a single link. Tatum tapped the link. The browser window opened slowly. The website was similar to the first—a video uploaded by Schrodinger titled "Experiment Number Two." For a while they just stared at the black video screen while the slow cellular connection accessed the stream. Then, suddenly, the face of a girl lying in the darkness appeared, the video in the same black-and-white hues of an infrared camera. She was yelling, thumping on something above her. The phone's speaker morphed the screams, making them sound grainy and inhuman.

"That's Maribel Howe," Zoe said. "I saw her photo."

"I need to go to the station. Let me help you get your suitcase, and—"

"No." Zoe stared at the screen. "I'm coming with you."

CHAPTER 40

Maribel's voice on the phone had set Delia's life back into motion. She hadn't even noticed it had stopped until that call. Time had stood still for weeks on end while Delia waited for her daughter to return. She and Frank had stopped talking; she'd rarely left the house, hardly bothering with any semblance of a routine. Only the pain she'd inflicted on herself corresponded to the rules of time, its intensity ebbing as the minutes ticked by.

But upon hearing her daughter screaming for help, she'd realized Maribel needed her help *now*.

She and Frank had tried talking the night before for the first time in six weeks. It had been a stunted conversation, full of pauses and half-finished sentences. As if their ability to communicate had gone stale after they'd left it untouched for too long. It had been a formal conversation, full of technicalities. What were the possibilities? How could they try to help Maribel? Frank, a man of action, had suggested hiring a private detective, kicking up a social media campaign, and trying to schedule an interview on the local TV.

Delia had agreed to everything he'd said while resolving that she would go to the police station and demand that their daughter's disappearance get the attention it deserved. There was a sort of bitter irony there—Maribel had said more than once that Delia's nagging skills couldn't be matched. And now her own plan to help her daughter was essentially nagging the police to make an effort.

She drove toward the police station, the window cranked open to let her cigarette smoke out. Since the phone call, she'd chain-smoked almost two boxes. The cigarette was held between the fingers of her right hand, which she used to shift gears as well, ash scattering everywhere.

Her phone blipped in her pocket. Another reporter, probably. They'd been nagging her. She had no idea how they'd even found out about the call. Had someone in the police told them? Frank said it was good—they needed the public interest. So far they had the public eye for sure. The *San Angelo Standard-Times* had an article on Maribel on page three. The bare facts were there—the phone call, the missing girl, an image of Maribel smiling, looking pure and beautiful. The press pointed accusing fingers at the police, who hadn't reacted when the girl had first gone missing.

How long before they started wondering why Maribel had left home at eighteen? How long before the accusing fingers would shift from the police to the parents?

She inhaled the smoke as she thought grimly of what she'd say when she got to the station. She had to make them see she'd never leave before they took her seriously. It was time to get Maribel back.

CHAPTER 41

The detective division was frantic. The video of Maribel Howe played on multiple computers and phones, her shrieks emitting from everywhere, creating a chilling cacophony of distress. Tatum stood in the division's entrance, momentarily paralyzed, as Zoe brushed past him to Foster's cubicle. Tatum hurried after her, trying to ignore the guttural screams of the girl calling for her mother, begging to be let out.

Foster was on the phone shouting at someone, the video running on his computer. He hung up as they reached him.

"When did this video go live?" Zoe demanded.

He glanced at her. "Twenty-five minutes ago. People began getting the link by email soon after. He's sending it to a lot more people than before. Dispatch is swamped by phone calls."

"Did you talk to Shelton?" Tatum asked. "Is he trying to trace the source of the video?"

"Lyons is on the phone with him right now," Foster said. "We also sent three patrol cars to search the vicinity of Nicole Medina's grave site in case he decided to bury Maribel nearby. And I just managed to get us permission to get a helicopter up in the air. Maybe we'll catch sight of the bastard still shoveling dirt on top of her."

"He didn't video himself this time." Zoe frowned. "Maybe the burial site is easily recognizable, and he didn't want to give it away."

"We can probably figure out areas that could be easier to spot," Foster said. "Any familiar landmark would be a dead giveaway, right? I'll get someone on that right away." He picked up the phone.

"Foster!" Lyons shouted from her seat and launched from her chair. "He's using one of the phones from earlier!" Her voice was almost drowned completely by Maribel's screams.

"What?"

"The phones he used—"

Tatum raised his hand to stop her and then shouted at the top of his lungs, "Everyone, mute your goddamn videos. Now!"

For a second, it seemed that no one had paid attention to him. But then, one by one, the screams stopped, until the room became reasonably quiet. Tatum shut his eyes in relief, unclenching his fists.

"I just talked to Shelton." Lyons's eyes were bright. "The killer is using the same phone as last time to stream this video. We have an approximate location. It's close to Route 67, just north of the Twin Buttes Reservoir. Near the trailer park they have there." She bent over his keyboard and tapped, getting a map on his screen.

"Holy shit, we got him," Foster spat, punching digits on his phone. "Dispatch, I need patrol cars on Route 67. And we need two . . . no, three roadblocks. One by the turn to Willeke Pit Road. One by the turn to South Jameson Road, and the third on that road that leads to the Twin Buttes Reservoir, just off 67 . . . yeah, that's the one. Don't let *any* car through until I give you further instructions, got that? Not even the police chief. The entire area is sealed."

He hung up, his forehead furrowed. "How dangerous would he be when cornered?" he asked Tatum. "Should we be worried?"

"He might try to run when cornered," Tatum said. "But not if it means risking his life. It's more likely he'll try to bullshit his way out, claim he doesn't have anything to do with it, that sort of thing."

He glanced at Zoe for affirmation. She gave him a distracted nod, her attention elsewhere. "Everything we saw so far matches a killer that preys on the weak. He used a knife to intimidate Nicole Medina, which makes me think he doesn't even have a gun."

Lyons's desk phone rang, and she went over to pick it up.

"I'm going over to monitor the search," Foster said. "I'd appreciate it if one of you would accompany me."

"I'll go," Tatum said. "We can—"

Lyons slammed down the phone, her eyes wide. "Delia Howe is at the front desk."

"Delia Howe?" Zoe asked. "Does she know about the video?"

"Doesn't sound like it. I think she just wants to talk."

Tatum looked around him, at the screens showing the girl struggling in the darkness, the detectives all working frantically to find her. "She can't get in here."

CHAPTER 42

Zoe and Lyons managed to get Delia Howe to an unused meeting room without her noticing the frantic activity in the station.

They went over the details of the phone call that Delia had received from Maribel the day before. Zoe had difficulties picturing the exact situation, and she kept hoping for a random detail to shed some light on that phone call. As the interview went on, frustration grew inside her. Nothing here felt right.

Lyons wrote down everything Delia said in a notebook. Delia seemed to get agitated as they went over the same details.

"I told you that already," she suddenly snapped. "I don't know why she hung up. Maybe she heard someone coming. Maybe someone took the phone from her. What are you people going to do about it? Are you even looking for her now?"

Zoe's and Lyons's eyes met for a fragment of a second, but Delia seemed to catch the exchange, tensing up.

"Mrs. Howe, we are doing our best to find your daughter," Lyons said.

"I don't believe you! I want to talk to someone else. I want to talk to the man in charge." She massaged her wrist, and Zoe glanced at it. A new burn mark marred Delia's skin, larger than last time. But no bruises around the wrist. No one had forced Delia's hand onto the flame. As Lyons tried to calm the woman down, Zoe attempted to put the sequence of events in order again. Six weeks before, on July 29,

Maribel Howe had disappeared, presumably taken by the unsub. Then, on September 8, Maribel managed to get to a phone and call her mother. One day later, the unsub buried her alive and published the video. Had he kept her imprisoned all that time?

"I want to talk to someone else right now!" Delia Howe shrieked, banging the table.

A sliver of truth floated just beyond her reach. She had to concentrate and couldn't do it in there. "Excuse me." She got up, leaving the room, shutting the door behind her. She leaned against the hallway's wall, deep in thought.

Suppose he'd held the girl captive for more than a month. And then she'd managed to escape, calling her mother. As retribution, he'd buried her alive. It was a good explanation, but it didn't fit. Why did he keep Maribel imprisoned while Nicole Medina was buried immediately after being taken?

Maybe Maribel hadn't been kidnapped. Maybe she'd really left home, and then the killer had kidnapped her recently from wherever she'd been staying. But that seemed far fetched. Why had she disappeared so suddenly, leaving everything she owned behind her?

That phone call was strange as well. Delia Howe was adamant that she hadn't informed the press about it. Maybe her husband had, or maybe there was a leak from the police, but there was so much detail in the news articles about the call, detail that only Delia could know.

It was possible that the killer had leaked the details, but it didn't seem to fit either. If he'd buried her as retribution for trying to escape and calling her mother, he wouldn't draw attention to his own carelessness.

Lyons got out of the room and stepped over to Zoe. "What's going on?"

"Something here is wrong. Do you think Maribel was imprisoned by the killer all this time?"

"I'm almost sure of it. That's the best explanation."

"Why?"

"I don't know yet, Zoe. Maybe he used her body. Maybe he enjoyed talking to her. Maybe he liked her cooking skills. We'll ask her when we find her."

"Why didn't he keep Nicole Medina? Why change the pattern so drastically? Why keep Maribel for so long only to bury her too?"

"Maybe because he's a sadistic psychopath," Lyons suggested.

"It doesn't work like that," Zoe said slowly. "The unsub doesn't do stuff because he wants to spread misery. He's not possessed by the devil. Everything he does is propelled by need. Some of it is his sexual need. He has an elaborate sexual fantasy in his mind, and these acts, burying women alive, are the consequence of that fantasy. He also seems to want attention. The attention of the press and the police. Fame." A detail in the video had snagged her attention, but she couldn't put her finger on it. Like a shadow glimpsed by the corner of her eye, gone as soon as she turned to face it.

"We can figure that out later," Lyons said. "Right now we need to finish this interview and . . ." The word died on her lips as she turned to the door of the meeting room.

Zoe followed her eyes. The door was slightly open, and the room was empty. While they'd been talking, Delia had slid out and left.

They both took off after the running woman. Delia brushed past a pair of cops, then darted to the right, straight through the door labeled "Detective Division."

Zoe and Lyons caught up with her a second later. She stood at the division's entrance, staring at the various screens displaying her daughter's crying face. Though the videos were muted now, the impact of the picture was enough.

Delia's eyes were wide, her lips trembling. "That's . . . Maribel."

Lyons grabbed her arm gently. "Mrs. Howe, please come with me."

The woman tore her arm away, never shifting her eyes from the screens. "What's going on?"

Lyons answered, but Zoe didn't pay attention. Now, watching alongside the girl's mother, she finally realized what had bothered her about the video.

The girl had a smear of mascara on her face. But if the killer really had taken her six weeks ago, there was no good reason for her to wear any makeup. Not unless the killer had demanded it from her.

And eyeing the girl's shirt, a strapless green top, Zoe could think of one reason.

CHAPTER 43

It was the first time since Tatum had landed in Texas that the heat was getting to him. A bead of sweat ran down his forehead and into his right eye, making it sting. Foster approached, handing him a large bottle of water. Tatum took it gratefully and drank half of it in one go.

"How long do you think she has?" Foster asked, his eyes glazed.

Tatum shrugged. They'd gone through similar conversations three times in the past hour. They had no way to know, even if they knew the exact time she'd been shut in the box. As far as he could tell from the video, Maribel was actually doing the one thing that could increase her chances of survival—she now lay still, consuming less oxygen from the very limited amount around her.

Foster's phone blipped. "Oh, damn it!" he snapped. "The press have the story."

He showed Tatum the screen. It was an article titled "Police Searching for Girl Buried Alive." A frame from the video was placed directly under the headline, Maribel Howe's face paused midscream. "Soon they'll connect it to the Nicole Medina case, and we'll have a panicked population to handle."

Tatum glanced at his own phone, where the video still ran. "He didn't stop the video feed yet," he remarked. "It's almost two hours long."

"What do you think it means?"

"Hell if I know," Tatum said tiredly. "Zoe would say his fantasy is evolving."

The constant sound of faraway honking set his teeth on edge. Route 67 was a few dozen yards away, and two police blockades had split it into three sections, resulting in long stand-still traffic jams in either direction. Though they let vehicles pass, they did it slowly, writing down the license plate of each car.

He stared at the lines of traffic, the sun glinting off their windshields, then turned around to survey the entire search perimeter. It was a plateau of sand and gravel spotted with dry shrubs and bare trees. A trailer park stood by the road, its inhabitants gathering with interest to watch the police search. Beyond it, he could barely glimpse a gas station. A long railway ran parallel to the road a few yards apart. Having studied the map, Tatum knew this railway and the road didn't diverge.

Several patrol officers were combing the ground with metal detectors, though all they'd found so far were beer cans. A K-9 handler who'd introduced himself as Jones was searching by the trailer park with his dog, Buster. On the other side of the perimeter, a technician was pushing a ground-penetrating radar over the gravel. It didn't look like a complex piece of technology. In fact, it was similar to a lawn mower. The radar technician seemed to struggle with the endless rocks, shrubs, and cacti in his way. As Tatum watched, he stopped, shaking his head, and took a step away from his machine. He walked over, his shoulders slumped.

"Now what?" Foster grunted.

"The GPR can't penetrate deep here," the man said. "Too much clay in the soil."

"What kind of excuse is that?" Foster asked.

"The clay interferes with the radar's effectiveness."

"You said this baby of yours can see fifty feet deep. So what are we talking about? Only fifteen feet? Ten? Five?"

"Fifteen inches."

"Fifteen inches?" Foster sputtered.

"Too much clay," the technician repeated. "I'm sorry."

"We should get more dogs here," Foster said to Tatum. "More metal detectors too. And—"

Tatum's phone emitted strange static. Tatum glanced at it, shielding the screen against the sun. "What the hell?" he muttered. Something was happening on the video.

The walls around Maribel were vibrating, something roaring around her. Sand filtered through the cracks. Maribel screamed uncontrollably.

For a second, Tatum's gut sank, and he thought of the physicist's words. *Einstein's experiment had a barrel of explosives.*

The technician let out a curse, looking over Tatum's shoulder. The walls kept vibrating. This wasn't an explosion. This was something else entirely.

"What is that?" Foster asked. "It looks like there's an earthquake in there. *Where is she?*"

Tatum raised his eyes, looking around him. He could see nothing that made that amount of noise and vibration, but Maribel's surroundings were definitely shuddering. Could they be in the wrong place?

And then he caught sight of the railroad.

His gut sank, and he glanced at the screen. Maribel had been taken weeks ago, but her shirt, though a bit rumpled, didn't seem to look like something that had been worn for more than a few days. Something was smeared around her eyes, and now Tatum knew what it was. Makeup.

They had assumed they were looking at a live video the entire time, just like with Nicole Medina. But they weren't.

"It's a train," he said numbly. "There's a train running above her. She's buried near the tracks."

"But there's no train here."

"There was one when the video was taken." Tatum's heart throbbed. "Back when she was kidnapped. You have the wrong K-9 handler here, Detective. We need a cadaver dog."

CHAPTER 44

He leaned back in his chair, smiling, the first article about him open on the browser. Already questions about his identity were rising in the text: Who was Schrodinger? What was this "experiment"? The article maintained a hopeful tone. A police source was quoted saying they were fairly certain they knew where the girl was.

Perhaps, the article suggested, the girl in the video could supply Schrodinger's real identity.

The girl in the video would not be able to supply them with anything. Had anyone figured that out yet?

Maybe Zoe Bentley had.

He switched tabs, rereading the article that described how she'd caught the Strangling Undertaker. She was, according to the article, experienced, brilliant, and thorough.

And they'd sent her to look for him. He felt a thrill of excitement. They already knew he was someone exceptional.

He opened a few more of the local papers and refreshed their pages, waiting for a new article to show up. Soon he had more than twenty open tabs on his browser. One of the tabs began playing an annoying jingle, and for the life of him, he couldn't figure out which one it was. He ended up muting the volume.

Another article popped up in a different paper. Parts of it were obviously an unabashed copy-paste job from the first article. Shoddy work. He despised amateurs more than anything else.

What about Nicole Medina? Had anyone in the press figured out the connection yet? Nothing in the articles. Maybe one of the readers would. It was an age of crowdsourced information. He browsed the comments, almost instantly regretting it. One commenter claimed the entire thing was made up by the media to distract the general public from what was going on in the Middle East. More comments postulated this was "terrifying" or "horrible" and "the work of a monster." No one mentioned Nicole Medina. Though someone did ask if there was an "experiment number one."

He sighed. He'd have to wait patiently for an enterprising reporter to make the connection. It would happen soon—he was almost certain of it. Maybe a police source would leak it, or maybe one of the reporters would just do thorough research.

By tomorrow they'd all know there was a serial killer in San Angelo.

He went over the websites again, clicking refresh, waiting, eyes skimming the screen impatiently. Nothing. Soon he'd have to leave for work.

He'd have to be patient.

Switching to the Instagram tab, he scrolled down his feed, a column of girls presenting themselves for his attention. Every now and then he'd pause, examine a girl in the image, hesitating. Would she be the next one?

And then she caught his eye, smiling at the camera while lying on the bed, the blanket covering her body. It was Juliet Beach. One of his favorites.

Last morning being eighteen, she'd written. He switched to her Facebook profile and checked her birthday. September 10. That was tomorrow.

Would she be partying tomorrow night? Of course she would. Experiment number three.

CHAPTER 45

Officer Victor Finkelstein parked his SUV on the side of the road and opened the back door for Shelley, his four-legged partner. She leaped from the vehicle, wagging her tail, her jaw open in a wide canine grin, tongue lolling, panting hard.

He grabbed her water bowl from the vehicle, put it in front of her, and rummaged in the small cooler for the ice-cold bottle of water he'd put there earlier.

"Glad to see you here, Finkelstein," someone said behind him. The man mispronounced his name, making it sound like *Fankelstein*, which Victor was used to by now. It was a sort of well-known joke in the San Angelo Police Department. He could see the humor in his name's similarity to the fictional nineteenth-century scientist, especially considering what he did for a living. In fact, that was why he called his dog Shelley, a sort of "wink, wink, do you get it," which no one ever did.

He glanced over his shoulder. Detective Foster walked over, another man by his side. Both of them seemed sweaty, cranky, and somewhat tired.

"Hey, Detective," Victor said.

"We need you by the railroad," Foster said.

"A few minutes, Detective. Shelley needs a drink."

Foster nodded irritably, as if he were obliging an unreasonable demand. People who didn't work with dogs didn't understand how it worked. Shelley was not Victor's pet, and she wasn't his damn slave. She was his *partner*. And Victor always took care to treat her that way: as his equal. Would Foster have looked as impatient if Victor had said that he needed a drink of water? Not likely.

He found the bottle, bits of ice still floating in the water inside. He poured half the bottle into Shelley's bowl, and she lapped at it with gusto. Victor took a swig from the bottle himself, capped it, and put it back in the cooler. Then he closed the back of the van and leaned on it, folding his arms. Shelley still lapped at the water.

Foster glanced at his phone and cleared his throat. "If you don't mind—"

"In a minute, Detective," Victor said steadily. "There's no rush. Not if you called *us* here."

The detective exchanged glances with the man by his side.

"I'm Officer Finkelstein." Victor extended his hand.

"Agent Gray." The man took a step forward and shook his hand. He had a firm handshake and a nice polite smile.

"A fed, huh?"

Shelley raised her head from the bowl and glanced at Victor. She gave her tail a small wag.

"Okay, Detective, lead the way."

The two men led him through a sandy patch of land. To his surprise, Victor saw Jones there. The two handlers rarely worked together. Jones and Buster were called to help the *living*.

If Victor had a small fault, it was that he often felt his and Shelley's work wasn't as appreciated as the rest of the unit's. Take Jones, for example. The man had been interviewed by local papers half a dozen times at least. People loved those stories: "Man's best friend saves two hikers lost in a canyon" or "Cop and his dog locate missing girl." Pictures with the survivors, flowers, chocolates, Christmas cards every year. Then there were the detection dogs and their yearly moment of glory, photographed by the shipment of cocaine they'd managed to sniff out.

But no articles or pictures in the papers for Victor and Shelley. No "Man's best friend finds decomposing corpse." No handshakes with the chief of police or the mayor.

Ah, well. He knew the value of his job. How many parents had received closure thanks to Victor and Shelley? How many murderers had been taken off the streets thanks to evidence the two partners, six legs and a tail between them, had found?

Buster barked once as they got closer. Shelley wagged her tail. She wasn't much of a barker, really. Silent and peaceful, like Victor.

"So we think there's a body buried somewhere here?" Victor asked.

"Agent Gray certainly thinks so," Foster said guardedly.

"We think the girl's buried somewhere near the railroad," the agent said. "We don't know exactly how long ago."

Victor nodded. "Hear that, Shelley? Let's find her."

Shelley glanced at him, her ears perking up, one leg in the air. Then she sniffed the ground tentatively.

"Which way?" Victor asked Foster.

"Probably west." Agent Gray pointed.

Victor began to lead Shelley, letting her sniff occasionally. She stopped to pee near a cactus, then kept walking. And then, all of a sudden, she led Victor and not the other way around. Pulling hard against her leash, her body tense, nose close to the ground. She led him five yards away from the railroad, behind a small knoll, then paused, sniffing around attentively. She scratched the ground a couple of times and gave a tiny whine.

Foster and Agent Gray showed up a few seconds later.

"Something here," Victor said.

"A body?" Foster asked.

Victor shrugged. "A cadaver. Could be a dead coyote or goat. Could be the girl you're looking for."

Foster sighed heavily. "Let's start digging."

Victor realized that up to that moment, they'd been hoping he'd fail. They'd been hoping the girl might still be alive.

He crouched by Shelley and scratched her neck and behind her left ear. "Good girl. You're a good girl."

Shelley gave him her canine grin, tongue lolling. It would have been nice if someone occasionally scratched behind Victor's ear and told him he was a good cop.

CHAPTER 46

Delia sat at the station by one of the desks, staring at the screen. They'd stopped trying to make her leave after she'd nearly clawed one of the detective's eyes out. Instead they'd given her a place to sit and placed a cup of water on the desk. The video was muted, and Delia didn't try to turn on the sound. She just stared at her daughter's face.

They'd told her they were searching for Maribel but wouldn't tell her anything else. That Bentley woman spoke in hushed whispers with Detective Lyons, but neither of them had said anything to Delia.

She'd never seen her daughter so frightened in her life. Maribel had always been a ferocious kid, even when she was a tiny toddler. Part of Delia's issues with her stemmed from the fact that Maribel was never worried about the repercussions of anything she did. She never cared about punishments or anything else. For Delia, who'd spent her entire childhood terrified of her father's temper, it was incomprehensible.

But Maribel was terrified now. And it tore Delia's heart to see it.

Behind her, she heard a phone ring.

"Hey, Tatum," Zoe Bentley said. "Any news?"

Delia turned around, looking at her. Bentley's body was tense, her expression focused. Delia tried to read the woman's face. It was like trying to interpret a marble statue. Bentley listened, occasionally emitting one of those vague words that were scattered throughout a conversation. "Okay," "Yes," "I see," "Uh-huh." And then finally, "I'll tell her."

Bentley's stare met Delia's. She hung up her phone and cleared her throat.

"Mrs. Howe, I'm sorry. They just found your daughter's body."

Delia gaped at her, confused, then glanced back at the screen. Maribel still lay there in the darkness, her lips moving slightly, eyes blinking. "But . . . this video . . ."

"The video isn't from today," Bentley's voice had no softness in it. "We don't know when it was taken, but it's likely that it was soon after your daughter disappeared."

Delia turned her focus to Lyons, as if hoping the detective would talk sense into this woman, but the detective just watched Bentley, mouth slightly ajar.

"Are you sure?" Delia asked. "There was a girl in Maribel's school that looked almost like her. Maybe it's her . . . you can't stop searching just because—"

"The clothes on the body match the clothing in the video, and the shirt is the one she wore on the day she disappeared," Bentley said. "We might need you to identify her later. But it's her."

She bent across Delia, switching off the screen. Delia gasped and reached out to turn the screen back on. To her surprise, Bentley grabbed her arm, holding her firmly. She was strong, considering her delicate body.

Delia tore her wrist away and let out a dismayed sob. Bentley stepped back and folded her arms, her gaze on Delia.

"Maribel is gone," Bentley said again. "Watching this video of her suffering won't bring her back. All it can do is cause you pain, the same as burning your wrist on your gas stove."

"If she hadn't left . . . if she'd only have listened and stayed here, this wouldn't have happened," Delia mumbled, looking away.

"She didn't die because she left home or because she didn't listen. She also didn't die because of anything that *you* did."

Delia flinched, praying the woman would leave her alone, let her be.

"She died because someone killed her. A man who didn't care about you or her. Do you understand that?" Bentley knelt by her side. "If you want to see your daughter's face, I suggest you look at her pictures. Not at the video that her murderer made."

Delia ignored her, shut her eyes. Bentley talked some more. Then Lyons said something. After a while, they helped her to her feet. She didn't struggle. Someone asked her if she had someone to be with, if she needed a ride home. She muttered she was fine, that she had a car. She could get home by herself. They let her.

The gas stove in her kitchen was only a short drive away.

CHAPTER 47

San Angelo, Texas, Thursday, March 24, 1994

His favorite table in the school cafeteria was at the far corner, where he had a perfect line of sight.

He sat there on his own, as always, sketch pad in hand, scribbling fast, his attention consumed completely. The Tater Tots, milk, chicken nuggets, and green Jell-O all sat untouched on his tray, forgotten.

Debra Miller was the only person he could see.

She sat at her regular table with her friends, five forgettable girls whose names he didn't know. At the moment she was laughing, palm over her mouth, eyes sparkling, her blonde curls tumbling hypnotically on her shoulders. Her shirt was wide, letting one shoulder peek from it slightly. He was well familiar with that shirt, that shoulder, and her beautiful neck. He sat behind her in math class, mesmerized for the entire lesson by her every movement.

His pencil scraped as he drew her hair, those endless waves of curls, as he imagined running his hand through them. He didn't even have to watch her to get it right anymore. Later, at home, he would page through his sketchbook, make corrections, add some color. Debra was on his mind from the moment he woke up until the minute he fell asleep.

And often she'd appear in his dreams.

He hardly noticed the noise, the three boys who were chasing each other between the tables, laughing. One of them, a boy named Allen, swerved just by his table, colliding with him, knocking the sketch pad from his hand.

"Sorry," Allen apologized breathlessly. "I didn't see you."

He didn't answer, his eyes fixed on the sketch pad that lay by Allen's feet.

Allen crouched and picked it up, glancing at the sketch. "Oh, that's really good. You drew that?"

He cleared his throat and held out his hand for the pad. "Yes," he said, his voice barely a whisper.

"You drawing the girls?" Allen asked playfully as he paged through it with his dirty hands. "You . . ."

His voice faded as he took in the images. He flipped a page—and another and another. His happy smile twisted into a grimace; the spark in his eyes disappeared. His whole expression morphed, overflowing with disgust and horror as if looking through the sketches, he'd been exposed to something he could never unsee.

Allen tossed the sketch pad on the floor and leaned forward.

"Listen to me, you freak." Allen's voice trembled. "If I ever catch you near any of the girls in this school . . . if you even accidentally bump into one, I'll kick the living shit out of you. You got that?"

He nodded, pulse quick, his breath held.

"If I ever see you *drawing* anything else, I'll kick the living shit out of you. You got that?"

Another nod.

Allen turned away, shoulders hunched, and walked away, a slight sway in his steps.

He picked up the sketch pad, flipped through it. Fragments of his own sketches caught his gaze. Debra's beautiful eyes wide with horror as mud was stuffed into her mouth. Her naked body trapped in a cage. That beautiful bare shoulder protruding from the earth as she tried to escape the quickening sand.

CHAPTER 48

Zoe gazed through the passenger window of Lyons's car as they approached the crime scene. The location did not possess the silence and privacy of the first burial site. It was near a highway, and vehicles drove by constantly. There was a trailer park, a gas station, and a bunch of warehouses nearby providing many curious spectators. And to cap it all, the media had gotten hold of the video link, and an enterprising journalist had managed to connect it to the phone call that was allegedly from Maribel to Delia and to the murder of Nicole Medina. Zoe counted five different media vans, and a sixth one pulled up just as they parked.

The officers that had been searching for Maribel Howe all morning were now trying to keep the crowds away using yards of crime scene tape. A large tarp tent had been raised around the grave site, hiding it from the prying eyes and camera lenses, but Zoe knew that images of this scene would be plastered online that very evening. And they would be linked to the killer's website. There would be endless debate about the ominous "Experiment Number One and Two" videos, as well as theories about experiment number three. People would talk about the two Schrodingers, the scientist and the murderer.

He'd gotten what he was going for. Fame.

Harry Barry had called her three times in the past hour, and she'd ignored the calls. He was probably furious at the loss of his big scoop, but Zoe couldn't care less. Her sister was being stalked by one killer while here another killer was accelerating. Should she leave right now and go back to Dale City? Should she stay? Both options seemed equally impossible.

She stepped out of the car and into the inferno of the high noon sun. Trying to ignore it, she followed Lyons, who strode toward the throng, homing in on the officer with the clipboard. They both signed their name in the log and moved into the crime scene.

Tatum was talking with an officer with a dog on a leash. Zoe walked over, lowering her head against the sun.

Tatum turned toward her as she got closer. "How's the mother?"

Zoe shook her head. "Not good. Lyons called someone from the local Victims Assistance Unit. She still claims her daughter phoned her yesterday."

"The killer must have used parts of the video's audio to cobble up a daughter crying for her mother's help," Tatum said heavily.

"The police can call off the search in the area where Maribel supposedly called from. Since it was the killer's doing, he probably called far from his home to throw us off."

"Foster already figured that one out."

"What do we have so far? The video is still running."

"I talked to Shelton," Tatum said. "They're trying to pull the website down, but it's tricky. Host and domain were registered via a Czech provider."

"What about the phone uploading the video? It's here somewhere, right?"

"We had officers canvassing the entire area with metal detectors, but no luck. Right now they're trying to search the nearby trailer park, but some inhabitants are making problems. Foster is working on search warrants, but it's a bureaucratic nightmare."

The dog sniffed Zoe's hand tentatively. She pulled it away, annoyed.

"This is Victor, the K-9 officer who located the body," Tatum said.

"It was Shelley who located the body," Victor said. "I was just tagging along."

Zoe nodded at him curtly, then turned back to Tatum. "Do we have time of death yet?"

"The ME is still in there." Tatum gestured at the tent. "Feel free to ask him. I saw enough."

Zoe made her way to the tent and lifted the flap. She almost turned around and left as the smell hit her. It was stifling hot inside, and the stench was so thick and sharp it felt malignant.

A large rectangular hole was located in the middle of the ground, and one spotlight shone down at it. Zoe took three steps forward and saw the doctor's bald head as he crouched by the body. It was horrifically decomposed, bloated, and misshapen, patches of black and gray on the skin. One glance was enough for her, and she took a step back to hide the body from her sight.

She tried to recall the doctor's name, but all she could think of was his idiotic nickname.

"Uh . . . Doctor? Curly?" she said.

He raised his head, a face mask hiding his nose and mouth. "Agent Bentley."

"Do you have time of death yet?"

"It's really hard to say. Liquids have been expelled from the body, and there's a buildup of gas as you can see—"

"I'll take your word for it."

"The body was buried deep in very dry soil, well beyond the reach of insects, so the putrefaction is not as bad as it would otherwise be. I'll be able to give you a good estimate after I check the stage of the internal organs' decomposition. But that requires a full autopsy. For now, I can estimate that the victim died at least two weeks ago and no more than eight."

"Thanks, Doctor," she blurted and lunged for the flap of the opening. Once outside, she took a deep breath, and that turned out to be a mistake. The tent gave the sense that it contained the smell inside, but in fact, the stench's presence was still very notable, and Zoe had managed to inhale a deep lungful of it. For a moment it was touch and go, and she almost threw up, but knowing she was being watched, she stumbled a few steps, taking shallow breaths through her nose until her stomach settled.

She took out her phone and wrote Andrea a quick message. Everything all right?

She watched the three dots blinking as Andrea wrote her response. Better. Your chief dropped by today. She's nice. And Marvin is making me his famous hamburgers.

Zoe hesitated, then tapped, I missed the flight. There was another murder.

Oh god. That's terrible.

I'll get on the next one. They can manage without me.

The three dots blinked for a long time. Zoe thought that she would get a manifesto as a response, but in the end, Andrea simply wrote, You can stay another day or two.

Zoe imagined her sister writing an answer, deleting it, writing another, deleting again, struggling to decide how she really felt. She pressed her lips tightly and wrote, We'll talk about it later.

Sliding the phone into her pocket, she scrutinized the area, trying to figure out what had made the killer choose this spot. It wasn't as isolated as the first one—plenty of potential witnesses within a hundred yards. Then again, the grave itself was reasonably hidden by a small knoll and a cluster of trees. Though it was close to the highway, it was far enough from it, and there was a road that broke off the highway that he could use to get nearby with a van. It was good . . . but not good enough. She was missing something important here, and it frustrated her.

She saw Lyons talking to a police officer a few yards away, her face animated. The officer was holding an evidence bag with something metallic in it. Lyons took it from him.

Zoe hurried over. "What's up?"

"They found the phone that's streaming the video. It's not connected to anything—the video is saved on the phone. Damn thing is *still* streaming."

"Where was it?"

"It was in the trailer park, in a pile of junk."

"The trailer park is fenced, right?" Zoe asked, excitement building. "Did anyone see a stranger drive in—"

"No one drove in for anything," Lyons said. "There's an old lady whose trailer is just by the gate. She says she sees everyone coming in or out. I believe her. She listed all the actions of her neighbors from the past week in a level of detail that makes me think she keeps a log. She didn't see any stranger enter the trailer park in the past twenty-four hours. Do you think it's possible the killer lives there?"

Zoe shook her head. "The killer is careful. He'd never draw us to his doorstep. Maybe he gave it to someone to plant there."

"Or maybe he just tossed it over the fence. The pile of junk is just a few feet away from the edge of the trailer park."

"This is what he wanted all along," Zoe said.

"What do you mean?"

"He could have streamed this video from anywhere. But not only does he put it here—he uses one of the phones that he used in the previous murder. Despite the fact that he'd carefully made sure they were turned off the entire time in between. Because he knew we'd be monitoring it and would instantly show up here once the phone was turned on. He's led us here because he *wanted* us to find the body."

"Why?"

"Because that's the point of experiment number two. The test subject of his experiment wasn't Maribel Howe. It was us. He wanted to see how we'd react if we assumed the video was live, like the first one was. He's playing with us."

CHAPTER 49

Tatum watched as Foster interrogated yet another witness from the trailer park. A few of them took affront to the color of Foster's skin. One of them was drunk to the point of slurred incoherent sentences, and a woman who lived in a ramshackle trailer painted a ghastly pink agreed to answer questions only through a closed door. It was not ideal.

The general consensus was that the residents hadn't seen any stranger enter the trailer park for the past twenty-four hours, and none of them knew where the offending phone had come from. No one had seen anyone dig the pit or place a coffin-size box in it. In fact, none of them had seen anything interesting, not to mention illegal, ever, since the day they were born. Lucky lot.

Two of the residents *did* point out that there was a suspicious individual living inside the trailer park, *right among them*. This man could very well be a sinister murderer.

The residents' names were Howard and Tommy. The suspicious individuals they referred to were, respectively, Tommy and Howard. Further questioning brought up an old grudge between the two originating in a drill one of them had borrowed and never returned, resulting in an escalating barrage of offenses that no one, not even themselves, could keep track of.

Tatum groaned, thrusting his hands in his pockets. It seemed like a pointless waste of time. He considered going to see how the officers talking to the gas station attendants were doing.

"Detective Foster," a female officer called, motioning with her hand. "You'll want to hear this."

Foster approached her. "What is it, Wilson?"

Tatum moved closer to hear the conversation. The officer had been talking to a young teenager, maybe sixteen. He mostly talked to the officer's chest, but she didn't seem to mind. She had a certain intensity to her eyes that Tatum knew well. She'd latched on to something good.

"Okay, Paul, tell Detective Foster what you just told me," she said to the boy.

He turned around, clearly miffed about the fact that he now had to address a middle-aged male detective who had nothing going for him in the cleavage department. "Well, like I said, me and Jeff—he don' live here no more because he moved out with his mother because his parents got divorced, so he and his mom moved in with his grandparents down south—we were walking around a while ago, I think it was a year and a half ago, yeah, definitely a year and a half ago, because Jeff moved away last summer and it was just before then . . . I remember he was talking about how his parents were getting a divorce because they were fighting all the time, and we saw this guy."

"What guy?" Foster asked.

"A guy where you built that tent over there. He dug a pit, he had a shovel and a bunch of other tools, and he wore some kind of maintenance suit, but we knew he wasn't maintaining shit, because there are no pipes or wires or anything there, right? Jeff's dad used to be a plumber working for the city before he got fired, because he drank all the time, so he knew there was nothing there—also this guy didn't look like a plumber."

"What did he look like?"

"I don't know, man. He was white for sure, but we were too far away, and we didn't want to get any closer because we didn't want him to see us."

"Why not?"

The rhythm of the conversation was hypnotic, Foster asking pointed questions fast and short and the boy answering in long, serpentine sentences, their structure mazelike. Tatum could almost imagine this being a stage act accompanied by the strumming of a single guitar.

"Because Jeff said he was someone from the Mafia and that he dug a pit to stash drugs in or money or a body, and we didn't want him to see us—we're not idiots—we stayed away, but we were careful to see exactly what he was doing, and this guy dug there *all day*, like nonstop."

"Did you tell your parents? Tell anyone?"

Paul seemed to hesitate for a moment and stared downward at his shoes, biting his lips.

"You didn't want to," Tatum said. "Because you were hoping he'd stash money there."

"It ain't against the law to say nothin'," Paul muttered.

"So this guy digs a hole." Frustration crept into Foster's voice. "Then what?"

"Then he left. So we waited until it was dark, and we went there, because we figured maybe he stashed some money there, so we could take some of it—not too much, y'know. Jeff really wanted cash because his dad was unemployed, so he figured he could maybe help out a bit, and I wanted cash because . . ." He paused. His own motives probably hadn't been as pure as Jeff's.

"Because cash is a good thing to have," Tatum said. "Go on."

"So we go there, and at first we couldn't find the hole, which was weird, man, because why dig a hole if you just fill it up, right? But after a while we hear this strange noise, and we notice that the ground is wobbling. It turns out this guy covered his hole with a few wooden planks, and then he hid them under the sand, so this hole was invisible if you didn't know where to look. We removed the planks, but we found nothing there, no cash, no drugs. So I said, or maybe it was Jeff—no, it was definitely me—I said, 'Maybe this guy dug the hole, and he intends to use it later, y'know?' Like a good hiding spot. So we were thinking we'd keep an eye on this hole, maybe see that guy again, and once he puts his stash there, we'll check it out, and if it's cash, we could maybe take some, and if it's drugs, we could, uuuuh . . . tell the police."

Tatum rolled his eyes. *Or steal it and sell it.*

"But this guy never came back, and I checked this damn hole every night for like . . . a whole year. He never put anything there, so I figured he forgot where he put the hole, and Jeff already moved away, and I got kinda tired of going every night to check it and also one time a scorpion almost stung me—it ain't fun to wander here at night, y'know?"

"And you never saw that guy again?" Foster asked.

"Nah, never. I mean, maybe, because I never got a good look at him, so I coulda seen him in the street or in the park or behind me at the movies, and I wouldn't know. But I never seen the guy come back to his hole. No one ever came to that hole. Until you lot showed up."

"And did you happen to see anything about him? Anything at all?"

"He drove a white van. Didn't get no license plate or anything, but it was white and looked kinda crap."

Tatum and Foster exchanged looks. Finally, something.

"Do you know how I can get in touch with Jeff?" Foster asked.

"No, man. He moved somewhere near San Antonio, I think."

"We'll find him. And can you tell us anything else about the van? What brand? Anything that stood out about it?"

"It was white," Paul said apologetically. "I was mostly paying attention to the hole."

"Thanks, Paul. You've been very helpful," Foster said.

The boy nodded and milled around, maybe hoping to talk to Officer Wilson again. But after a while he must have realized it wasn't in his immediate future and shuffled away.

"Could the killer have been planning this thing for a year and a half?" Foster asked Tatum in a low voice.

Tatum glanced sideways, seeing Zoe approach them.

"What's up?" she asked.

"We have a witness who saw our man dig the hole," Tatum said, "a year and a half ago."

She paused, stunned. "A year and a half?"

"He's clearly been planning this for much longer than you thought," Foster said. "You were wrong."

Tatum expected Zoe to snap back. *You were wrong* were not her favorite words to hear, and certainly not in that order. But instead she just gazed ahead. He knew that look. An idea was taking shape in her mind.

CHAPTER 50

Zoe paced back and forth in the station's meeting room, her mind churning. Tatum sat by the table, chewing a pizza slice. They'd bought a whole pizza on the way, a replacement for both lunch and dinner.

"Sit down," he said. "Eat. We don't brainstorm on an empty stomach."

She sat down, forgot why she was sitting, and stood up. Sat down again. Grabbed a pizza slice. It was topped with grilled ham and pineapple. The pineapple debate was a sore spot between Zoe and her sister, but she was happy to discover that Tatum was not as averse to the idea as Andrea. They'd ordered half with pineapple and ham and half with pepperoni and hot peppers. She took a bite, making sure it contained both ham and pineapple, and shut her eyes.

The ham was grilled to perfection, its edges crispy, and the contrast with the pineapple sweetness, the thick layer of mozzarella, and the garlicky pizza sauce managed, for one blessed second, to drive everything else from her mind. She was in pizza nirvana. She was one with the pizza. She chewed carefully and swallowed. When she opened her eyes, Tatum was looking at her, a small smile tugging at the side of his mouth.

"What?" she said, feeling defensive.

"It's nice to see you enjoy something for once. It doesn't happen much."

She cleared her throat. "It used to be more frequent before . . ." *Before Glover reentered my life.* "Before things became so hectic."

"Right."

She sighed and checked her phone. She'd talked to Andrea half an hour ago, and her sister had sounded fine. Marvin kept her company; the police watched outside; she felt safe. Still, Zoe wanted to be there. Wanted to hug Andrea, to tell her nothing would happen to her, that her big sister was there for her.

"Let's talk about Schrodinger's Killer," Tatum said.

Zoe rolled her eyes. The press had nicknamed the killer, and it threatened to stick. Zoe hated this particular nickname because the killer had chosen it for himself. He'd baptized himself Schrodinger, knowing it would end up being his nickname.

"Our initial theory seems to be wrong," Tatum said. "We assumed he began planning these murders a few months ago, after succumbing to his fantasy for the first time. But it now looks like he's been planning this for years, preparing the graves, planning his websites, stalking potential victims—"

"No," Zoe interrupted. "I stand by my initial assessment. He began planning this whole thing with Schrodinger and the weird experiments a few months ago. After he killed for the first time."

"He was seen digging the pit over a year ago."

"This guy's sexual fantasy revolves around burying women alive. But he didn't, for years. Instead, he fantasized. And part of his fantasy was digging those pits. He probably dug them imagining he *could* use them. I'm betting that he'd sometimes masturbate near these pits. He'd leave them covered, knowing he could, potentially, one day use them. That thought must've excited him."

"So you're saying when he dug that pit a year and a half ago, he never planned to really use it."

"I'm saying he toyed with the idea, but it was a fantasy. Then, a year later, he snapped. Decides to bury his first victim, and he already has pits ready all over the place. All he has to do is choose one."

Tatum took a slice of pepperoni pizza. "So why does that help us?"

Zoe eyed the pizza box. She still hadn't finished her slice, but Tatum seemed intent on eating just the pepperoni slices, and there was only one of those left. She took a huge bite from her slice, knowing that time was of the essence. "At first," she said, her mouth full, "we thought he'd dig a pit, kidnap a victim, then bury her in the pit, right? But that's not the case. He already has pits. Dozens of them, probably. All we have to do is find them."

Tatum paused, the slice halfway to his mouth. "And we wait for him there. A stakeout."

"That's right."

"These damn pits could be anywhere."

"Not anywhere." She stood up, approaching the map on the wall. She marked a small red *X* in the spot where they'd found Maribel Howe. "This is where Maribel was buried. And *this*"—she pointed at another *X* that was already there before—"is where Nicole was buried. Both are about four to five miles from San Angelo. Our guy gets an urge, he drives a few miles out of the city, digs a pit. So these pits are several miles out of the city, near roads, but hidden enough so he doesn't get interrupted."

"That's still a shitload of ground to cover."

"Maybe there's a way to locate these holes efficiently. We need to talk to an expert. Some . . . dirt expert."

"You mean a geologist?" Tatum smirked.

"Whatever." Zoe finished her slice and snatched the last pepperoni slice before Tatum could get to it. The smirk disappeared from his face.

"Okay." Tatum grabbed one of the pineapple slices. "Along with the hotline that Foster started this morning, that's two proactive steps we're taking. I like it."

"We know something else about the killer," Zoe said, her tongue starting to prickle from the hot peppers. "He stalks the victims. That's almost a certainty. Both Nicole and Maribel were taken when they returned late at night to their homes. The killer *waited* for them there. He was probably staking out their homes for days, waiting for an opportunity."

"So he'd be someone who wouldn't be easily noticed. Dressed as a maintenance man, like that kid in the park said."

"That sounds like the most reasonable conclusion," Zoe agreed.

"We can tell Foster. Have the police patrols check out maintenance people working alone, make sure they're actually working, and take their names. Check the type of van they use. Look into the ones that fit our profile."

"Good idea. Number four." Zoe raised four fingers. She huffed heavily through her mouth, trying to get more airflow to soothe the burning. "I want to establish a dialogue with the murderer."

"Like a public letter in the newspaper? They tried it with the Son of Sam—it didn't work."

"The Son of Sam was *already* talking to them, writing his weird poetic letters. And he wasn't stupid enough to answer directly. He just enjoyed the attention. If we publish a public letter for this killer—"

"You can call him Schrodinger's Killer. I won't judge."

"We'll get a similar result. He'd never answer us. He communicates very little as it is."

"He isn't communicating with us at all."

"He named himself Schrodinger. He's telling us his murders are experiments. *And* he sends us videos. These are all forms of communication, but he's given them a lot of thought, made sure to keep them to a minimum. He's careful. We need to establish a mode of communication that would catch him off his guard. That would make him answer impulsively."

Tatum frowned. "What do you have in mind?"

"I want to get an unflattering article published."

"Online media is already calling him a maniac and a monster."

"He's been expecting that. That wouldn't enrage him." Zoe shook her head. "I want to make him sound like a bungling idiot. Maybe we can get him to comment on the article."

"That sounds . . . volatile. How do you know he won't react by killing another victim? Showing us how capable he is?"

"He is planning to kill another woman soon—he pretty much told us that with his experiments," Zoe said with certainty. "And his murders are well planned and calculated. I believe when we finally find him, we'll see he has a list of potential victims. Maybe even dates. He won't change his plan because of us. But with a bit of luck, we can get a gut reaction from him."

"You're thinking of using that guy Harry Barry, right?"

Zoe nodded, taking a swig from her Coke can. Coke was by far the most useless liquid when it came to negating spicy foods.

Tatum leaned back in his seat. "You don't sound like you're flying home tomorrow morning."

Zoe bit her lip. She still hadn't decided, but Tatum was right. She was thinking and talking about it as if she intended to stay, at least for a day or two more. She felt a stab of guilt. Shouldn't she be with her sister right now?

"Nothing changed yesterday when Glover showed up," she said. "For the past month I've been feeling as if I was sitting with a wasp in the room. I couldn't see it, but it was there."

Tatum looked at her, saying nothing.

"Glover is the wasp," she clarified.

"I got that."

"Now I *know* where he is. And everyone else does too. I've been trying to get Mancuso and Caldwell to take this threat seriously. Now they know I was right. They're watching out for Andrea. And Glover wouldn't attack now. Not when he knows we're watching. He'll wait. He's always been careful and patient."

Tatum nodded in agreement.

"I'm going back as soon as possible," she continued. "But not yet. The San Angelo police isn't equipped to deal with this killer. I'll stay for a day or two more, make sure the investigation is progressing in the right direction, and then I'll fly to be with my sister."

"All right, then. There's just one thing you didn't think of."

Zoe tensed. "What?"

"Andrea's with Marvin. That's the real risk. By the time you get back, he's going to drive her insane."

CHAPTER 51

As soon as Juliet Beach dropped by her parents' home, she saw they were having one of their nuclear, take-no-prisoner arguments. Her brother, Tommy, hid in his room, literally under the blankets. She shut the door to his room behind her, muting her mother's hysterical monologue.

"Oh," she said. "I thought Tommy was here, but I guess he went somewhere."

The blob under the blankets shifted.

"That's too bad." Juliet sighed. "I really wanted to go for some ice cream."

A sharp intake of breath expelled from the blob. In the background, Mom called Dad a useless bastard. Her parents' fights were the main reason Juliet left home. Though weirdly enough, when they weren't fighting, they clearly adored each other.

"Maybe I'll rest a little before I leave," Juliet said.

A slight giggle from the blob.

She lay down on the bed, squashing the blob with her back. "Oh, what *is* that?" she groaned. "This bed is so uncomfortable!" She shifted, poking the blob, getting another giggle.

Beyond the door, Dad's muffled voice called her mom a leech. Lovely. She needed to get out of there, but no way was she leaving Tommy behind.

"I think maybe this bed needs tickling," she announced, and her fingers went for the blob's soft spots. After three seconds, Tommy let out a shriek of laughter, his head poking from the bedsheets, a mass of blond curls, his eyes crinkling with amusement.

"I was here all the time. I was hiding!" he said, brimming with joy for outsmarting his sister.

"You *were*?" Juliet said, shocked. "I didn't even see you."

He was smiling at her, his button nose teasing her to kiss it. She grabbed him in a big hug. "Wanna go for some ice cream?" she asked.

"Can I get *three* flavors this time?"

"I'll have to ask the ice cream man if it's allowed."

"Okay." He bounded from bed, already putting on his shoes. "Can I take Ted with me?"

Ted was his Darth Vader doll. Juliet used to call it his "Teddy Vader," and Tommy, assuming Teddy was the doll's first name, had shortened it to Ted.

"Sure, but he isn't getting ice cream."

"Okay."

Beyond the door, Mom shrieked something unintelligible. Tommy paused, stiffening.

"They'll stop fighting by the time we get back," Juliet said.

"How do you know?"

Nineteen years of experience, that was how she knew. These fights were fast and furious, always ending with Mom crying and Dad apologizing. "I just do."

"Promise?"

"I promise. Now get Ted—I want my ice cream."

He snatched Ted from the bed and was about to open the door.

"Wait." Juliet took out her phone and knelt by his side. "Say ice cream." She raised the phone so that the camera caught them both.

"Ice creeeeeam."

CHAPTER 52

Harry sat by the bar, drinking his second Miller and feeling very much like he'd been played.

He'd become too sentimental: that was the problem. He'd developed a soft spot for Zoe Bentley, thinking she'd never break her word. He should have known better. Words were just that, words, and they were fragile things, bound to be broken. After all, he'd broken his own promises more times than he could count.

And now every damn reporter in the country had the scoop. A serial killer in San Angelo. Tomorrow they'd all write about the FBI presence in the case, and Harry would have absolutely nothing.

Zoe had messaged him half an hour ago, asking him to meet. He'd named this place, hoping he could get her drunk enough to let slip a tasty morsel. But now she was late, and he suspected he was being stood up.

Oh, sure, he had already written his own article naming both Zoe Bentley and Agent Tatum Gray, referencing the Strangling Undertaker case, as well as Zoe's encounter with a serial killer at a young age. But he knew it wasn't enough. It didn't have that extra spice that made an article viral.

He scanned the bar. Though it was Friday night, it seemed empty. News about the serial killer was spreading fast. People were scared.

A woman slid onto the empty barstool next to him. Zoe. She raised her hand to draw the barman's attention. "A pint of Guinness, please."

The barman smiled at her. "That's a serious drink for a woman."

"Is it?" Zoe held the barman's gaze for a long second.

The barman's smile faded, replaced with a perplexed, somewhat intimidated expression. He cleared his throat. "Sure, coming right up."

Harry emptied his own glass. "And I'll have another Miller."

They sat in silence as the barman poured their drinks. Finally, Harry said, "You screwed me."

"No, I didn't. Settle down."

"You told me you'd have something for me. Now everyone has it."

"All they have is a stupid nickname and a bunch of conjectures."

"They'll have more tomorrow. Reporters in this town have their sources in the police. You know what I have? Nothing."

The barman placed the drinks in front of them, avoiding Zoe's gaze. Harry almost found it amusing.

Zoe took a deep swig from her glass, shutting her eyes, breathing through her nose. "God, I needed that," she muttered. "It's been a very long day."

"You want me to feel sorry for you?"

"I want you to stop bitching, for a start," Zoe said sharply. "You act like I'm your girlfriend. Let me remind you that *you're* the reporter that's actively badgering me."

Harry grinned at her, cheered up by her annoyed tone of voice. "I'm not *badgering* you. I'm . . . tailing you from a respectable distance."

"You booked a room in my motel!"

"It's a good motel. It has a nice swimming pool."

"Oh, give me a break!" She gave him a furious gaze.

He raised his glass in a mock toast. "Now who's bitching?"

She blinked, then took another sip of her beer. "Listen, I want to give you an interview, but you have to publish it tomorrow morning."

"I already wrote my story for tomorrow. My editor is working on it right now."

"Tell him to trash it. We need a new one."

"We?"

"I'm willing to give you an interview every day. An update on the case. I'll talk to no other reporter."

Harry peered at her skeptically. "Why?"

"I want to catch the killer off balance."

"Are you talking about Schrodinger's Killer?"

"That's a dumb nickname."

"It's what everyone's calling him," Harry pointed out, starting to feel excited. "So . . . what exactly do you want to do here?"

She looked at him thoughtfully. "Who in the BAU is your source?"

Harry leaned back, confused. "What source?"

"Someone told you I flew here on a case. Who was it?"

Harry grinned. "Forget it. That's off the table. You should know that. A reporter who gives away his sources is useless."

"We'll find him."

"I'm sure you will. You're so very clever. Now . . . we were talking about my daily interview."

Zoe took a swig from her beer, licking the foam off her top lip. "I want to make this killer sound incompetent. To prod him, make him lash out. Maybe he'll comment on the article. Do you have data on the people commenting on your articles? IP addresses, that sort of thing?"

Harry knew exactly how thorough their data was because he'd tracked down people who'd commented on his articles more than once. It was important to have a well-documented shit list. "Sure. We can get quite a lot from a comment."

"Great." Now it was Zoe's turn to get excited. Her eyes sparkled in a way Harry found quite fetching. "If he comments, we might be able to track him down."

"What makes you think he'll react to the article?"

"He takes himself very seriously. So you'll interview me, and I'll slip in some details about how he keeps making mistakes. That we'll catch him in no time. That sort of thing."

Harry rolled his eyes. "And that'll infuriate him and make him react?"

"He won't like how I'm belittling him."

"Don't take this the wrong way," Harry said. "But when it comes to hurting people's feelings, you're like a six-year-old girl yelling at a boy who pulled her pigtails that he stinks."

Zoe furrowed her brow in annoyance. "I'm good at what I do."

"You're good at getting into serial killers' minds and understanding the way they tick, no doubt there." Harry grinned. "But if you need to annoy people? I suggest that you let me take the wheel for a bit."

"I suppose I can't argue with that."

"What you want to do is compare him to others. People are competitive, men in particular."

"Serial killers often relate to other serial killers when talking about their own actions," Zoe said. "BTK used to compare himself to the Son of Sam and the Green River Killer."

"See? You tell everyone that he sucks, and he won't bat an eyelash. But tell people that compared to Manson, he's a clown, and this guy will blow a gasket."

"That's . . . that's a good idea. So when we talk about it, we'll compare him to some other serial killers. And he'll come up short. That'll get him riled up."

"But that's deep in the text, right? We need a headline. A headline sets the tone for the article. The headline can't be 'San Angelo Killer Isn't as Good as Ted Bundy.'"

"Well . . . no. But I don't think we can really get him annoyed just with a headline."

"Can't we?" Harry raised his eyebrow. "He named himself, right? Calls himself Schrodinger?"

"Yeah. And the press call him Schrodinger's Killer."

Harry folded his arms, smirking. "The *Chicago Daily Gazette* might have a different name for him."

CHAPTER 53

San Angelo, Texas, Saturday, September 10, 2016

"The Digging Killer Strikes Twice in San Angelo."

He glared at the article in disbelief, his fist spasming. He skimmed the article, feeling his heart pounding. It was one of the most detailed articles he'd found that morning, and while it linked him to both victims and even provided good images from the video clips, there were certain sentences that seared themselves into his retina.

"Profiler Dr. Zoe Bentley stated that the Digging Killer is inefficient . . ."

"Though he dubbed himself Schrodinger, he seemed to have misspelled the name, omitting the umlaut that the original Schrödinger had in his name . . ."

"When asked if this 'Digging Killer' is the next Ted Bundy, Dr. Bentley answered, 'Not by a long shot.'"

It was worse. This was the only reporter Zoe Bentley had agreed to talk to. As a result, various *other* articles had quoted this article, and he constantly saw phrases like, "The Digging Killer, a.k.a. Schrodinger's Killer." The new nickname seemed to stick. It was mind boggling.

His eyes watered. He bit the side of his mouth, the taste of blood on his tongue. Before he knew what he was doing, he was already typing furiously, the comment box below the article filling up, a scroll bar appearing as he kept on going, correcting inaccuracies, explaining that Schrodinger was a completely legitimate way to spell the name, warning that by the time he was done, Ted Bundy's body count would seem meager . . .

He paused and pushed his chair away from the computer. Scrutinizing the comment box and the wall of text within, he shook his head. What the hell was wrong with him?

Taking a long breath, he browsed back to Juliet Beach's Instagram page. He scrolled through the images he knew so well, scrutinized the new picture Juliet had taken with her brother. He then read a few of the birthday greetings that showed up in the comments. Imagined his upcoming evening, feeling the excitement building up in his chest. Slowly, his frustration and anger dissipated.

Glancing at the time, he decided he had just long enough to write a short email to the article's reporter. The man's name was H. Barry. The article wasn't badly written. The man had done his research, gotten all the facts right, and managed to snag a good interview. It was a man who was proud of his work.

He could relate to that.

Locating H. Barry's email, he wrote his reply to the article. He kept reminding himself to be short and concise. It was important to get this right. It was possible, and even likely, that the reporter would publish this email. He had to sound like the man he was.

Ted Bundy?

By the time he was finished, people wouldn't even remember who that was.

CHAPTER 54

Zoe was relieved to find out there were no morning meetings on Saturday. In fact, the lieutenant hadn't shown up yet, and they could all work efficiently without needing to explain their every action to the annoying man.

Foster told her the hotline had begun receiving an endless onslaught of tips ever since the public had found out about the serial killer. Lyons and he were sifting through the call logs, determining what was relevant. Foster also had a long list of people he needed to interview—Maribel Howe's friends and relatives. He promised to find a geologist who would talk to them as soon as possible.

Though the man was one of the most energetic detectives Zoe had ever met, Foster was clearly running on fumes. His eyes were bloodshot, his shirt rumpled. She wondered if he remembered to eat and sleep.

Zoe opened Harry's article on her laptop again. There were about twenty comments, and she read through them quickly. None of them seemed to be relevant.

It was time to get to work. She shut the room's door and browsed her music library, finally deciding on Katy Perry's *One of the Boys* as her soundtrack. She needed a quick pick-me-up. No slow instrumental bit to get the album started. Katy understood that sometimes, you just needed to get going.

She'd printed out the whole crime scene report and spread the pages on the desk, her head bobbing with the beat, humming quietly to herself with the chorus.

"Too-doo-doo no-fingerprints no-DNA outside-the-box.

"Too-do-do-do-do-do infrared-camera in-the-box, same-setup as-the-first-time.

"Too-doo-doo box-dimensions identical-to-first-box.

"Too-do-do-do-do-do phone-used is-clean-of-fingerprints, screen-cracked probably-from being-thrown."

She sorted through the images while Katy kissed a girl and liked it.

Holding the panoramic view of the crime scene between thumb and forefinger, she frowned. "Why did you dig here?" she muttered. "What's so exciting about this place?"

She glanced at the images of the first crime scene. It seemed similar. A lot of rocks, dry plants, uneven ground.

The door to the meeting room opened. Foster stood in the doorway, frowning as he listened to the music. She glared at him, daring him to say anything about it.

"The geologist told us to drop by his home," he said. "We'll be going in about half an hour if you want to join us."

"Cool. Thanks."

He began closing the door.

"Foster," she called. "Hang on."

"Yeah?"

"Take a look at this." She held up the images. "What do you see?"

He entered the room and took a look. "The crime scene."

She rolled her eyes. "Imagine driving by this area. Not knowing it's a crime scene. What would you think?"

He shrugged. "Nothing. It looks like everywhere around here. Dry. Hot."

"But it's not exactly the same." She opened Google Maps. "Look here."

She clicked on a point in the map. The image of the area appeared on-screen. A completely flat, sand-covered landscape. Hardly any plants, no rocks to speak of.

"Okay," he said. "I don't follow your point. This isn't the crime scene."

"When you see those places, when you drive around San Angelo, what do you think?"

"I don't know. I don't pay attention. I grew up around here."

"But the killer *does* pay attention. Do you know what he thinks when he looks around?"

"No."

"He thinks, 'This looks like a good place to bury my next victim.' Or he might think, 'This doesn't do it for me at all. This place is a turnoff.' For him, choosing a place to dig is *exciting*. This is his porn."

Foster seemed distinctly uncomfortable. Zoe was used to that reaction.

"Why is this"—she gestured at the rocky terrain with the plants—"a better turn-on than this?" She pointed at the sandy terrain. "Doesn't the sandy field look more fun to dig in?"

"I don't know, Bentley." He sighed. "Did you see that we have a definite time of death?"

"Really?" Zoe's interest was piqued.

"Yup. Curly estimates it to be between the thirtieth and the thirty-first of July."

"That's remarkably accurate."

"Apparently there's an advantage to our killer burying the victims alive. He buries them deep, no insect activity, no exposure to heat. So Curly can nail the time of death quite precisely, just by checking the putrefaction of the internal organs. He really outdid himself this time."

"So she died within a day or two of disappearing. It matches the same pattern as Medina. He doesn't waste any time. Takes the girl and buries her alive almost immediately afterward."

Foster nodded. "What else?"

"We know he had this fantasy of burying women for a long time. He is obsessed with his own fame. He killed at least three victims—"

"*Three?*" Foster stared at her. "We know of two victims. He even numbered them experiments one and two."

"No. I told you—this whole thing with the infrared camera and posting the videos online? That's something he planned *after* killing his first victim. The original fantasy was just burying the victim alive. For a long time it was just a fantasy. He probably never thought he'd go through with it. He dug some pits as a sort of make-believe. Maybe he buried some animals alive. Then came the stressors causing him to snap. He killed his first victim, fulfilling his urge. Only *then* did he figure out he could film the victim inside the box. See how they struggle and die."

"How do you know?"

"Because this is what I do. This is what all these people are like. The original fantasy is never so elaborate. It *definitely* doesn't cater to external factors, like fame. There's another victim, Foster. Call her victim zero if you need to. She wasn't filmed. And if we find her, we might even get fingerprints or DNA. He was probably less careful with the first one."

Foster eyed her skeptically. "You talk like you already know everything about this guy."

"Not everything. I still don't know why he chooses these locations."

CHAPTER 55

The home office of Dr. Andrei Yermilov was barren and devoid of character, the desk clean and neat, the walls decorated with maps or diagrams of soil layers. Zoe sat on a chair taken from the kitchen, to the left of Foster and Tatum. While Foster explained what they were looking for, Andrei kept looking around him sadly, as if he constantly wondered how he'd ended up there.

"So," he said, his accent heavy, "you search for hidden holes."

"Most likely covered with planks and sand," Foster repeated.

Andrei sighed and looked around him again. He eyed one of the posters with particular dismay.

"Why don't you use"—he waved his hands vaguely—"radar?"

"The radar didn't work when we tried it," Foster said. "The technician said there was too much clay in the ground."

"Too much clay?" Andrei seemed perplexed. "There is no clay in the hole. There is only a hole."

A second went by as they all considered this philosophical statement.

"So you're saying," Tatum said, "that if we're looking for actual holes, the radar will work just fine."

"Of course!"

"Last time we were searching for a box that was buried deep in the soil," Tatum told Zoe. "So presumably, there was a lot of clay in the soil. But if the hole is just covered with a few inches of sand—"

"I got it, thanks," she said, annoyed. "No need to mansplain."

"It'll be slow going, though," Foster said. "I mean, that guy pushing the radar took forever."

"Man pushing?" Andrei's eyes widened. "Why don't you use a car?"

"Uh . . . what do you mean?"

"You hook the radar to a car. Drive." He moved his hands, pantomiming driving. "The radar finds holes. It's easy. We do it every day."

"Can you show us exactly how?" Tatum asked.

Andrei sighed again and tapped at his keyboard, spitting short impatient sentences as he explained. Zoe half listened, already trying to think of the best way to approach this task. They'd have to focus on the areas that the killer had most likely dug in. It would have to be outside the city, and not too far. But just searching in a certain perimeter around San Angelo could take weeks. They had to find a way to narrow it down.

Her attention was snagged back to Andrei, who seemed to have stopped talking about the radar and now explained something in general.

"Very hard, tools break every day. It's frustrating. Research is stalling. The funding is almost gone." He glared at one of the topographical maps and groaned. "I have a birthday next week."

"Happy birthday," Tatum said helpfully.

"It is not happy."

"Right." Foster shifted his chair closer to the door, as if he intended to make a break for it. "I'm sorry your research about the Angelo bedrock layer is difficult—"

"Difficult? Pah! It is disastrous. Sample taking is terrible. Three drills broken last week."

"Why?" Zoe asked.

Foster tried to catch her eye, emphatically motioning for her to shut up, but Zoe ignored him.

"You said you're researching the Angelo stone? Is it called that because of San Angelo?"

"Of course. Do you see any other Angelo here?"

"And the ground is . . . what? Hard?"

"Hard? It is like steel! I need expensive drilling technology—I can't use cheap drills. This is no Minecraft."

"What's Minecraft?" Zoe asked.

Everyone stared at her in astonishment.

"Even *I* know what Minecraft is," Tatum said. "And I don't have kids."

"What's Minecraft?" Zoe asked again, annoyed by her own ignorance.

"It is stupid video game!" Andrei roared. "Terrible! My son plays all day long; he thinks there is ten kind of stones in the world. Ten! I tell him, no, it is much more complicated, but he tells me there is sand and rock and gravel and coal. To dig, he punches floor!"

"He actually needs to use a pickax," Foster said. "There are all sorts of pickaxes and—"

"It is impossible to dig so fast with pickax!" Andrei was apoplectic with rage. "He digs until he reaches lava. Absurd! And now he wants my help to get to Nether. Says I know about digging. He says I don't respect his hobby. Minecraft is no hobby! Stamp collecting is a hobby. Piano playing is a hobby. We argued yesterday all evening." He switched to Russian, carrying on his tirade, while specks of spittle shot from his mouth.

This is all your fault, Tatum mouthed at Zoe.

Once Andrei paused for air, Zoe quickly interjected. "So the ground around here is hard to dig in. Right?"

"The Angelo series is."

"But our guy digs holes," Zoe said.

"Not in Angelo soil." Andrei let out a small desperate laugh. "Trust me."

"But he did."

"Where? Show me on map." He gestured at the topographical map on the wall.

Zoe got up and pointed to the locations of the crime scenes. "Here. And here."

"It is not Angelo soil there. It is Tulia soil. Much better for digging. Look." He turned to the computer and opened a browser. A diagram of several layers in different colors filled the screen. "This is Tulia. Five layers, yes? Some hard, but not terrible. A lot of clay. Unpleasant, but you can dig. Now." He opened a different window. "*This* is the Angelo series. You dig twelve inches, you reach this layer." He stabbed his finger at the screen with vehemence. "The bane of my life. *Suka blyat!* Thick and hard. The tools break all time."

"That's why he chooses his locations the way he does," Zoe muttered excitedly. "He digs where he can!"

Andrei let out another short angry laugh. "If only I was so lucky."

"This Angelo series . . . where is it?"

"Everywhere. Almost everything on that side of map." He motioned to the area east of San Angelo.

"And the rest? It's Tulia?"

"A lot of things. Some hard, some not."

"But these two are Tulia, right?" She pointed at the two crime scene locations.

"Yes. Definitely Tulia."

"Can you tell us which areas are Tulia as well? And maybe other soil types that are easier to dig in?" Tatum asked.

"It will take hours. No."

"Dr. Yermilov," Foster said, "it will help save innocent lives."

Andrei sighed. "Fine. Research is crap anyway. I go get coffee. This will be very long and . . . what's American word? Boring."

It was. The doctor painstakingly went over each area in the map, explaining about the various layers, the tools that would be needed, while Foster compounded a list. Zoe listened, trying to take it all in. Though this was mind numbing, she was sure the killer obsessed about these details. For him, researching the best areas to dig in was foreplay.

Her phone blipped, and she glanced at it. It was an email from Harry. She skimmed it, her heart pounding hard.

> You were right. The Digging Killer wasn't partial to our unflattering article. But he didn't comment on the site. He sent me an email, forwarded below. H.
>
> Dear H. Barry.
>
> I still remember my parents talking about Henry Lee Lucas's confessions. Everyone back then had a friend or a family member in the jury. We had a guest in town, our very own serial killer. But he was just passing through. This time, it's the real thing.
>
> Back then, he claimed he killed thousands of people, and the reporters lapped it up, giving up their professionalism for a bit of sensation. Unlike Lucas, I will give no false claims. But I won't accept inaccuracies.
>
> 1. Nothing was inefficient in my methods. You were misinformed. Every step I took was necessary and unavoidable.
>
> 2. I do not enjoy the suffering of my subjects. I do what I must. There's a reason to all of this.
>
> 3. Any comparison of my work to anyone else's is absurd. If you had one page from Einstein's *Annus Mirabilis,* you couldn't compare it to another

scientist's work, could you? Wait until you have the full story.

And one more thing. "The Digging Killer"? I think you can do better than that.

Schrodinger

With a few sentences, the killer had managed to shed endless light on his psyche. Despite his attempt at being cordial and warm, anger seethed underneath. They'd managed to rattle him. Now they had a line of communication.

CHAPTER 56

Baltimore, Maryland, Friday, September 15, 1999

"When she dropped his wedding ring, I thought I was going to scream," Elise said as he walked her back to her dorm room.

That would have been her fourth scream during the movie. He'd counted. Her screams made him think of his mother encountering a large cockroach. They grated on his nerves. Perhaps *The Sixth Sense* hadn't been the best choice for a date movie.

Then again, after each scream, she'd buried her face in his chest, refusing to watch as the little boy faced the dead people trying to talk to him. She'd shivered in his arms. It had made him feel good. Made him feel like a man.

It was the second date, and unlike the first date, which had been a series of awkward silences glued together by small talk, it was going more or less well. He'd followed his roommate's suggestion and taken her to a movie, because the movie did the talking for you. And he'd been right: it was as if the movie provided the meat for the conversation. Before the movie had started, it was logistics: *Which movie should we go to; do you want popcorn; do you want to sit in the front or the back*. And after it ended, they could talk about the movie and its oh-so-surprising twist. Which he had seen coming a mile away. For the past week, all people had talked about was "the amazing surprising twist," pretty much guaranteeing the twist would be neither amazing nor surprising.

"What was your favorite part?" Elise asked him.

He took a moment, not because he didn't know which part was his absolute favorite but because he had to find an alternative. "The part in the end," he said dutifully. "The twist."

The best part had been when they'd locked the kid in the small dark room. It had set his heart racing. But she might not understand.

They reached her dorm, and she invited him inside for a little drink. He was tense when he followed her to her room. Unlike him, she had the entire room for herself. Her dorm was an apartment of five bedrooms with one shared bathroom and kitchen. After he'd been smelling his roommate's socks for an entire week, it was paradise.

She brought them two glasses and a bottle of cheap wine and poured each a large glass. The wine's taste lingered unpleasantly in his mouth, and he was dizzy in minutes. He hardly ever drank, hated the sensations that followed. But his roommate, an ever-flowing fountain of unsought-for advice, had told him it would help him loosen up.

It was Elise that loosened up first, though, kissing him. She pushed herself on him in a needy and aggressive manner, her fingers scratching at his back, removing his shirt. He tried to be more active, to kiss her back, to caress her, to lead. But when he touched her waist, she grabbed his hand, moved it to her thigh. When he kissed her neck, she whispered that he should bite her. When he struggled with her bra, she lost her patience, removing it herself.

Endless instructions and corrections. She took control. And the good feeling that had settled in him during the movie, when he'd felt like a man, dissipated. He was a kid again, getting lectured about how to eat politely, how to dress, how to talk when there was company, how to be a good boy.

And despite the fact that usually he couldn't go an hour without getting an unwanted, potentially embarrassing erection, now there was nothing. He had a condom in his pocket, and Elise had another one she took out of her purse, but both were equally useless.

She tried to help him, but that only made it worse. He could feel rage building up. It was *her* fault, not his. The way she pawed at him, the way she acted as if nothing he did was right. He could do her all night if she'd just stop nagging and interrupting his focus.

He grabbed her wrist and squeezed it, pulling her hand away.

"Hey, you're hurting me!" she hissed.

He didn't let go, clenching his jaw, his heart throbbing, pulling at her hand, twisting it, until she fell from the bed.

"What the hell is your problem?" she half screamed at him. He knew that tone of voice. His mother used it often. When she wanted to scream but knew people might hear them. Of course, it was still a dorm room with four other bedrooms and paper-thin walls.

He didn't answer, just stared at her.

Her eyes filled with tears. She wrapped herself with a towel. "I'm going to wash up. You better get out of here."

She stumbled out, leaving the door open, although he was naked. He heard the bathroom door close.

He put on his clothes, a steady ring in his ears. His mind was filled with violent images. He would follow her into the bathroom, grab her head, smash it against the wall. Then he'd show her he could function just fine. He'd use *both* condoms.

But he also knew he wouldn't. No. He would leave and go home. And when his roommate asked him how the date went, he'd just say *A gentleman never tells*, har-har. And perhaps, if he was really careful, he could go through the rest of his college studies without running into Elise or any of her friends.

He stepped out of the room, closing the door behind him. He was about to walk out of the dorm, but then he glanced at the bathroom door. He heard the noise of water running beyond it.

A bunch of chairs stood in the shared kitchen, and he took one of them. He jammed it under the doorknob of the bathroom. He tried the handle softly, making sure it couldn't budge.

Then he flicked off the bathroom light.

"Hey," Elise said from inside. "I'm in here. Hello?"

The sound of water stopped. He put his ear to the door, listening. He heard a thud and a grunt of pain as she ran into something. Then a slight rattle as she tried the doorknob.

"Hello? The door is stuck. Hello?"

She spoke in a low voice. Four bedrooms. She wouldn't want to wake them all up, let them find her locked naked in the bathroom. Wouldn't that be humiliating.

His rage ebbed as she tried the door again. Locked in a dark place. A good place to think. A good place to contemplate her behavior.

"Hello? Let me out!" Alarm filled her voice now.

She thumped at the door and raised her voice, calling for help again. Soon, she was screaming. And her screams didn't grate on his nerves anymore.

There was that erection after all.

CHAPTER 57

As soon as they reached the station, they went straight to the situation room. Foster eyed the map on the wall. It was a large-scale map of San Angelo and the area around it, spanning about ten miles in each direction.

"Okay." Foster handed Zoe and Tatum blue markers. "Let's mark the areas that Yermilov said were easier to dig in."

"We should mark Tulia soil in a different color," Zoe said. "So far the killer always focused on Tulia."

"A different color." Foster muttered. "You feds sure have fancy ideas." He left the room and returned a minute later, clutching a bunch of markers in his hand. "Here." He tossed a green marker over to Zoe.

She caught it in her left hand, feeling ridiculously proud of herself, and tried to act as if she always caught things thrown at her and it was no big thing.

"Okay," Foster said. "You have the list?"

"I have it." Tatum unfolded a page. It was a list of areas they'd composed from Dr. Yermilov's instructions.

He took it to the nearby photocopier and copied it twice, handing one page to Zoe and one to Foster. Zoe located the cluster of Tulia locations. Each was a list of a pair of coordinates and a radius. She marked them on the map with her green marker. One area around the place where Nicole Medina was buried, another for Maribel Howe. And then additional areas all over the western part of the map.

Foster and Tatum stood by her, crowding her, drawing circles of their own. Soon, the entire map was filled with green and blue circles.

"We can narrow it further, at least for now," Zoe said. "Both victims were buried less than six miles from town. I think we can focus on a six-mile radius for the initial search. We can widen it later."

Foster drew a squiggly circle on the map, using a bit of crime scene tape as an improvised drafting compass. It defined a six-mile radius around San Angelo.

"The pits the killer would dig will be nearby roads, but they'd be side roads," Tatum said. "Also, he'd avoid any highly populated area, so we can ignore the area around Grape Creek. And we only need to mark the roads in the easy-to-dig soil."

They marked the relevant roads painstakingly, one after the other. There were still a lot more than Zoe would have wanted, but searching that area with a ground-penetrating radar sounded doable. The work of a few days.

Finally, all roads were marked. They stepped back, staring at the map.

"I'm going to talk to Jensen," Foster said. "Wrangle the budget for at least one radar from him. We need to start working on this as soon as possible."

"Maybe the FBI field office can give you a hand there," Tatum said. "I'll check."

"I need to talk to Harry," Zoe told them. She'd filled them in regarding the email from the killer in the car. "Get another article ready."

"I'll also ask Shelton if we can get anything on that email address," Tatum said.

Zoe nodded distractedly. "It's a temporary email address. I doubt he'd ever use it again, but it's worth a try."

Foster and Tatum left to make their phone calls, leaving Zoe alone in the room. She was exhausted. Opening her laptop, she read the email the killer had sent several times more. Then she got up and wrote three phrases on the whiteboard.

Every step I took was necessary and unavoidable.

There's a reason to all of this.

Wait until you have the full story.

She regarded the sentences, tapping her lips. Then she dialed Harry.

"I was just about to call you," Harry said. "Did you read it?"

"Yes," Zoe said. "I have a few ideas."

"I looked into this Henry Lee Lucas he mentions. I suppose you already know who that is."

"He was a serial killer. No one knows exactly how many people he killed, but he was prolific. At one point he claimed he killed three thousand people, which is what the unsub is referring to."

"Yeah, but do you know where he was tried?"

Zoe frowned. "Somewhere in Texas. He was caught by a Texas Ranger, if I'm not mistaken."

"He was supposed to be tried in Austin, but due to pretrial publicity, they moved the trial to San Angelo."

Zoe exhaled and read the email again. "Everyone back then had a friend or family member in the jury," she said.

"Your serial killer was raised in San Angelo." Harry sounded pleased with himself. "He's a local boy."

"He mentions his parents talking about it," Zoe said. "When was the trial?"

"It was . . . 1984."

"So assuming he was between five and ten years old, that'd mean he's now around forty, perhaps just a bit older."

"Why assume he was between five and ten? What if he was thirteen?"

"Then he probably wouldn't say he remembers his parents talking about it. He'd say he remembers the kids in class talking about it." She recalled her own experience as a teenager, how the kids in school would talk about nothing else except the Maynard serial killer.

"Good point."

"And I know how to talk to him now," Zoe said. "This guy has concocted a whole story about his mission. This comparison to Einstein's *Annus Mirabilis*? This is him telling us that he has a grand plan. A vocation. His email is full of it. This is what he wants to share."

"And what will his vocation tell you?" Harry asked. "How will that help the profile?"

Zoe snorted. "I couldn't care less about his vocation. It's just a story he tells himself. But talking about it might get him to accidentally give us a real hint, something we could use."

"What do you mean, a story he tells himself?"

"People lie to themselves all the time, Harry. You should know it better than most. And this guy is telling himself one big elaborate lie to avoid seeing a very simple truth."

"What truth?"

"That he gets off on burying women alive."

CHAPTER 58

Zoe was reading a report about Henry Lee Lucas in the *American Journal of Forensic Psychiatry* when the door to the situation room was flung open. Lyons stood in the doorway, her face flushed.

"I have a suspect," she said, out of breath.

Zoe felt a jolt of excitement, almost as if it were an airborne virus, highly infectious. "Who?" she asked.

"His name is Alfred Sheppard. He called the hotline."

"When?"

"This morning." Lyons paced back and forth in the room, her face animated. "This guy Sheppard phoned an hour and a half ago, said he remembered he saw someone who looked like Maribel Howe with a guy in a local pub."

Zoe nodded, her attention rapt.

"They took some details from him. It turns out his van was one of the vehicles that drove through the roadblocks at 67 yesterday. It's a white Ford Transit. We figured it merited closer inspection. And guess what?"

"I don't guess."

"He showed up *twice* at the Medina memorial site. His face matches one of the people we photographed there."

There it was. Too many coincidences to ignore. Zoe stood up, unable to stay still any longer. "Do Nicole's parents know who he is?"

"Not by name. I sent someone over with a picture to interview them, see if this guy looks familiar."

"Is his story being verified?"

"Maribel Howe took a selfie in that pub with a friend, tagged the location, and posted it in her Instagram profile. The photo was posted three days before she disappeared. It checks out, but anyone could have come up with it."

Zoe nodded. "Do you have enough for a search warrant?"

"Looking into it."

"Maybe a professional opinion from me will sway a judge's mind."

"Couldn't hurt."

"Where is he now?"

"We asked him to come over and tell us more about Maribel Howe and the guy she was with. He's in Interview Room One. As far as he knows, he's here to help us out."

"Anyone in there with him?"

"No. I took a quick statement from him and then asked him to wait. He's been there for about fifteen minutes now. Foster was just about to enter, but we thought we'd talk to you about how to proceed. You can watch the interrogation from the monitor room. Come on."

Zoe followed Lyons down the hallway, deeper into the station. The interview room was almost at the farthest side of the station, and that was not by chance. Anyone taken there would have to walk by the different departments, brushing past uniformed cops, detectives, detainees. Closed doors with plaques like "Homicide" and "Evidence Storage" and "Armory." Civilians who were unused to the scenery of a police station were set instantly on edge by it all. And nervous people made mistakes.

The monitor room was small and dimly lit. Both left and right walls had large darkened one-way mirrors in them, looking into the adjacent interrogation rooms. Detective Foster, Lieutenant Jensen, and Tatum were already there, looking through the left mirror at the man who sat in Interview Room One.

He was bald and wore a white T-shirt and a pair of worn, stained jeans. His right foot tapped on the floor rapidly, his arms folded. He glanced at the mirror and then quickly looked away.

"How did he get here?" Zoe asked without preamble. "Did someone pick him up, or did he drive over?"

"He drove over. The van's in the parking lot," Foster said. "Someone's checking it out right now."

"Just from outside, I hope," Jensen said. "We don't have cause to—"

"Just looking through the van's windows and taking some pictures," Foster answered briskly. He was impatient and didn't seem in the mood to coddle Jensen as he usually did.

"Okay," Jensen said, his voice clipped. "Was he Mirandized?"

"No. He's not under arrest," Foster said.

"I don't want another mess like the one with the Whitfield case, Detective. I want you to Mirandize him."

"If you Mirandize him, he won't say a word," Zoe said. "We can't let him know that he's under suspicion. Not at first. And you aren't required to Mirandize him yet if he wasn't arrested."

Jensen shook his head stubbornly. "He was taken through the police station into the interrogation room and left with the door closed for a long time. A skilled lawyer would argue that he felt as if he was being held."

"He came in his own van." Foster raised his voice. "He can leave whenever he wants! If he says anything, that falls under spontaneous confession."

"Does he know he can leave? No, he doesn't. Don't make a big deal out of it. Just tell him it's something that you have to do before you start talking to him. Let Detective Lyons say it, make it sound like a bureaucratic hassle."

"Tell you what." Lyons laid a hand on Foster's shoulder, almost as if she held him back from punching the lieutenant. "We don't Mirandize him until we're deep into the interview, and then we'll make the call. We won't make any outright accusation before Mirandizing him, okay?"

Jensen seem to hesitate for a moment, then muttered, "That's acceptable."

Zoe looked through the one-way mirror at Sheppard. "We have to do this carefully. If he's our guy, he'll be ready for any obvious questions. We need to catch him off guard."

CHAPTER 59

"Sorry to keep you waiting, Mr. Sheppard. We had some things we needed to verify first." Foster's voice buzzed from the speaker in the control panel. The sound system gave it a slight echo, which Tatum found distracting. He watched as Foster and Lyons sat in front of Alfred Sheppard. Lyons had a laptop bag slung on her shoulder. Both had thick folders in their hands. Foster's folder was the actual crime case file, thickened with some extra pages. Lyons's folder was a fake.

"It's okay. I'm sure you're very busy," Sheppard said. His voice was a bit gravelly, making Tatum think of a man who smoked.

"We really appreciate you doing this, Mr. Sheppard," Lyons said. "As you may have heard on the news, the investigation has a few concrete leads, and a testimony from you can really help us narrow our suspect pool."

Zoe leaned forward to the mic. "Don't mention the news. We want him to feel like anything you tell him is classified. He doesn't want to know what's already in the news."

Lyons blinked once in something that might have been affirmation. Or maybe just a regular blink. Then she began outlining some of the case's details. She didn't say anything that wasn't publicly known, but she did a good job of making it seem as if she was disclosing it for the first time.

"She's good," Tatum said.

"Can you please tell us about the night you saw Maribel Howe?" Foster put his folder on the table with a slight thump and pulled a small notebook and pen from his shirt pocket.

"Uh, sure. It was . . . a few weeks ago, on the twenty-sixth of July. I went out with some friends. One of them just had a birthday. And I saw the woman—"

"Maribel Howe." Foster removed a large color photo from the folder and placed it on the table. It was an image of Maribel Howe in a park, a river in the background. She was smiling at the camera, the wind playing with a strand of her hair. It was a beautiful picture and one of the sweetest images in her Instagram account.

"Uh, yeah, her. I saw her with a guy. He was about six feet tall, black hair, had a beard. I noticed them because they were arguing about something, and she looked kinda upset. I wanted to intervene, but my friend convinced me not to."

"This is really very helpful, Mr. Sheppard," Lyons said. "We're trying to make a list of possible suspects, and currently we're focusing on a few in particular. Your description definitely matches one of our prime suspects, and it might be invaluable in building a case."

This was an utter fabrication, but its impact was instantly visible as the man relaxed and smiled at the detective. "I'm really glad I can help."

"So tell us in your own words what you saw," Foster said.

"Well, they were sitting in a booth, but this guy was acting a bit aggressive. I couldn't hear what he said, but the woman . . . Maribel seemed upset."

"Upset how exactly?"

"I don't know. She seemed unhappy."

"Was there any other indication they were having an argument? Aside from the way the guy talked?"

"No. Like I said, I couldn't hear them. And they left soon after."

"Try to nudge him a bit," Zoe spoke into the mic. "See if you can get him to change his story."

"Was he violent in any way?" Foster asked.

"No. I mean, I would have intervened if he hit her."

"But he made no physical intimidating gestures?"

"Uh . . . no, I don't think he did."

"Maybe he crowded her? Invaded her personal space?" Lyons suggested, sounding hopeful.

Sheppard seemed to pause for a second. "Now that you say so, yeah, he *was* kinda leaning forward in a sort of threatening way. That's part of the reason I wanted to intervene."

"Was she simply upset? Or did she cry?" Lyons asked.

"I don't know. I think she might have been crying when they left."

"It definitely looks like he's catering to what they want to hear," Tatum said.

"Yeah," Zoe agreed. "He won't say anything someone else would later contradict, but he's willing to change his story to fit the mold."

Lyons told Sheppard again how useful everything he said was. As she spoke, she dropped the occasional tidbit about the case that they'd agreed beforehand to share with him. The man's attention was rapt.

"I'd say with your help we have a good chance to catch the Digging Killer," Lyons said.

"Good. I'm really glad," Sheppard said.

"He didn't flinch at the nickname," Tatum said.

"Maybe he got used to it," Jensen suggested.

"Maybe," Zoe muttered. She watched the man intently as Foster spread the photos on the table. "This guy isn't fazed by seeing pictures from the crime scene."

"What does that mean?" Jensen asked.

"It means he's desensitized, but these days there's a lot of violence online. Anyone who's interested in violence can get it in vast quantities. Of course, it's one thing to see a random gory picture and another thing entirely to look at a picture of a decomposed body of someone you saw alive."

"Is he the killer?"

"He's someone who's fascinated by this case, but that doesn't make him the killer."

They talked some more. Foster dropped the Digging Killer nickname a few times more.

"Clothing now," Zoe said.

Jensen nodded, grabbing the evidence bags from the table. He left the room, and a second later, the interview room door opened, and he strode inside.

"Detective Foster." His voice was ridiculously mechanical, like a man who'd practiced his lines for hours. "The clothing."

"A five-year-old could see through that act," Tatum muttered, frustrated.

"It doesn't matter," Zoe said. "Look at Sheppard—he didn't even notice."

She was right. Sheppard stared at the translucent bags intently. Inside them were the clothes Maribel Howe had been wearing when they'd found her.

"Do these clothes look familiar?" Foster asked, spreading the bags on the interrogation room table. "Did she wear any of them when you saw her?"

"The . . . the shoes, I think."

Jensen hovered, uncertain. Foster gave him a meaningful glance, and the lieutenant blinked and left the room.

The interview room table was now a well-orchestrated scatter of photographs and evidence, and the effect seemed to be getting to Sheppard. His right knee bounced even more nervously than before. Foster and Lyons took him through his testimony again, asking further questions about Maribel Howe. Had there been any other friends with her? The night she'd disappeared, she'd been with some friends—had he seen any of them in the pub?

Foster got up, pacing around the room as they were asking the questions. When he sat down, he dragged his chair and sat to Sheppard's right side. Since the table sat against the far wall, this had the effect of hemming Sheppard in. If he wanted to leave now, he'd have to ask Foster to move.

"I don't like that," Jensen muttered. "The suspect looks trapped. A good lawyer could claim that by this point, the suspect felt he was being held."

"It's a completely standard interrogation technique," Tatum said casually. "We use it all the time in the bureau. There, see how he's pointing out the pictures? We can just say he sat there to be closer to the witness."

Jensen didn't answer, but he seemed at least momentarily reassured.

"I want to show you some footage from the Digging Killer's videos." Lyons unzipped the laptop bag.

"Okay," Sheppard said.

Tatum watched the man intently as Lyons opened her laptop and started the first video. Nicole Medina, screaming for help. Sheppard was clearly mesmerized. He stared at the screen, his mouth ajar.

"He definitely looks excited by this clip," Jensen said.

They let the video play for several minutes. Sheppard's eyes didn't budge from the screen.

"Do you know who that is?" Lyons asked.

He glanced at her, then back at the screen. "The other victim."

"Had you seen this video before?"

"No. Just images in articles."

She kept asking him questions about Nicole Medina. He was vague, his answers short. He didn't play dumb, didn't act as if he didn't know who that was. His eyes kept going back to the monitor.

"I think this is our guy," Tatum said.

"I don't know," Zoe muttered. "I don't think his response fits."

"Why not?" Tatum asked. "He looks almost excited by it. Isn't it what you were expecting?"

"The killer has the two videos at home. Probably the full videos. I'm willing to bet he's watched them dozens of times. He probably has favorite segments. Does this guy look like he's watched the video dozens of times? Look at him. He's completely enthralled."

"Maybe it's just really good stuff. Every time he watches it, it's as exciting as the first."

Zoe glanced at him, raising an eyebrow. "If that was the case, he wouldn't need to kill more girls. This is the last reaction I would have expected from the killer. I thought he'd act as if he finds it abhorrent. Or maybe he'd watch a few seconds, cool and detached. But this?" She shook her head. "I don't know."

A few minutes went by. Lyons let the video run. The sounds it emitted, accompanied by the mild echo of the monitor room's sound system, were getting on Tatum's nerves.

"Okay, I think it's my turn." He grabbed an earpiece and plugged it in his ear.

He stepped out from the monitor room, blinking at the sudden harsh light outside. He took a moment to get used to it. He wouldn't be very imposing if he barged into the interrogation room blinking like a frog in a hailstorm. After a second, he pushed open the door to the interrogation room.

The room smelled of sweat. This was something they couldn't have known in the monitor room. Sheppard was sweating profusely. All eyes in the room went to Tatum.

"Mr. Sheppard," he said. "I'm Agent Gray, from the FBI. I'll join in for the rest of this session."

"Uh . . . okay. Sure."

Tatum leaned against the wall and folded his arms. That was the extent of his job there. To stand by the door, blocking the way out, a federal agent.

To make the pressure rise even further.

Foster and Lyons resumed the questioning. Had Sheppard ever seen Nicole Medina before? Had he seen her with the man who'd been with Maribel Howe? Was he sure? More photos were spread on the table, whose surface was hardly visible by now. Foster and Lyons were doing their job splendidly.

"Mr. Sheppard," Foster suddenly said. "Can you tell us where you were on August twelfth at eight p.m.?"

This had been another of Zoe's ideas. The date was insignificant. None of the girls had disappeared on that date. As far as they knew, nothing had happened then. Zoe theorized the killer would have prepared an alibi for the nights of the kidnappings, but he would be caught unprepared if asked about a different date. It would make him wonder what they had. It would unbalance him.

And it did.

"Uh . . . what? When? I don't see what that has to do with—"

"It ties in to your testimony," Lyons said smoothly. "To this guy you saw. So where were you?"

"I . . . I would have to check. Am . . . am I a suspect?" His eyes shifted, glancing at Tatum, then back at Lyons.

"Of course not," Lyons said. "You're just here to help."

"That's right."

"Do you remember what you did that night?"

He looked around him frantically.

"I don't like this," Jensen's voice buzzed in Tatum's ear. "You're asking him direct questions, Foster. I want him Mirandized. I don't want another Whitfield incident."

"No need," Zoe's voice sounded in the background. "They're asking about an unrelated date. We agreed on it beforehand."

"I . . . think I was home," Sheppard said.

"Can anyone corroborate that?" Foster asked.

"A skilled lawyer could make the entire footage from this interrogation inadmissible!" Jensen sounded hysterical. "Foster, Mirandize him, now!"

"You're being an idiot!" Zoe snapped sharply. "There's absolutely no need to act like a—"

The feed was cut as Jensen presumably removed his finger from the mic's button. Tatum cursed inwardly, realizing their mistake. When Tatum had entered the interrogation room, he'd increased the pressure on the suspect. But he'd also left Jensen alone with Zoe. And if there was something she absolutely *couldn't* do, it was handle someone like the lieutenant.

"Uh . . . I think maybe I was alone . . . no, hang on." Sheppard licked his lips. In the background, Nicole Medina let out a long desperate moan. His eyes shifted to the screen, then to Tatum. He seemed like a cornered animal. A cornered animal that was about to make a mistake.

The door to the interrogation room flew open, and Jensen strode inside, brandishing a Miranda slip.

"Mr. Sheppard," he piped. "Before you go any further, would you mind signing this? It's just a bit of bureaucracy. It states that you know your rights. That you have the right to an attorney and that anything you say can be used against you in the court of law. You know, all that stuff from the movies."

He put the paper on the table, over Maribel Howe's picture, and smiled.

Sheppard's eyes went to the Miranda slip. He frowned.

"Why would I need to sign this?" he asked. "I just came to help."

"It's really just procedure," Jensen murmured.

Every moment in the interrogation was a careful thread, weaving the web tighter around Alfred Sheppard. Each subtle move tightened the trap, making it harder for him to get out safely. And Jensen had collapsed this carefully laid snare with one bumbling, heavy-handed move.

"Am I under arrest?" Sheppard asked.

Foster sighed. "No, Mr. Sheppard. You're just here to help."

"Well, then I think I gave you all that I can. It's getting late. I really need to go home now."

CHAPTER 60

"I was surprised to get your phone call," Joseph told Zoe after they'd ordered dinner. "I thought you were back home with your sister by now."

They were sitting at the restaurant where they'd met for the first time. Zoe had ordered the same steak, and her stomach made a little rumble when she thought of it. "I was delayed. I'll probably fly back on Tuesday."

"Is she okay?"

"Andrea's fine." Zoe smiled, thinking of the message her sister had sent her an hour ago. Ever since Marvin had temporarily moved himself to the apartment, Andrea had begun sending her endless GIFs of the two grumpy old men from the Muppets. Though she couldn't be sure, she got the sense that Andrea couldn't get enough of Marvin's company.

The barman placed their drinks in front of them. Zoe had asked for Guinness; Joseph had ordered a pint of Shiner.

Zoe took a swig of her beer, licking the froth from her upper lip, enjoying the heavy creamy taste. She was glad Joseph had come. Though Tatum had wanted to get some takeout and keep talking about the case, Zoe needed a break. The bitter taste that followed her after Jensen had ruined their interrogation mingled with exhaustion that followed the constant attempts to guess the killer's motives. It was overwhelming. She wanted to talk to someone outside the case.

"So how did you spend Friday evening?" she asked.

"Went to see a movie with some friends." He shrugged. "We had some laughs."

He told her about a girl who'd sat in the seat in front of him. She'd apparently kept overreacting to the movie scenes to the point where he'd been more invested in her reactions than in the movie itself. Zoe listened with a smile, her mind slipping in and out of focus, thinking of Andrea, of Schrodinger, of Alfred Sheppard. She was almost sure Sheppard wasn't their guy. If she had to guess, she'd peg Sheppard as a man obsessed with serial killers who reacted to an actual killer hunting in his city. If Lyons received the search warrant, Zoe was willing to bet they'd find endless serial killer paraphernalia in his home.

But she didn't think he was the killer.

They put surveillance on him for now, just in case. She felt a fresh surge of anger at how effectively Jensen had managed to demolish their efforts.

"What are you thinking about?" Joseph asked her.

She looked around her. Half the tables were empty. The atmosphere seemed subdued. "This place is a lot emptier tonight. Is it always like that on Saturday?"

Joseph raised an eyebrow. "I don't know if you've heard, but there's a serial killer on the loose."

"Oh. Right."

"Any progress there?"

"We have some very good leads. It looks promising."

"I read an interview you gave to the press," Joseph said. "You sounded very sure of yourself."

"We have a lot of experience finding these people, and in this case in particular, we have a bit of an advantage."

"What advantage?"

"I'd rather not talk about—"

Her phone rang. She sent an apologetic look at Joseph and picked it up. It was Tatum.

"I don't want to interfere with your date," he said, giving the word *date* a strange inflection Zoe couldn't figure out. "But I got something for you."

"What?"

"Shelton got a crew driving with a GPR running—"

"GPR?"

"The ground-penetrating radar. They already found one of this guy's pits."

She smacked her palm on the bar, eliciting several frowns from people around her. "Where?"

"To the north, about half a mile north of Grape Creek. In one of the Tulia soil areas."

"North of Grape Creek?" She got up, mouthing *be right back* to Joseph. "How far from San Angelo?"

"Five and a half miles."

"Almost at the edge of our search area." She pushed open the door and walked outside. Despite the night's darkness, it was dry and hot. She was slowly getting used to the climate and didn't find it nearly as unbearable as she had the first day she landed. "Do you think we should widen our perimeter?"

"We still have a lot of ground to cover," Tatum said. "They stopped for the night, and it's the weekend, so I doubt we'll be able to get another GPR before Monday. I think we're good for now."

"How does it look?"

"Six feet deep, rectangular, covered with two large boards, and about fifteen inches of soil on top of them. It was a few yards away from the road, hidden from sight. About what you'd expect."

"Did Foster get surveillance on it?"

"He's working on it now. Jensen's in a huff, because we already added one surveillance tonight, and it's the weekend. More overtime,

I guess. Anyway, Lyons told me it'll be fine. They'll get the surveillance running even if they need to be there themselves."

"This is fantastic news, Tatum."

"I know." She could hear the smile in his voice. "You can go back to your dinner now. I'll let you know if anything else happens."

"Thanks."

She hung up the phone, walking back past empty seats until she reached the bar. Their dishes had been served while Joseph was waiting.

"Good news?" Joseph asked.

"Some progress on the case," she answered. "God, this smells fantastic—I'm starving."

She sliced a large bite of steak and put it in her mouth, shutting her eyes with pure joy. She chewed and swallowed, then smiled at Joseph. "I'd never tell Andrea this, but the steak here is infinitely better than hers."

"Welcome to Texas." Joseph smiled at her. "I have to say I don't recall ever seeing a woman enjoy food the way you do."

"Maybe you were dating the wrong sort of women."

"If I'd dated the right kind, I'd have a ring on my finger by now."

"You want to get married?"

"Sure." He gave her a look. "But no need to be alarmed. I'm not going to pop the question."

She let out a snort. "Well, I'm leaving in two days, so I doubt you would, anyway."

"Don't underestimate me. Let me remind you I've chased women across the country before." He burst out laughing. "Don't look so worried. I'm not going to stalk you back to your home."

A moment later he seemed to realize his comment was a bit in poor taste, because he became deadly serious. "Sorry, I didn't mean . . ."

"Don't worry about it." Zoe shook her head, smiling.

They ate a bit in silence. The place *really* was mostly empty. That would hamper the killer as well. She tried to imagine him right now.

Was he outside his chosen target's house, like he had been with Maribel and Nicole, hoping she'd leave home soon? It might take weeks before that happened. Maybe they'd manage to catch him watching his target's house before he struck again. Or maybe he'd visit one of his pits and stumble into a stakeout.

A sudden bright light snapped her out of her focus. A group of young men and women had clustered their heads together and were now snapping selfies of their night out.

Zoe peered at them, biting her lower lip. What if she'd been wrong? What if the killer wasn't hiding by the victim's house, waiting for her to leave?

"Oh, shit," she muttered.

"What is it?" Joseph asked.

Lyons had said that Maribel Howe had an Instagram account she kept updating. Nicole Medina's mother had said her daughter was constantly on the phone chatting with her friends. Both victims had a prolific social media life. How had she missed it?

Rummaging in her bag, she took out her phone again. She opened Maribel Howe's Instagram account. It was full of comments from mournful friends. The account was public. She then searched for Nicole's account, finding it easily. Public as well.

"I missed something big in my profile," she said.

Nicole Medina had posted on her Instagram account the night she'd gone out to that party. She'd even tagged her location. *Anyone* who checked could know she was out with friends. All he'd have to do was drive to her home and wait for her to come back.

"What did you miss?" Joseph asked.

Zoe ignored him, going back to Maribel Howe's account. Yup, there she was. Tagging herself outside the movie theater.

The killer stalked his victims through their social media accounts, waiting for them to go out. Once they did, he'd drive to their home, wait for them to come back. When it was late. When everyone in the vicinity was already sleeping. When home was just a few steps away and their guard was down.

The implication hit her hard. That meant the killer didn't necessarily have *one* target victim. He might be looking through dozens of accounts. Hundreds. And he could check out their homes at leisure when he had free time, plan his hiding spot for the moment when he chose.

Even now, with everyone scared, surely some of his designated victims might go out.

She instantly had half a dozen ideas. They could do a bait operation, creating a profile for the kind of girls he targeted—she'd done something like it before. They could find accounts of girls at risk, warn them, monitor them. They could maybe get a list of accounts who'd visited Maribel and Nicole's pages and see if any of those visited a lot of other profiles.

"I have to go," she said. "I'm sorry."

"But you haven't even finished your steak." Joseph looked dismayed.

"I . . . right." She motioned to the barman. "Can I take this to go, please?"

"Can I see you later this evening? I'm planning on going to sleep pretty late. You can call me whenever you want."

She looked at him for a long moment, the prospect alluring. "Yeah," she finally said. "I'll call you."

CHAPTER 61

This had to be the shittiest birthday Juliet had ever had. And that included her seventh birthday with that horrendous party bear that had given her nightmares for weeks *and* her fourteenth birthday, when Roger Asshat Harris had broken up with her. She always told herself to keep her expectations low for her birthdays. Low expectations mitigated disappointments. And yet even her lowest expectations weren't *that* depressing.

Yesterday, she'd looked forward to a fun party. Nine of her friends had marked the event as "coming" and five more as "maybe." She had called in advance to book the long table at Ronny's, already imagining herself sitting in the middle while everyone sang "Happy Birthday," a chocolate cake with a tiny sparkler in front of her.

Low expectations, Juliet. Low expectations.

Because apparently there was a serial killer in San Angelo, and he hadn't scheduled with Juliet before making himself known *on her goddamn birthday.* And those five "maybes" had quickly morphed into "not attending," and the nine "coming" had suddenly become "maybe," followed by apologetic messages and cancellations.

The final count of friends who showed up?

Two.

Tiffany and Luis, Tiffany's boyfriend. Luis, it was worth mentioning, was not even Juliet's friend. She thought he was a douche. But hey, he wasn't a coward.

At least she was spared the humiliation of sitting at that huge table with two people. Ronny's was almost completely empty, and they could choose whichever table they felt like. She eyed the large table every few minutes, thinking that if only that creep had waited a bit more before killing two women, she'd be sitting there surrounded by her cowardly bunch of friends.

She refused the damn chocolate cake with the sparkler.

Tiffany did her best to be cheerful, but a constant twinge of hysteria made her voice crack, and she kept checking the time, mentioning they should probably leave early. As if serial killers stuck to some sort of timetable. *Oh my, look at the time—it's half past murder o'clock.*

Not that Juliet minded. The entire place was on edge. The waitress had already warned them they were closing early. The few patrons kept looking around them, as if verifying they weren't the last to leave. Safety in numbers seemed to be the phrase of the day, which had been what Juliet had kept telling her canceling friends.

The only one who seemed cheerful was Luis. And for Luis, being cheerful meant he was being a total horntoad. He pawed at Tiffany above the table and, Juliet quickly found out, below the table as well. *Twice* he accidentally brushed her leg with his foot trying to reach for Tiffany's. Or maybe it wasn't an accident at all. Who knew. When Tiffany suddenly gasped, reacting to some invisible under-the-table action, Juliet asked for the bill.

They all drove back in Luis's car, and his right hand sneaked under Tiffany's skirt over and over again. It was mesmerizing and disgusting at once, and all Juliet wanted was to get home and go to sleep.

Halfway to her home Luis jokingly suggested a birthday ménage à trois. It was one of those ha-ha jokes that you just knew was meant to be taken half seriously.

Ew, ew, ew. This ride couldn't end fast enough.

He pulled up by her home, and she opened the passenger door.

"Hey, want us to walk you to the door?" Luis asked, his tone suddenly serious.

She almost said yes, because the serial killer news was actually getting to her too, but his hand was still under Tiffany's skirt when he asked, and Juliet suddenly wondered if he'd make the same ménage à trois suggestion when they were by the door.

"Nah, there's really no need." She smiled at them, doing her best to be nice because at least they'd shown up. "Thanks for coming."

"Happy birthday, sweetie," Tiffany said. "I'll call you tomorrow."

"We'll wait here until you get inside," Luis said.

Maybe he wasn't a douche, after all. He was a bit horny. So what?

She got out of the car and closed the passenger door behind her. The darkness was stifling. She suddenly thought of all those times her mother had asked her if she couldn't get the landlord to install some lights outside. She'd brushed it off as another of those things her mom nagged about, but now she yearned for two or three lights along the way.

The door was less than twenty yards from her. It was no big thing.

She walked down the sandy path, stumbling as her right high heel snagged a root or something. High heels were not the right footwear for this path. After a few yards she heard a rustle in the bushes. She froze. Luis's car was still behind her—she could hear the engine running—but could they even see her in this darkness? What if someone pounced at her right now, dragged her into the shadows? What could Luis and Tiffany do?

And then she ran, panic taking control over her body, her pulse running high, her breathing short and wheezing. She nearly fell again, righted herself, got to the door. She rummaged in her bag for the keys, fingers trembling. Where were they? Where were they?

She felt the familiar shape of the dolphin key ring, pulled it out, keys jingling. Found the key, inserted it into the lock, heard it click.

Breathless, she hit the light switches by the entrance. Both the light in the living room and the light above the front door turned on. She gulped air, trying to calm her trembling breath. She wanted to cry.

She stepped into the house and turned around. Luis and Tiffany waved at her from the car. She waved back, trying to smile.

The car drove off.

God, what a shitty night. She couldn't wait to pee and go to bed. She turned around, giving the door a kick.

She'd expected it to slam shut. But there was nothing. No slam, not even a light thud.

She was about to glance back when something pressed to her throat, just as a hand gripped her right arm.

"Don't scream, or I cut. Got that?" The voice was gravelly, angry.

She froze, unable to move, unable to breathe.

"Just nod your head slightly so that I see you understand."

She let out a tiny nod.

"Walk. Straight to the kitchen. Don't make any sudden moves."

She took one step after the other, her body feeling as if it were made of Jell-O. Even if she dared to struggle, elbow him in the stomach and run or grab the hand with the knife and bite it, she couldn't. She could hardly stand upright.

He must've waited in the shadows after all. Waited patiently until Luis had driven off. Then he'd moved, gotten to the door just before it had closed.

"My boyfriend is in the bedroom," she said, her voice hoarse. "He'll wake up in a minute."

"You don't have a boyfriend. You broke up four months ago, remember? You wrote a really touching post about it."

"What are you going to do to me?" Her vision clouded with tears as they entered the kitchen. The kitchen window was just in front of them, and she saw herself in the reflection and the man behind her. She quickly looked away, whimpering with fear.

"Don't cry. It's your birthday, right?" He forced her to the kitchen table. "Sit down."

The kitchen chair lurked in the dark. If she sat, she knew she would never be able to get up. As long as she remained standing, she had a chance. She could bolt and run. She could struggle. She could grab something, hit him, and—

A sudden blinding pain on her neck made her gasp.

"That was just a shallow cut," he whispered. "You don't want me to cut deeper."

She sat, every movement slow and precise. She let out a hiccuping sob, then another. She couldn't stop. She felt the sticky trickle of blood running down her neck.

"Try to calm down. Here, drink this." He let go of her arm and put a bottle of mineral water on the table in front of her.

"I . . . I'm not thirsty—"

"Drink." His hand grabbed her again, squeezing.

She uncapped the bottle and took a few gulps. Then a few more. She put the bottle back on the table.

"Feeling better?" he asked.

"Please don't hurt me."

He didn't answer. She waited for him to do something. *Anything.* But he didn't. The blade stayed at her throat. His hand still clutched her arm. Had he fallen asleep? She considered lunging off the chair, kicking him in the balls, running outside.

She made a tiny move with her head.

"Don't move."

She froze.

Seconds ticked by. She had no idea what was going on. The blood soaked her shirt, ran down her collar. Was it really a shallow cut? Or was she about to die?

She felt a bit of nausea, a dizziness. Her limbs were heavy, impossible to move. Blood loss, probably. Except it didn't feel like there was that much blood.

No. Not blood loss. He'd put something in the water.

"What." Her tongue was heavy. "What."

He leaned forward and sang softly in her ear. "Happy birthday to you, happy birthday to you, happy birthday, dear Juliet. Happy . . ."

CHAPTER 62

San Angelo, Texas, Sunday, September 11, 2016

He'd gotten less than three hours of sleep, waking up before dawn. He'd have loved to sleep a couple of hours more, but the girl would wake up soon, and it was safer to do the work just as the day started, before the rest of the city's residents woke up.

It was almost worth it, just to listen to the silence. Early morning on Sunday. *Everyone* was asleep. It almost felt as if he were alone in the world.

The soil bins and the box with the girl inside were already loaded in the van. He'd done that last night before going to sleep. All he had to do now was slide into the driver's seat, open the garage door, and drive out.

Halfway down the street, he suddenly wasn't sure if he'd remembered to take all he needed. He parked by the sidewalk, checked the bag. Laptop, burner phone, cable, gloves. The digging tools were in the handbag in the back.

He'd forgotten his shades. It would make the drive back annoying as hell. He contemplated returning for them but finally decided not to. He'd drive without them, and the annoyance would help him remember them next time.

The sky had that dark-blue hue that you got just before the sun rose, a few exceptionally bright stars still barely visible. He hummed to himself as he drove, feeling a twinge of excitement building up.

The last stretch of the way was rough driving, his van bumping on the rocky terrain. The pit was less accessible than the previous times. His wheel hit a rock, and for a moment he was worried he might have gotten a flat tire. But it seemed fine.

In the back, he heard a muffled noise. The girl had woken up.

He stopped the van, opened the door, grabbed the bag, and hopped out. The pit was completely invisible, of course, but he knew where it was by heart. He took out the shovel from the bag and cleared the soil away from the planks that hid the pit. It took him less than five minutes. If there was anything he was exceptionally good at, it was digging.

He stuck the shovel in the ground, lifted the left plank . . .

His heart sank.

Part of the pit's wall had caved, crumbling into the bottom, filling it almost halfway. He let out a sharp curse. When had that happened? He'd checked this place just two weeks ago, and it was fine. Shoveling all of this out of the way would take about two hours.

The girl screamed in the back.

He wavered in indecision. What if he drove to a different location? He had several options, but he hated to make last-minute changes. And the police had already found out about the closest spot.

No. He could see no reason to make a big deal about this. The pit was still perfectly usable; he'd just have to suck it up and bury her only three feet deep. Buried was still buried, after all. No one but him really cared how deep it was.

He felt better after making the decision, the excitement building again. He opened the back of the van and dragged the box out just like he'd practiced a million times before. It was probably the trickiest part, getting it into the pit aligned and straight without jostling the girl inside too much.

He paused just before reaching the pit and connected the wire to the camera. With Maribel Howe, he'd forgotten to do it before placing the box in the pit, and it had been a *nightmare* to plug it in afterward. But he was more experienced now. He had the routine nailed.

The box hardly made a sound as it landed in the pit, but the girl still let out a muffled scream. Ignoring it, he unloaded the soil bins one at a time. He plugged the wire to the laptop and turned it on. The image of the girl inside materialized on-screen. He let out an eager sigh. Perfect.

He picked up the shovel again and scooped the first lump of soil onto the box. The girl's muffled screams intensified.

CHAPTER 63

It was clear to Zoe that none of them had slept much. The dark patches under the eyes of Tatum, Lyons, and Foster matched the ones that she'd seen in the mirror when she'd woken up. Despite the fact that it was Sunday morning, the four of them had all showed up at the station before nine. Foster brewed them a very strong pot of coffee to get started.

She'd gone to sleep after two in the morning . . . and alone. She'd texted Joseph when she and Tatum had finished discussing the case, but he'd never replied. He'd probably gone to bed after all.

They sat in the Schrodinger situation room. The map on the wall already had a new *X* northwest of Grape Creek—the pit they'd found.

"Okay." Foster massaged his forehead. "I gather from the emails I got from Agent Gray *at two in the morning* that you have some new ideas."

"Yes," Zoe said. "Originally, we assumed the killer picked his target and then stalked her house, waiting for her to go out. That way, he could grab her just as she was coming home, late at night, with no witnesses to see."

"Uh-huh."

"What if he isn't stalking one target? What if he has a selection of targets that he found via social media? Probably mostly through Instagram. He checks out those girls' profiles, and when they post online that they're going out or tag themselves out of home, he knows he has a window of opportunity. *That's* when he goes to their home and waits for them."

"Does that check out with the profiles of Maribel Howe and Nicole Medina?"

"Yes," Lyons answered instantly before Zoe could. "Maribel posted she was going to see a movie, and Nicole tagged herself at the party."

"And both profiles are public," Zoe said.

"Hmm. In the original scenario, I assumed he followed the girls to their home, which is how he knew their address. How does he know where they live if he just found them online?"

"There are a bunch of ways to find out addresses," Tatum answered. "In Nicole's case, she constantly tagged her location when she posted photos, so all he had to do was follow the location of the pictures she took at home."

"Maribel Howe was a bit more careful," Zoe said. "She never actively posted her location. But she did use Musical.ly."

"I'm a bit slow when it comes to the social media networks," Foster said. "What exactly is Musical.ly?"

"It's a social media app for people who post themselves singing," Tatum replied. "Mostly teens, but they have some older users. And Musical.ly posts have the location of the user by default. The majority of users don't even realize it's there."

"Maribel's Musical.ly and Instagram profiles are connected," Zoe said. "Anyone could find her address in less than five minutes."

Foster sighed heavily. "That definitely sounds plausible. What do we do about it?"

Zoe's phone rang. It was Harry. He probably wanted to talk to her about the article. She declined the call, resolving to return it in five minutes.

"We can canvass the local users of social media and warn potential users, for one," Tatum said.

"We can create a bait," Zoe said.

"Zoe and I discussed this last night. I'm not a fan of the bait idea," Tatum said.

"I've done it before."

"And you said the girl almost got killed."

"Because the people monitoring her were inept. In this case, it would work."

Foster interrupted them. "Tell me more about the bait idea."

Zoe nodded. "Well, we need to create—" Her phone rang again. Harry. She sighed. "Hang on—this might be important."

She answered the call. "Harry? You're awake early on Sunday mor—"

"I got another email." Harry's voice was edgy, tense. Completely unlike the annoying man she knew.

She frowned. "What does it—"

"It just says, 'Maybe this will make you think.' And there's a link. A third video."

Foster's phone rang, making Zoe jump. He answered. "Foster. Slow down, what?"

"What video?" Zoe asked Harry urgently.

"A third girl. I'm sending you the link now." He hung up.

Her phone blipped with the video link. She clicked it, and the familiar website layout appeared on-screen. Schrodinger. "Experiment Number Three."

And then the video started. A girl in a tight space, her mouth gagged, yelling hysterically.

"Dispatch just got a phone call from the mother of a girl named Juliet Beach," Foster said. "She couldn't get Juliet on the phone this morning, so she went to her home and saw a spatter of blood in the—" He paused and stared at Zoe, her phone in hand.

She showed him the phone's screen. "Just got it from Harry, the journalist."

Lyons was already tapping on her own phone. After a second, she showed them the screen—Juliet Beach's Instagram page. "It's her. Last post from yesterday evening. She went to celebrate her birthday."

"Then this is recent," Foster said. "Maybe even live."

They all crowded around Zoe's phone, staring for a few seconds.

"Why is she gagged?" Lyons said. "The first girls weren't gagged."

"Because now that the killer's methods are public, the victims know they're being filmed. He doesn't want the victim to say anything that might help us," Zoe said.

"What's that in the corner there?" Foster asked. "It looks like a box."

Zoe saw what he pointed at. A small metallic box with a green inscription and a very familiar-looking icon.

Skull and bones denoting poison.

CHAPTER 64

The map in the situation room seemed huge, the possible locations for the victim endless. Zoe surveyed it helplessly.

"I need that GPR out there as fast as possible," Foster shouted into his phone. "Every minute counts!"

The GPR probably wouldn't help anyway; they all knew that. If the victim was buried in Tulia soil, there would be too much clay for the radar to work.

Foster instructed dispatch to get hold of all the K-9 rescue dogs in the area and to ask for help from the Abilene and Midland police forces as well.

"State police too!" Foster told her, phone still to his ear. "I want every damn dog here looking for that girl."

Tatum talked to Shelton, outlining the email to Harry, the website, the cellular feed, Juliet's Instagram feed visitors. A plethora of digital footprints that could potentially lead them to the girl. Or not.

The three-phone conversation intermingled into a shouting match, and Zoe found it hard to concentrate. Where could the girl be?

"That box with the girl." Foster was by her side, talking quietly. "It's acid, right? Just like the physicist said. The bastard's third experiment has acid."

Zoe bit her lower lip. "It's . . . possible. But I think it's unlikely."

"Why?"

"Because that's not what turns him on. He clearly enjoys burying women alive, letting them suffocate to death. Exposing her to acid would be too far from his preference. It would require a higher engineering ability than what he's demonstrated so far."

"So . . . what is it?"

"It's a prop," Zoe said, trying to feel certain. "That's all."

"Are you—"

"The feed stopped," Tatum suddenly said. "The girl's gone."

"Already?" Foster rushed to the screen. "It's barely been fifteen minutes."

But Tatum was right. The girl was gone, replaced by a black screen.

He sat in the basement, a small smile on his lips, watching the girl as she struggled, tears running down her face. She was the best so far. He'd chosen well. The one thing he couldn't tell beforehand when picking his victims was how they'd react in the box. It was hardly something people posted on their profile. But she was perfect. The screams, the struggles, the helpless wide eyes.

The gag and the bound hands turned out to be an improvement as well. He'd never contemplated using them before, but it definitely made the struggles more . . . desperate.

"You really need some time to think," he whispered to the girl on the screen.

The toggle button underneath the video was marked offline. He hesitated. Long enough?

Let's give them a few more seconds.

He drank from his glass of water, hummed a catchy tune he'd heard on the radio a few days ago.

Okay. Long enough.

He clicked the toggle button. *Online.*

"It's back!" Lyons shouted.

The girl was back on-screen.

"He seems to be having technical problems," Foster said. He was on the phone again with dispatch, coordinating the patrol vehicles on the way to Juliet's home, to her mother's home, to talk to the friends she'd met with the night before.

"I don't think it's technical problems," Zoe said. "See the video running time? It never stopped. This is intentional. He's turning the public feed on and off."

"Why?"

"*That's* experiment number three," she said. "Not the acid. He's playing with us again. Remember what that physicist told us? A state of superposition. Every time he stops the feed, we don't know if Juliet Beach is alive or dead. She's in both states at once. The acid container is there to make us *think* that it might open at any moment. To increase our uncertainty. To make us wonder if she's alive or dead."

"Or it's real."

"It's not real."

"Fine," Foster spat. "Give me something I can use. This map is huge, and for now I have two dogs and one clunky GPR that just broke down. Where should they look first?"

Zoe hesitated. "There's a geographic profiling formula. It calculates the distance where a criminal might strike next on the basis that, statistically, criminals strike farther from their home each time. It's . . . highly inaccurate and demands that I guess some variables that denote elements in his psyche."

"That sounds complicated. We don't have time, Zoe."

"It's not complicated. It's just an estimation." She sat down and scribbled in her notebook, recalling the formula from memory. She never trusted the method completely; she'd seen too many criminals work outside the buffer zones that the formula predicated. And she *hated* inaccuracies.

But they had to start somewhere.

"Well?" Foster asked, impatient.

"Hang on," she said testily, eyeing the variables one more time, trying to see if they matched the geographies of earlier crimes. More or less. She could give a better estimate in half an hour, but for now . . .

"Six to eight miles from his home," she said. "I'd say we can treat his home as the center of San Angelo, for now. It seems to fit the previous crime scenes."

Lyons was already on the map, calling out locations to Foster, who rattled them off to dispatch, ordering them to send the K-9 units there.

Juliet couldn't breathe. That was the first sensation she had, and it stayed with her. The darkness was so complete it had a texture of its own, like a weightless material draped over her body, clinging to her, never letting go.

She'd screamed for so long she'd nearly thrown up, managing to stop just in time. With the gag in her mouth, she'd surely suffocate and die.

She would probably die anyway.

If she lay perfectly still on her back, she could almost imagine she was in a vast dark room. But every single movement dispelled this notion. The walls of her prison were closing in on her from all sides. The wooden plank above her was less than two inches from her nose. Kicking with her foot had resulted in a bruised knee and ankle.

Her throat was hoarse, her crotch itchy and damp. She'd wet herself earlier, the pressure in her bladder unbearable. Her recollection from the night before was in tatters. She'd gone out with Tiffany and Luis . . . remembered riding the car, and then . . . ?

Sensations and fragment of images, blinking in and out like fireflies. A blade held to her throat. A grip on her arm. The sour smell of a stranger's sweat.

She screamed again. And wept. And then let the silence creep in again.

And then . . . another sound. What was it? Thumping? A steady thump, so familiar but hard to pinpoint in this prison.

Bass. This was the rhythm of music. Somewhere, not too far, someone was listening to loud music.

She screamed again, gathering all her strength, feeling her throat give.

The music faded.

And then, unable to stop herself, she threw up, the vomit filling her mouth, up her nose, clogging her nostrils, and there was no air.

"What's that sound?" Tatum asked.

"What sound?" Zoe asked, frowning. There were about a bazillion sounds, with Foster and Lyons talking over each other on the phone and a portable police radio unit that Foster had dragged into the situation room crackling with the channel dedicated to the search. The video had already blinked in and out four times, and each time the tension in the room rose higher as they all wondered if the feed would return or if this time, the killer would leave it off.

"There's a sound in the video." Tatum looked around him. "Foster! Lyons! Shut up for a goddamn second."

They did, and Foster switched off the radio. All that was left was the video's sound. Juliet's whimpering. And a steady sound of bass.

"Music," Tatum said.

"Someone's listening to music nearby?" Foster asked incredulously. "Do you think it's possible she isn't buried at all?"

"No, listen—it's fading," Zoe said.

At that moment, Juliet began screaming through her gag desperately, and the bass became impossible to hear.

"I think it was a car playing loud music that went nearby," Zoe said. "This victim is buried a lot shallower than the other victims."

"Good, that'll help the K-9 dogs," Lyons said.

"Something's wrong." Tatum tensed, crouching over the screen. "Look at her."

Juliet bucked and struggled uncontrollably. Froth bubbled at the corner of the gag. A blob of liquid spurted from one of her nostrils. Zoe glanced at the metal contraption, wondering if she'd been wrong, if it was poison after all, but it was still shut. Then she realized what had happened.

"She just threw up." Foster's voice was strained. "She's choking. Damn it!"

The sensation of helplessness was devastating. All they could do was watch as the girl struggled, her eyes widening, her throat contracting. She shook her head, slammed it against the lid of the box, scratching her forehead. Zoe held her breath, almost as if identifying with the girl's horrific situation.

And then another glob of liquid spurted from Juliet's nostril, and she stopped struggling. The girl blinked, the nostril contracting and expanding. She'd managed to clear a way to breathe the limited supply of air she had. A steady trickle of blood ran from the gash in her forehead, but it didn't seem serious.

Tatum exhaled slowly. "That was close."

"Too close," Lyons croaked.

"The music," Tatum said. "Maybe we can somehow locate the vehicle that played it. Backtrack his route and figure out where Juliet is."

Foster stared into space.

"Foster, are you with me? We can tell the patrol vehicles to look for someone who's playing really loud—"

"The hell with that." Foster was already fiddling with his phone. "We can do so much better." He put the phone to his ear. "Listen. I want you to tell all patrols to start playing loud music using their siren speaker. As loud as possible, okay? We'll be able to hear it if they go past where she's buried. That's right. And tell them to pick songs with bass. As much bass as possible. You need to coordinate between them so that they don't play the same damn song."

He flipped on the radio. It already crackled with the dispatcher's voice as she relayed Foster's instructions. He grinned at the rest of them.

"We might actually find her."

CHAPTER 65

Juliet's throat was raw, the taste of vomit a constant, nauseating sensation in her mouth. She didn't move much anymore; she didn't have the strength. She wondered vaguely if the air had run out, if she'd finally die soon.

Her head throbbed. A wet trickle of liquid ran down the right side of her forehead—she was pretty sure it was blood. She wished she could wipe it off.

Her shoulders were in agony, a consequence of lying for hours with her hands pulled behind her back. Whatever bound her hands had a nasty bite. At first she'd kept moving her fingers to make sure the blood flowed to her palms. Now she couldn't bring herself to care. One way or another, she wanted this to end.

How long had she been lying there? It must have been days. The memory of the thudding bass music seemed unclear. Perhaps she'd imagined it.

Almost as if conjuring the music with her mind, she began hearing it again. It sounded different now. Screechy, static, unpleasant. She shut her eyes. She couldn't find the power to scream for help, and she was afraid she'd throw up again.

The music faded. Juliet was fading too.

"Every second it's offline, we might be missing the sound of our patrol cars' sirens," Foster said broodingly.

The video had been offline for three and a half minutes already—the longest duration so far. If the killer decided to leave it offline, Juliet was probably doomed. And like Foster had pointed out, even if he did return it, there was a chance they'd missed a patrol car that had just gone by. Foster did his best to coordinate the search, telling the patrol cars to stop where they were whenever the feed froze, but by now they had fourteen patrol cars screaming through the streets, and it became cumbersome to control.

Even worse, dispatch was overwhelmed with phone calls. The San Angelo citizens were not happy with their Sunday morning peace and quiet being interrupted by patrol cars driving by playing noisy music at full volume. People were dialing 911 nonstop, and with dispatch answering those calls and the calls of distraught people stumbling onto Juliet's video and managing the search, their reaction time was slowing down considerably. Lieutenant Jensen, who'd shown up in the station an hour before, was trying to handle *that* problem, but Zoe doubted he improved the situation.

"It's back," Zoe said, relieved, as the video of Juliet flickered onto the screen again. Her eyes were shut, but her chest was rising and falling—just barely.

"There's some music," Foster said. "Hear that?"

It was fading, but he was right. There was definitely the faint sound of bass, steady and slow.

"What song *is* that?" Tatum asked.

Zoe listened, ears straining, trying to match it to anything she knew. "It's . . . is that rap?"

"Hang on," Foster said. "I'll ask dispatch for the list of songs the patrols are playing."

"It's 'Swing My Door'!" Lyons shouted.

They all gawked at her.

"By Gucci." She rolled her eyes at their confused stares. "Seriously? Do you all live under a rock?"

Foster grabbed the mic of the portable radio. "Dispatch, this is five-thirteen. Do we have anyone playing Gucci?"

A moment of silence. "Five-thirteen, dispatch. Affirmative. Search car nine-oh-two."

"Copy. What's his location?"

The radio crackled as another male voice answered, slight static accompanying his voice. "Five-thirteen, this is nine-oh-two. I'm on South Burma Road, arriving at Arden Road in about a minute."

"Copy nine-oh-two. Stop where you are. Are you playing, uh . . . 'Swing My Door'?"

"Five-thirteen, that's affirmative."

"Nine-oh-two, this is five-thirteen—I want you to turn around and drive back. I'll tell you when to stop."

"Copy five-thirteen, on my way."

Foster let out a long breath. "Dispatch, this is five-thirteen."

"Go ahead."

"Send the GPR and the K-9 units to nine-oh-two's location."

"Five-thirteen, on it."

Foster lowered the volume of the radio as dispatch talked to the K-9 units.

"Okay," he said. "Where is he?"

"This is the road here." Lyons pointed at the map. "And there's a Tulia patch nearby. I'd say it's a good candidate."

"Excellent," Foster said. "We'll see where our guy is when we hear the music on the—"

"The feed stopped again," Zoe said.

The screen was dark.

His heart beat wildly, staring at the *offline* toggle, his mind spinning with the sudden, horrible idea that had occurred to him.

The first time he'd heard the sound of the passing car's music, he'd been mildly annoyed, realizing it was because of the shallow grave. If he had buried the girl deep enough, nothing would have disturbed the experiment, and the only sounds would have been the sounds of her crying.

The second time, the music was even louder, and a scratchiness in the sound set his teeth on edge. Someone was playing their music really loudly, and their sound system was terrible.

It had taken him five minutes before he realized what it reminded him of.

The sound of a patrol car's sound system. Usually used to direct drivers to stop at the side of the road. It almost sounded as if someone was playing music through it. But why would they—

And then it dawned on him. They were using it to search for the girl. Trying to get a feedback on her location from his *own damn video.*

He killed the feed, trembling, trying to tell himself he was just imagining things. It was some teenager driving by with a shitty sound system and bad taste in music.

But he couldn't shake the feeling that maybe it wasn't.

He searched through his phone contacts for Officer Richard Russo. Dick Russo was a friend of his; they sometimes went out for a beer together. He dialed the man.

Dick answered the phone after three rings. An abysmal noise filled the background. Loud music.

"Dick!" he said. "How are you?"

"Hey, man," Dick answered. "I'll have to call you back—"

"Listen," he interrupted Dick. "I have two steaks I bought yesterday and a six-pack. I wondered if you want to drop by for lunch."

"I can't." Dick was almost shouting over the loud music. "I'm on duty. They called us all. That serial killer buried another one, and we're looking for her."

"Oh, crap, that's terrible. What's that music? Are you looking for her in a club?"

"Nah, man. Dispatch told us to play it. They're hoping it'll help the search somehow."

"Oh." He wanted to say something else, but his throat clenched, all words gone from his mind.

"I'll take a rain check on that steak, okay, man?"

"Sure. Good luck, Dick." He hung up.

He was totally screwed. They'd already heard one of the patrol car radios via the video. They'd find the location. He tried to recall the evening before. Had the girl seen his face? Maybe. Maybe not. He'd have to hope she hadn't. She'd been distraught, and—

The laptop.

It was still at the crime scene, connected to the camera feed. They'd find nothing incriminating on the laptop itself—he only used it for the videos. But there could be fingerprints on the keys. And he knew damn well that any keyboard was an endless repository of skin cells, fingernails, half-eaten crumbs. All with his DNA on it.

His first instinct was to grab a bag and drive south. He'd reach the border in three hours, cross over to Mexico.

No. Don't panic. Think it through. He had some time before the police found the girl. There was a delay in the video feed, it would take them time to pinpoint the exact location. He could get there before them. Yank out the laptop and take it with him.

He bolted for the door. Every minute counted. And if he was there, he might as well dig up the shallow grave and strangle the girl. By the time the police reached her, there'd be no evidence linked to him.

CHAPTER 66

Every second that passed made Zoe's heart sink a bit more. More than six hours since the video had started. And thirty-seven minutes since it had stopped. The two K-9 teams had reached the area and were searching with no luck so far. The hope that the feed would resume had dissipated completely. The killer had decided they'd seen enough, leaving Juliet both alive and dead in their minds.

"Let's assume that the video wasn't live." Foster voiced Zoe's gnawing worry. "There's a small delay. Hopefully no more than a few minutes. We should determine what are the likeliest areas in the route of nine-oh-two."

He took a marker and drew a circle near the crossroads where they'd stopped the patrol car. "This is where he reached. He drove down Burma Road, all the way from 87. Before that he drove up to 87 from Fisher Lake." Foster drew the route. It crossed some of the areas they'd marked as good digging areas.

"You can ignore all this section, I think." Tatum pointed at the northern part of the route. "Too close to Grape Creek. He wouldn't dig so close to a large population."

"My thoughts exactly," Foster said. "What about the rest?"

Zoe looked down at her page of scribbles. For the past hour she'd been playing with the variables of Rossmo's formula—the formula used for geographic profiling. She'd managed to nail a set of variables that worked well for both Nicole and Maribel. She could shift the values a bit, according to her estimation of the killer's psyche.

How confident had he been with his third victim?

She thought of Harry's email. Short message, with none of the rage of the previous email. The tone was almost smug. He was *very* confident. She jotted a few numbers.

"Do we have an area that's between eight and ten miles from his home?" she asked.

"Earlier you said six to eight," Foster pointed out.

"I told you it was inaccurate," she said irritably.

"Well . . . that rules out the road by the lake completely. And South Burma Road."

They all scrutinized the map.

"So either here . . . or here." Lyons pointed out two digging areas on North Burma Road.

"Any guesses?" Foster asked.

"The southern one," Zoe said. "It's not Tulia—it's a different type of soil that Dr. Yermilov said was okay for digging but not ideal."

"So?"

"He buried her in a shallower grave. There must have been a good reason."

Foster grabbed the mic of the portable radio. Zoe listened to him dictate the coordinates, feeling numb. She prayed she'd gotten it right.

He drove past three patrol cars on the way, and his heart thudded like a hummingbird's when he arrived at the spot. He looked around nervously as he got out of the car. Being spotted now would be the end.

He was so nervous and dizzy that it took him a few minutes to find the exact spot where the girl was buried. He was sobbing in frustration by the time he finally noticed it. It was irony at its worst—thumbing his nose at the police for being unable to find the victims, only to be thwarted by the same problem. But there it was—he saw the imperceptible signs. The layout of the pebbles scattered on the sand. The slight irregularity in the slope of the soil. No one but him could have possibly found it.

The laptop and the burner phone were inside a bag covered in sand next to the pit. He unplugged the laptop from the cable, turned off the phone, and tossed them both into the back of his van. His anxiety abated as he did it.

Now for the girl.

On the way to the spot, he'd managed to convince himself that she'd positively seen him. He had to get rid of her before the police found her.

He grabbed the shovel from the back of the van and plunged it into the soil. The grave was shallow, he knew, and he could dig down to the box in a few minutes.

He had no intention of digging it up completely. All he needed was a narrow hole all the way to the box.

Scoop after scoop, the pit in the ground grew deeper. The sun was high and blazing with infernal heat. He was drenched in sweat, the back of his neck tingling with sunburn. His motions were jerky and quick, fueled with fear and rage.

The shovel thumped against the wooden box. He scooped some more sand and widened the hole, uncovering the box's brown surface.

Any hope he had that the girl was already gone evaporated as she began screaming through the gag.

He ran to the van, put back the shovel, and picked up a large sledgehammer, congratulating himself for keeping it in the van. He dragged it back to the pit, his muscles screaming with pain.

Two or three blows on the box's top was all it would take. The girl's head was just beyond the wood.

He raised the hammer and swung. The angle was awkward, and he twisted his hands at the last second, his shoulder nearly dislocating itself. The hammer hit the wood sideways without much strength. It barely scratched the surface.

The girl's screams became frantic as he swung again, hitting sand this time. Damn it! The hole was too narrow to get a good swing.

He shifted the hammer, tried for another tactic. Bringing the hammer vertically down with all his strength.

Slam.

A large piece of wood shot up, tumbling in the air. This was better. This would get it done.

Slam.

Another dent. Good.

Slam.

He was sweating, his arms trembling. Just a few more of those, and he'd—

And then he heard them. The sirens.

He frantically slammed the hammer down again and again.

Slam. Slam. Slam.

But the wood was too tough. If he had a few more minutes, he could get it done. But they were getting close. He had to run.

Letting out another sob, he ran back to the van, pulled the door open, and jumped in. The sledgehammer's handle jammed into his chest painfully, and he whimpered, struggling to move it out of his way as he started the engine.

He couldn't go back the way he'd come. He heard the police sirens from that direction, knew they were hurtling over the dirt road in his direction right now. Instead he drove forward, van juddering over the rubble, its frame creaking noisily as he accelerated, driving off.

"Five-thirteen, this is nine-oh-two—do you copy?"

The patrolman's voice vibrated as if he was running. He'd addressed Foster directly, disregarding dispatch, protocols bending and breaking under the strain everyone could feel in their guts. Everyone was silent in the room. Zoe's eyes locked on Foster as he answered.

"This is five-thirteen, go ahead."

"I'm here with kilo twenty-two," the patrolman said. That was the K-9 unit they'd sent to the northern part of Burma Road. "The dog's pulling hard, and there are fresh tire marks on the ground, over."

"Nine-oh-two, five-thirteen. Which way are you headed?"

"Five-thirteen, nine-oh-two. We're heading west. I . . . hang on." A pause. "There's a pit ahead. Someone was digging here."

Zoe and Tatum exchanged looks.

"Why isn't it covered?" Zoe muttered. "I don't like this."

"Nine-oh-two, proceed with caution," Foster said. "Suspect could be nearby."

"Copy, five-thirteen. We're getting close to the hole. The dog is heading straight to it."

They waited, time ticking by, nerve racking. The rest of the channel went silent, all radio chatter lost as dispatch and the rest of the patrol vehicles listened in.

"Five-thirteen, this is nine-oh-two. We reached the pit. There's definitely something wooden buried here."

"Nine-oh-two, this is five-thirteen. Can you hear the girl?"

"Negative. Digging."

"She might have run out of air," Tatum said.

"Or maybe there was acid in that thing after all," Lyons said.

"There was no acid." Zoe gritted her teeth, hoping she was right. Facing a dead, acid-burned corpse would be devastating. She tried to convince herself she was right, but she couldn't. She had no way of knowing what the killer was really thinking.

"Nine-oh-two, this is five-thirteen," Foster said but then didn't continue.

Of course. What could he possibly say? *Dig faster? Let us know what's going on?*

All they could do was wait.

The world was a blur. Juliet was dizzy, exhausted to the brink of unconsciousness. Her entire body ached. She could hear vague sounds above her and knew she was supposed to care. That it mattered. But she couldn't make a sound, couldn't even move. She thought back to last night, to her birthday party.

She should have agreed to the cake and the sparkler. Right now, telling the waiter not to bring it seemed like a sad mistake. It would have been nice. Sweet chocolate, a shiny light, her friends singing to her. She wished she could go back in time and make it happen. She wanted to tell Tiffany how grateful she was they'd come to celebrate her birthday.

She wished she could hug Tommy, kiss his nose, hear his laughter.

Something scratched against the wood on top of her. What was it?

And then, light, impossibly bright. She shut her eyes, moving her face aside, and felt something amazing. A draft of wind. And fresh air. She inhaled deeply, sensing . . . something. Something so immense she couldn't even process it.

"Hey, are you all right? Can you move? Oh god."

Hands on her face, removing that awful gag from her mouth. She couldn't say anything, but she took a lungful of air through her mouth.

A voice by her side. "Five-thirteen, this is nine-oh-two. We have the girl. She's alive."

CHAPTER 67

Juliet lay in the white hospital bed, feeling a bit fuzzy, her limbs too heavy to move. It was hard for her to focus on anything for long. After she'd been trapped in utter darkness, the amount of color and light in the room was slightly overwhelming. She kept shutting her eyes to rest, then opening them when she suddenly worried it might all be taken away, slamming her back into that box.

The police told her she'd spent between eight and fourteen hours in the box, but she knew they were wrong. She'd been there days. She'd insisted on it several times, in fact, grabbing the woman detective's wrist hard to make her understand. And then they'd given her something. Now nothing seemed particularly important or pressing. She drifted in and out of consciousness as if she were occasionally dipping her toes in a cold pool. The only time she'd become alert was when the nurse had turned off the light. They'd switched it back on when she wouldn't stop screaming.

Her mom had been with her for a couple of hours and promised to bring Tommy the next day. Juliet had been relieved when she left. Her mother's tendency was to talk incessantly when stressed, and she wore Juliet down.

Now someone was in her room again. The female detective who had talked to her before, and two strangers, introducing themselves as

Agent Gray and Zoe Bentley. Juliet wasn't sure if Zoe was a federal agent or a detective or what, but maybe it was a bit rude to ask.

"Juliet," Zoe said. "We were hoping you could try to remember more about the encounter. It would really help us to catch the guy who did this to you."

Remembering. Now there was a thing she didn't want to do right now. "I told the detective . . . it's all gone. I remember getting home, but then . . ." She shook her head softly.

"You were drugged," Agent Gray said. "He gave you Rohypnol. Short-term amnesia is a common side effect of the drug."

Juliet blinked. "Roofies? Isn't that a rape drug? Did he—"

"He didn't," Zoe quickly said.

How did she know? Had they done any physical tests on her when she was asleep? Her skin crawled at the thought of that man touching her. Her eyes blurred with tears.

"I don't remember anything. I don't know what to tell you." Her tongue was thick in her mouth; talking was impossibly hard. She wished they'd leave.

"Even the tiniest detail could help us a lot," Zoe said. "You remember the ride home, right?"

Luis and Tiffany in the front seats, Luis's hand under Tiffany's skirt. "Yes."

"You got home. And then what?"

"I . . . walked to the door."

"Do you remember unlocking it?"

Had she? She clenched her fist. "No . . . I don't think so. But I remember it being open. I waved Tiffany goodbye."

"And then what did you do?"

"I went to the kitchen."

"Why?"

"I think I was thirsty." No. That was wrong. She needed to pee. And she'd drunk a lot in the pub. "I don't remember. Maybe I went to the bathroom."

"You didn't." Zoe's voice was intent. "You went to the kitchen. Why?"

"I . . . I don't remember." Tears were running down her cheeks. Her lips were trembling.

"Zoe," Agent Gray said softly to the woman. "She doesn't remember. The Rohypnol—"

"Don't think with your eyes," Zoe told Juliet, leaning closer. Her stare was so intense Juliet wanted to flee. "Think with all your senses. What did you smell? What did you feel? What did you hear?"

"I don't know." Juliet's voice broke. "Nothing!"

"The door was open when the police went to your home. Did you close it?"

"I must have."

"Do you remember closing it?"

"I . . ."

"Zoe," Detective Lyons said firmly. "Juliet went through a lot, and—"

"Your arm is bruised," Zoe said. "Someone grabbed you."

All the people Juliet had seen since she'd been rescued had been so kind and full of sympathy. But this woman seemed mostly annoyed with her.

"Sweat," Juliet blurted. "I remember the smell of sweat. A stranger's sweat."

Zoe leaned back.

"And a knife at my throat. I think it was a knife. He . . . he forced me to the kitchen."

"Did you see his face?"

"No. He was behind me."

"When you entered the kitchen, the window was just in front of you. At night, with the light on, you would have seen his reflection. Do you remember seeing that?"

Juliet tried to recall that night, but her memories slipped away, like mist. "No. I just remember the knife. And his voice. It almost sounded as if he was mocking me. I don't know how to explain—he was . . ." She struggled, searching for a word.

"Smug?" Zoe asked.

"Yes." Juliet exhaled. "He was smug."

A small smile tweaked Zoe's lips. "Thank you." She gave Juliet's hand a squeeze.

Juliet pulled her hand away, hating this woman, the way she forced her to look back. She said nothing, just glared furiously. But Zoe didn't seem to mind. She probably didn't care how Juliet felt at all.

CHAPTER 68

It was half past nine in the evening when Zoe realized she hadn't eaten an actual meal since breakfast. When Juliet had been found alive, Lyons had bought celebratory doughnuts for everyone, and Zoe had had one. And on the way out from the hospital, she'd bought a Snickers bar from the candy dispenser.

She sat in her hotel room, crime scene photos spread on the bed, her notebook in hand, dozens of ideas that required a thorough investigation scrawled on the page.

Her stomach rumbled noisily.

She sighed and put the notebook on the bedsheet. Taking her phone, she opened her recent calls, scrolling for Joseph's number, and was about to tap it, but her finger paused, hovering above it unsteadily.

Joseph was a nice guy, and she enjoyed going out with him. Spending another night with him was an alluring prospect. But she also knew it would lead nowhere.

At the time, she'd needed a distraction. She'd been worried sick about Andrea, needed something, *anything*, to take her mind off the idea of Rod Glover stalking her sister. And Tatum had been unavailable, still angry at her for . . . whatever reason. But now, meeting with Joseph was just a way to pass the time.

Eating dinner with Tatum was different. It was a struggle to put her finger on the exact reason. Perhaps because they worked together.

Though she'd partnered with people before, and she wasn't sure it felt the same. It had bothered her when he'd been furious with her, and she didn't usually care what people thought about her.

They'd never really talked through their argument. The Schrodinger case and the urgency with Andrea had swept it down the current of time. It was for the best.

Or maybe it wasn't?

Maybe giving the matter the closure it deserved was better. She'd tried to apologize once, but Tatum had been furious at the time, and perhaps she'd managed to botch the entire thing. It was time she apologized again. And then they'd have dinner because she was *starving*.

She left her room and walked over to Tatum's door. She rapped on it, and a moment later she heard him say sleepily, "Just a moment."

As she waited, her thoughts went back to the last crime scene. Different than the previous ones, for sure. The box with the girl hadn't been entirely covered, for some reason. And the network cable hadn't been clipped—it had simply been disconnected. Why had the killer changed his pattern?

Of course, serial killers changed their signatures and MO all the time. It was part of the fantasy's evolution. With every murder, every iteration, they fine-tuned their methods to match their experience and their needs. So why had he left the coffin partly uncovered? She frowned.

The door opened, and Tatum stood in the doorway, blinking at her sleepily. His shirt was a bit rumpled, his hair shooting to all sides.

"I just fell asleep with all my clothes on," he said. "I guess I was exhausted."

"I know how you feel," Zoe muttered. "Listen . . . I wanted to . . ."

Why had the camera been disconnected? Surely the killer wanted the entire video of the buried girl and not just part of it.

"Something you wanted?" Tatum asked.

She looked at him, her mind spinning.

"The killer," she said. "He figured out we were about to find her. That's why he disconnected the camera. And that's why . . . oh! He tried to dig her up to kill her. So she wouldn't be able to give us anything!"

"I guess it's possible."

"I'm sure of it!" She brushed past him into his room, pacing back and forth excitedly.

"Why don't you come in?" Tatum raised an eyebrow. He shut the door.

"He doesn't have a gun, just like you said," Zoe said. "Or he would have shot Juliet through the lid." Her heart thrummed in her chest.

"So . . . why didn't he finish the job?"

"He must have heard the cops approaching. He panicked and fled. They must have missed him by minutes."

"Do you want to grab something to eat?" Tatum suggested. "I'm a bit hungry."

She glanced at him. Right, that was why she'd come here. To eat. "Good idea. Let's order a pizza or something. I want to think this through."

CHAPTER 69

He sat in the basement for hours, waiting. Coming up with endless plans and actions and panicky ideas, letting them spin and churn in his head while his body hardly moved. Every second, the cops might barge into his house. Maybe someone had seen his van driving away from the burial site, mere minutes before the police showed up. Maybe the girl had seen his face, had described it in perfect detail, enough for even the shabbiest sketch artist to come up with a reasonable impression.

He'd always known the chances were against him. After all, he was hardly trying to keep a low profile. Eventually he would slip up or miss something, and he'd be caught.

But so soon?

He had a list he kept on his desk in the basement, a numbered list of all his planned experiments, slowly escalating. He crossed off each experiment as he finished it. There were twenty.

He'd managed *two*. And botched the third.

Grabbing the list, he tore it up in rage, crumpling the pieces in his fist.

And then kept waiting.

He contemplated checking out the unfinished video of the girl, but his heart wasn't in it. He kept imagining he heard footsteps upstairs, that the SWAT team was just outside the basement door. Soon they'd break open the door, shouting, "Move, move, move," perhaps tossing a flash grenade to stun him, before filling the room, slamming him to the floor, hands behind his back.

Finally, he couldn't take the tension anymore and dialed his cop friend, Dick.

The phone rang. Was Dick at the station right now, mouthing to the surrounding cops, *It's him*? Maybe they were motioning frantically for someone to trace the call. Telling Dick to act natural. He could feel his heart in his throat, nearly hung up.

"Hey!" Dick sounded cheerful when he answered. *Too cheerful.* It was probably a trap. They knew.

"Hey yourself," he said, trying to keep his voice steady. "How'd it go today?"

"We found the girl. *Alive!* She's in shock but unharmed."

"That's amazing."

"You're telling me! I was sure it was going to end up with another body. This is one of those rare days that it's good to be a cop."

"Wanna celebrate with some steak?" he asked, stopping himself from asking the question on the tip of his tongue: *Did she see his face?*

"Nah, sorry. I'm exhausted. I spent the whole goddamn day securing the scene. Next week?"

"Sure. So the girl's all right?"

"Yeah. Doesn't remember a thing, though. I guess it's shock. Doctors say it's possible the memories might return later."

He shut his eyes. Dick *could* be stringing him along . . . but he was such a bad liar. He remembered that time they'd thrown a surprise birthday party for Dick's wife. He hadn't been able to stop fidgeting the entire day.

"Here's hoping," he said, realizing he'd let the silence stretch out.

"I'm holding on to that promise for steak, okay?"

"If you bring the beer."

"Don't I always?" Dick laughed. "See ya, man."

"Bye."

His palms were sweating as he put the phone on the table. Was he really off the hook?

For now, apparently he was.

But it was only a matter of time. The girl might remember. Or they'd match the tire tracks at the burial site to his van. Or they'd figure out he'd been tipped off about the search, start questioning everyone, asking who they talked to. And Dick would say, "No one. Who would I tell? Oh, right, I remember—it's probably nothing, but . . ."

He unfurled his left fist, the torn, crumpled pieces from the list of experiments still in it. He wanted to go on. How many more experiments would he manage before they got him? Two? Three? Five?

One?

He had to make it count.

Item twenty on the list was his masterpiece. The one that would nail his spot in the pages of history. He could afford to skip a few. He'd have to buy a signal booster for it to work, but he'd already done his research. He knew where to get it so it would be delivered the next day.

And maybe this time he could take the one victim who could really turn him into a legend.

CHAPTER 70

San Angelo, Texas, Monday, September 12, 2016

The constant noise in the police station on Monday morning reminded Tatum of an angry swarm of bees, if bees constantly drank coffee, shouted instructions on the phone, and walked briskly down corridors, muttering to themselves. There was a definite sense that stuff needed to get done, and if you weren't getting things done, you'd better make damn sure you found something to get done or at least look like you were getting something done.

As far as Tatum could see, the entire police force was now tasked with finding Schrodinger's Killer. Petty thieves, abusive husbands, drug dealers, and drunk drivers all got the day off from police scrutiny, free to break the law at leisure. Because unless you happened to bury women alive, the San Angelo police didn't care.

Officially, Jensen was in charge of the operation, but a tectonic shift was transpiring. The Texas Department of Public Safety had joined the circus. Texas Rangers roamed the division, and one of them, a gray-haired, stocky man, was slowly taking control of the investigation. Jensen appeared helpless against the sudden coup. Tatum guessed they'd have a day or two at most until DPS would be formally in charge.

Meanwhile, Foster was the one who actually called the shots. He assigned people to go through security cam footage, interview witnesses who had seen Juliet the night of the party, go through social media profiles of possible future victims, and do whatever else occurred to him.

They had no morning meeting, no time to *talk*. It was time to *do*. Talking could come later. And besides, Jensen was distracted because there was a press conference at nine in the morning, and the DPS major intended to join him. The citizens of San Angelo—and, in fact, the rest of Texas—all wanted to hear about the brilliant police operation that had led to the rescue of the beautiful and heroic Juliet Beach. Those were actual words Tatum had heard on the radio that morning. *Beautiful and heroic.*

Tatum found it hard to concentrate. His desk was opposite Foster's, and every few minutes someone would approach Foster, often leaning on Foster's desk and thus pointing their ass toward Tatum as they reported their findings or asked a question. The narrow passageway between the desks guaranteed that the said backsides were often inches from Tatum's head. He'd seen a plethora of rear ends that morning, of all kinds and shapes. That was not a position he enjoyed.

He gritted his teeth as yet another bum was pointed at him, this one belonging to a uniformed cop, and continued reading through the crime scene report. This time, they had a lot more to work with.

Juliet Beach had been buried inside a box almost identical to the previous boxes. A metal contraption was placed in one corner with the drawing of a skull and bones—the supposed acid container. It was empty and wasn't wired to anything—a prop, just like Zoe had intuited. Tatum saw the twisted sense in it. The so-called "experiment" involved constantly turning the feed on and off, leaving the viewers in suspense when the feed was offline. But there wouldn't be enough suspense without an imminent threat.

Several dents and scratches marred the box's wooden lid. One dent was 0.6 inches deep, and its shape indicated a heavy tool with a blunt rectangular edge, which didn't match the shovels the police had used to dig up the box. The tool had nearly gone through the lid, which was just over an inch thick.

Tatum imagined the murderer, a shadowy, faceless man slamming the heavy tool at the lid, trying to smash it to kill Juliet Beach before the police could get to her.

As in the previous instances, they found no fingerprints, hairs, fabrics, or anything similar on the box's exterior. The interior was filled with fingerprints, broken fingernails, blood, and skin cells, all probably belonging to the victim. It had all been sent to the lab.

They'd found track marks in the sand, and some were fairly recent. They'd matched a portion of the tracks to similar markings found at Nicole Medina's crime scene.

The cable that ran up from the infrared camera in the box was unclipped this time, protruding from the sand. They'd found a single fingerprint on the plastic plug. It had been checked against AFIS, the Automated Fingerprint Identification System, but the print was partial and smudged, and they'd found no match.

Contrary to popular belief, fingerprinting wasn't a magical method of identification. Given a good fingerprint or two, the system could spit a long list of possible matches after a couple of hours. But there was only so much it could do with a smudge. The database was just too large.

Still, Tatum mentally noted this. He had an idea that he wanted to check later.

The box had been buried about three feet below the surface. Underneath it was a hollow space that had caved in. This was the reason the killer hadn't been able to bury Juliet as deep as before, and this lucky happenstance was the only reason Juliet was still alive.

There were several photographs of the crime scene. Tatum wished that someone had taken a photograph before they'd begun digging. But of course, their attention had been elsewhere. Even Zoe didn't grumble about it this time. The location was a bit more remote than before, in a large field of fenced private land. The killer had presumably opened the unlocked gate in the fence to drive through. Numerous fingerprints on the gate had been matched to the officers who'd opened it and to the owner. The tire tracks of the killer's vehicle led to a different portion of the fence, which had been cut with wire cutters. No fingerprints anywhere.

How close had they been to catching him?

Tatum couldn't dislodge the "could haves," "should haves," and "if onlys" that always followed moments like these. He let himself drift on a daydream in which they'd thought to set up roadblocks on Burma Road, the serial killer had been caught, and the San Angelo citizens were throwing a parade in their—

A set of buttocks brushed his shoulders.

"Oops, sorry," the young detective apologized, shifting a bit closer to Foster's desk.

Tatum got up and strode outside. Somehow, the baking sun was better than the air-conditioned chaos inside the station.

He took out his phone and dialed the one and only Sarah Lee, his private analyst.

"Tatum, I'm not your private analyst," she said as she answered the phone. "I have actual important work here."

"That's what I admire about you—the way you manage to multitask all those different things. *And* on top of that to take care of a dog. How *is* Grace, by the way?"

"Grace is fine, Tatum." She tried to hide the smile in her voice, quite unsuccessfully. "What do you want?"

"I have a fingerprint."

"I'd say you have ten. That's how fingerprints usually work."

"It's from a crime scene."

"Run it against AFIS, and you'll have your results in no time."

"It's a crap fingerprint. AFIS can't match it."

"What do you want from me?"

"You remember the Klaus case back in LA? It was . . . about three years ago."

She took a second to recall it. "Oh yeah, bank robbery, right?"

"Right. We had two partial fingerprints, and you did some magic incantation and got a match to a similar crime."

"It wasn't a magic incantation."

"You mixed it in your witch's cauldron—"

"Tatum."

"And added a newt's eye and some pixie dust, and then opened your spell book—"

"That's not how it went."

"And spoke the magic words—"

"I just ran it against a much smaller database."

"Well." Tatum grinned. "It felt like magic to me. Can you do it with my fingerprint?"

She sighed. "What I did then was run it against fingerprints found at other robbery crime scenes in the area in the previous three months. And even then, you might remember, I got a bunch of false matches."

"And one true match," Tatum pointed out.

"Okay, fine."

"Can you run my fingerprint against crimes in Texas from the last ten years?"

"That's your definition of *small*?" she asked. "I'd never get a match like that."

"Okay." He hesitated. "Make that the past three years, and just San Angelo."

"Mmmm." She didn't sound thrilled. "It's going to take a bit of work, and you know I do have people I actually *need* to do stuff for—"

"But none of them are as charming as I am."

"You'd be surprised. Let me see what I can do."

"Thanks, Sarah. You're the bee's knees."

"Yeah, yeah." She hung up.

Smiling, Tatum slid the phone into his pocket. He nipped inside and sent Sarah the image file of the smudged fingerprint. Then, not wanting to endure the ongoing butt parade, he decided he could go grab a coffee and a sandwich somewhere nearby.

Sarah's email landed in his inbox just as he returned to the station's parking lot. He read it on his phone, leaving the engine on for the sake of the air-conditioning. There was a possible match to seven crime reports. Three gang-related shootings, two break-ins, one auto theft, and one rape. There were no details on the files, just names and local case file numbers.

He walked inside and crouched over Foster's desk, pointing his own butt at the back of his empty chair.

"I have some possible matches to the fingerprint," he said. "One is a rape."

"Seriously?" Foster tensed. "Do you have a name?"

"Derek Woodard."

Foster's shoulders sagged. "That asshole. He's in prison. We got him for a series of sexual assaults. He targeted old pensioners."

"Damn." Tatum ignored the twinge of disappointment in his mind. "Well, I have six other matches here."

"Let's see them."

They went over the list, checking the case file numbers. Three more were incarcerated, one was dead, and one had been shot in his back and was now in a wheelchair.

The only two remaining cases were the auto theft and one of the break-ins. Although no one had been caught in the auto-theft crime, it involved three perpetrators who'd broken one of the car's windows and taken the car for a ride, finally leaving it discarded, all of its tires flat, outside San Angelo. It had happened nine months before, and Tatum couldn't think of a crime that was less likely to involve their killer.

The other, which Tatum thought was a break-in, was just an attempted break-in of a local gas station, four months before. A window had been smashed, and once the alarm had sounded, the perpetrator had fled. This wasn't likely to be related either, but the case file did note that the unknown person had been caught on the security camera trying to break in. The actual footage was missing. The fingerprints didn't hit a relevant match on AFIS.

"I'll go have a look," Tatum said.

"I can send someone over," Foster answered. "You don't need to trouble yourself."

Tatum glanced around him, the busy, angry hum feeling almost unbearable. "It's okay. I could use a break."

CHAPTER 71

The gas station was on the outskirts of San Angelo, and only one other vehicle was there when Tatum parked his car. A woman stood by the pumps fueling her car while three children sat in the back seat. She seemed tired to the point of exhaustion and ignored her kids as they made faces at her through the back window. Tatum smiled at her, trying to convey sympathy, and entered the station's store.

A thin man stood behind the counter, and as Tatum approached him, he let out a hiccup.

Tatum pulled out his badge. "Agent Gray, FBI. I wanted to ask you about the—"

"Hic."

Tatum blinked. The hiccup had been somewhat violent and had broken his train of thought. "Uh . . . I wanted to ask you about the attempted—"

"Hic."

"Sorry. Um. Do you want a drink of water?"

"No," the man said. "Hic."

"It could help with your hiccups."

"It won't."

"Right." Tatum slung his thumbs through the belt. "I wanted to ask you about the attempted break-in that happened four months ago. Did you work here back then?"

"Hic. Yes."

"I understand that the man who tried to break in was caught on camera."

"Yes." The man gestured at a screen that was split to four, displaying the security feeds of the gas station's cameras. Two displayed the inside of the store. One showed the front door. The fourth was aimed at the gas pumps. Tatum saw the woman outside on the screen. She had finished filling the gas tank and stared into space as her kids took turns mashing their faces against the window.

"Can I see the footage?"

The man raised an eyebrow. "Hic. It was a long time ago. The computer only retains footage a month back. Hic."

"And you didn't save a copy of that film?" Tatum asked incredulously.

"No. Why—hic—would I? The man wore a mask."

"What kind of mask?"

"A ski mask. It hid his face almost completely. He broke that window over there." The man pointed at a window near the door. "Then the alarm started, and he ran. Not much of a movie."

Tatum kept waiting for the next hiccup, feeling a strange tension coiling inside him. The man met his eye calmly. The hiccups were apparently gone.

"Can you tell me—"

"Hic."

"Are you sure you don't want a drink of water? It really helps with hiccups."

"It won't help me."

"Why not?"

"I've been—hic—hiccuping for a while now."

"Maybe drinking water would fix that."

"Hic. It didn't fix it for the past four years."

"You've been hiccuping for . . . four years?"

"Hic. Yes. And drinking water didn't help. You know what else didn't help? Holding my breath. And—hic—drinking water from an upside-down glass. And being surprised or—hic—frightened. And biting a lemon. And helpful suggestions by—hic—FBI agents."

"I'm sorry."

"I don't like hiccuping. It doesn't help my sex life. It wakes me up at—hic—night. So I'm tired, which makes me hiccup even more. Also some people think it's funny. Hic." The man eyed Tatum suspiciously.

"I don't think it's funny," Tatum said, feeling a bit guilty.

"Anyway, there's no footage. Hic. But I watched it several times. Just a guy with a mask and gloves. He broke the window with a hammer, then ran. Hic."

"Gloves?" Tatum asked, surprised. "I thought there was a fingerprint."

"There was." He indicated the window. "He wore latex gloves, and they—hic—tore when the window was broken. So he got a fingerprint on the glass."

Tatum nodded, distracted. It didn't sound like their guy. "Thanks. And good luck with the—"

"Hic."

"Yeah."

He left the store, the blazing heat hitting him straight in the face. For a moment, his eyes adjusting to the bright light outside, he could almost imagine he'd walked into the middle of the desert. Across the road, he could see nothing but a flat expanse of sand, spotted with cacti and numerous rocks.

He frowned, then looked behind him. The security camera was easily visible above the automatic glass door. And looking from where he stood, it was impossible to tell its exact angle. He turned back to the large empty field, then glanced at the camera.

He had a crazy idea. Pulling his phone, he dialed Zoe.

"Are you near the map?"

"Yes."

"Can you check something for me? I'm at a gas station on Route 67, about a mile outside San Angelo's south side. Can you see if it's one of our easy digging spots?"

"Hang on."

He waited, feeling as if he was wasting his time and hers along with it.

"Yes, it's in one of those areas," she finally said. "Why?"

"Well . . . there's a gas station here, and there was a break-in attempt four months ago. The fingerprint they found in the crime scene yesterday might match the one here. The security camera above the front door looks like it's aimed straight at the area across the road."

A second passed as Zoe processed this. "You think the unsub tried to break in to the gas station to destroy the security footage?"

"That's what I had in mind. I mean . . . if he suspected the camera caught him killing someone. What do you think?"

"He's pretty careful. But if it was an early killing, he would have been very agitated. It could spur him to react fast . . . like he did yesterday, trying to dig up Juliet to kill her. It's the same reaction, a sudden gut fear that prods him into a risky maneuver. I can see it happening."

"Right," Tatum said, encouraged. "I hope that guy with the cadaver dog isn't busy. I've got a job for him."

CHAPTER 72

It took Shelley, the cadaver dog, less than ten minutes to home in on a spot deep in the field, half hidden from the road by a few dry shrubs and cacti. Once there, the dog paused, scratched the earth, and whined. And Victor looked at him and said, "She found something all right."

This time, there was absolutely no urgency, and they did it right. The crime scene technicians showed up and set up a crime scene tape and a wide three-walled screen to hide the excavation from the road. Several cops were dispatched to stop any curious onlookers or journalists from getting near. And the grave was dug carefully while Tatum and Victor watched, soon joined by Zoe and Foster. The entire crime scene was filling with cops and rangers, and Curly had already shown up as well, standing by Tatum's side, waiting for the remains.

"Second body in five days," Victor said sadly.

"Third for me," Curly said.

"This city never used to be so violent back in the day," Victor muttered.

"Yeah, it's a terrible business."

Tatum glanced down at the dog, who was sniffing at his shoe. "Your dog . . . Shelley is amazing at what she does."

"She really is." Victor sniffed. "Saw that Jones and Buster were on the front page of the *San Angelo Standard-Times* with that girl, Juliet."

"Jones and Buster?" Tatum asked, confused. "Oh, that guy with the dog who found her? Yeah. It was a nice picture."

"It was."

The officers got out of the grave one by one, and then one of them leaned forward into the hole and yanked the lid. All of them turned away, grunting in disgust.

Victor sighed again and shook his head. "Come on, Shelley—let's go write our report."

The K-9 officer left, and Tatum approached the grave, Zoe already two steps ahead of him.

This one was definitely different.

For one, these remains were much older. The body had suffered from insect activity, and putrefaction was very advanced. The insects could reach her easily, since the box was not as well made as the previous ones, and there were thin gaps between the planks. The box was square, not rectangular, more like a crate. The skeletal body was curled inside in a fetal position. If this girl had been buried alive like this, her death must have been even worse than the other victims, with her body forced into this unnatural position just so she could fit into the box.

Tatum turned away, feeling sick. In the background he heard some muttering from the people around him.

"No camera," Zoe said dryly.

Tatum felt a flash of anger, and he wasn't sure if he was angry at himself for not seeing it or at Zoe's ability to notice such a detail when faced with such a horrid scene. He forced himself to look again and saw she was right. The box was as plain as could be. Perhaps its original use had been to contain fruits or vegetables. No infrared camera was located inside or a hole through which the cable could be fitted.

"Excuse me." Curly shouldered his way through.

"We'll need to lift the box out," Foster told him. "No room for you in the pit."

"Just take care not to spill dirt into the box while you dig."

They ended up closing the box before they commenced digging again, freeing it from the soil. Tatum took a few steps aside, watching them. He'd followed a threadbare lead, and it had ended up leading them to another dead girl. He was anything but victorious.

"That's his first victim," Zoe said, joining him by his side.

"You sure?"

She shrugged. "Can't be sure of anything. But it looks like it. Just the basic fantasy, bury a girl alive. He didn't even have a box in the right size. The location is far from perfect, too close to the city. Not well hidden. He was lucky no one saw him."

"He probably buried her at night. It must have been pitch dark."

"Yeah. But still, there are markings of inexperience everywhere. Then, once he was done and had his sexual relief, he became focused enough to notice the gas station. And he began wondering."

"About the security cameras."

"He was worried that the cameras might have caught him. He put on a ski mask and some gloves . . . I'm guessing he had both of those handy. And he tried to break inside to destroy the footage."

"The camera isn't even aimed at this area," Tatum said. "What a dumb asshole."

"Right." Zoe raised her eyebrow, clearly surprised at his angry tone. "He isn't dumb anymore. He had plenty of time to think about his mistakes and to avoid making them again."

Tatum nodded, not wanting to debate it. He was tired of analyzing the killer, trying to get into his head. For once, he just wanted to think of him as a monster, a vile evil creature that couldn't be explained, that should be hunted with pitchforks and torches and destroyed.

"He might have a link to the victim," Zoe added. "Maybe he lived close to her; maybe she was an acquaintance. If we figure out that link, we might catch him."

"Maybe," Tatum grunted.

Perhaps sensing his mood, Zoe walked away, probably trying to imagine what the killer had seen that night. By tomorrow she'd have a perfect picture of how the event of that night had taken place.

The officers managed to pry the box out of the pit, and Curly approached it, instructing them to be careful. He opened the lid, his hands gloved, and leaned into the box, inspecting the body. Tatum imagined him taking the skeleton's pulse to determine if it was really dead and let a humorless smile stretch his lips.

Curly pulled out a small purse and handed it to Foster without a word. Tatum stepped forward, feeling curious.

Foster opened the purse and took a cursory glance at it. "Some money here, forty dollars and change. A crumpled bus ticket . . . ah. There's the driver's lice—" His mouth went slack, eyes widening, filling with surprise and pain.

"What is it?" Tatum asked.

"I know this woman," Foster croaked. "She . . . we went to school together. Debra Miller. Aw, shit."

"I'm sorry."

"She was so lovely," Foster said. "Everyone adored her. But she left town after school. Pretty sure I heard she moved to California."

Tatum said nothing, watching as Curly examined the body. Despite her supposed move to California, this woman had ended up in a crate, buried under the soil of her hometown.

CHAPTER 73

Zoe joined Lyons to notify Debra's parents.

"Why tag along?" Lyons asked her on the way. "There's literally nothing harder in this job than notifying family. Do you like suffering?"

Zoe wasn't sure if Lyons meant to ask if she liked to suffer or if she enjoyed other people's suffering, but the answer was the same in any case. "No, I don't. But people reveal a lot when their guard is down."

"This is the worst kind of notification," Lyons muttered.

"We don't need to give them the gory details," Zoe pointed out. "Especially since we don't know."

"That's not what I mean. Yeah, sure, notifying parents about a violent death is terrible, but it's even worse when we don't know it's her for sure."

"Oh, right." Zoe knew what Lyons meant. They would tell Debra's parents that they found her body . . . but then they'd ask if there was anything to assist in verifying it was her, because of the body's decomposed state. And then, as predictable as the sun in the morning, hope showed its ugly head. *Maybe it's not her,* the parent would point out. *You could be wrong.* Suddenly, they saw a lifesaver they could cling to in this terrible storm of grief and loss. They'd refuse to entertain the almost certain outcome that no, it wasn't a pickpocket who had stolen their daughter's purse and then gotten killed. It was their daughter all along.

Which only meant they'd end up being notified twice. The first time when the body was found and the second when its identity was confirmed.

They parked next to a house painted in a cheerful white and yellow, a nice green picket fence surrounding the yard. But as they got out of the car and walked to the front door, Zoe noticed signs of neglect everywhere. Wilting flowers in the garden, surrounded by weeds. Grimy windows. Peeling wall paint. She could hear the faint buzz of flies all around her.

Lyons knocked on the door, then knocked again.

"Just a minute," a man said from inside.

They waited for what seemed like much more than a minute, and just when Lyons was about to knock again, the door opened. The man who opened it was bald, his face crinkled and weary. He wore a stained white shirt. On first glance, Zoe guessed his age to be around eighty, and then she realized he was younger than that. Probably not much more than sixty. But he seemed like a man whose life had worn him down.

"Mr. Miller?" Lyons said.

"Yeah."

"I'm Detective Lyons. Can we come in?"

His shoulders slumped. "Is this about Debra?"

"It's better if we discuss this inside."

He folded his arms. "How much trouble is she in?"

Lyons hesitated. "Sir . . . it might be best if you sit down for this."

His eyes widened. "Is she . . . hurt?"

Lyons sighed, clearly deciding they weren't about to be invited inside. "Mr. Miller, I'm afraid that Debra is dead."

"Dead?" The word came out as a whisper.

"We believe so. Yes, sir."

"You . . . *believe*?" There it was. Hope. "You aren't sure?"

"We're reasonably sure. We found a body with your daughter's driver's license in its purse."

"Does she look like my daughter?"

Lyons swallowed. "The body is in a bad shape. We believe she was murdered four months ago."

"Four months ago?" The hope seemed to evaporate. "That's quite accurate."

"When was the last time you saw your daughter?" Lyons asked.

Mr. Miller took a shuddering breath. "Well . . . last time was around the beginning of May."

Zoe and Lyons exchanged looks. The gas station had been broken into on May 6.

Mr. Miller turned around and scuffled inside, leaving the door open. Zoe and Lyons followed him.

The house had a cold and abandoned feeling to it. Dust and dirt were everywhere. The lights were turned mostly off, the curtains drawn, leaving just enough light to walk without stumbling into something. Miller shuffled to the kitchen and turned on a neon lamp that hummed noisily, glowing with a white hostile light. He slumped onto a chair by a small, peeling wooden table. There were two other chairs, and Zoe sat in one, letting Lyons take the other.

"You say she was murdered. Who did it? How?" he asked, his voice raspy, his eyes gleaming wet.

"We don't know the exact details yet," Lyons said.

"What *do* you know?"

"Four months ago you saw your daughter, and you haven't talked to her since," Zoe said softly, ignoring the question. "Why didn't you report her missing?"

"We thought she just left." He shook his head. "She was always disappearing for months at a time. Showing up unannounced, looking like hell. We knew she was using. Sometimes she had a black eye or a swollen lip, but she always said she was fine, refused to give us any details. Sometimes she'd call from jail. I went to bail her out three times."

He let out a long, hopeless groan. A tear materialized and ran down his cheek.

"She'd been the sweetest, happiest kid when she was at school. So popular, surrounded by friends. When school ended, she just got . . . lost. She started working a minimum wage job at the nearby cinema, didn't want to go to college, began smoking. We didn't know what to do. Then she announced she was going to California, that she found a marvelous job opportunity there. We were so relieved. But she stopped calling after a while, and when she showed up next, it was easy to see that a good job was the furthest thing from her life."

He looked at the wall, his eyes white, empty, and quivering, tears rolling from them steadily, following each other in the grooves of his face. "The men in her life were the ones who destroyed her—I'm sure of it. They say a girl learns how a man behaves from her father, but I never laid a hand on her. I swear."

"Some women find the wrong men despite their parents," Zoe said. She wasn't trying to comfort him, just pointing out a flaw in his reasoning, but he smiled at her sadly.

"Was it one of them who did it?" he asked.

"We don't know yet," Lyons said. "Do you have any names?"

"None. She always said she was done with them. I'd ask who gave her that bruise or broke her finger, and she'd say it didn't matter, that she was done with him for good. I don't know if she always returned to the same guy or if she really ditched them every time, finding others just as bad."

"And what happened the last time you saw her?" Lyons asked.

"She showed up a day before. Looking worse than ever. Thin. Broken. Do you ladies have children?"

They both shook their heads.

"You have no idea how it feels to have your child show up like that. And Martha and I decided that this time, she wasn't going to just disappear with some money in her hand. No, we were going to save her." He snorted, then hid his face in his palms, shaking.

A clock hung on the wall of the kitchen, and it ticked. Zoe could almost swear the seconds were slowing down, each longer than the last.

Finally, he removed his hands. His face was a mess. "We told her she had to stay. That we were taking her to rehab. To therapy. We were going to help her get better. She said she didn't need that. She shouted at us, that she didn't need our help, that she was leaving forever this time. I . . . I said some things I shouldn't have. Oh god, the things I told her. If you ever have children, never show them your disappointment in how they turned out."

Zoe wished Tatum were there. He always seemed to know what to say to make people feel better.

"She left. And we didn't hear from her again. We thought she'd return, like she always did, but she didn't. And then Martha died, a month ago. She just . . . died. Her heart stopped working. It broke, I guess."

He folded his arms. "And that's it."

Lyons asked him questions, tried to get a better idea of where she'd gone, if she'd had any friends she'd get in touch with, anything at all. But Debra's father's answers became shorter and shorter all the way to monosyllabic words and then nothing at all.

Finally, after Lyons ascertained he didn't need any help, he gave her the name of Debra's dentist, who could probably assist in verifying it really was her body. And then he shut down completely, like a toy that had run out of batteries.

CHAPTER 74

San Angelo, Texas, Thursday, May 5, 2016

He pushed the door and walked into the pub, sat on a stool, jaw clenched in anger. This was how every day ended. His entire body clenched tight, as if about to explode. It only became bearable after a few beers.

For the past few days, he'd begun drinking earlier than usual. He'd done his job properly, but at the end of the day, it didn't matter, did it? Failure was still failure, even if it wasn't his fault.

The barman didn't even ask him what he wanted anymore. He just nodded at him and poured his beer. He'd become a regular.

"Hey," a woman said as he emptied his first glass. "Don't I know you?"

He was about to shrug, to shake his head, to tell her that no, she didn't. He glanced at her, and the words died on his lips.

"Yeah, I know you," she said brightly. "You . . . we went to the same school, right?"

"Debra?" he asked, not believing.

Was it really the same girl? The lovely, pure girl he'd fantasized about in all those long classes? Same lips, same nose . . . but that was where the similarity ended. She was almost skeletal, her cheekbones protruding sharply. Her hair, once a cascade of curls, was a tangled mess, looking almost sticky. Her skin had a strange tone to it, oily. And her eyes. They were so . . . dull.

"That's right." She smiled, happy to be recognized. It probably didn't happen too often. "How have you been?"

It took him a few seconds to figure out she didn't know his name, which was no big surprise. He bought her a beer and casually mentioned his own name as he told her a dumb story about a letter that he'd gotten from school. He saw the relief in her sunken dead eyes when she caught it, didn't have to skirt around it in her conversation, calling him *babe* and *dude*.

She was impressed when he told her what he did, and it made him feel better about himself. When he asked her what she'd been doing, mentioning he'd heard that she was in California, she looked away. She talked vaguely about a good job she had there and an asshole boyfriend. But now, apparently, she was done with both the job and the boyfriend. And California, as well.

"I was actually just about to get on a bus," she said. "Maybe tonight."

"A bus where?"

She shrugged. "Who knows. Somewhere far. I need to start again. Clean slate, you know?"

"Yeah."

"What I really need," she said, "is some time to think."

His body clenched as if she'd kicked him in the gut.

"I know exactly what you mean." His voice cracked, and he stuck a hand in his pocket. The plastic bag almost felt hot to his touch. He'd bought it a few months earlier and carried it around, thinking of it as just one more fantasy. He never believed he'd have the courage to use it. He opened it, sliding out one round pill into his palm.

She had to go to the bathroom a few minutes later, perhaps to avoid the apparent lull in conversation. When she was gone, he took his hand from his pocket, palming the pill. He glanced around, already drenched in sweat. No one was looking. One quick move and the pill was in her half-finished glass. It seemed to take forever for it to dissipate into nothing. Any moment the barman or one of the people around him would ask and point at the fizzing pill.

But no one did.

She was half out of it by the time he told her he'd give her a ride to the bus station. She confessed she didn't have money for the bus, and he shoved a hundred-dollar bill into her hand, which she took without complaining, stuffing it into her pocket, clearly used to taking money from men she hardly knew.

Her eyelids were half-closed within seconds of her entering the van. She never even noticed the crate in the back. The digging implements.

For a moment he considered dropping the whole thing. His heart thumped so loudly it almost sounded as if it were plugged into the van's stereo system. But his mind was already in high gear, imagining the act. And *she'd asked for it.*

He drove them to the nearest location. It was dark, of course, but he knew the way. He stopped the van a few yards from the pit's location. He got out, taking a small LED light and a shovel with him, and walked to the pit, finding the mark he'd left there. He shoveled off the sand from the pit's cover and removed it. Just looking at its yawning dark abyss made a shiver run through his body. This was actually happening.

He opened the back of the van and pulled the crate out. He dragged it through the sand, already regretting not parking the van closer, its back pointed at the pit.

Next time, he thought, and it startled him. There wouldn't *be* a next time. This was a onetime thing.

Then he strode to the front side of the van, opening the passenger's door. He unbuckled her seatbelt, smelling her as he leaned across her body. She smelled of perfume and rot, and he shuddered. She muttered as he helped her out, and he half cajoled her, half dragged her to the crate.

It had always seemed like a huge crate to him, but now that he needed to push her into it, he realized how small it was. Why had he never searched for anything bigger?

Because you never really thought you'd go through with it.

He began shoving her inside. She muttered angrily. He pushed harder. She started to resist, but he forced her with all his strength. She shouted faintly, but there was no one around to hear. She scratched him, whimpering, and he gave her one final shove. She fell inside, hitting her head, crying. He closed the box just as she reached out to grab the edge, and the wooden lid hit her fingers. She cried again, pulling the fingers away. He latched it shut.

Pulling the crate into the pit in the darkness was the hardest thing he'd ever done, and he almost fell inside himself as he did it. When it finally tumbled inside, he heard her muffled shriek. He was breathing hard from the effort and the excitement.

Shoveling the soil on top of the crate, he quickly saw the problem. There wasn't enough soil around to cover it easily. He should have brought soil with him. Stupid. Stupid!

Instead he shoveled soil from all around, trying to keep the surface uniform so that it wouldn't look strange come morning. He used large rocks lying around to fill the empty space, and they landed on the crate with a loud thud, eliciting more screams.

He worked hard, not daring to stop. Soon, he couldn't hear her screams anymore, and he regretted it. He wished he could still hear her. He wished he could see her terrified face as she thumped on the lid. But of course, that was impossible.

And then it was covered. He was about to explode. He needed release.

It took only seconds, and the feeling that followed, that complete, wonderful nothingness, was the best thing he'd ever felt. He stared ahead at the dark, empty road, the silhouette of the closed gas station, the starry sky. He wondered how Debra was using her time to think.

His eyes focused on the gas station. He hadn't been worried about it earlier; it was closed. But now it hit him. What if there was a security camera there?

It would have night vision capabilities for sure. And if, by chance, it was aimed at where he was . . .

He swallowed. How had this never occurred to him before?

And the answer came to him again. Because he'd never really thought he'd go through with it.

He considered digging Debra up, telling her it had been just a joke. He'd drive her to the bus station, put her on a bus to New York. The woman was a drug addict—no one would believe a word she said.

But they might. And if there was footage . . .

Oh god.

He could destroy the footage.

No way this gas station paid for some fancy cloud storage for their footage. Their security cameras would be hooked to a computer inside. All he'd have to do was break a window, walk in, and delete the footage, and he'd be done. Among all his gear, he had a ski mask. And he always had gloves with him.

He rummaged for his toolbox. Break a window, get inside, delete the footage. It would only take two minutes. And he'd be safe.

CHAPTER 75

Dale City, Virginia, Monday, September 12, 2016

Andrea woke up with a start, knowing that something she'd heard had jarred her out of her sleep, but she wasn't sure what. Then it came again. A knock on the door. She frowned at the clock. Half past eleven. What the hell?

She got out of bed, padding barefoot to the living room. Someone knocked on the door again. A polite knock, unhurried.

"Yeah?"

"Ma'am, I'm Officer Browning from downstairs." The voice came, muffled, official. "We got a report of a stranger in your building. Are you all right?"

"There's no one here. The door was locked."

"Are you sure, ma'am? A neighbor said she saw someone climbing the emergency stairway. Do you want me to have a look around?"

Andrea's heart froze. The emergency stairway was just outside her bedroom window. She was sure it was latched, but . . . a terrible image of Rod Glover sliding through the window, hiding under her bed, waiting, like a child's nightmare. *There's a monster under the bed, Mommy.*

"Uh, hang on." She considered getting her robe, but it was in the bedroom, just next to the window. And the emergency stairway. Officer Browning would have to deal with her tank top and bralessness. She shuffled to the door, glancing through the peephole. The uniformed officer stood by the door, his face turned away from the peephole as he watched around him impatiently.

She unlatched the door, unlocked it, and pulled it open.

"Come in, but—"

He turned to face her, and her world shifted, shattering, the threat no longer behind her, no longer imagined.

His hand shot forward, grabbing her throat, squeezing, and the scream that hurtled up her throat came out strangled, croaky, weak. Glover took a step inside the house, kicking the door closed behind him. He was dressed in a cop's uniform, but his sneer was as far from a law officer's expression as anything.

"Hello, Andrea," he hissed. He put a knife to her cheek, just inches below her eye, and pressed it, letting the tip puncture the skin lightly. "Don't struggle, or Zoe will have a one-eyed sister. Don't scream. Don't do anything. You got that? Blink if you do."

Andrea blinked, terrified. Her lungs spasmed as she tried to breathe, her mouth opening and closing desperately.

"Here's the good news," Glover said. "I want you alive. I want Zoe to see the fear in your eyes when she gets back. I want her to feel like the shitty sister she is, leaving you all alone. So if you just stay still, we'll be done in no time. You got that?"

Another blink and a tear. Even if she wanted to struggle, she couldn't. Her muscles felt like butter. Spots were dancing in her vision, her lungs burning for air.

His grip slackened, and she managed to take a wheezing breath.

"Let's go to the bedroom," he suggested.

He stepped forward slowly, and she had to stumble backward to keep pace. A thought struck her—he knew where he was going. He moved calmly, his eyes already flicking to the right door, as if he had learned the apartment's layout by heart. She let out a sob.

"Shhhhh."

Step. Step. One hand on her throat, the other with the knife, dancing in front of her left eye, the tip almost close enough to touch, forcing her to shut her eyes.

"Open your eyes. Walk."

And then, just as they passed the guest room, the door opened. Glover didn't seem to realize, his eyes focused on his destination and on Andrea's terrified face. Marvin stepped out, looking confused, his eyes locking with hers. She saw the understanding there. He began moving, when Glover whipped around, fast as a snake. He slammed Andrea against the wall, the hand with the knife darting forward, stabbing Marvin's chest. Marvin gasped, his eyes glazing, and Glover punched him in the face, emitting a crack. Marvin stumbled back, falling, head hitting the doorknob. Blood pooled almost instantly on the floor by his lax body.

"No!" Andrea let out a scream, and the knife was back at her eye.

"Interesting bodyguard you had here," Glover hissed. Fury filled his eyes. "For this surprise, I'll give you something to remember me by when we're done."

He pushed her hard to the bedroom, his movements rougher than before, his face hard, angry, his teeth bared in an inhuman snarl. He whipped her around, and it was almost a relief, not being able to see his face. He pushed her hard against the bed.

There were a few seconds of nothingness, and then a cloth clenched around her throat. She remembered what Zoe had told her. Glover had a fixation with strangling his victims.

She wasn't going to make it.

Even if he really intended to keep her alive, he wouldn't be able to control his urges. He'd rape her and strangle her to death, just like he had with every other victim.

But now it was too late to do anything. The cloth bit into her throat, and she had no air. Her fingers clawed at the noose, while Glover ripped her pants, muttering curses, growling, the noises he made more bestial than human.

An image popped into her mind, from her childhood. Locked in the room, Glover pounding at the door, and Zoe hugging her, protecting her. But her sister was thousands of miles away now.

She faded into unconsciousness, the dark oblivion welcoming, but then the cloth around her neck shifted, its grip lessened by a fraction, and she could draw a quick breath of air. That was also something Glover did. He knew how to keep his victims alive and conscious till the end.

She inhaled his smell, and it was rank, sweaty, unclean. She struggled, not wanting this thing to touch her anymore. He laughed, pushed her face into the mattress, his fingers on her skin, groping, probing.

An explosion.

It made her ears ring, and she let out a terrified scream. The cloth had disappeared from her throat, and she could scream freely now, over and over, as much as she liked, and she did. She turned around, seeing the blurry shape of Marvin standing inside the room, leaning against the wall, a gun in his hand.

She searched for Glover, glimpsed him in the corner, holding his side, grimacing. His predatory eyes locked on Marvin, and indecision flickered in his gaze.

Another explosion roared as Marvin shot again. A shattering as the window broke, and she knew he'd missed; he was dazed and weak from blood loss. Glover would realize this, would pounce on him, kill the old man in seconds.

But he didn't. She saw fear in his eyes now, the fear of a monster used to easy prey, unaccustomed to pain. The fighting had caught him by surprise. He lunged forward, not for Marvin and the gun but for the door. Marvin moved, tried to get a third shot, but Glover was already out of the room.

For a moment none of them moved. Then Marvin stumbled to the floor, still gripping the gun hard.

CHAPTER 76

Zoe sat on her bed, pages scattered all around her. Some were photos of the crime scene; others were handwritten summaries of what she could glean about Debra Miller. She had a feeling that Debra was more significant than the other victims. She was different—no Instagram or Facebook account as far as Zoe could tell, so the killer hadn't stalked her like the others. And, of course, she was older than the killer's other victims.

Something about her had prodded him into action. What was it? Had she reminded him of someone he knew? Maybe his mother? Or maybe something had attracted him in her appearance—Debra's father said she looked worse than ever before. Understandably, he didn't have a picture from that time, but Zoe could make educated guesses. She was probably thin. Bad skin and teeth. Broken fingernails. Nervous tics. Maybe this was what had made the killer act.

She was doing her best to avoid thinking about it from Debra's perspective. That was a rabbit hole she didn't want to go down into. Of all the victims, she estimated that Debra had suffered the worst.

Her phone rang, and she let it ring for several seconds, her attention elsewhere. Then she fumbled for it, still reading her notes.

"Hello?"

For a second all she heard was a shuddering breath, and Zoe's focus sharpened. "Andrea?"

"Zoe . . . I . . . can you please come home?"

"What's wrong?" She was weightless in a pool of anxiety. "What happened?"

"Glover broke into the apartment. He . . . attacked me."

"Are you hurt?" Zoe was already off the bed, grabbing her bag, throwing everything at hand inside it. It seemed impossible. Why would he attack now? She was so sure he'd wait for them to lower their guard. He'd always been so patient.

"Yes . . . no. I don't know. There's a paramedic here. Marvin shot Glover."

"*Marvin* shot Glover? Where were the police? Is Glover dead?" She needed more information. Where were her damn shoes?

"Please come home. Please. I need you, Zoe. Please just get here. I need you now. Come home. Come home!" Andrea's voice rose, becoming hysterical. In the background she heard a stranger's voice saying that he needed a sedative.

"Andrea, I'm on my way, okay? I'm on my way right now."

Her sister sobbed on the other side, just a series of hiccuping whimpers, each of them tearing at Zoe's heart like a serrated blade. And then the line went dead.

Zoe's shoes were in the bathroom. She put them on, mind blank, each action automated, her movements feeling jerky, unreal. She grabbed the bag on her way out, vaguely aware that she'd left some things behind, not caring. She half walked, half ran to the stairs before realizing she couldn't get home to Andrea by running. Her mind scrambled for answers, came up with the best solution she could think of, and she turned around, hurried to Tatum's door, and banged on it.

"Tatum, open up!"

He did, wide eyed and confused, gun in hand, as if he expected to shoot someone. Which perhaps made sense, considering her screaming. "What happened?"

"Glover attacked Andrea. I need to fly back. Give me the car keys."

Tatum frowned at her, and she nearly hit him to get him to move. "Car keys! Now."

"Is she all right?" he asked, stepping back into his room.

"She's alive. I don't know anything else. Marvin shot Glover."

"*What?* Is Marvin okay?" He asked her some other things, words coming out of his mouth; she was unable to connect them into sentences in her mind.

"I don't *know*!" she screeched at him. "Give me the fucking keys!"

He located the keys in his jacket's pocket. Pulled them out. Said something else she didn't catch. Something about how she intended to get there.

"I'll drive to Austin. There are planes flying from there all the time," she said, snatching the keys from his hand. She turned around, bolting for the door. Behind her, Tatum was talking, calling her, but she couldn't turn back—there was no time. Andrea's screams were still ringing in her ears, yanking her onward, toward Virginia.

CHAPTER 77

Tatum watched Zoe disappear into the darkness and turned back to his room, shocked. He'd never seen her like this. Her eyes, always so sharp and keen, had been glazed in a look of abject fear. Her face had been wet with tears she hadn't even seemed to notice.

Shaking himself from his torpor, he lunged for his phone, dialed. Waited impatiently as the phone rang once. Twice. Three times.

Marvin answered. "Tatub?"

"Marvin, are you all right?"

"I shot hib, Tatub. I shot the bastard. He was bessing with the wrong guy!"

"Why are you talking like that?"

"He broke by dose, Tatub. But I shot hib."

In the background someone said, "Sir, *please* put that gun down."

"Like hell I will!" Marvin shouted. "What if he comes back—who's godda shoot hib? You?"

"Sir, if you don't put the gun down, I will have to—"

"You stay away frob be!"

"Marvin," Tatum shouted into the phone. "What's going on?"

"They want the gun, Tatub. I'm not giving it up."

"Watch where you're waving that thing, old man!" someone said sharply.

"Marvin, give the cops your gun." Tatum gritted his teeth.

"No way, Tatub. Who's godda look after Adrea if I do that? The fish?"

Tatum massaged his forehead, heart thumping. "Let me talk to the officer."

"Here. By grandson wadts to have a word. He's frob the FBI."

A moment of silence and then another voice on the phone. "Hello?"

"This is Special Agent Gray," Tatum said. "Who's this?"

"I'm Officer Collier. Are you this man's grandson?"

"Yes. What's going on there, Officer?"

"Listen, Agent, you need to tell your crazy grandfather to put that damn thing down. He nearly shot us when we came inside, and he doesn't seem too stable."

"Don't worry—he won't shoot anyone." Tatum fervently hoped he was right. "What about Andrea? Is she all right?"

"She's in shock but mostly unhurt. The paramedics are looking after her. But if your grandfather won't put down the gun, he'll bleed to death."

"Bleed to death?"

"He was stabbed. The paramedics won't get near him; he's acting like a loon. He's probably in shock."

"No, that's his regular behavior," Tatum said. "Put me on speaker."

"Uh, okay. Hang on."

A second later there was a crackle as Tatum was presumably put on speaker.

"Marvin?" he called.

"Yeah, Tatub, what's up?"

"I need you to give the officer the gun."

"I don't think so, Tatub. I need this gun. To shoot that bastard if he comes back."

How was it that even bleeding to death with a broken nose, this man managed to be so infuriating? Tatum almost screamed at him, but he knew that would only make the old man dig his heels farther into the ground. "Okay, listen. Can you give the gun to Andrea?"

"Baybe," Marvin said grudgingly.

"Just until they patch you up."

"I don't deed patching up. It's just a scratch."

"Do it for me, okay, Marvin? Give the gun to Andrea, and let them have a look at you."

"You're a paid in the ass, Tatub."

Tatum sighed in relief, listening to Marvin call Andrea to give her the gun. There was some back and forth, and finally, Officer Collier got back on the line.

"Your grandfather is being taken care of," he said.

"Thanks."

"He's a piece of work."

"That he is."

"But from what we could figure out, he saved this girl's life. He's one tough son of a bitch."

"He's that too." Tatum sat on the bed, exhausted. "What about Rod Glover? Is he dead?"

"He ran away. He's currently missing."

"Missing?" Tatum gritted his teeth. "Weren't you people watching the damn building? How could he be missing?"

"We're still looking into that. Don't worry—we'll find him in a few hours. He won't get far. He bled all over the place."

"Right." Tatum grunted. "I have to go, Officer. Thanks for your help."

He hung up and shut his eyes, worried about Zoe. She'd been in a hell of a state when she'd left, and he should have never let her drive like that.

CHAPTER 78

San Angelo, Texas, Tuesday, September 13, 2016

Despite the chaos of the night before, Tatum showed up for Nicole Medina's funeral. The priest's voice droned, echoing in the church's packed sanctuary. The constant sound of people murmuring served as background noise. Tatum regarded the people around him, estimating that probably only one out of ten actually knew Nicole Medina or her parents. Most were reporters or just curious onlookers.

Tatum was edgy from lack of sleep. He'd spent hours the previous night talking with Mancuso, with the police officers handling the manhunt after Rod Glover, and with the medical team looking after Marvin and Andrea. Then he'd lain in bed, trying to sleep. He wasn't sure when he'd fallen asleep, but he had a hunch it wasn't long before the alarm had buzzed him awake.

Remembering that he didn't have a car, he'd called Foster, filling him in, asking for a ride. Foster had told him he wasn't coming—he was too busy managing the investigation—but that Lyons would pick him up. She'd shown up fifteen minutes later, and he'd had to update her regarding Zoe's absence as well, a duty he hadn't relished.

Now they sat next to each other, surveying the crowd, searching for a killer. Tatum doubted he'd show up there, but you never knew. He scanned the faces around him, trying to gauge who matched the killer's profile. A whole lot of people, really. Though he and Zoe knew a lot about how the killer's mind worked, they'd never progressed very far when it came to knowing how he looked. About forty, quite strong, Caucasian. Also, Tatum had a very vague idea of his build from the first video.

A familiar face caught his attention, and he frowned, trying to place it, until it clicked. It was Harry Barry. He sat in the back, jotting in a small notebook. Their eyes met, and Harry nodded at him.

A police photographer was there as well, taking pictures of the people who showed up. Later, Foster and Lyons would have a field day, sorting the images. Tatum had already decided he wouldn't be joining them. After the funeral, he would tie up loose ends and go back home. Marvin needed him. And so did Zoe.

"One of the GPR teams found another of the killer's pits," Lyons whispered to him, reading a message on her phone.

"Good," Tatum muttered. The noose was tightening. He was quite certain by now that it was only a matter of days until this killer would be caught. The San Angelo police didn't need him there.

Still, he scrutinized the faces around him, wondering if the man they'd chased for the past week was in plain sight.

He focused back on the priest, who seemed to be finishing up the ceremony, standing above the coffin. It was a closed-casket funeral. Nicole's body was past the embalmer's abilities.

His phone buzzed, and he checked it. He didn't recognize the number. He declined the call, put the phone back in his pocket.

"They're about to wrap up here," he said. "I'll stand outside, watch everyone as they're leaving. Maybe you should stay behind."

"Okay." Lyons only half listened. She was reading another email on her phone. Glancing over her shoulder, Tatum saw it was the crime scene report from Debra Miller's grave. It seemed disappointingly short. Nothing found in the crime scene aside from the body and the crate it had been buried in. Unlike the other murders, there had been no objects found in the crate—no camera, or cable, no props—and nothing had been found on the body except her purse. Lyons flipped a finger over her screen and began reading the autopsy report.

He stood up discreetly and walked outside. It was the hottest day since they'd gotten there, and the fact that he wore a suit didn't help. He was sweating already. He decided to go for a swim once he returned to the motel, then figure out what flight to take.

He watched as the church doors opened, and people milled outside. More than a dozen press photographers hurried forward to video the procession. Tatum shook his head and focused on the rest of the crowd. Could the killer be hiding under the guise of a photographer? It wasn't likely.

His phone buzzed again, the same number as before.

He put the phone to his ear. "Hello?"

"Um . . . is this Tatum?" A female voice, fragile. Somewhat familiar.

"Yeah, who's this?"

"It's Andrea. Zoe's sister."

"Oh, right." She sounded like a ghost of her former self. "How are you feeling?"

"A bit better. Woozy. They keep sedating me. Listen, do you know where Zoe is? Her phone is unavailable."

He felt a stab of worry. "Well, she said she's flying back from Austin, so she's probably on the plane. That's why she's unavailable."

"Oh, okay, that makes sense." Andrea sounded relieved, a sensation Tatum didn't share. "If she contacts you, can you tell her to give me a call, let me know when she's getting here?"

"Sure."

"Thanks, Tatum. Bye."

She hung up. Tatum eyed the procession distractedly as they carried the coffin to the graveyard. Lyons was in the back of the procession, and he drew her attention, signaling he'd join her in a minute. She nodded.

He dialed Zoe, and the call went straight to voicemail. He hung up and dialed Foster.

"Yeah?" Foster answered, sounding impatient.

"Foster, listen, it's Tatum. Uh . . . sorry to bother you, but Zoe's phone is offline. She might be on her flight right now, but she drove off in quite a state last night. I'm worried that . . . something happened."

"You want me to check the accident reports from last night?"

"If it's not too much trouble," Tatum said, feeling relieved that Foster had offered. "She drove a silver Hyundai Accent to Austin."

"Sure. I'll call you back in a few."

"Thanks, Foster. I really appreciate it."

He hung up and followed the procession, watched them lowering the coffin into the grave. Nicole's mother wept uncontrollably. Tatum decided to drop any pretense that he was looking for a killer and just pay his respects to the woman they hadn't managed to save.

His phone buzzed, and he stepped away from the crowd. It was Foster.

"Listen, Tatum. There was no accident involving a woman with Zoe's description. Two accidents with silver Hyundai Accents, but both were not rentals, and the people involved weren't Zoe."

"Then I guess she's on her flight." Tatum exhaled with relief.

"There's no flight currently en route between Austin and any airport in Virginia."

Tatum frowned. "Maybe she forgot to turn on her phone after the flight?"

"Maybe. The last flight landed two hours ago."

Tatum's heart sunk. In that case, Zoe would almost certainly have reached Andrea by now. "Thanks, Foster."

"Keep me posted when you talk to her."

"Sure. Bye."

He hung up and dialed Zoe's number, getting the voicemail again. He tried twice more with no success. A vague sensation of dread began spreading in his gut.

CHAPTER 79

Tatum's internal clock kept tallying seconds and minutes. Fifty minutes since the moment he'd realized Zoe had disappeared.

He paced in his motel room, calling different people in San Angelo, in Austin, in Quantico, anyone who could help, give him a shred of information. He kept thinking of the way she'd left, half-coherent, eyes dull. He should never have let her drive like that. But he had been worried about Marvin and had had a momentary lapse of judgment. He kept thinking of the Hyundai lying upside down at the foot of a ravine along the way or in a ditch. Images of Zoe in the car bleeding, unconscious, or dead flickered in his mind.

His phone rang. Mancuso.

"Zoe never checked in to any flight." Mancuso's voice was high with tension. "Any news on road accidents?"

"DPS sent patrol cars on every main route between San Angelo and Austin searching for her," Tatum said. "But she must have taken Route 71, and it's a good road. It's not likely she would have lost her way. And if she had an accident on it, we'd have already . . ." His gut sank. "Known. Shit. Mancuso, I'll call you back."

He hung up and dashed out of the room.

She hadn't gotten on any flight, and they couldn't find her on the way to Austin, but there was one place he'd never checked. It hadn't even occurred to him.

The parking lot was on the other side of the motel.

The rental still stood there. Zoe hadn't taken it after all.

Could she have decided to take an Uber, realizing she couldn't drive? Tatum doubted it. He doubled back, deciding to check her room.

He strolled inside the lobby, trying to seem as casual as he could. He could pull a badge to get a key to Zoe's room, but the desk clerk might call the manager, and they'd say he needed a search warrant . . . he had no time. The girl behind the desk had seen him and Zoe pass through together multiple times. He forced a smile onto his face.

"Hey," he said. "My friend locked herself out of her room. Do you have a spare key?"

She looked at him uncertainly. Tatum broke eye contact and coughed, feigning embarrassment. "She's . . . um. Waiting in my room. She doesn't have her clothing with her at the moment."

The girl blushed and tried to hide her smile. She located a spare key and handed it to Tatum. It took a lot of self-control not to dash away with it.

His heart was in his throat as he opened the door. Zoe's room was a mess. Papers were scattered on the bed, some on the floor. He went through them quickly—they were all related to the Schrodinger case. He found a pair of discarded stockings in the corner by the bed. Her toothbrush and the rest of her toiletries were still in the bathroom, and he guessed she'd forgotten to pack them in her haste. There were some pictures of the latest crime scene on the night table, and he picked them up to flip through them, then noticed a business card underneath.

Joseph Dodson. Air-conditioning technician and electrician. Tatum frowned, confused, then recalled the man he'd seen leaving Zoe's room that morning a few days before.

A very large man.

He held the card between thumb and forefinger, trying to think this through, when his phone rang. The number was one he didn't know, but he'd called a lot of people in the past couple of hours.

“Hello?” he answered.

“Agent Gray?” The man on the other side breathed heavily, voice unsteady. “It’s Harry. The reporter.”

“I don’t have time right now to—”

“I just got another email from Schrodinger. A video.” This didn’t sound like the cynical, smooth-talking reporter Tatum had spoken with. The man was on the verge of hysteria. “I’m sending you the link.”

He hung up.

A second later, the phone bleeped as it received an incoming message. It wasn’t one of the regular random URLs from before. This was a link to a YouTube video. Tatum tapped the link, and the video showed up on-screen.

Tatum’s knees buckled, and he sat on the bed heavily as he stared at Zoe’s face.

CHAPTER 80

Darkness.

For a second, Zoe thought it was still night, that she'd pulled the blinds down. Her mouth was dry, woolly. She shifted, perhaps to reach for her phone, see what time it was.

She couldn't move her hands. They were bound behind her back; she could feel the hard bite of something holding her wrists together. Her mouth was gagged.

A jumble of sensations and fragments of memory surfaced. Pain. Her body ached all over, an echo of a much worse pain from before.

She kicked with her foot, hit something hard just above it. She was dreaming. It sometimes happened—she was so focused on her cases that she had nightmares about them. But the pain in her body, the bite in her wrists, the feeling in her mouth: it was all too real.

And the darkness was absolute. The sort of darkness where she couldn't tell the difference when she shut her eyes.

She tried to pull her hands free, wriggled, hitting wooden walls on both sides. Panicking, she tried to sit up, hit her forehead.

It wasn't silent in the cramped, dark space. A muffled, consistent screeching filled the void around her. Only when her throat began burning did she realize it was her, screaming through the gag, consumed by terror.

It wasn't a rational fear; it was something primal, the acute fear of being trapped in the dark, unable to move, the walls of the box closing in on her. Anywhere she moved, she felt the outline of a wall, sturdy, impregnable. And beyond it she suddenly knew was only earth. Rocks and soil in all directions. Even if her hands were untied, she'd still be trapped in this tiny abyss.

Zoe's body took control as she shrieked, wriggled, and shook her head, all rational thoughts fading in the hurricane of fear that stormed through her mind.

CHAPTER 81

She screamed again. Tatum stiffened; the sound was unbearable.

"Mute the damn thing," Foster said, his voice cracking. He was talking on the phone.

Tatum was in the situation room with Foster and Lyons. They'd set a laptop on the table, the video constantly running on it. He knew that throughout the station, screens were displaying the same video, speakers emitting the same screams. He checked his watch, as he'd done more than a dozen times since he'd entered the room. It'd been an hour and twenty minutes since the video had started. It was impossible to know how long Zoe had been in that box. Two hours? Three?

Eight?

Lyons sat in front of the computer, her eyes shimmering. She didn't mute the video, and they all knew why. There was a chance, however slight, that the same trick they'd used for Juliet Beach would work here. Foster had sent patrol cars blaring music at full volume as soon as Tatum had told him about the video.

But when Zoe was quiet, they could hear nothing else. And Tatum knew Schrodinger would never make the same mistake twice. Wherever she was buried, she was buried deep, well beyond sound.

"Another comment," Lyons said. "'This is a fake.' *Fake* spelled with *ck*."

For the first time, Schrodinger's video had comments. They had a view count and even a "thumbs up, thumbs down" indication. Schrodinger had embraced YouTube wholeheartedly, creating his own channel, called Schrodinger. The video was named "Experiment Number Four." FBI and DPS cyber fighting teams were attempting to trace the feed, but Tatum wasn't hopeful.

He paced the room, but now he paused and stared at the screen again. The video feed was darker than before; it was hard to see the details. Zoe lay on her back, a gag in her mouth, hair disheveled, face wet with tears. Beyond her, Tatum could just glimpse the darkness of a wooden wall.

There were no props, no metal contraptions labeled as poison or explosives. The feed ran steadily, with no changes.

For a moment, his mind clouded, blind panic flooding his brain, his thought process washed away by huge frothing waves of pure fear for Zoe's life. He forced himself to breathe, to think of it rationally. He would be of no use to Zoe like this. He checked the time again. An hour and twenty-three minutes since the video had started.

They had two GPR teams searching as fast as they could. Tatum had used Zoe's formula to figure out the wider radius of the search perimeter, and they were focusing on it, but of course, since Zoe's grave was probably filled with a clay-rich soil, the chance they would find anything was almost zero, even if they stood right on top of her. The K-9 units were searching the same areas as well.

"Sheppard's out." Foster put down his phone. "I just spoke with the surveillance crews that were on him. He had no opportunity to take Zoe."

Tatum nodded. "Zoe thought he wasn't a likely suspect." He still felt his heart clench. Sheppard was one of the few leads they had.

"The only suspect we have for now is that guy Joseph Dodson," Foster said. "They should be picking him up any minute now. Any thoughts about him?"

Thoughts. Tatum forced himself to concentrate, to think about it clinically. "He's approximately the right age. He's strong. He works as an electrician and an air-conditioning technician, so he probably has a van he works with. It's likely he could acquire the relevant technical knowledge that was needed to film the girls he'd buried and to broadcast it. Also, he was close to Zoe, so he could get details about the investigation from her."

"I like him for it," Foster said darkly.

They all became silent. Zoe's frantic breathing emanated from the computer, and Tatum clenched his fists.

"Why YouTube?" Lyons asked, for the third time in the past hour.

"Probably because of the comments," Foster said impatiently. "He wants to see the shocked and horrified comments of the viewers."

Tatum frowned, thinking about it. "It doesn't fit the profile. This guy doesn't want to engage. He wants to show people he's smart. If he wanted comments, he could have let people post comments on the previous experiments as well. My guess is he doesn't care about the comments. It's just random noise."

"What then?"

Tatum looked at the video. What did YouTube give its users aside from comments? It had to be something the killer couldn't do on his own website. All he could think of was ads, and he doubted the killer was concerned about revenue.

"Traffic." Lyons suddenly pointed at the view count. It had just become four digits and was climbing steadily.

"That's it," Tatum agreed, trying to ignore the nausea in his guts. "With Juliet Beach, people already reported they couldn't get the feed. The website couldn't handle the traffic. And this time, I think he wants to go big. He wants everyone to see. He wants his precious fame."

"YouTube will remove the video once it's reported," Lyons said. "What then?"

"We can't let them," Tatum said, his heart missing a beat. "I'll handle it." He would call Mancuso, tell her to contact YouTube, explain the situation, and stop them from removing the video until Zoe was safe. Even as he thought it, he realized he was doing exactly what the killer wanted. He was carrying out the bastard's job for him.

Foster's phone rang, and he answered it. "Yeah. Bring him here, and get him to Interview Room One." He hung up.

"Joseph Dodson?" Lyons asked.

"Yes," Foster said. "They just picked him up. We're working on a search warrant."

"We might not have enough for a search warrant," Lyons pointed out.

"We'll search his home no matter what," Foster said grimly. "We'll get what we need to find her."

CHAPTER 82

Zoe lay exhausted, not knowing how much time had passed since she had woken up. She felt like she occasionally blacked out but wasn't sure if she really did lose consciousness or if her mind simply disconnected, leaving her body to flail blindly in panic. She had no way to measure the passage of time aside from the slow, relentless increase in the pressure of her bladder and the close to unbearable thirst. Thinking back on the day before, she realized she hadn't drunk much and now paid for it dearly.

But it would be suffocation that would kill her long before thirst.

For the first time since she'd woken up, she was exhausted enough to stop thrashing and to slowly think of her situation.

When they'd started the investigation, the analyst had estimated that Nicole Medina would run out of air in twelve hours. Juliet Beach had been buried alive for about nine hours, and she'd been almost dead when they'd found her. Zoe had no idea if the box she was in was the same size, but it was safe to assume it was close enough. She was smaller than the average woman, meaning that maybe there had been more air in the box when she'd been shut there.

All her thrashing and screaming had significantly lowered that amount.

The best thing she could do to maximize the time she had was sleep, lowering her breathing rate significantly. But that wasn't an option right now; the discomfort she was in was too severe. So she'd have to lie still and stay calm.

It was the "stay calm" she had an issue with. She could still feel the cavernous terror just at the edge of her mind, waiting for her to touch one of the walls, feel the space closing in on her again, think of the tons of sand and dirt that lay on top of her small, confined space.

She tried some basic relaxation techniques, focusing on her body, trying to loosen her muscles, breathing steadily. But she couldn't focus properly, and frightened thoughts kept assaulting her. She lost control for a while, kicked around the walls of her enclosure. Cried.

She'd have to try something else.

If she couldn't calm herself by emptying her mind, she'd have to calm herself by filling it. This was something she found much easier to do. In fact, it was her default state.

She tried to think about Andrea, but there was too much uncertainty there, too much fear of a different kind, and she quickly shied away from those thoughts. Her sister was alive and, for now, probably in a much better situation than Zoe was.

Then it occurred to her that she was probably being filmed. If she could glean anything about her situation, perhaps she could somehow let her viewers know about it. She could save herself. The idea that she would be able to extract herself from this situation immediately reduced her terror of being trapped.

She wiggled a bit, got her cheek against the wall of the box. It was wooden but somehow smooth. She tried to recall how smooth the boxes of the other victims had been. Was this box different somehow? She tried to sniff the interior, maybe smell something that could help, but all she could smell was herself. Then she lay silent and listened hard for what felt forever.

Nothing.

Of her five senses, taste and sight were out of the picture. So far touch, smell, and sound had given her nothing.

She tried to remember what had happened the night before. The memory was fragmented, and she estimated it was probably because she had been so distraught. She recalled deciding to fly from Austin. A brief interaction with Tatum—she couldn't remember anything they'd said. She'd walked to the parking lot, and then . . .

Pain. All of her muscles had been rigid with pain. She hadn't been able to move.

He had tased her. And then, somehow, had knocked her out. A shift from his previous strategy. He was clearly even more confident than before. Or more desperate. Perhaps a bit of both.

She tried hard to remember whether she'd managed to see anything helpful. She remembered seeing the rental in the dark and then . . . nothing, just pain.

She didn't let herself lose hope. She knew how memory worked. It often returned in surprising bursts of clarity. She would wait. But she had to keep her mind busy. She had her eyes closed, and as long as she didn't move, it was possible to almost forget where she was.

She focused on the case. That was the best way for her to keep busy. When she worked, she could think about a case for hours, trying to get into the killer's mind-set, figuring out his motives, compulsions, the things that made him tick. Usually, she would surround herself with photographs of the crime scenes and the victims, but she had to work with the hand she'd been dealt.

Last night, before Andrea had called—her mind lingered there for a second, and she forced it away—she had been focused on Debra Miller. Debra Miller was the first victim, the one who'd prodded the killer to act.

If the killer knew who Debra was and that she was running away, he could figure no one would report her missing. Could that be all there was?

No. There were endless homeless girls who had no one to look for them. They'd probably be easier to pick up since many of them were prostitutes. But this killer always focused on girls who had a home and a life. Debra might have been messed up, but she also came from a family who loved her, and she had a place to come back to.

She tried to find a common trait between Debra and the rest of the girls, but there was none. Debra was significantly older than the rest of the victims. She was a drug addict, unhealthy; the others were fine. Debra was searching for a way out of her current life, which might resemble Maribel Howe, but not Juliet and Nicole.

She decided to try to attack the problem differently. See what the three other victims had in common and try to figure out how this applied to Debra Miller.

Physically, the three women were different, but all three were good looking. Juliet Beach was quite stunning, in fact, but all three would make heads turn. Could the killer have seen Debra as good looking? She was thin, as were Juliet and Nicole, but Maribel was curvy and had plump cheeks. Zoe doubted just looks could be the answer.

He stalked the girls using social media. She'd reviewed the accounts of all three extensively. They all posted frequently. All seemed happy, though that was hardly extraordinary on social media, the land of fake smiles. All took photos with various men—maybe that was what set him off. Perhaps Debra Miller had propositioned him somehow, making him think of her as slutty, just like the other girls.

But that felt wrong. As far as Zoe could tell, all three girls' profiles were quite pure, in social media standards. No teasing photos, no bikinis or bare-backed shots or even kissy faces. Just photos of girls having fun, going out with friends.

Friends. They were popular. Or at least, the social media equivalent of popular. A lot of pictures with different people and lots of followers. All three had over five hundred followers in their Instagram accounts.

So the three girls were beautiful and popular while Debra was lonely and sick looking.

Did he target them because they were the opposite of Debra or—

Her mind latched on to something Debra's father had said. *She'd been the sweetest, happiest kid when she was at school. So popular, surrounded by friends.* In the sensory-deprivation chamber Zoe was trapped in, she could hear his voice in her ear, as if he were next to her.

When she was at school.

As far as the killer was concerned, the four victims were the same. Beautiful. Popular.

But Debra had become unhappy and lonely as soon as school had ended.

He was a local boy. He'd gone to school with her.

She was suddenly completely sure of it. He'd gone to school with her—she, the popular, happy girl; him, the weird kid who had no friends. Hours upon hours to fantasize about her in class. His profile clearly painted him as obsessive, and the same tendencies would have been there as a boy. It would be a fixation that would never completely dissipate. Then he met her, all those years later. Already stressed, probably because of something at work—maybe he was fired or skipped for promotion or got a boss who hated him. And there she was. After more than twenty years, back in his life. It would be enough to trigger a reaction to fulfill his fantasy.

That was enough to hone down on him. How many students in one high school? A thousand? Cross-check them with her profile, maybe fingerprint them to match the partial fingerprint they already had, and that was it.

Unfortunately, those were not things she could do right now. But the police could. And Tatum. She had to communicate this somehow.

CHAPTER 83

A uniformed officer opened the door of the situation room. "Foster, Joseph Dodson is here."

"Good," Foster said. "Be right there."

The man closed the door, and Foster turned to face Tatum.

"Okay, we need to be smart here. We don't have much time."

Tatum nodded. Usually, they'd let the man sweat a bit before storming in, playing good cop, bad cop. But every minute the suspect was waiting, Zoe was suffocating. Tatum glanced at the screen. For the past twenty minutes, she'd been lying with her eyes closed, not moving. It was almost worse than before, when she'd struggled and screamed.

"How do you think we should play this?" he asked.

"You go in first," Foster said. "He already saw you once; he knows that *you* know who he is. It might unsettle him. We should probably get you some props like last time with Sheppard. Pictures from crime scenes, a thick folder, his business card in an evidence bag. We already have the phone records, so we can act it out a bit, make it sound like we know a lot more than we actually do. Then I come in, tell him I can keep the feds off his back if he tells us where Zoe is right now . . . something like that?"

Tatum hesitated. It sounded like a reasonable strategy with an everyday criminal, but for this serial killer?

"What about the warrant to his house?" he asked. "We might be able to interrogate him better if we had something concrete."

Foster sighed. "Lyons is working on it. If we don't get it in ten minutes, I think we'll just . . ." He waved his hand ambiguously, clearly not wanting to spell it out. Tatum already caught the drift. Foster was intent on searching the man's house, legal or not. He appreciated it.

He had something else that held him back.

Zoe had apparently slept with this man. Would she really have been so blind, not to see the signs? As a child, she'd been on friendly terms with Rod Glover, and she still carried the emotional scars. Tatum wanted to believe his partner would never let herself be intimate with someone who could possibly be a killer.

Of course, some psychopaths were *very* good actors.

This interrogation could take hours. If they were wrong about Dodson, Zoe's chances would decrease from slim to none.

"Tell you what," he said. "You go first. Props and all. Then, in half an hour I'll join in, do the whole FBI spiel, while hopefully Lyons gets whatever we need from this guy's apartment."

"You sure?" Foster frowned.

"Yeah. I want to think it through a bit. Get my ducks in a row."

Foster glanced at the laptop for a long second, exhaled, and left the room, closing the door behind him.

Tatum turned to the laptop. Zoe lay with her eyes open now, still not moving. The only thing that indicated she was still alive was her occasional blinking. The view counter was in six digits by now. The story had hit all the main news channels, and the link to the video had become viral. The killer was getting what he wanted. The world was watching.

"What would you say if you were here?" he asked the screen. He got up and paced back and forth in the room. Even if Joseph was the wrong man, what else could he do? What would Zoe do?

She'd analyze what they knew. Estimate what it meant. Try to reach new conclusions.

Zoe screamed through her gag again, thrashing from side to side. Tatum took three steps to the laptop and muted the sound. Enough people were watching the damn video. If there was anything worth hearing, they'd let him know.

He sat by the table, took out his notebook, and bit his lower lip. Then he wrote down, *The unsub attacked her in the parking lot.*

That much was almost a certainty. The parking lot was dark, and Tatum doubted Zoe would have headed anywhere else once she had the keys. He tapped the pen on the notebook and then added, *He was stalking her, waiting for the right moment.*

This was a shift in the killer's strategy. He'd chosen Zoe as his target and was actively stalking her. Why? Fame? Or did he get a kick out of taking the one who was closest to finding him? Zoe had publicly shamed him in that article. Maybe that was what had made him act.

Tatum tried to imagine this guy Joseph doing something like that. It didn't fit. If Joseph wanted to take her, it would make more sense for him to knock on her door. She already knew him. She'd open the door, and he could incapacitate her in the room, maybe drug her like he had with the others.

Once he questioned it, other things began to feel strange. When the killer had tried to break in to the gas station, he'd had latex gloves on. But Joseph was an electrician. Tatum's uncle had worked as an electrician. Tatum recalled that he'd used special rubber gloves when working, much thicker and sturdier than simple latex gloves. Joseph would have used those.

Joseph was big. Though it was hard to estimate the killer's size in the first video, Tatum doubted he was that big. He also doubted that knowing how big he was, the killer would film himself.

Besides, Zoe would have *known*.

CHAPTER 84

Zoe tried grunting into her gag, nearly threw up, had a brief panic attack, and forced herself to stop. Could she remove the gag? She tried to push it out with her tongue, then froze.

Not only the police were watching. *He* watched her as well. And if she'd manage to get the gag out or to signal *anything*, he'd kill the feed. And her chance to help them would be gone.

It would have to be something he wouldn't notice. Or that he'd figure out only after someone else got the message. No hand messages, no words, no sounds.

Blinking: that was the only safe course of action.

How she would have loved to know Morse code right now. Did *anyone* still know Morse? Just a few short and long blinks, and she could pass any message to the people watching her. But no Morse for her. The only other possibility was blinking letters according to numerical value. One blink for *A*, two blinks for *B* . . . and twenty-six damn blinks for *Z*. A significant pause between each letter. They'd have to insert the spaces between the words themselves.

She composed a short message in her head. *The killer knew Debra Miller at school.* She could definitely make it shorter. Do her best to avoid the second half of the ABC. *He knew Debra at school.* Much better.

Okay. *H* was eight, *E* was five, *K* was eleven . . . she began blinking.

It was nearly impossible.

She had to blink naturally, or the killer would notice something was wrong instantly. That meant short, light blinks. She had to count them carefully. And counting blinks in complete darkness, where she couldn't really distinguish if her eyes were open or shut . . .

She got all the way to the *W* of *knew*. And she was pretty sure she'd screwed up the *H* and the *N* on the way.

She let out a frustrated sob. She'd have to start over until she got it right. But the killer was smart. He'd notice something irregular with her blinking. This would never work. She'd have to make the message shorter. *Much* shorter. She'd have to trust someone to figure out what she was trying to say.

Tatum. She'd have to trust Tatum would figure it out. She'd talked to him about the connection between the killer and Debra. She'd left all the notes about Debra in her room. Tatum would know it was what she had in mind.

Her new message was simply *school*. Nineteen, three, eight, fifteen, fifteen, twelve.

It still felt impossible. She decided to try.

But if she didn't give the killer what he wanted, he might shut off the feed out of frustration or boredom. She couldn't let that happen.

She bucked and screamed again.

He sat at work, door locked to make sure no one came in, and watched her. He knew he had things to do, but he just couldn't pull his eyes away from the feed. The first hour was the best; she'd been completely out of control, and he'd felt an unimaginable thrill as she'd cried and screamed. Not so cold and calculating now, was she? That was what happened when people were shut in the darkness and had time to really *think*.

But when she calmed down, he began to feel frustrated. She was cheating him. The video was only seventy-three minutes long so far. He needed *more*.

She lay still for an eternity, and he wished he could prod her into moving again. Maybe that was what he should do in future experiments. He'd have to think about it.

She opened her eyes and for a while just blinked. What was wrong with her eyes? A nervous reaction of some kind?

And then she bucked and screamed again. Even wilder than before, and it was a thrill to watch. Soon, lust came over him, and he fumbled for the Kleenex on the desk, breathing hard, face flushed.

By the time he was done, she'd stopped screaming and was lying with her eyes closed. He let out a shuddering breath. This was the best experiment he'd done so far.

Tatum's phone rang. It was Harry. Tatum answered quickly.

"Yeah?"

"Are you watching the video?" Harry asked, sounding tense.

"No, why?"

"Watch the damn video. I think Zoe is trying to signal something."

Tatum hurried to the screen and watched. At first, he didn't see anything unusual. She just lay there, blinking. But then he realized she was blinking fast. And then pausing. Blinking fast. And pausing.

"She's . . . blinking in a pattern."

"It's not Morse—I already checked."

Zoe suddenly shut her eyes. After a few seconds she began twisting and kicking again. Tatum tensed in sympathy, glancing away.

"I think she's acting," Harry said.

Tatum turned back to the screen. "How can you tell?"

"I've been writing about sex scandals and celebrities for years. Trust me—I know when someone's acting fake." Harry sounded annoyingly smug. "She'll stop in a bit. She's already done this twice before; you'll see."

Like Harry said, Zoe suddenly stopped. Eyes shut, seeming exhausted.

"Prepare for the blinking."

Suddenly Zoe opened her eyes and blinked. It took Tatum a second to react.

"Count them!" he barked into the phone. "Count the blinks."

He counted them himself, scribbling the results in his notebook. After a minute, she shut her eyes and lay still.

"Okay," Harry said. "I have eighteen, three, eight, fifteen, twenty-seven."

"I have seventeen, three, eight, fifteen, fifteen, eleven," Tatum muttered. "I'm pretty sure there was a pause after the second fifteen."

"If there was a pause, you'd get fifteen twelve to make twenty-seven."

"You counted wrong. It's fifteen eleven. It's not Morse, so it's probably letters. The number is the letter's position in the ABC."

"Okay. So let's see. Seventeen is . . . A, B, C—"

"Do it quietly," Tatum snapped. "I can't think like that."

He jotted the ABC and the corresponding numbers. Then he matched it to what he'd counted. On the laptop's screen, Zoe was thrashing again.

"Right," Harry said. "I got . . . rchook. That doesn't make any sense."

"I have qchook," Tatum muttered.

"If I counted right and just missed the pause, it would be twelve at the end, which would mean . . . rchool."

"School!" Tatum shouted. "It's school."

"Right." Harry sounded excited as well. "So . . . she's telling us she's buried in a school?"

"That makes sense . . ." Tatum hesitated. "How would she know where she's buried?"

"Maybe she heard some school noise before she was buried."

"That's probably it," Tatum agreed. "I'll get people looking into it right now."

"Great, keep me updated."

"Uh-huh," Tatum said, hanging up. He was about to hurry out of the room, then paused.

Zoe had been trying to search for a link between Debra and the killer. Could that be what she meant?

It was that feeling of indecision again. The wrong decision could waste precious time, cost Zoe her life. He decided to follow both leads. He'd tell Foster and Lyons about the school, get them to search for Zoe in local schools. That was the more likely scenario.

And he'd look into Debra's school life on the off chance that this was what Zoe had meant.

Chief Christine Mancuso talked on her phone nonstop, the video playing on her screen. She'd muted it long before but couldn't bring herself to turn it off. It felt like by turning it off, she'd be betraying Zoe somehow, abandoning her to the darkness.

She'd just gotten off the phone after a long conversation with the special agent in charge of the San Antonio Division. He'd sent six of his top men to San Angelo, and his analysts were working around the clock to find Zoe. Words, Mancuso guessed, that were mostly aimed to reassure her or to cover his ass. Maybe both. But it was all she could do. Talk to anyone who could help.

She dialed Tatum again to get an update, but the line was busy.

Then the phone rang in her hand.

"Hello?"

"Is this Agent Mancuso?" the voice was familiar, but she couldn't place it.

"This is Chief Mancuso."

"Oh, Chief, right. This is Mitchell Lonnie from the Glenmore Park PD. Remember me?"

It took her a moment to place him. Pretty boy, sad green eyes. "Yeah, Lonnie, I remember."

"Listen, I'm watching the video—"

"Me too, Lonnie. I don't have any update right now—I'm sorry."

"No, listen. I figured out something. Zoe's trying to tell us something. She's blinking letters and—"

"School," Mancuso cut him off. "She's blinking the word *school.*"

Silence stretched. "Right," Mitchell said at last.

"I know. I had Zoe's partner and three analysts tell me that already."

"I just want to help."

Mancuso shut her eyes, frustrated at herself. "I know," she said, her tone softer. "Thanks. We're doing everything we can."

And that was the real snag. Lonnie or her or anyone around her couldn't do anything. Zoe was beyond their reach in almost every way, and all they were able to do was watch.

In complete and utter darkness, Zoe kept on acting her routine. Thrash in panic for thirty seconds, count to ten, blink her message, rest for a minute. And again. Panic, pause, blink, rest. Panic, pause, blink, rest.

She had no idea if anyone was seeing her. Had no idea if they got the message. She knew she would have to stop soon. She was consuming too much air.

But for now, she kept going, blinking into the abyss and hoping.

He began to suspect something the fourth time she went into a screaming fit. Her moments of hysteria were too regular. Almost like they were regulated somehow. With a woman like her, it almost made sense that even her loss of control would follow some sort of pattern, but still.

He watched as she jerked and bucked, shaking her head. Her eyes were shut, but something was wrong. He'd seen several women in these situations, including her, and she was acting . . . off somehow.

She stopped. And then began that nervous blinking again.

No, not nervous. Something else. Methodical.

He watched closely, feeling his gut sink. It was some sort of signal. How had he missed it before? He'd been too consumed with his private emotions and lust, too engaged with her fear.

She'd played him.

He quickly paused the video, killing the feed. Then, after a moment, he read the comments below the video.

School! She's blinking the word school!

This video is so fake

I think it's schoon.

It's definitely school.

I keep getting lost in the count

FAKE

School

Yeah, school

Hundreds of people had noticed it before him. He was close to panic, but then he forced himself to calm down. School? What did that even mean? Did she think she was buried in a school?

He shook his head, bemused. There was nothing there. It was a good thing he'd figured it out before she managed to signal anything else.

CHAPTER 85

The man who opened the door for Tatum looked terrible. Bloodshot eyes, pallid skin. His smell reminded Tatum of the way his aunt had smelled in the days before she'd died in the hospital. It didn't matter how much the nurses had aired her room and cleaned her; they couldn't clear the stench of death's proximity.

"Mr. Miller?" Tatum asked.

The man nodded, a weary what-the-hell-do-you-want nod. Tatum caught a whiff of alcohol on his breath.

"I'm Agent Gray from the FBI." He flicked his badge, though Miller didn't even glance at it. "Can I have a few minutes of your time?"

"Sure," the man rasped. "Is this about Debra?"

"Yeah. I wondered . . . do you have Debra's yearbooks?"

He expected some questions, maybe an angry reaction, but Mr. Miller just nodded and motioned Tatum to follow him inside. The house was dark, and the same smell clung to every corner. Tatum found himself taking shallow breaths.

Mr. Miller led him to a room that could only belong to Debra herself. Unlike the rest of the house, this room was bathed in light—a large window was positioned above the bed, and though it was dusty, it let the sun in. There was a depression on the bed, as if someone had sat on it recently. Tatum was willing to bet that Mr. Miller had spent a lot of the past twenty-four hours there, grieving for the daughter he'd found out was long dead.

A small bookcase stood in the corner with some books, albums, scrapbooks, and four yearbooks.

"Can I take them?" Tatum asked.

"I'd rather you didn't," the man said. "But feel free to look through them."

Tatum didn't argue. He took the last one, from 1993.

"Do you want to drink anything, Agent Gray?"

"Just water, thanks." Tatum was already flipping the pages one by one. He had no actual plan, nothing to go on, but he figured it would be easy to peg the weird kids. The ones who dressed differently, who didn't appear in group photos, who didn't smile in their own photograph. That would be a good place to start.

One thing was clear: Debra had been incredibly popular. She'd been stunning, appeared in endless photos, and in the most cliché manner had been a part of the cheerleader squad. A lot different than the woman she'd become just before the killer had found her—an abused drug addict.

Tatum paused as a familiar face caught his eye. A photo of a grinning African American teenager. Samuel Foster.

Of course. Tatum could kick himself. Foster had said he knew this girl from school. He'd just wasted valuable time, when he could have done this with Foster all along, get firsthand knowledge about any of those kids. He was about to put the yearbook away, thank Miller, and return to the station, when another face drew his attention. A boy with a pair of large spectacles and messy curly hair. The name underneath the picture was Clyde Prescott.

Tatum frowned at the image, unable to shake the feeling that he'd seen this fellow Clyde a bunch of times. He flipped through the yearbook, but Clyde wasn't in any of the group photos or in any of the clubs.

Clyde Prescott. Tatum took another look at him, at that solemn face. At the curly mass of hair.

Curly.

This was the medical examiner. Suddenly, the nickname he had made perfect sense. He *had* been curly once. And he'd been with Foster at school.

Curly had shown up at the scene the day before when they'd dug up the body, unlike the previous times. He'd hurried to the body as soon as he could, as if to make sure he got to it first. Had he been trying to remove something? A piece of evidence?

And though Foster had reacted when he realized the victim had been at school with him, Tatum didn't recall Curly saying anything. That was downright bizarre. *Anyone* would have said something.

Unless they wanted to avoid being associated with the victim.

Tatum took a long breath, focusing, trying to see if more pieces fit. The killer had figured out they were about to locate Juliet Beach, as if he'd been tipped off. Curly could easily have found out, either by hanging around the police station or by calling one of his many acquaintances in the force, what was going on.

What about the profile? Very intelligent, around forty, white. Working at a job that demanded thoroughness but not speed.

And there was his manner—always trying to show off. Trying to prove how smart he was. That estimation of Maribel Howe's time of death. Ridiculously specific. It was the same with Nicole Medina's time of death. A demonstration of his capabilities.

The time of death. Tatum suddenly recalled the details of the Whitfield case, the dead prostitute who had been found buried in the desert. During the trial, it had turned out that the time of death had been off. Curly would have been one of the main people who'd be blamed when the suspect walked. Would he really have risked it happening again by estimating the time of death of Howe and Medina so specifically? Never. Not unless he'd *known* he was right. And it was easy to know it, if he'd killed them himself.

That was the recent stressor in his life, the thing that had finally pushed him over the edge. The Whitfield case had been opened eight months before. The trial had probably taken place a few months after that . . . the blaming fingers would have started pointing at Curly around April or May. Just when Debra Miller had been murdered.

They'd thought the killer would want to insert himself into the investigation—that was why they'd begun the hotline, requesting information. But Curly was already a very integral part of the investigation. Tatum bunched his fists. Curly had easy access to the situation room, to their map, the outline of their profile, the crime scene photos.

It was all very vague and circumstantial. But it felt *right*.

He checked the time. It was almost two. Zoe had been buried for about six hours. Right or wrong, they didn't have long to find her. All he had was a hunch. He had to verify it fast, see if he was right, and if not, he'd sit down with Foster, go over the rest of that school's students one by one. Which would take too damn long.

Zoe's life depended on him. He *had* to be right.

CHAPTER 86

Clyde Prescott irritably prepared the toxicology samples for the bureau's lab. He'd already done blood and vitreous fluid and now removed a portion from each of the organs, labeling them methodically. He was completely exhausted, having slept less than three hours the night before, and the task seemed Sisyphean and redundant.

He wasn't thrilled with the upcoming visit of Agent Gray, who'd called him twenty minutes before, asking if he could drop by and check Maribel Howe's body for something. The agent was quite vague about what he needed, only saying it was related to Zoe Bentley's burial location.

Clyde couldn't imagine what the agent was talking about. The rest of the police were concentrated in the widespread search of the local schools.

He heard the steps of someone approaching and raised his eyes. It was Samuel Foster.

"Hey, Curly." Foster smiled at him wearily.

"Hey, Samuel," Clyde said. "Any progress?"

"Nah. We still don't have enough K-9 units for the search. They're sending additional units from Austin and Houston. But so far, nada."

"How's Zoe doing?"

"The feed stopped about an hour ago," the detective said grimly. "We're hoping she's fine, but we're estimating she's been in that box for seven hours, could be more. I'm not optimistic."

"It's a terrible business." Clyde marked the container with the kidney portion using a black marker and set it on the counter. "How can I help you?"

"I'm here to meet Gray. He said he's coming over with a witness."

Clyde tensed slightly. "A witness?"

"Yeah. Didn't really catch the details. Something about Maribel Howe's body . . ." Foster shrugged. "He said it'd just take a minute. He was very distraught."

"That's understandable."

"I can't imagine what the man's going through."

Clyde nodded, and they both lapsed into an uncomfortable silence. Foster seemed about to say something when Agent Gray stepped into the room.

"Oh, good," Foster said. "You're here. What's this about?"

"I just wanted my witness to have a look at Maribel Howe's body," Agent Gray said. He turned around. "You can come in, miss."

There was the sound of the hesitant footsteps of high-heeled shoes. And then Juliet Beach stepped into the room. Her gaze met Clyde's, and she froze. Her eyes widened, and she let out a sharp exhale, her hand flying to her mouth.

Clyde's gut dropped. He leaned on the counter, trying to act casual, but his fingers trembled.

"Now, miss, if you don't mind having a look at—" Tatum paused when he saw Juliet's face. "Miss?"

She let out a gasp and dashed out of the room.

"Agent Gray," Foster said. "What—"

"Neither of you move!" Tatum barked. "Both of you stay right here."

He ran after the girl.

"What was that all about?" Foster asked. "What was he doing, bringing that girl here? She's already traumatized enough without walking into a goddamn morgue."

Clyde cleared his throat. "Maybe I should go after her," he croaked. "This place is not for civilians."

"No offense, Curly, but you're not exactly a people person. I suppose I should follow him and see what this is all about, though."

"You probably should," Curly said hurriedly. "The sooner we—"

Gray stepped back in the room, blocking the doorway. His expression had morphed, his jaw clenched, eyes blazing in anger.

Before he realized what he was doing, Clyde took two steps back, placing the autopsy table between them.

"Well, Prescott," Agent Gray growled. "Guess what? It's over."

"What are you talking about?" Clyde blurted. "What's that girl—"

"What should I call you? Curly or Schrodinger? Which do you prefer?"

"What?" Foster sputtered incredulously. "Agent Gray, what are you—"

"He knows what I'm talking about." The agent pointed a shaking finger at Clyde. "Don't you?"

"I don't!" The blood drained from his face. The girl had recognized him. One glance and her memory had come back. "I have no idea what's going on." He was thinking furiously. All he had to do was bullshit his way out of there. Get to his car. Drive off.

"Agent Gray, are you saying Dr. Prescott is . . . that he is the serial killer?"

"Go talk to Juliet," the agent said. "She has a very interesting story to tell."

For a moment no one moved.

"It's ridiculous," Clyde said. "Even if that girl thinks she recognizes me . . . she's been through a lot. She might be making accusations all over the place. Just before she said she didn't remember who had taken her, right?"

Foster stared at him, his eyes narrowed.

"Go get her," Clyde urged. "Bring her here. We'll talk about it."

"You're right," the agent suddenly said. "We don't have time to throw wild accusations around."

"Right."

"We can clear this up fast. Let's take your fingerprints."

"W . . . what?"

"Compare them to the partial fingerprint we have. And the fingerprint from the attempted break-in into the gas station. It'd take only fifteen minutes. I have a contact who can compare them super quick."

Foster watched Clyde intently. "What do you think, Dr. Prescott? Would you mind giving us your fingerprints?"

He'd always known it would come to that. The least he could do was to act respectably.

"No need," he answered, feigning calm. "You got me."

He thought of Zoe Bentley, deep below the ground. His final experiment. The one that would make him famous.

He would *never* tell them where she was.

CHAPTER 87

Tatum left the morgue, feeling exhausted. He strode through the hallway to the station's entrance and stepped out. Prescott had already made it clear he wasn't about to give up Zoe's location. They would have to crack him, and do it fast.

Juliet waited by the door.

"Did . . . did you arrest him?" she asked. She was trembling.

"Yeah. He already confessed." There was a small puddle of vomit a few feet away. Poor kid.

"He'll go to prison, right? They won't let him, like . . . pay bail or something?"

"No. He's too risky."

"And I won't have to testify, right? In court? I mean, he confessed."

Tatum hesitated. "I hope not."

Juliet exhaled, and a single tear ran down her cheek.

The door opened, and Foster walked out, looking shaken.

Tatum turned to him. "Where is he?"

"The interview room. But he won't say a thing."

Tatum nodded. "I'll go to Prescott's house. Maybe he left something there. A map or a journal or something."

"Hurry. We don't have much time left." Foster turned to Juliet. "It's a good thing you identified him, miss. You may have saved Zoe Bentley's life."

Juliet gaped at Foster blankly. Tatum snorted.

"I didn't identify anyone," Juliet said. "I just did what the agent told me to. I don't remember what happened that night—I already told you. I don't think I even saw his face."

Foster blinked, then turned to Tatum. "A bluff?"

"He was dying to confess. Just needed a bit of prodding."

"But how the hell did you—"

"Later, Detective. I'm going to look in that asshole's house. Did you send a patrol car there?"

"They'll meet you there."

"Okay, and get someone to drive the actress of the year back to her home. You did an amazing job, Juliet. You deserve a goddamn Oscar."

CHAPTER 88

The interrogation room was stifling hot. Tatum forced himself to shut the door, leaving the cool air of the other room behind him. Prescott was used to working in the morgue, where the temperature was significantly lower than the rest of the building. It was a reasonable bet that the heat made him uncomfortable.

Then again, he was also used to digging in the blazing sun.

While Tatum had searched the man's apartment, Foster had released Joseph Dodson, who was now obviously in the clear. Then he began interrogating Prescott, grilling him for over an hour. Prescott had asked for no lawyer and had been happy to talk about his previous murders. But when it came to Zoe, he'd stayed silent.

Tatum sat down, saying nothing, looking at the man. Prescott seemed at ease, almost bored. It was a mask; Tatum was sure of it. He'd seen the fear in the man's eyes when confronted with Juliet. Seen the color drain from Prescott's face. It had taken him a few moments to get his act together. But Tatum had glimpsed the real man behind it.

And he needed to find him again and make him crack.

Unfortunately, he'd lost the interrogator's most valuable tool. Time. Zoe would be dead in a few hours; he couldn't afford to waste a single moment. But he also couldn't let Prescott see that.

He let the silence stretch, counting the seconds in his mind, each one heavy and loud.

"There's a password-locked application on your laptop," Tatum finally said. "Controlling the video feed from wherever Zoe is."

"That's right," Prescott said. His voice was cool, distant. A note of smugness there as well.

"I have a deal for you. Give me the password. And I'll turn on the feed."

Prescott raised his eyebrow. "And in return?"

"I'll let you watch it."

Prescott folded his arms, smiled slightly, saying nothing.

"I know you want to."

"You know nothing about me, Agent."

"This is your last opportunity to glimpse any of your precious videos. There'll be no movie time in prison."

For one moment, the man seemed to hesitate, and Tatum forced his own face to remain expressionless. He needed to know if Zoe was alive more than anything. He estimated that she'd been in the coffin for almost ten hours. Maybe more. Not knowing gnawed at him, emitted a constant white noise of panic in his mind.

Prescott shook his head. "No."

Tatum didn't expect any other reaction. This was part of Prescott's mask. It wasn't likely he'd let it drop that easily. Still, Tatum couldn't resist the temptation to ask. Already, he regretted giving the man this little victory.

He took a notebook from his briefcase, flipped a few pages. "I don't suppose you saw the profile we composed of the Digging Killer?"

Prescott cleared his throat. "No, I didn't. It would be interesting to hear what you think."

"Aged between thirty and forty-five. White. Has a van. Works in a job that emphasizes thoroughness. Not very riveting stuff. There are some things here that match your background quite well. But the part where it gets really interesting is—"

The door opened, and Foster walked inside carrying a few evidence bags. He placed them on the table. Lyons followed him, carrying a portable paper shredder, which she placed by the evidence bags, not glancing at Prescott. Both of them left, closing the door behind them.

Prescott scrutinized the evidence bags. Tatum got up, grabbing the power cable for the shredder.

"Where was I? Oh yeah. It gets really interesting when we started estimating what makes you tick." He plugged the shredder into the wall, then sat back down. He opened one of the evidence bags, took out the laptop that was in it. "You really should have locked the entire thing with a password. It's amazing the kind of things we found here."

"Maybe I wanted you to find them."

Tatum turned on the laptop, which had been hibernating. "Maybe you did. But people often forget the astounding amount of information their computer collects about them." He looked at the screen as the computer whirred to life, forcing himself to ignore the sluggish pace of the ancient hardware, doing his best to avoid glancing at the clock on the bottom right corner. Time—it was everywhere.

"One of the things that stood out about you is that you are driven by fame."

Prescott snorted in derision. "Right. Hollywood is just around the corner, waiting for me."

Tatum raised an eyebrow. "Not Hollywood, maybe. But you have your own hall of fame, don't you? Let me read you some of the search queries from your browser." He opened the history tab on the browser. "Most famous serial killers. Infamous serial killers. Famous serial murderers . . . nice trick there, swapping *killers* for murderers. Let's see what else . . . oh, I like this one. Important serial killers. Almost every day, you look those things up. Are you imagining your name in those articles and charts? Here's an article you keep returning to. 'Twenty of the Most Infamous Serial Killers America Has Ever Seen.' Where do you think you measure there? Number thirteen? Nine? Seven?"

"I couldn't care less."

"Well, that's good, because I have news for you. A serial killer who managed to kill only three or four people doesn't really get to those charts."

Prescott just smirked, shuffling in his chair to make himself more comfortable.

"But of course, you don't really care about numbers, do you?"

"No, I don't."

"What *do* you care about, Prescott?"

Prescott folded his arms. "Humanity."

The man inserted a lot of pathos into that one word. Tatum felt like wrapping his fingers around the doctor's neck and squeezing. Instead, he smirked. "Of course. You're a regular humanitarian."

"Sometimes you need to kill a few to save many."

Tatum quirked his eyebrow. "Save them from what?"

"Themselves." The cool facade dropped off. A fervor filled Prescott's eyes. "No one has time to *think* anymore, do they? We all used to have time to think. Waiting for the bus to come, standing in line in the supermarket, maybe just sitting in your living room. But what do we do now when that happens?"

Tatum said nothing, letting the man preach his sermon.

"We whip out our mobile phones. Check Twitter or Instagram or play a game of Candy Crush. Because god forbid we actually *think* for five minutes. What do you think this will do to us in the long run? The whole human race, avoiding their own thoughts?"

"And that's what you gave your victims. Time to think."

"It was more than that. I gave *everyone* time to think. Whenever I stopped the video feed, everyone would start wondering. Is she dead? Is she alive?"

"Superposition."

"*That's right.* Superposition. A question with no answer. I forced their hand. They had to think."

Tatum sighed and let a small weary smile show. "Yeah . . . your mission, right? I know all about it already. Do you know what Zoe wrote down on your profile? She wrote that you are so obsessed with yourself and your so-called mission that she expects to find a meticulous journal about it in your possession." Tatum opened another evidence bag, taking out a stack of papers. "Look what I found. Not a journal, even better. A partial draft of your autobiography. There's a preface where you wrote down what you just said. Humanity, time to think, mobile phones, blah blah blah—it's tiresome stuff. But you were *invested* in this thing. These pages are full of your own corrections and editing notes. You were working really hard, getting it just right. I bet you can't wait to write the final two or three chapters and find a publisher. In fact, I even saw in your browser history that you were researching agents. Methodical planning there."

Tatum picked up the top page. "I hope you remember your own notes." He skimmed it, a bored expression on his face, then turned to the shredder and slid the page in. The shredder buzzed to life, whirring as the page turned into long, thin ribbons.

Tatum took another page and shredded it, then the third. He watched each page as it shredded, the ribbons piling on the floor in a growing heap.

"You're destroying evidence," Prescott said. His voice was cool, but Tatum could feel something else underneath the surface.

"We have evidence up the wazoo, as far as you're concerned." Tatum shredded the fourth page. "How many chapters do you think you have left to write?" He shredded another page.

"Some. This interview would make for a great scene."

"You know what *I* think?" Tatum shredded another page. The sound of the shredding was very satisfying. He hoped Jensen wouldn't barge in, screaming that he was destroying evidence. "I think you have maybe . . . three chapters left. One for Zoe. One for your capture, and one covering the legal proceedings that follow. Maybe an epilogue for your time waiting for your death sentence."

"Is that your professional opinion as an editor?"

"As an avid reader." Tatum put the stack of pages down and picked up the last evidence bag, opening it. He slid the book out. "*The Bundy Murders*. Found it in your library, along with four more like it. You liked to read about Ted Bundy, didn't you?"

"I found him interesting."

"There are some pages here that are underlined and earmarked repeatedly. Do you know what I'm talking about?"

Prescott said nothing. Tatum let the silence stretch while he shredded a few more pages. Every second, Zoe's death inched closer. He wanted Prescott to feel there was a price for the trickling of time as well.

"I'm talking about the pages about Bundy's escapes." Tatum said. "Tell me, Prescott. Do you really think you might be able to escape prison?"

"I never considered it."

"Ted Bundy escaped in 1977. We've improved since then. And I'll personally make sure you're placed in the most secure, isolated vault available, watched twenty-four seven. Trust me—there'll be no chapter in your autobiography about how you managed to get away." It was Tatum's turn to smirk.

"You're wrong about me, Agent. I'm done."

"Of course you are." Tatum raised a page and skimmed it. "I like this note of yours. 'This section needs work; it feels trite.' I have to say I agree with your assessment. Also, you misspelled the word *rhythm* here. There should be an *H* after the *R*. Ah well." Tatum shredded it too.

Prescott's mask was hanging there well, but Tatum was sure now that there was a tension in the man's posture. He was getting to him. How much further would he need to take it? How much longer?

"There were no other copies of your autobiography, as far as we could tell. The forensic team is looking further, but I'm pretty sure there's only one. I found a five-hundred-page package of paper on your desk, and it was about half-empty. This draft is—well, *was*, really—two hundred and thirty pages long. Double spaced so there's room for your notes, right?" Tatum shredded another page. "Yeah, it's the only copy. Aside from the one on the laptop." Tatum put the pages down, turned to the laptop. "There it is. The file name, as you probably remember, is 'Time to Think.'" He clicked it. "If I were to delete this . . . would you be able to rewrite it?" His finger hovered above the delete button.

A few seconds passed. Prescott didn't budge, his face blank. Not calm anymore. Not at ease. Simply contained.

"We'll just have to find out." Tatum hit the keyboard with two fingers. "Shift delete. Don't want you to get it from the Recycle Bin, do I?"

There it was. The first spark of anger, the first twitch of fury in Prescott's lip. Tatum leaned back and shredded pages again. Now, Prescott's eyes were intent on Tatum's hand as he shredded each page in turn, and Tatum knew he was right. Prescott had no other copy of the file.

"Are you already planning to rewrite it?" Tatum asked. "Trying to remember your favorite paragraphs for later? Maybe a sentence you were particularly pleased with? Do your best, Prescott, but you better remember hard. Because I'll make sure you won't get anything to write with. No pens, no pencils, no goddamn crayons. And paper? You won't get a single Post-it. When you go to the toilet, you'll have to wipe with your fingers, because you can forget about toilet paper. This autobiography will *never* see the light of day, unless I get what I want. And you know what that is."

Another paper shredded. And another. And another.

"Where. Is. Zoe?"

Prescott clenched his teeth tightly, as if forcing himself to be quiet.

"I saw on your laptop that you bought a cellular signal booster online on Sunday. Why? Where did you put her that you needed a cellular booster?"

No answer.

Almost there. Just a bit more. Hang in there, Zoe.

"You know what?" Tatum said brightly. "I didn't even tell you the best part of our profile. Zoe figured it out, and seeing your library at home, I realize she was spot on. You had some medical books, a bunch of serial killer biographies. And a book called *Buried Alive*, which I didn't need to open to guess what it's about."

"So what?" Prescott asked, sneering. "I do my research."

"Right! Except you know what was missing? I didn't find one book about Schrodinger or physics or quantum mechanics. And I didn't see even a pamphlet about humanity or the process of thought or any sort of philosophy. Almost as if those things didn't really interest you. Isn't that strange?"

Prescott didn't answer.

"Here, let me read you from Zoe's notes." He put down the pages left from the draft, picked up the notebook, flipping another page. "The unsub is obsessed with his mission, his goal. He wants to believe this is what drives him, what makes him kill. This is why he created the website, why he streams those videos, why he's constantly naming himself Schrodinger, and why he calls the murders 'experiments.' But it's a lie he tells himself."

Tatum paused, raised his eyes for a moment to meet Prescott's, then kept reading. "The truth is, the unsub kills those women for one reason. He derives sexual stimulation from the act of burying women alive. He uses his obsession as a facade to avoid the shame in acknowledging that to himself."

Tatum put the notebook back. Took a page from the leftover autobiography. Shredded it. Shredded another one.

"She used big words. Zoe's like that," he said. "But what she meant was this dude has a kinky taste and likes to get it off while burying women alive. And he's so damn embarrassed by his weird fetish that he invented a whole story just so he doesn't feel like a weirdo loser."

Another page shredded. Prescott's body was trembling.

"What I'll do once I finish shredding this piece of shit you call a book here," Tatum said, "is call a press conference. And tell them we caught the Digging Killer. And this sad sack of shit used to polish his knob while watching his own videos. And that's why he did all this. That's how people will remember you."

Page shredded.

"Unless you tell me. Where. Zoe. Is."

"You can keep going," Prescott said, his voice trembling with rage. "But you won't get anything from me. And your precious Dr. Bentley can rot underground. She was right under your noses, and you never even realized it."

Tatum put down the draft, feeling a twitch of excitement. "She *was* right under our noses."

"That's right," Prescott sputtered, flushing. "She's right under your fucking noses."

"Language, Doctor. You didn't say she *is* under our nose. You said she *was* under our nose. Did you move her?" Tatum looked at the man intently, thinking hard. He'd bought a cellular signal booster. What had changed?

For some reason, Prescott hadn't been able to stretch a cable from the box to the surface. He'd had to boost the signal of the transmission. The puzzle pieces shifted, the truth taking shape. "No. Of course you didn't move her. It was us. We're the ones who moved her. She was under our noses just *before*."

Tatum lunged from his chair, and Prescott tightened, as if worried that he would strike him. But Tatum was already striding toward the door. He knew where Zoe was.

CHAPTER 89

It was hard to tell how long she'd been there. Zoe knew she couldn't trust her own measurement of time. Sleep tried to grab hold of her, and she struggled to stay awake. It didn't make sense. She would spend less air if she were sleeping. But she knew that in all probability, once she fell asleep, she would never wake up. She couldn't make herself give up. Not yet. She kept wondering whether there was anything else she could do. Any message she could try to pass along.

After her initial message of *school*, she'd switched to *Debra school*, which was a nightmare to get right. She'd tried three times, feeling that she managed to garble it completely each time, blinking too much, pausing in the wrong moments, fumbling a letter. Her focus and concentration were shot to hell.

Finally, she'd given up and just lay there, thoughts flickering in and out in her mind like a swarm of fireflies, out of sync with each other.

She was dizzy, and her head pounded. Was it exhaustion, thirst, or the low amount of oxygen in the air?

For the millionth time, she wondered if she'd screwed herself by trying to communicate with people outside. After all, they'd been searching for her, and then she'd given them a single word, *school*. It must've been easy to assume that she meant she was buried in a school. Had she pulled them away from a promising lead, sending them on a fool's errand?

She wanted to believe that Tatum, at least, would know the killer would never risk burying her somewhere so public, with so many possible witnesses.

Fading away, she began hallucinating again, hearing voices. Andrea, her parents, old colleagues and friends. It was reassuring that her mind had finally stopped obsessing about serial murderers and psychopaths, letting her relax, surrounded by people who cared about her.

A sudden thunk made her eyes open wide to no perceivable effect. It was still dark.

But she heard sounds, real sounds. The muffled voices of people, the scraping and thumping. After so long in a dark silence, it was an overwhelming sensation to *hear* something aside from her own breathing and sounds. She tried to let out a scream for help, couldn't.

A creaking sound was followed by sudden sunlight. She instantly shut her eyes, and even through her eyelids, the light shot a sharp pain through her skull.

Someone was by her side, pulling the gag from her mouth. She moved her tongue around, the sudden freedom of it feeling sublime. She wanted water but couldn't ask for it, couldn't talk.

A voice murmured by her ear, soft, tense, full of worry. Tatum. His arms helped her up, pulling her close. She let go then, her feet buckling, and he had to grab her to keep her upright. Someone cut the binding on her wrists. People were shouting around her, hurried instructions for a medic.

A bottle to her lips, a slight sip of water. She let it roll in her mouth, almost crying at the sensation.

An arm around her shoulders, a strong hand, and Tatum's voice. "You're all right. We got you, you're—"

She shifted, pulling herself away from the hand sharply. She didn't want anyone to touch her. It was too close, too limiting, like the box. She wanted *nothing* to contain her body.

Forcing one eye open to a slit, she expected a familiar scenery from the previous crime scenes. Desert soil, pebbles, rocks, and cacti around her.

But that wasn't what she saw. The ground was green, for some reason, and there were trees around her and large white shapes . . . rocks?

She opened the other eye, holding a hand to shade her face, feeling Tatum's silent presence by her side.

A . . . cemetery?

"Where?" she croaked.

"Fairmount Cemetery," Tatum said. "We're in San Angelo."

A cemetery. She'd been buried alive in a cemetery. Her brain was already churning up ideas, but they were disjointed, broken. She turned around, stared at the large pit they'd pulled her out of and the coffin at the bottom. A coffin, not a box.

"This is . . . a grave?"

"It's Nicole Medina's grave," Tatum told her. "He switched you with her body just before the funeral."

She looked down at the pit. The coffin lay inside, and something metallic flashed in it—the infrared camera. Her breath shuddered. *Just before the funeral.* Who was it? The priest? The funeral director? She hugged herself, her body rocking, already knowing the answer. "It was the medical examiner. He fits the profile. The stressor?"

"The Whitfield case," Tatum said. "Zoe—"

"The wrong time of death. Of course. We should have seen it straightaway. We should have known. Did you get my message? I tried to communicate by blinking, but I couldn't get the letters right—kept losing my count, but I tried to tell you."

"We got the message. That's how we found him. He was with Debra in high school. Listen, let's step away . . ."

"When did he switch between me and the body? How long have I been in there?"

"You should rest." Tatum motioned the paramedic over.

"*Tell me.* How long?"

Tatum cleared his throat. "From what we could tell, the only time he had to switch the body was last night. He arranged it with the funeral home, told them he had some final urgent tests to do on the body. They brought the coffin to the morgue in the evening, picked it up at five in the morning."

Zoe looked back at the coffin, realizing that its walls were bare, the lining missing. He must have removed it so that anyone watching the video wouldn't see the lining and figure out where she was. "He would have waited for the last moment to make sure I was anesthetized for long enough so I wouldn't wake up during the funeral. And to make sure I'd last longer. So probably four thirty. What time is it?"

A paramedic approached her with a small medical bag. She took a step back. "*What time is it?*"

The paramedic glanced at Tatum, who raised a hand to stop him. "It's just after six thirty."

Zoe blinked. "Fourteen hours." A constant clicking noise that distracted her. "Fourteen hours." It was her teeth, she realized. They were chattering. "I've been in there for fourteen hours. He put me there. I was . . . it was . . ." Strange, how cold she was. It was always so hot in San Angelo. But she was trembling, cold.

"Miss, I'm going to give you something to calm you down, okay?" The paramedic asked warily.

She took another step back, shaking like a leaf. Her palms were clammy, and she couldn't stop her teeth from chattering. She glanced at Tatum, not knowing what she needed, only knowing she needed him to do *something*. To help her.

"I'm right here," he said.

She glanced at the paramedic. He held a small needle. "Miss?"

Her head jerked, giving him a quick reluctant nod, and he took her hand. She had to force herself to freeze so she wouldn't hit him. The needle pierced her flesh, and she had a flicker of a memory, standing in the parking lot, her body rigid with pain, and a sudden sting in her neck. That was how he'd taken her.

"Don't go," she told Tatum.

"I'm not going anywhere."

CHAPTER 90

Dale City, Virginia, Monday, September 19, 2016

Zoe knew only the basics when it came to PTSD, but she was pretty sure that people who suffered from it shouldn't be taking care of each other. Despite that, it was what she and Andrea were doing, and it worked reasonably well, considering the circumstances.

There were some problems. It felt like their traumas were dueling each other. Zoe wanted every window in the apartment open at all times. She needed light and air, and the busy street noise was music to her ears. Andrea wanted the windows closed, the door locked. She'd turned the apartment into her own cocoon and wanted to make sure there was no way for any intruder to creep in. But they tried to compromise—the living room window would be open, but the window next to the emergency stairs would remain latched. The door would be kept locked at all times, of course. Zoe would go out for very long walks, feeling the wind on her face.

They both had nightmares.

They slept in the same room and in the same bed, though that arrangement had to change soon. Zoe had a long scratch on her face from last night, when Andrea had nearly clawed her eye out, trying to struggle against someone who wasn't there.

Still, that morning almost felt normal, in a weekend vacation sort of way. Zoe woke up to the sound of frying, Andrea banging pans and pots in the kitchen. She got out of bed and padded to the kitchen, blinking.

Andrea hummed to herself, sounding more cheerful than she had since Zoe had returned home. A tall pile of pancakes sat on a plate by her side, and she was making another one, flipping it, smiling with pleasure at how it turned out.

Zoe reached out for the pancakes, and Andrea swatted her hand with the spatula.

"Ow!"

"Not yet," Andrea said. "I had this all planned out. With butter and maple syrup on top. I bought some orange juice to go with it."

"But I'm hungry," Zoe complained. "Just one." She reached for the pancakes again.

The spatula landed, missing her fingers by an inch.

"Watch it." Andrea waggled her eyebrows and waved the spatula menacingly.

"Can I have a cup of coffee at least?" Zoe grumbled, eyeing the pancakes yearningly.

"One cup."

Zoe prepared herself a cup, waiting patiently for the dark liquid of life to fill the mug. She sipped from it, breathing in the smell of coffee. Sublime.

Then, with one sharp movement she stole the topmost pancake and stuffed it into her mouth hurriedly, nearly choking herself.

"You should see yourself." Andrea snorted. "Your cheeks stuffed with pancake—you look like a hamster."

Zoe grinned at her, mouth full, and walked over to the living room, swallowing.

"Can I put on some music?" she called. That was another thing she needed almost constantly. Music.

"Fine, but no Beyoncé or Taylor—I can't take it anymore."

"Katy Perry?"

"Okay." Andrea groaned.

*Zoe put on T*eenage Dream and stepped over to the living room window, which Andrea had closed, opening it again, staring at the cars driving back and forth.

She didn't need to be an expert in trauma to know that one thing was emphatically different between Andrea and her. Zoe's attacker was in a federal prison, awaiting his trial. Andrea's monster was on the loose. Despite the cops watching every exit of the building, despite the roadblocks, despite the citywide search, Rod Glover had disappeared, like a malicious ghost.

"I wish I partied like that last Friday night," Andrea said behind her.

"What?" Zoe asked, startled.

"The song."

"Oh." She hadn't even been listening to the music; it was just one more relaxing sound to accompany her.

"Breakfast is served, madam. Can we turn off the noise?"

"Uh . . . just a few more songs? 'Firework' is just about to play."

Andrea sighed, shaking her head, stomping back into the kitchen. Zoe followed her, embarrassed, not willing to admit how much she needed the music.

It would get better. She hoped.

Each of them had a plate with a monstrous pile of pancakes, a block of butter on top, floating in a lake of maple. A third plate contained sliced fruit—bananas, strawberries, apples, and some blueberries and pecans. It was an Instagram-worthy type of breakfast, if either of them was the type to post meal images, which they weren't. Both Bentley sisters believed food was meant to be eaten, not posted online to tease.

Zoe sliced into the pancakes, forking three maple-soggy pieces. She then topped the fork with a banana and put it in her mouth. She shut her eyes, breathing through her nose, letting the sweetness flood her body. Katy obliged with the chorus of "Firework," and there it was: a perfect moment, a peaceful second that she wished could last.

"I heard you on the phone yesterday," Andrea said, "talking with your boss about the leak."

"It's nothing. Don't worry about it. Someone told that reporter I was—"

"I'm the leak."

Zoe stared at her, dumbstruck.

"He was writing a book about you, and he called me. He kept talking about how if he could get a close look at how you worked, you'd really shine. And there were all those assholes in your unit giving you crap for not being an agent and—"

"Andrea, do you have any idea how much trouble this could have caused?" Zoe wanted Harry Barry to be there right now so that she could stab his eyes with her fork. "I don't do this job to be famous. I don't care about his dumb book or what people say about me."

"You should. People's opinions are important."

"Don't ever. Do that. Again. You understand? I can't have you walking behind my back, talking to reporters. Especially not now, when we're living together."

"You don't have to worry about that."

"Good." She was still furious, but it was mostly aimed at Harry. She knew how conniving and convincing the bastard could be. It didn't surprise her that he'd managed to sway Andrea.

"I'm going to visit Mom," Andrea said after they'd eaten in silence for a minute.

Zoe nearly choked for the second time that morning. Coughing, she took a swig of orange juice. "You're going to do what?"

"She's been hassling me nonstop these past few days, Zoe. She's worried. She needs to see at least one of us face to face."

"You can do a video chat."

"Zoe, don't be ridiculous."

"Fine! Go—she'll drive you insane in three seconds. When are you flying?"

"Tomorrow. I already bought a ticket."

"And when are you flying back? I can pick you up if it's not in the middle of the night."

"I . . . don't know."

Zoe took another bite, feeling suddenly tense. Andrea gazed down at her plate, not eating. Her expression was guilty.

"This is not about visiting Mom," Zoe said.

"It's also about Mom."

"You're leaving."

"I don't know what I'm doing yet." She raised her face. Her eyes were wet. "I need some time away. Away from this city, away from those memories, away from—"

"Me?"

Andrea drank from her glass, not answering.

"I don't want you to leave." Zoe felt like she was drowning.

"It might be just for a few days, Zoe, just to clear my head. Don't make this into a big deal—"

"Clear your *head*? With Mom?"

"With myself. This isn't just about Glover. It's about me needing a change, okay? I followed you here without a plan, and it hasn't exactly been great for me."

Zoe put down her fork, biting her lip.

"I love you, Zoe," Andrea said. "But I need this, for me, okay?"

"Okay."

"Are you mad at me?"

"No, Ray-Ray. I'm not mad." She forked a small piece of pancake and put it into her mouth, chewing listlessly. "Eat your pancakes."

CHAPTER 91

When Tatum approached Marvin's room in intensive care, his heart clenched with worry. The day before when he'd visited, the old man had been sedated, his speech slurred, his skin pale, almost translucent. Tatum hadn't grasped the details, but there had been some sort of infection. For the first time in a long while, he'd realized how old his grandfather really was.

He was steeling himself for another difficult visit when he heard a burst of womanly laughter from inside the room. A playful shriek followed it, and then a middle-aged nurse came walking out, shaking her head, a wide grin on her face.

She paused when she saw Tatum. "You're Marvin Gray's son, right?" she said. "You're his spitting image."

"I'm actually his grandson," Tatum said, nonplussed.

She let out a giggle. "Uh-huh. Sure you are."

Tatum sighed. "Is he better?"

"I'd say he is. Your father will outlive us all. I think by tomorrow he'll be able to come home."

"Are you sure you don't need him monitored for an additional day or two?"

"I doubt we'd be able to hold him here even if we wanted to." She winked at him and strode away.

Tatum entered the room, where Marvin lay in the bed holding a piece of paper, frowning at it. His nose was still swollen and red, though it did look a bit better than the day before.

"What's that you have there?" Tatum asked, sitting on a chair by the bed.

"Tell me, Tatum, is that a seven or a one?" Marvin asked, showing him the paper.

"I think it's a seven . . . is that the nurse's phone number?"

"Mind your own business, Tatum." Marvin put the paper on his night table and picked up his phone. "Oh, that reminds me. If anyone asks, tell them you're my son. It's very important."

"I'll keep that in mind. Sounds like you'll be able to leave tomorrow."

"It's about damn time, Tatum. I can't do anything here. I can't drink, I can't smoke—"

"You quit smoking seven years ago."

"You'd think so, right? It's all been great until they told me I can't smoke. Now I feel like I need a cigarette all the time." Marvin tapped on the phone's screen. "I've been reading about your guy."

"Which guy is that?"

"This Prescott guy." Marvin turned the phone so Tatum could see the screen. It di*splayed the Chicago D*aily Gazette's article, of course.

Tatum rolled his eyes. Harry Barry was milking this story dry. "Don't believe everything you read."

"Guy sounds like a real treat. He was the medical examiner at the s*tation*? You worked with him?"

"Yup. You never can tell."

"You should have, from the moment you met him. You don't look into people's eyes enough, Tatum—I already told you that. You can always see the truth in the eyes."

Tatum met his grandfather's gaze. "What's my truth right now?"

"Looks like you're pissed off." Marvin grinned at him.

Tatum had to smile back. Marvin was in a good mood. He suspected the old man enjoyed his painkillers a bit too much. "Andrea says hi."

Marvin's face morphed, concern seeping in. "How's she doing?"

"I think she's fine, under the circumstances. She's a tough girl."

"Not as tough as you'd like to believe," Marvin grumbled. "Poor kid. When are you going to get that bastard, Tatum? Why don't you do your job?"

"I'm enjoying a bit of a vacation. A few days off, and I've got the apartment all to myself." Tatum sighed again, remembering he probably had only one day left.

"Oh! Is the fish okay?" Marvin asked, his eyes widening. "Damn, I'm sorry. I didn't feed him after I got stabbed, Tatum."

"The fish is fine—swimming in his bowl."

"Oh good." Marvin relaxed. "And the cat?"

"Freckle's fine too. Don't worry about it."

"Ah." A brief look of disappointment. "Well, can't win 'em all."

"He misses you."

"Yeah, yeah, you're hilarious. What about that internal investigation? Are you off the hook for making the world a better place?"

"Sounds like it. The witness is a friend of Wells's mother. Apparently he wasn't even there when it happened."

"Who's Wells?"

"The pedophile I shot."

"Then call him the pedophile, Tatum. I can't keep track of all the nutjobs you shoot."

"There were only . . . never mind that." Tatum paused for a moment. "Would you mind talking about . . . that night?"

"Why would I mind?"

"The police got the basic gist of what happened from Andrea's testimony and the evidence in the scene. But I want to hear about it from your point of view."

"Hmph. Yeah, well, I woke up from the noise of someone knocking on the door. It took me a bit of time to get up, and by that time, Andrea was at the door. She opened it."

"Did you hear him come in?"

"I don't know what I heard, Tatum. The door closed, and there was some sound. Something that made me feel wrong. Maybe she called out or something; I don't know. I opened the door of the room just a bit, saw this guy pushing Andrea to her bedroom. I stepped forward—"

"What were you going to do? Beat him up?" Tatum's voice was much sharper than he'd intended.

"Look, Tatum, do you want my version, or do you want to lecture me? I did a lot more than the damn cops did."

"Fine. Then what?"

"He hit me. Wasn't too hard. Let me tell you: he acts big, but he hits like a girl, Tatum."

"He broke your nose, stabbed you, and gave you a concussion."

"Who's telling the story, Tatum? Me or you? Were you there? If that's the way you conduct your interrogations, it's no wonder this fellow keeps getting away."

"Fine. He hits like a girl."

"Right. So I walk back to my room, get my gun, then follow him to the bedroom. I shot him once, hit him in the side. He turned to face me, so I fired a warning shot at the window."

"You mean that you missed."

"You're a pain in the ass, Tatum. Yes, I missed. It was dark, it was a small room, my nose hurt, and I didn't want to hit Andrea, okay?"

"Okay."

"Then he got away."

Tatum leaned forward. "How?"

"Through the door, Tatum. He ran past me through the door."

"How did he seem?"

Marvin thought about it for a moment. "You remember that time Freckle scratched my ankle, and I went after him with a frying pan?"

"And broke my TV set. Yes, Marvin, I have a vague recollection of that wonderful day."

"I cornered him in the bathroom. And the expression on his face—that was how that guy looked."

"Like a trapped animal," Tatum said.

"Yes." Marvin seemed satisfied. "Maybe I shoulda gone after him with a frying pan instead of a gun."

CHAPTER 92

Dale City, Virginia, Tuesday, September 20, 2016

Zoe had managed to wear the face of a supportive, loving sister until Andrea got into the Uber that took her to the airport. Then she let herself fall apart for a while. Fear lurked, waiting for her, its presence almost like an actual shadow stalking in the corner of a hallway or an unlit room or beyond a closed door.

She opened all the windows in the apartment. Went for a very long walk. Switched on the music in the apartment, turning up the volume to fill the empty rooms with noise.

For a while, she tried to force herself to work. She read the transcripts of the interviews with Clyde Prescott, frustrated that she hadn't talked to him herself. Why hadn't she? She'd done it with Jeffrey Alston. She'd interviewed several serial killers before. But she hadn't been able to bring herself to face Prescott.

She read through his partial autobiography. Though Tatum had pulled an act, deleting it from the laptop, he'd made sure to save a copy beforehand. The same couldn't be said for the printed draft with the notes, which he had actually shredded. She wished she had those pages with Prescott's handwritten comments.

It almost worked. She managed to spend long stretches of time—fifteen and twenty minutes—consumed by work, writing notes, tightening the profile, knowing it might be invaluable to another profiler someday. But then she'd realize she was staring into space, her body tense, breath held, the silence around her oppressive and consuming.

The sudden knock on her door nearly gave her a heart attack. She was about to run to the kitchen and grab her largest knife when Tatum spoke through the door. "Zoe, are you there? It's me."

She unlocked the door, letting him in, half hating herself for how relieved she felt.

"You're reading that thing?" he asked, noticing the pages on the table.

"It's fascinating," she said. "Prescott could be quite articulate, and I'm learning a lot about him just by reading it."

"The less I know about that monster, the better."

"He's not . . ." Zoe shook her head and swallowed the rest of the sentence. "I wish you hadn't shredded his notes. I would have loved to have seen them." To her surprise, her tone was angry, accusing.

"I was too busy saving your life to worry about that."

"You could have shredded blank pages; you didn't need to use the actual thing. You could have made a copy before. You could have—"

"What are you talking about?" Tatum blinked, clearly bewildered. "I was worried sick . . . do you have any idea what I was going through?"

"No!" she screamed—she didn't know why, her mind short-circuiting. "But it wasn't as *b*ad as what I was going through."

She was frustrated by her own tears and irrational behavior. She didn't want him to see her like that.

Tatum took her hand and pulled her, very softly, toward him. She let herself be pulled, and then her cheek touched his chest. He hugged her but did so gently, the touch feather light, as if he knew that she couldn't stand being con*strained* by anything. She shut her eyes and listened to the beats of his heart.

After a while she let out a shuddering breath and pulled away. "Sorry."

"You have nothing to be sorry about."

"Do you want something to drink?"

It was three p.m. She expected him to refuse.

"That would be perfect," he said.

She opened the cupboard and took out a bottle of Talisker Skye and two lowball glasses. She poured a bit of the amber liquid for Tatum and a much larger portion for herself.

"Is that my ration?" Tatum asked, holding the glass to the light.

"It's the middle of the afternoon," Zoe pointed out.

"Your glass has four times *as* much!"

"I'm traumatized. I'm allowed."

"Well, I've been visiting Marvin in the hospital. I'm traumatized too."

Zoe added some more whiskey to Tatum's glass. He took it from her and clinked it with her own glass.

"To trauma," he said.

She snorted. "To trauma."

They sipped from their glasses. She let the smoky taste linger on her tongue, then swallowed, feeling the warmness spreading in her chest. They drank in a comfortable silence, and Zoe found her thoughts just wandering around pleasantly, going nowhere in particular. It was refreshing.

But finally she sighed. "So. Mancuso told me that you're on the Glover case."

He looked surprised. "She did? She told me not to tell you."

Zoe didn't answer, her lip twitching upward. After a second, Tatum let out a soft curse.

"You were bluffing. She never told you anything."

"She didn't." Zoe sipped from her glass, pleased with herself. "But you just did. I had a feeling you'd ask to be involved."

"Okay, yes, I did."

"Any idea how he got away?"

“The police think that he may have gone up to the roof. From there, he could have scaled down a drainpipe into an alley that wasn’t watched by the cops and fled.”

“He sounds like a ninja. And then he presumably used some sort of getaway vehicle to escape, managing to avoid the citywide manhunt after him.”

“That’s the general idea.”

“While bleeding heavily.” She finished her glass.

“They think Marvin may have been confused about how hard he was hit.”

“What do you think?”

Tatum’s gaze met hers. “It doesn’t feel right.”

“Let’s go see,” she said.

They walked to her bedroom. Tatum had never been in her bedroom before, obviously. She kicked herself for letting him in without tidying a bit first. Clothes were scattered everywhere, including some underwear; there were three half-empty mugs of coffee on the desk and papers on the bed and the floor.

“Ignore the”—she waved her hand vaguely at the room—“everything.”

“Right.” He smirked.

“According to blood spatter and Andrea’s testimony, Glover was here when Marvin shot him.” She stood by the bed.

“So Marvin is by the door.” Tatum surveyed it. “He has a concussion and a broken nose. He’s probably leaning against the doorway or the wall.”

“One shot hits Glover in the side.”

“Glover isn’t used to extreme pain,” Tatum said. “As far as we know, he wasn’t abused as a kid. He didn’t get into fights, not ones he couldn’t win easily. He preyed on the weak.”

“I cut him with a knife in Chicago,” Zoe said, recalling that day. “It was a shallow cut, but it scared the shit out of him.”

"So he's in pain."

"A second shot blasts the window. Marvin misses, but maybe Glover thinks otherwise."

"He sees an immediate threat, Marvin, aiming a gun at him. And he knows the shooting probably alerted the cops." Zoe bites her lip. "He wants to run."

"The window is broken, sharp shards of glass everywhere, and he doesn't want to turn his back to Marvin." Tatum's eyes seemed distant, as if he were seeing it happening. Zoe knew that expression. Andrea sometimes told her *that* was how she looked.

"So he bolts for the door."

"Right." Tatum turned to the door, preparing to leave.

"Tatum." Zoe blurted. She didn't know why she'd stopped him.

"What?" He looked at her, confused.

"Nothing. Let's go to the front door."

She followed him out of the bedroom. They opened the front door, regarding the hallway. There was a door to the staircase, an elevator, and some doors to other apartments.

"Which way did he go?"

"He was scared," Tatum said. "And hur*t.*"

"And he knew the cops were outside," Zoe added. "We know that because he was dressed as a cop."

"How did he get into the building dressed as a cop?" Tatum asked.

"How did he get into the building at *all?* It was late—the cops would have been alert to anyone leaving or entering."

Zoe was used to thinking alone. Even when she'd worked with Tatum before, she'd used him as someone she could test her own theories with. But now it was as if something had clicked, and they were in sync. Their minds worked together, like gears in a clockwork mechanism. She saw the man who'd sat in front of Clyde Prescott and methodically cracked the killer like a walnut.

"We know he was in Dale City weeks ago," Tatum said.

"Coming out of the woodwork once I was away."

"Andrea told the cops that he appeared to know the layout of the apartment," Tatum said. "They thought he may have broken inside before to take a look."

"Maybe he didn't need to." Zoe was nauseated. "The apartments here have the same layout."

"He'd been waiting." Tatum glanced around him. "That was his MO, right? He waited for his prey. He'd choose a good spot and just wait."

Zoe nodded. "He'd choose the perfect spot. Wait for a girl to walk by, alone."

CHAPTER 93

It took Zoe and Tatum seven minutes to convince the superintendent of Zoe's apartment building. He was an old gruff man whose initial stance was that unless they had a warrant, he had nothing to say to them. But they talked in that same sync Zoe found so exhilarating and confusing. She played the victim, the resident whose apartment had been broken into, while Tatum took the role of the imposing federal agent.

After seven minutes, the super would have given them his firstborn child, if they'd been so inclined. But they weren't. All they wanted were names and descriptions of the new residents.

The super wasn't very good at describing people, but it didn't matter, because only one of the new residents was a middle-aged man who lived alone, going by the name of Daniel Moore.

He wouldn't give them the key but insisted he come with them for some reason Zoe couldn't fathom. Perhaps it was some sort of ancient superintendent code of honor she didn't know or care about. But he unlocked the door for them.

The flies and smell in the apartment easily clarified no one had been there for a few days, at least.

A bunch of half-eaten takeout boxes were tossed in the kitchen's sink, all from the same Thai food place around the corner. They stank up the entire apartment, and the superintendent muttered about insects and cleaning bills and lawsuits.

Zoe ignored him. She strode to the bedroom, Tatum in her wake.

Dry blood was spattered on the floor and the bedsheets. It was where Glover had fled to. Like any hurt animal, he'd bolted to his lair to lick his wounds.

He'd left in a hurry. Papers were scattered in the room, some clothes. Zoe frowned, trying to figure this out. He was already safe here, and then he'd bolted out . . . why?

"Something spooked him," Tatum said behind her.

"There was a door-to-door investigation a day after he assaulted Andrea," Zoe said. "Cops talking to the residents, asking if they'd heard anything."

"They knocked on the door to the apartment."

"Probably *calle*d out police." She imagined him here, curling in the corner, trying not to make a sound. It gave her a small jolt of satisfaction, knowing he was hurt and scared.

"He waited for them to go, then took what he needed and ran." Tatum inspected a paper on the night table. "Phone bill for Daniel Moore. He faked the entire identity."

"Identity theft, probably," Zoe said. "The police have been searching for him for years. He managed to keep out of their reach."

"Look at this." Tatum handed her something else. "A hospital bill."

For a moment, Zoe thought Glover had been brazen enough to go to the hospital with his gunshot wound. But no. This was dated three weeks before. It was a bill for an MRI.

She found the results on the floor, crumpled into a ball. She read them repeatedly several times, her eyes widening.

"What is it?" Tatum asked.

"Suspicion for a malignant brain tumor," she said. "I think he might be dying." The final puzzle piece clicked. That was why he hadn't waited for them to lower their guard. He didn't have time.

"Couldn't happen to a better person," Tatum said with grim satisfaction.

Zoe didn't answer. An inkling of dread settled in her gut.

A wounded animal went to its lair to lick its wounds.

A dying animal had nothing left to lose. And that made it unpredictable—and dangerous.

CHAPTER 94

They sat in a bar in Woodbridge because Zoe didn't want to go back to her apartment. Tatum had been drinking the same pint of Blue Moon since they'd sat down. Zoe was already on her second pint of Guinness, and the glass was half-finished. She was, for the first time in a long while, drunk. Usually, the slightest loss of control made her edgy. But right now, she enjoyed the way alcohol blurred away the sharp edges of reality.

"You know what's good?" she said.

"What?" Tatum asked.

"Beer."

He raised an eyebrow. "You probably drank enough from that good beer."

"You're not my mother," she drawled.

"Thank god for that."

"My mother is unbearable. I don't understand why Andrea went to stay with her."

Tatum sighed. "She's probably not that bad."

Zoe didn't argue the point. "Tatum, you know that night?"

"What night?"

"The night when I said maybe you shot that guy because you thought he deserved it."

"Yeah." He took a long drink from his glass.

Zoe was pretty sure she was supposed to apologize, though she suddenly wasn't sure what had triggered the argument in the first place. She still thought she might have been right, though that probably wasn't the best thing to say at the moment. "I was dumb," she finally offered. It wasn't something she said often—or, in fact, ever. But it seemed like a safe bet.

"Well, thanks for saying that." He smiled at her gratefully.

She had no idea how she'd managed to navigate through that thorny issue. It was like she'd been running with a blindfold in a minefield, missing the mines by pure chance.

"I also wanted to thank you for saving Andrea."

"I didn't save Andrea," he said, surprised.

"Yes, you did. You told your grandfather to look out *for* her, and he shot Glover and saved Andrea. So I owe you Andrea's life. Or she owes you her life. Or maybe we split it. Split the tab." She let out a small hiccuping laugh. "Each of us owes a bit of Andrea's life."

"Okay, you definitely had enough to drink. Let's get you home." He got off the barstool.

"Wait." She grabbed his wrist. "Not yet."

He sighed, sat back down. "You'll have a hell of a hangover tomorrow."

"I don't get hangovers."

"You're in for a surprise."

"I think I don't dehydrate easily."

The song in the background changed to Cyndi Lauper's "Girls Just Want to Have Fun."

"Oh, I love this song," Zoe said.

"You would."

"What's that supposed to mean?"

"Nothing." Tatum smirked at her.

They sat in silence for a bit, listening to the song.

"I need to find Rod Glover," Zoe said, the words sobering her up slightly. "I know it makes me sound obsessive, but—"

"You're right."

"What?"

"You're right. You need to find him. And I'll help."

"Okay then." She had a strange fuzzy feeling that had nothing to do with the alcohol in her bloodstream. "Thanks."

"You're welcome." Tatum pried the glass, still almost half-full, out of her hand. "Partner."

She tried to be serious; they were talking about an important matter. But that warm feeling settled in her stomach, and girls just wanted to have fun in the background. A smile crept to her face and wouldn't go away. For the first time in days, she felt almost safe.

ACKNOWLEDGMENTS

This book would never have seen the light of day without my wife, Liora. She's there to brainstorm with me, read and edit my work, and supply endless support whenever I need it. Although she often asks that I write about flowers and butterflies, she's always there to help me write about murderers and psychopaths. One day I will write a flower-and-butterfly thriller just for her.

Christine Mancuso, who taught me much of what I know about writing, received the first draft of this book. She gave me a lot of notes, helped me develop Juliet Beach and the interactions between Zoe and Joseph, and much more.

Jessica Tribble, my editor, gave me amazingly helpful editing notes. With her help, I trimmed what desperately needed trimming, fixed the mystery so that it actually works, and completely rewrote the book's start, making it punchier and stronger.

Bryon Quertermous did the developmental editing on this book. He fixed glaring pacing problems, helped the dialog shine better, and assisted in removing two unnecessary and weak chapters.

Stephanie Chou did the final editing on the book, smoothing out my clunky grammar and endless spelling mistakes and catching some sneaky errors, among them a sunset that lasted for way too long.

Sarah Hershman, my agent, showed faith in me and helped this series get published and succeed as much as it did.

Thanks to my friends in Author's Corner, who gave me support and help and cheered for me when this series first went live. I couldn't ask for better friends. Thanks to my parents, for giving me all the support I needed in this roller coaster ride called "being an author."

ABOUT THE AUTHOR

Photo © 2017 Yael Omer

Mike Omer has been a journalist, a game developer, and the CEO of Loadingames, but he can currently be found penning the next in his series of thrillers featuring forensic psychologist Zoe Bentley. Omer loves to write about two things: real people who could be the perpetrators or victims of crimes—and funny stuff. He mixes these two loves quite passionately into his suspenseful and often macabre mysteries. Omer is married to a woman who diligently forces him to live his dream, and he is father to an angel, a pixie, and a gremlin. He has two voracious hounds that wag their tails quite menacingly at anyone who dares approach his home. Learn more by emailing him at mike@strangerealm.com.